PRAISE FOR A. C. ARTHUR

THE AFTER PARTY

"A sexy thrill."

—POPSUGAR

"This is *Homicide: Life on the Street* meets *9 to 5* meets *Bridgerton* in a story that screams to become a TV series. Part thriller and part mystery, this delightful story of friendship also celebrates sex, love, and family."

—*Kirkus Reviews* (starred review)

"*The After Party* by A. C. Arthur is a thrilling head trip! This seamless blend of beautiful women's fiction and exciting murder mystery gives the reader everything—homicide, twists, laughs, sisterhood, growth, triumphs, WITH moments, and even some romance. *The After Party* is simply unexpected and fantastic. It's also your next must read!"

—*USA Today* bestselling author Naima Simone

HAPPY IS ON HIATUS

"Arthur writes strong female characters, compelling story lines, and the message that family always has your back. Her fluid writing with touches of humor, romance, and enough issues to keep things interesting will keep readers engaged. Will appeal to fans of Terry McMillan and Eric Jerome Dickey."

—*Library Journal*

LEAVE
IT TO
Us

LEAVE IT TO Us

A NOVEL

A.C. ARTHUR

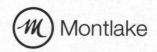 Montlake

Published by Montlake, Seattle

www.apub.com

Amazon, the Amazon logo, and Montlake are trademarks of Amazon.com, Inc., or its affiliates.

ISBN-13: 9781662511158 (paperback)
ISBN-13: 9781662511165 (digital)

Cover design by Caroline Teagle Johnson

Cover images: © scisettialfio / Getty; © Cierra Ayers / Getty; © OGphoto / Getty; © Natspace / Getty

Printed in the United States of America

To Joncquay M. Berger,
the sister God blessed with me because I didn't have a
biological one.
Thank you for being with me through it all.

Sisters . . .
the biggest, longest, surest, strongest friendship of
them all.

Chapter 1

TAMI

When you come from a long line of strong, successful Black women, the bar is already too high to reach. Even on something as basic as choosing an outfit to wear to a meeting with a lawyer.

Tami hadn't been around lawyers since she'd walked out of Hagen & Hagen, LLC, three years before. She'd been a legal secretary at the medical malpractice firm for nearly a year, and each one of the six lawyers who worked there had been an ignorant, arrogant jerk she hated with a passion. It had been her first job in the "real world," as her mother and sisters had put it, so she'd stuck it out for as long as she possibly could—ten months, to be exact—without catching a charge for stabbing one of those pompous idiots in the neck with the envelope opener.

Today she'd be walking into a totally different office. At least, the name of the practice was different, and the reason she would be there was too. Rosen, Crawford & Milligan was the firm handling the reading of Grandma Betty's will. And Tami had to be there in the next hour or she'd be late.

Yvonne hated when Tami was late. Hell, Yvonne hated when Tami breathed. Or so it had seemed all Tami's life. Older than she was by eleven years, Yvonne more often served as Tami's second mother rather than her oldest sister. Correcting everything from the way Tami combed her hair to the way she walked, her overly critical sister was just another voice of condemnation in Tami's head. A voice she swore she'd never be rid of.

"Jeans?" she asked herself while standing at the end of her bed.

She'd pulled piles of clothes from her closet in her search for the perfect outfit to wear today. But in the last hour, she'd narrowed the contenders down to three outfits: distressed light-blue jeans and a simple white shirt, which she'd pair with navy-blue flats; black jeans that seemed a bit dressier, with a denim button-front shirt and cheetah-print flats; or rose-colored slacks with a sleeveless white blouse and strappy, natural-hued high-heeled sandals.

If you don't look like you're about your business, nobody will think you are.

That's something Yvonne had said years ago, when Tami was dressing for an internship interview during her college years. Tami had still been living in their childhood home then, and Yvonne had come by to see their mother, Freda, who'd only shaken her head during the exchange. Something she often did when Yvonne was chastising Tami, most likely because Yvonne's thoughts generally mirrored Freda's. And Tami had tried valiantly to ignore them both, since they rarely had anything nice to say to her anyway.

Still, she spent another ten minutes staring at the three outfits, trying her best to make the right decision . . . for once. Finally, she opted for the middle ground, choosing the black jeans. With that decision made, she went to the bathroom to apply her makeup. Her hair was already done, pulled up into a neat bun on top of her head.

"Dammit!"

Stomping back into her room, she searched every bottle, cup, and tray on her dresser, then groaned. Making her way into her apartment's second bedroom, which was now mostly empty, she grumbled, "If that heffa stole my moisturizer, I'm beatin' her entire ass!"

Moving through the room, she looked in the few plastic bins that Shana had left when she moved out a week ago. Then Tami stomped into the second bathroom, which her former roommate had used, opening and slamming the empty drawers of the vanity. She rolled her eyes as she made her way back to her own bathroom, this time muttering, "Guess that's her get-back for me supposedly trying to steal her boyfriend. But ain't nobody want that funky-breath, unemployed, dirty-fingernail-having James."

The thought of that sleazy bastard being up in her face when Shana had walked into the apartment last week still gave Tami a raging headache. She'd just slapped his hand away from her breast, which he'd attempted to grope, when his girlfriend came in. Shana had immediately taken his side when he'd sworn, "Your girl's been tryin' to get in my pants for weeks now."

"What?" Shana had yelled, stalking over to where they were standing in the kitchen. She'd grabbed James by the arm, pulling him away from Tami, then stepped up into Tami's face.

Shana's scowl had told Tami this wasn't going to end well, and so she had squared her shoulders in preparation for whatever was coming. "He's lying," she'd said blandly, because Shana's lips were already turned up in distaste.

"If that's true, why were you all up on him?" Shana questioned.

Shaking her head, Tami had replied, "*He* was all up on *me*. Again." Then she'd crossed her arms over her chest. "I'd been trying not to spoil your delusions about his no-good ass, but like my grandma always said, *When someone shows you their true colors, don't try to repaint them.*"

"She's lyin', baby. Don't nobody want her flighty ass!" James had countered.

To that, Tami had only rolled her eyes. "Look, I don't have time for this silliness. Just tell your man to keep his hands to himself, or the next time, he'll be missing a few fingers." She'd nodded toward the block of knives on the kitchen counter and then moved to walk around them.

Two days later, there'd been a note from Shana taped to Tami's bedroom door that read:

I can't live with somebody who's trying to take my man.

That was it, and Shana—plus her half of the rent and utilities—was gone. Oh, and apparently Tami's favorite moisturizer too.

She didn't have time to keep harping on the fact that she was now totally responsible for all the bills in this apartment and was—as of two days ago—unemployed as well. She had forty minutes to get her face done, climb into her car, pray it started, and then drive to the law firm.

She was definitely going to be late.

✉

"Hey, gorgeous. Where you rushing off to today?"

Her steps barely slowed as she tossed a glance over to Gabriel Taylor, the day-shift security guard in her apartment building and her part-time lover.

"Got a meeting with a lawyer in like . . ." Her words trailed off as she twisted her arm to look at the watch on her left wrist. "Seven minutes."

Gabriel fell into step beside her, the crisp, earthy scent of his cologne wafting up to her nostrils as she approached the side door that led to the garage.

"You finally catch a charge for that temper of yours?" he asked, and then chuckled.

"You're not funny." But he was cute. Dangerously cute with his tall self—Tami loved a tall man, especially in contrast to her five-foot-two-inch stature.

But Gabriel had so much more than just his height going for him. His beautiful pecan complexion was perfectly accented by black, wavy hair, which he kept cut low; a thin mustache; and full eyebrows that secretly made her jealous. He had an athletic build and soulful eyes, and he was quick to laugh—at his own corny jokes. Still, he was fun to be around most times, and on a few occasions, those fun times had turned into sexy times. But they were just friends, because that was all Tami had room for in her jumbled mind.

"Yeah, I am, and that's why you love me," he continued, stopping at the door when she did.

She straightened the strap of her purse on her shoulder and then propped a hand on her hip before staring up at him. He wasn't lying—she did love him. In a best-friend, buddy with-benefits sort of way. "Anyway," she said with a grin that couldn't help spreading, since he was looking at her with his own goofy smile, "I have to meet with this lawyer about my grandmother's will. Hopefully, it won't take too long, because I have a Zoom interview scheduled for later this afternoon."

"Still looking for another job, huh?" he asked, and leaned his shoulder against the door. "I told you I can put in a good word for you with my supervisor. You don't even need experience. Just have to pass a background check and drug test. You know the drill."

He shrugged and she inwardly groaned. She didn't know who would lose their shit faster, her mother or Yvonne, if she announced she was going to be a rent-a-cop in the apartment building where she lived. Mama would go on and on about wasting the business administration degree it had taken her six years to obtain, and Yvonne would run down how financially irresponsible it would be for an almost-thirty-year-old woman to take a job that barely paid minimum wage.

"Thanks, but no thanks. I've got a little stashed away—and remember that contest I told you about? The one where some ad agency was asking for jingle lyrics?" His forehead scrunched as if he were trying to recall, so she just waved her hand and continued. "It was about five or six months ago. Anyway, I won! Wait . . ." She paused, and this time she was the one to frown. "I thought I told you about this. Guess I didn't. So anyway, I won, and they sent me a twenty-five-hundred-dollar check."

"Really? That's what's up! Look at you, following your dreams," he said before tweaking her nose. "Annnnnd making money."

She smirked, even though she knew his comment was meant to ease her ire at her family's lack of belief in her ability to make a stable living in the music industry. "One twenty-five-hundred-dollar check isn't exactly fantastic money," she said. "Considering I now have to pay my eleven-hundred-dollar-a-month rent on my own."

"But it's a start," he told her. "A damn good start."

A shrug was all she could muster at Gabriel's positive words. He meant well, and she appreciated him for being her biggest cheerleader. She was just in a mood. This meeting with her sisters and this lawyer had kept her anxiety on one hundred all through the night and that morning.

And now she was on her way to what was sure to be another sister showdown. That's what she called it whenever she had to be in the same room with her two older sisters—a showdown to see who would get angry enough to walk out first. It was usually Lana, because she had no backbone and/or time in her busy bougie-ass life to be bothered with her family.

"Okay, well, until you make it big-time in music—which I'm positive you will—my sister manages the Starbucks in the credit union building downtown. I can call her to see if she needs some help."

"Nah, I can barely remember how to order the simple hot chocolate I get when I go in there. I'd never get anybody's order right." Which meant she'd end up either getting fired or quitting before they fired her, because she was known for doing that too.

Plus, she didn't want Gabriel getting her a job, especially not through his sister. What if his family started thinking of her as the hot mess her own family did? Not that it mattered, since she and Gabriel weren't in a real romantic relationship, but that didn't stop the thoughts from jacking up her anxiety.

"True, true," he said with a nod. "Which is why I always make the coffee-and-hot-chocolate run for us."

Gabriel did a lot of things for her. He was a good guy and a great friend. Which was precisely why the last thing she wanted was to be indebted to him for finding her a job. That thought immediately brought forth a question: What *did* she want from Gabriel?

"Look, thanks. I really appreciate all your help. But I've got a feeling about this interview this afternoon. I think things are about to start looking up for me."

His smile spread. "That's my girl—always optimistic. So, you wanna catch a movie or something tonight? I get off at six."

Like he had to tell her what time he got off work. He'd been on the day shift, ten to six, for the past year and a half that she'd lived there. It was how they'd met and started this friends-with-benefits situation they had going on.

"Ah, I don't know. Might have to . . . um . . . do some studying in case I get this job." Did that sound like a brush-off? She hoped not, because she never wanted to hurt Gabriel's feelings. And she did like being with him. She just didn't feel like it tonight. The one thing she did agree with her family about was that she needed to find a steady-paying job and keep it while she still tried to pursue a career writing and producing music. That meant she had to focus on figuring out what would be a good—even if temporary—job for her. She couldn't do that while watching some comedy with Gabriel—because those were his favorite—or, a better probability, having sex with him.

"Hey, I really gotta go. I'll text you later if things change."

And then she pushed through the door, barely acknowledging his reply: "Okay, drive carefully."

She would drive carefully, but she'd also drive fast, because she really didn't want to give Yvonne any ammunition to come at her. Not again.

Chapter 2

LANA

37K in 37 days. No extensions.

Thirty-seven. Thousand. Dollars.

Lana cleared her phone of the screenshot she'd taken on her husband's device and texted to herself that morning. She'd made sure to delete the text to herself and screenshot from Isaac's phone before dropping it back onto the bed, where he'd left it. He'd come in from his workout at their building's gym at eleven forty-five. A time he should've been in his office at Sable Systems, the computer-engineering firm where he'd worked for the last ten years.

Isaac hadn't spoken a word as he waltzed past her. Sitting on the white leather-backed stool at their kitchen island, she'd watched him over the rim of her mug as she slowly sipped on her second cup of coffee. He wore dark-green basketball shorts with black compression leggings beneath them, black running shoes, and a white T-shirt stained with sweat at the armpits and wide patches down the front and back. Despite that and the fact that he'd acted like he had no home training—entering a room without speaking—Isaac Camby was still one of the finest men she'd ever seen. With his milk chocolate–hued skin, slim build, mesmerizing eyes, and silky voice, he'd claimed her heart fourteen years ago. And no matter what had happened during that course of time, she hadn't been able to break free of the trance his smooth lines, romantic interludes, and bone-melting sex had placed her under.

Not that he'd done anything particularly brutal or dirty during their marriage. No, Isaac was a good man. He worked hard, gave her the time and attention she deserved, supported and encouraged her dreams, made good money, and pleased her sexually. He was the ideal man for her—except when he gambled and lost, which he did more often than not.

She set her mug down and moved into the bedroom, giving a cursory glance at the expansive primary suite of their condo, which was situated in the center of Back Bay. The floors were wide-planked gray hardwood, with a plush, abstract gray-black-and-white area rug covering a good portion of the space. Their tufted-headboard California king bed was centered against one wall and had matching pewter nightstands on both sides. She'd made the bed once she'd climbed out of it a few hours earlier, smoothed the stone-gray duvet over pristine white sheets, fluffed the white-cased pillows they slept on, as well as the four decorative ones that Isaac had never understood the need for.

Sunlight poured through the windows, brightening the soft-gray walls and giving the space an airy feeling she relished on good days but still managed to feel trapped by on bad ones. Today was shaping up to be a bad one. This was the life she'd always wanted: the beautiful home, the handsome husband, a successful career—it was all she'd dreamed of and more. And yet it wasn't everything.

For as lovingly as she'd decorated the eighteen-hundred-square-foot three-bedroom, two-bathroom, there was still something missing. And that something had left a gaping hole in her soul that she desperately needed to fill. Luckily for her, she and Isaac were on the same page about what was missing—at least, they had been the last time she'd checked. The problem was, Lana hadn't checked in with Isaac on their baby timeline in almost a year. Not because she didn't still want to hear the shuffling of tiny feet over these immaculate floors or pick up dolls, trucks, and whatever other toys she knew they'd happily buy for their toddler from the living room or their room—because she still desperately wanted to do those things. But honestly, she'd started to wonder how that scenario would fit into the steadily growing tenuous vibe that permeated within these walls.

Crossing the space, she went to stand in the doorway of their primary bathroom. The floor was lighter here, a hexagon pattern of narrow gray and white tile; there was also a marble-top double vanity, a sunken tub, and floor-to-ceiling glass shower doors. Isaac stood behind those doors now, clouded by steam from the water spraying over his naked body. She watched as he dragged the cloth covered in soapy suds up and down his toned limbs, across his torso, and between his legs. Her breath hitched slightly at the sight, and she let a small, soft smile flutter over her lips. The spark was still there. She still wanted this man physically, and if the way her heart ached each time she thought about the very slim possibility of walking away from him and all they'd made together was any indication, she still craved him emotionally as well.

But there was no denying the cracks in their foundation, the places where this addiction that he had yet to claim—at least, not openly to her—was steadily creeping in, threatening to shatter their entire world.

"You gonna keep staring or come over here and join me, beautiful?"

The rich timbre of his voice yanked her out of her thoughts, and that small smile she'd allowed spread into a wider, more seductive one.

"Well, you walked by like you hadn't noticed I was there, so I wasn't sure you wanted company," she replied, and stepped fully into the room.

He moved farther beneath the water, which came down from the rainfall-jet panel system, and she watched it wash away all the soap, leaving his fit body glistening. She'd undone the belt of her robe, letting the silky green fabric fall to the floor, and was just pulling the cami nightdress she'd slept in up and over her head when he said, "I always notice you."

Then he moved from beneath the water and pushed the door open for her. The moment she stepped into the shower, he snaked an arm around her waist and pulled her naked body flush against his. His other hand immediately eased around the nape of her neck, fingers traveling up to twist into her hair, which she hadn't even thought to cover before hopping in with him. He leaned in, positioning his lips directly at her ear. "I can't breathe without you," he whispered.

And every worry, every doubt, every one of those cracks in their foundation that she'd just been contemplating, dissipated, leaving only his words of adoration, of desire, of love. Words that she drank thirstily, absorbed with every fiber of her being, and returned with honesty and fervor. She loved this man, and in this moment, she needed him more than she needed to figure out how their marriage was going to survive.

But just like many others before, that moment passed—blissfully so, but still, it was gone—and what was left two hours later as she sat in her car, replaying the morning's events, was despair. Leaning forward, she rested her head on the steering wheel and closed her eyes. How in the hell was she going to come up with $37,000? And why was she even trying to come up with it on her own, anyway? It wasn't her debt. But he *was* her husband.

What's hers was his, and what was his was hers. Or some other mess that preacher had said to them during their premarital counseling.

"It's going to be fine," she whispered. "It's all going to work out."

Just as it had the last time.

And the time before that.

Her phone dinged with a notification, bringing her attention abruptly back to the present, and she cracked open an eye to look down at her device. A reminder that she needed to be at the lawyer's office by one o'clock flashed on the screen. It was twelve thirty, and she had something she needed to do first. Now that she felt like she was being rushed, she put the useless pity party she'd been about to have on hold and sat up straight in her seat. Clearing her throat, she grabbed her purse with one hand and reached for the door handle with the other. She was dreading this meeting as much as she dreaded having to think about how she was going to pay her husband's latest gambling debt.

Five minutes later, Lana was walking into the bank and being directed to a set of chairs situated about six feet from a cluster of cubicles. Crossing one leg over the other, she smoothed down the soft material of the purple-and-white floral-print sundress she wore. Moving the Hermès clutch from where she'd tucked it under her arm, she set it in her lap and spread her fingers over it. Then she looked around to the people standing in the lines on the other side of the floor. Tellers worked behind clear glass, counting and disbursing money. An older woman, with one of those rickety metal shopping carts she hadn't seen since her grandmother had walked from the marketplace in town back to her waterfront house in South Carolina, came through the revolving doors at the front of the bank. Of course, that cart got stuck because those slices of space really were meant for only one person to fit in at a time. She was just about to get up and go help the woman when the security guard finally decided he'd leave his post, where he'd been standing with his back propped against the wall, eyes glued to his phone.

"Mrs. Butler-Camby?" a woman called.

Snapping her head around to the cubicles once again, she replied, "Yes. That's me."

The woman showcased her perfectly straight white teeth in a smile and waved a hand. "Great, you can come on over with me."

Lana followed her and took a seat in the guest chair directly across from the woman's desk.

"You know, you're welcome to use our business line at the far end of the counter anytime you come in," the woman—the placard on the front of the desk displayed her name as BRENDA JOHNSON—said.

It would've been nice if Brenda had introduced herself, but Lana wasn't here to tell these people how to do their jobs. At least, she prayed she didn't have to do that.

"I prefer to handle my business in a more discreet way," Lana replied.

Brenda blinked ridiculously long fake eyelashes at her in response before folding her hands over the desk blotter. "Well, then, how may I help you?"

Unsnapping her clutch, Lana dug her hand inside and pulled out the check she'd already endorsed with her signature and account number. "I'd like to deposit that into my account and check the balances of all of the other accounts with my name on them."

Brenda reached for the check. "We also have online banking, and our ATM machines can accept deposits."

It was Lana's turn to paste on a fake smile as she glanced at Brenda. "Then it's amazing that you still have a job, with all the other ways customers can be assisted."

The dismayed look that crossed Brenda's face only amused Lana, because hell, she hadn't told the woman to keep pushing her buttons. All she had to do was smile and do her job.

Lana wasn't the confrontational type like her baby sister, Tami. That girl was always looking for a fight—physical, when she'd been in middle and high school, and verbal, now that she'd entered the land of adulthood. If Tami didn't like something or felt she was being wronged in some way, she was damn sure letting you know. She'd been a spitfire since she'd first learned to talk and had gotten herself into more than a few bouts of trouble because of her sassy mouth and bristly attitude.

No, Lana was the calmest of her sisters, the most levelheaded, and the peacekeeper. Or, as Tami often said, she was "the bougie bitch." She didn't mind that title as much as she probably should've, because she'd always been well aware that she was nothing like Tami or Yvonne. Never had been. In fact, she'd often wondered if she'd been adopted, since Tami and Yvonne resembled each other, with their brown-sugar complexions, round faces, and pert noses. They were the cute sisters, while she'd been blessed with blunt good looks—a toasty-brown complexion; wide, full mouth; long nose; and expressive eyes. Her tall, slim frame had even landed her two years in modeling school, where she'd discovered she preferred being behind the camera and controlling the shots rather than posing in them.

"There are four accounts with the name Alana M. Butler-Camby on them. One as the sole owner of the business AMB Photography, and the remaining three as co-owner with Isaac J. Camby," Brenda said, reading from her computer screen.

"Correct," Lana told her. "I'd like that check deposited into the AMB account."

It was her payment from the gallery where she'd had her third showing last summer. The yearlong contract was ending next week, and she would need to decide whether to allow the three photos that hadn't been sold to remain at the gallery. If not, she would put them on her website with the other prints she sold directly.

Brenda's lilac acrylic nails danced over the keyboard before pausing to pick up the check and run it through some type of imaging machine. Then she pulled a deposit slip from her drawer and filled that out before attaching it to the check. She pushed another button, and a receipt printed from yet another machine. She pushed that across the desk toward Lana.

Lana picked it up and slid it into her purse.

"That gives you a balance of $10,367.89 in the AMB account," Brenda told her before pushing more buttons. "And $3,665 in the joint checking account. The savings has a balance of $264.95, and the money market account is at the minimum amount to keep it open: $3,501."

Dammit.

Of course, Lana didn't say that out loud. Instead, she nodded and snapped her purse shut. "Thank you so much for your help, Brenda."

"Oh," Brenda said, and looked at Lana as if she couldn't believe the woman wasn't asking her to do something else. "Will that be all for you today, ma'am?"

A few minutes ago, she hadn't wanted to do the two things Lana had asked, and now she was asking about doing more. "Yes, that sure will be. Again, thank you."

With that, she walked out of the woman's cubicle and out of the bank.

She was back in her car again before she slammed her palms against the steering wheel. "Dammit! Dammit! Dammit, Isaac!"

Chapter 3

YVONNE

"As you know, I was contacted by Jeremiah Sinclair about six months ago to assist in executing the directives in the will of Elizabeth Lorraine Coleman-Butler," Robyn Crawford said.

Yvonne thought the attorney was probably around her age, but she presumed the woman was a lot less stressed than she was at this very moment. The attorney they'd met a couple of weeks ago, when she'd called them to this same office, wore a nice royal-blue skirt suit and kept her gaze level with Yvonne's and her sisters' yet discerning. Robyn—as she'd asked them to call her—was another professional Black woman focused on doing her job to the best of her ability. Yvonne could respect that. Even if she envied the fact that Robyn also looked like she enjoyed doing her job.

"Yes," Yvonne said evenly, when she really wanted to yell for Robyn to hurry up and get this over with. "We understand that because Grandma Betty passed away on Daufuskie Island, the correct jurisdiction for all of her legal dealings is in Beaufort County, South Carolina."

"That's right," Robyn replied, with a nod toward Yvonne.

There was a snicker to her left, but Yvonne didn't turn to see which one of her sisters had made the sound. She figured it was Tami—the youngest, at twenty-nine, and still the most impetuous and irritating of the threesome. Lana, at thirty-five, had grown into exactly the type of woman Yvonne had thought she would—professional, powerful, and perfect.

"You've already told us about the cremation and the memorial service that we didn't get the chance to attend," Lana said. "What else is there to discuss? Why are we here now?"

Grandma Betty—or Elizabeth Lorraine Coleman-Butler, as Robyn and the obituary that Yvonne had printed and still carried around in her purse referred to her. Or Betty Butler—the renowned, award-winning R & B singer of the sixties and seventies—as a good portion of the world had known her. However she was known, she was gone. Yvonne's father's mother, the only grandmother the sisters had ever had a relationship with, had passed away.

Two weeks ago, Robyn had contacted them and told them Grandma Betty had suffered complications from pneumonia. She'd been immediately cremated, as per her instructions. By the time Robyn had gotten them all together for that first meeting, the memorial service—which Grandma Betty had also preplanned—had already taken place because their grandmother had left strict instructions for everything to be done within three days. Like she hadn't been raised a Black Baptist in the South, where the whole family gathering—funeral, burial, and repast— could take up to two weeks. And really, that wasn't even something that was relegated to the South. Yvonne recalled when they were younger and their uncle, Mama's only brother, had passed. It had taken a week for Aunt Irene to get all her family in town, then wait for donations toward the funeral expenses, before the funeral home would even set a date for the services.

Anyway, Yvonne had the same question Lana did, so she waited impatiently for Robyn's response.

"Mrs. Butler was adamant about every one of her wishes being carried out in exacting order," Robyn continued.

Yvonne wasn't shocked; Grandma Betty had always been a bossy one. How many times had Daddy shaken his head and said, "You're just like your grandmama"? Too many for Yvonne to count, although the memory had the corners of her mouth threatening to tilt into a smile.

"Of course she was." Lana sounded less than surprised, as they all probably were. She'd crossed one leg over the other so that the red bottom of the expensive pump she wore was visible to everyone sitting on this side of the desk.

"What wishes does she need carried out now?" Tami asked. "The cremation is done, and we didn't even get a chance to contest it."

Robyn shook her head. "Her request was made clear in the will that was witnessed and filed in the state of South Carolina. And her closest friend on the island knew of it and made sure it was executed expeditiously. Even if you were on the island the day of her death, you most likely would not have had enough time to petition the court and get a hearing date to request a change." She flipped open the clay-colored folder on her desk. "The rest, however, can be handled in a few ways."

Yvonne sighed. She had a feeling that whatever fell from Robyn's lips from this point forward wasn't going to be much better than finding out their grandmother was gone and not being able to get down to the island in time to pay their respects.

"In South Carolina, an estate can skip probate if it's less than twenty-five thousand dollars," Robyn began.

It was Tami's turn to sigh, and Lana's head tilted as if she were suddenly extremely interested in what was being said. Yvonne shifted her gaze from her sisters and locked in on Robyn and the glossy black curls that fell over her shoulders. It was one of several styles the woman wore, according to the pictures on the credenza by the door. One, a wedding photo, in which her hair had been pulled into a top bun cradled by a sparkling tiara. Another, with those lustrous curls draping over one shoulder. The final one, where she wore her natural dark coils and was flanked on either side by adorable twin girls. That one had held

Yvonne's gaze both times she'd walked into this office, but she resisted turning her attention to it now. There were more important matters at hand than wondering how this woman had managed to capture it all: success *and* joy.

"Anything above that amount, and the estate must go through probate to be settled," Robyn continued. "There's informal probate, which is most commonly used when all parties are in agreement regarding the distribution of the estate. No quarreling, no formal disputes." She gave each of them a quick nod, but Yonne wasn't fooled—the woman was waiting for one of them to go off about something.

To be honest, Yvonne was too. And, like Robyn, she knew that when and which sister would speak up first depended solely on what else Robyn had to say.

"Then there's unsupervised formal probate, which must go through the court to have the judge approve some of the actions regarding distribution." Robyn took a breath and continued. "Finally, there's supervised formal probate, in which the court oversees all aspects of the probate process."

"And now that we've had our lesson in estates and trusts, can you tell us what any of that has to do with us?" Lana asked, impatience lining her every word.

"Absolutely," Robyn replied, with a lift of her brow that seemed to acknowledge Lana's sarcasm. "There's the matter of Elizabeth's house." Robyn pushed her chair back and stood. She grabbed a small stack of folders on the edge of her desk and came around to offer one to each of the sisters. She continued to talk as she returned to her seat behind her desk. "It's located along the intracoastal waterway on Daufuskie Island."

Tami opened her folder first and gasped. "It's the summerhouse."

Yvonne opened her folder and stared down at a picture of a house she knew just as well as her younger sister.

"This house, the smaller blue one behind it, and the entire 2.94-acre lot, have been left in equal parts to Yvonne Renee, Alana Marie, and Tamela Michelle Butler," Robyn said, reading from a sheet of paper in the file.

"What?" Lana asked.

"The whole house?" was Tami's follow-up.

There were words running around in Yvonne's mind. Of course there were; she always knew what to say and when to say it. But at this very moment, she remained silent, one shaky finger gliding over the picture of the house by the water—the place she'd imagined princesses lived and would one day be swept into a fantastical life of love and happiness. The forty-year-old woman she'd become scoffed at the seven-year-old girl who'd dared to dream.

A slow smile crept along Robyn's face. It was a pretty smile, a peaceful one that again had Yvonne unfairly disliking her. Because really, it wasn't Robyn's fault that she'd found a way to have all the things in life Yvonne had secretly wanted—a great job *and* a loving family. That was all her fault because, as Mama had told her far too often for her to ever forget, *Your life is what* you *make it*. The fact that Yvonne had made her career a priority—sacrificing romantic relationships that might've, at some point, led to her having daughters, whom she'd teach to love and cherish each other the way she wished she and her sisters did—was all on her.

"Yes, both houses and the land now belong to the three of you," Robyn said.

"Why?" Yvonne's tone echoed Lana's previous bewilderment. "Why would she leave all that to us? Outside of spending Thanksgiving with her every year, we haven't spent any significant time there since we were teenagers." A fact that had made her extremely sad in the last year, and even more so the moment she'd learned that her grandmother had passed.

"Since I was sixteen," Tami stated quietly. "We haven't all spent a summer there together since I was sixteen."

Her youngest sister's voice pricked Yvonne's already annoyed state because she was right. Tami had loved when it was time to pack so they could go and visit Grandma Betty for the summer. It was the happiest Yvonne had ever seen her sister during their childhood—that and the months when they were actually on the island. For all her annoying traits, Tami's best features were her zest for life, her courageousness, and her ability to make the best of any situation. All things that Yvonne feared she'd never possess.

"Because you went to band camp that next summer and then that Jamaica trip you insisted you needed before going off to 'adult school,' as you called it," Yvonne said in a level tone that could—and where the prickly Tami was concerned, probably *would*—be construed as derision.

"College wasn't everybody's wet dream like it was yours, big sister," Tami muttered.

Yvonne loved both her sisters through all their faults and positives, but this one right here . . . she never disappointed. Tami could always be counted on for pushback, a confrontation, an argument. Grandma Betty had called her *spirited*, but Mama saw her youngest as defiant. Yvonne put her firmly in the exasperating category and clasped her fingers together in her lap. She took a steadying breath and continued. "Why would she leave the house to us?"

Robyn shrugged. "It was her last wish that the three of you have this house."

"To keep?" Lana asked. "I don't want to live on that island. There's nobody there, nothing to do."

"You mean no high-society parties for you to attend. No stores where you can buy those ridiculously expensive—yet admittedly cute—shoes you love so much," Tami tossed at Lana with a half smile.

Lana's shoes *were* cute . . . *and* expensive, but Yvonne tried not to care. Her perfect middle sister had it all, and Yvonne was both proud as hell and envious of her.

"Wait, that's not it, is it?" Yvonne asked. "We don't have to move to the island to claim this house? And why are you just telling us this now? Why didn't you just tell us everything a couple of weeks ago?"

"Elizabeth wanted to give you time to deal with her passing first," Robyn replied. "And Jeremiah and I took that time to make sure we had all the necessary paperwork in order to pass it on to you ladies at one time. Deeds, property maps, contractor and account information . . . We thought it would be simpler if all of this was verified and clearly documented for you when the additional terms of Elizabeth's will were explained."

"Contractor and account information? Additional terms?" Yvonne asked and then sighed. "Why don't you just tell us everything right now, Robyn. This piecemeal thing you're doing is starting to get annoying."

"Agreed," Lana said.

Robyn gave a nod as if she'd expected that sentiment. "It's all in the files I had my assistant compile for you. There's a lot of information there, so you don't have to try and digest it all now. But to sum this all up, your grandmother wants the three of you to renovate the house and then decide whether you'll keep it or sell it. She selected the contractor—a native to the island—who she trusted would preserve the historical integrity of the place but also respect your 'more modern opinions,' as she wrote in her notes."

That last part was said with a sort of chuckle from Robyn, which irked the hell out of Yvonne. Robyn hadn't known Grandma Betty. How could she have known that something like this would've totally entertained the old woman?

Her grandmother had known the sisters were like oil and water; she'd been the one who'd told them that time and time again, with a slap of a hand to her knee as she sat in one of those big white rocking chairs on her front porch—diamonds glittering from the rings on her fingers, her hair perfectly styled as if she had a show to do later that night. Grandma Betty had also known that Tami loved the island and the summerhouse way more than Yvonne or Lana ever had. Her slick comments each year when they arrived for Thanksgiving, wishing that there'd be some situation that forced them back to the island for more than a long weekend once a year, were a sure giveaway.

That quick flash of memory had Yvonne releasing a quiet gasp, her eyes shifting from Robyn down to the open file on her lap, the picture of that house with its huge front porch staring up at her.

"So we just need to fix this house up and sell it?" Lana said. "That shouldn't take too long."

"Hold up," Tami said, shaking her head. She closed the file on her lap and looked to her right and then her left—from where Lana sat to where Yvonne sat. Then she looked at Robyn. "This house, both houses, and all this land is ours now? And Grandma Betty wants us to sell it?"

Robyn sat back in her chair, her hands falling into her lap. She tilted her head as if she'd been expecting that question from this sister—and again, Yvonne was totally annoyed. This woman didn't know them well enough to expect any specific reaction, and she certainly didn't know how they were going to handle all this new information. Well, Yvonne was clueless on that point, too, but she suddenly wanted to leave this office and this entire will and inheritance business behind.

"It doesn't say specifically that you have to sell," Robyn answered. "It just says that she wants you to fix up the house and decide."

"Okay, there's a number right here," Lana said, flipping through some of the papers in the file. "All we have to do is call this contractor and have him get started. Then we can get this process underway."

"With what money?" Yvonne asked. "We don't have any money to fix up anything. If we did, our mother would have the accessibility she now needs in her house."

Those words were laced with all the ire Yvonne had been holding toward her sisters for the last year. It had been a little over two years since their mother had suffered a hemorrhagic stroke, and just about twenty-two months since Yvonne had uprooted her life so that she could provide Freda with the care she needed.

Probably sensing there was about to be an explosion of epic proportions between them, Robyn quickly spoke up. "The account I mentioned—it's an escrow account the contractor has been holding for this very purpose. Elizabeth knew that if she left the money in her account for you ladies to use, it might get tied up in the estate paperwork and legalities. She didn't want your efforts hampered in any way, so the contractor has fifty thousand dollars and is waiting for the three of you to arrive on the island to begin discussions on the work to be done."

Yvonne was shaking her head before Robyn finished speaking. "I can't go to that island. Who's going to take care of Mama?"

"I have a show to dismantle and meetings with my agent about a book pitch and other possible exhibits," Lana interjected. "I can't leave the city."

"I have to . . . I, um . . . I-I need to, uh," Tami stuttered and then grinned. "I'd love to go back to the island."

After rubbing her temples to calm a slow-brewing headache, Yvonne used both hands to form a T and called, "Time out. I feel like there's more to this you're not telling us. So before we all get into our minds what the next step is, I'd like you to just spill it."

"I'm telling you exactly what I've been instructed to tell you via Jeremiah and the terms of Elizabeth's will," Robyn stated.

Yvonne only blinked. "What's the 'out' clause?" she asked. "There has to be a way we can avoid all of this construction, escrow accounts, and the dictating of our steps and time. Grandma Betty would've given us a choice." Wouldn't she? There'd never been a time that her grandmother had come right out and said, "I want the three of you to live in this house," or done anything regarding this house. There were undertones of wanting them to visit the island more, but that was it. So this will and these stipulations were weird as hell.

"You sure about that?" Tami asked. "She never gave us a choice about eating that nasty okra."

Now, *that* was a memory Yvonne could have done without. She hated the vegetable too.

"If you do nothing, the house will continue to fall into disrepair and eventually be taken over by the historical society or the bank, who—because of the high value to prime intracoastal property like this—would get at least a million dollars only to have the new owners demolish both houses and build something new."

Tami gasped. "Demolish the summerhouse?"

"It's just a house," Lana said. "And we can delegate the renovations."

Robyn shook her head. "Elizabeth wants the three of you to stay on the island while the work is being done and leave once you decide what to do with the property."

Yvonne smirked. "Of course she does."

"How can she dictate to us from the grave?" Lana asked.

A wry chuckle bubbled up and out of Yvonne then. She rubbed a finger over her chin as the laughter continued. "Because she's Grandma Betty—the woman who always got her way, no matter what."

Chapter 4

LANA

"I'm not going back there," Lana said thirty minutes later, when they'd traded Robyn Crawford's office for a booth at Rabe's, a corner bar masquerading as a soul food restaurant, where Tami had insisted they stop to eat and discuss their newfound dilemma. "This isn't some Hallmark movie where we all pack up and go down south to save the family home. I have a real life right here in Boston. I don't have time to be fulfilling someone else's quirky last demands."

"Even if that someone is your grandmother?" Tami shook her head. "Don't answer that, because I already know what you're gonna say. And whatever, I'm going down there to do what she asked." Tami hummed as she perused the menu without a care in the world—or rather, without a care for what anybody wanted besides herself. "I always loved it there. Ohhhh, hush puppies. I haven't had those in forever. Remember, Grandma Betty used to make them on Friday nights with fried catfish, and we'd burn our fingers grabbing them off that plate as soon as she scooped them outta the grease?" Tami let out a blissful sigh.

"Mama used to make them too," Yvonne added as she reluctantly looked at the menu.

Tami frowned. "Hers weren't as good as Grandma Betty's."

"Well, everybody cooks things differently, Tam," Yvonne replied without bothering to look up at her sister.

"I know," Tami chirped. "Some people cook better than others. And some people don't cook at all." Her gaze immediately landed on Lana, who refused to look at that menu and was running her finger along the rim of the water glass in front of her.

She'd resisted the urge to grab the napkin and wipe the glass, because she didn't want to hear any of her sisters' smart remarks about her being a germaphobe. "I don't need to cook when there are perfectly good meal services here in the city that keep me and my husband well fed," she replied, and reminded herself to pay that bill when she got home—that one and all the others, since managing the household finances had always been her job. Isaac made the higher, steady salary between them, and after they'd moved in together, he'd suggested she quit her job at the magazine where she'd been photo editor to focus on her own photography career. Elated by his unwavering support, she'd hopped on that opportunity, and after a year of focusing on building her portfolio, she had booked her first small showing at a local gallery.

"And that's the most important thing, right?" Tami asked. "To make sure you and Isaac stay on top of the world, living your high-class lives and looking down on everyone else?"

"What are you even talking about? This isn't about Isaac and me. It's about what's feasible for our schedules. Grandma Betty always did that." Lana sighed heavily and rolled her eyes. "She used to call Mama late Thursday night to tell her to have us in Hilton Head in time to board the last ferry over to the island on Friday. And it was never a question of whether that was feasible or not. She said it and she meant it."

"And Mama did it," Lana continued with a huff. "That will always baffle me, since Mama didn't even like her."

"I don't think it was so much that Mama didn't like her but that she thought Grandma Betty was a little weird," Yvonne said.

"She was *a lot* weird," Lana countered, sending a curt glance to Yvonne, who was now sliding the black-framed glasses she'd put on to read the menu off her face. "Remember that time she had us participate in a séance? Tami didn't sleep in her own bed for the rest of the year, and Mama was livid."

"Yeah," Tami said with a slow nod. "All Mama kept saying when we got home was that Black folk don't play well with the dead. That might've been the only time Mama and I agreed on something."

Yvonne sighed. "You were six," she said to Tami. "Big Bird scared you when your class went to see *Sesame Street Live!*"

Tami wrinkled her nose. "And I still don't like birds."

After a heavy sigh, Lana continued. "My point is, why are we even considering this? It's ridiculous and intrusive. We have lives too; Grandma Betty never did appreciate that, with the way she used to fuss when we stopped coming down there for the summer and then insisted that every Thanksgiving we spend Wednesday through Sunday with her. She was so bossy." But Lana still loved her like she'd never loved another relative, except her father. The woman could work her nerves, with her lectures about life hidden in meat loaf, mashed potatoes, and green beans. Lana loved green beans.

"Maybe she was lonely," Yvonne said.

"Yeah," Lana agreed. "That's what I thought sometimes too. Especially after Daddy died and we stopped going down for the summer. That's why I never made excuses to get out of the Thanksgiving visits."

Tami looked around the restaurant. "Where's our server? I'd like to have something other than this lukewarm water for lunch."

"But I know you're not defending her," Lana said to Yvonne after giving up on trying to appeal to Tami and her wayward attention span. "You were the first one to stop going down for the summer visits."

"Because I was the first one to go to college. And then, when I finished school, I went straight to work," Yvonne said.

Tami rolled her eyes. "In the school system, just like Mama. Yeah, we know the story. But you were also off during the summer."

"I took classes during the summer to get my master's degree," Yvonne added, the ever-present irritation in her tone clear. "And for the record, I say we sell both houses as quickly as we can."

"Thank you!" Lana almost clapped with glee, relieved that somebody was actually on her side for once. "I think we should do the same. Just get it sold, divide up the money, and go on about our business."

She'd thought about it during their walk down the street to the restaurant. This could possibly be the answer to her current dilemma. If they could sell the house quickly, there was a good chance she could use her portion of the proceeds to pay off Isaac's debt. Then she could move on to the next steps in growing her career and her family without having to argue with her husband. That was what she wanted, right? To save her marriage and continue with the life she and Isaac had planned? That hadn't changed, had it?

"I'm going to call Robyn when I get back home and ask her about contesting just the terms that say we have to renovate before selling. It's such a weird clause, anyway—and really, I don't understand why Grandma Betty insisted on it. If it's our property now, we should be able to sell as is, if that's what we want." Yvonne paused briefly and shook her head. "Then I'll check to see what the value of these homes are now. Robyn said the bank might get a million dollars."

"Hold up," Tami interjected just as the server appeared. "I'll have a martini, an order of hush puppies, and a bacon cheeseburger. Cheddar cheese instead of American, and fried onions. No fries because I'm watching my carbs."

"You do know that hush puppies and the bun from the cheeseburger have carbs, right?" Yvonne asked, her face bunched into a frown as she looked over at Tami. "I'll have a chef's salad and a pink lemonade."

Lana drummed her fingers on the table. How could they think about food at a time like this? *Easily,* she surmised, since their husbands weren't in danger of being beaten to death by a bookie if they didn't come up with $37,000 in thirty-seven days. Of course, she didn't know if things were that dire with Isaac. She had no idea who his bookie was. Each time he owed a debt, she would just find the money by selling some prints, finagling this bill or that one to get it resolved. Then she'd give Isaac the money and pray that he did what he was supposed to do with it. But this was a lot more than Isaac had ever owed, and the tone of that text message didn't seem like there was room for negotiation or a missed due date.

Every aspect of this scenario had tipped the scales on the already precarious situation her life was in. She gritted her teeth—something she did only when she was stressed—and searched for some level of calm to at least get through this lunch with her sisters. The three didn't get together like this often enough, each of them busy with their own lives—or busy trying to stay *out* of each other's lives. It hadn't always been that way, but the last few years, and then Mama's illness, had put a strain on what Lana had assumed was a normal love-hate relationship between sisters.

"And for you, ma'am?" asked the server, who looked like she was no more than eighteen or nineteen years old. Lana hated being called *ma'am*. She wasn't old enough for that yet. Then again, looking at this girl—with her black lipstick, ear gauges, and ink-black hair and nails—Lana definitely *felt* old.

"Cheese fries and a fresh water with lemon," she said, and held her menu out for the server to take.

"I call dibs on some of your fries," Tami said when the server walked away.

Yvonne gave her a deadpan stare, but Lana scowled. "Fries are also carbs, Tami."

"That's why I didn't order them," Tami said. "Now, back to the houses. I think we should all pack our bags and head down to the island. For one, it would be like old times, and for two, it's what Grandma

Betty wanted us to do. And if we couldn't continue our summer trips to make her happy when she was alive, I think the next best thing to do is carry out her last wishes to the absolute detail."

Yvonne sat back in her chair and stared at Tami. Lana couldn't help it; she glared at Tami too.

Eventually—after a few moments—the corners of Yvonne's mouth turned up, and her eyes narrowed. "Did you quit or get fired this time?" she asked Tami.

Lana waited for Tami's response. She could not keep a job. For whatever reason, it just never worked out for her. Lana had actually started to believe that her baby sister was allergic to working.

Folding her arms over her chest, Tami sat back with a huff and then pouted. This child was twenty-nine years old and still pouting like she was three. Lana rolled her eyes so hard she felt a headache coming on.

"I didn't go to college and apply for a management position to be told I had to substitute in the infant classroom and change shitty diapers," Tami quipped. "I don't have any kids, and I'm not cleaning up after anyone else's."

Yvonne sighed. "So you quit."

"What other choice did I have?" Tami asked.

"Work until you find something better, for one," Lana replied. "But this is an old conversation that I do not feel like having."

"Same," Yvonne replied wryly. "So since you have time on your hands and will probably need a place to live because you don't have a paycheck to pay any of your bills, you can go on down to the island and babysit the renovations—"

"Wait," Lana interrupted. "Renovations are going to take too long. Why can't we sell as is?"

Tami made an annoyed face. "Because that's not what the will says. We—all three of us—have to go to the island and, as you call it, 'babysit the renovations.' And then we—all three of us—have to figure out what to do with the house."

"We're selling the house," Lana said.

"Exactly," Yvonne added. "And each of us will put up a certain amount from our proceeds to get Mama's house renovated to accommodate the ramp, bathroom, and kitchen changes she requires."

"I thought you were going to see if you could cash in one of her insurance policies to get that work done." It was a discussion they'd had months ago, after Yvonne had sent them both an angry email. Lana suspected that it had been Yvonne's attempt to avoid an in-person argument, but an online argument had ensued instead.

"And then we start a GoFundMe when it's time to come up with burial expenses? No thank you," Yvonne replied.

"You're putting her in the grave right behind Grandma Betty, huh?" Tami asked.

Yvonne slammed a hand on the table. "No. I'm thinking ahead, planning for the future—something I know is a foreign concept to you."

"Here's your martini," their server said when she returned and extended the glass to Tami, who had just sat up in her chair, ready to go in on Yvonne. "And your pink lemonade and your water with lemon."

Lana picked up her glass and immediately took a gulp. Just as Yvonne and Tami did the same.

"I should've gotten something stronger," she quipped.

"You and me both," Yvonne said while Tami took another sip from her glass and did a little shimmy that said she was pleased with her selection.

Chapter 5

TAMI

Twenty-four hours ago, she'd felt like she was just a little bit on the brink of a breakdown. She hadn't quite made it there yet, because if nothing else, Tami liked to believe she was an optimist. She also believed that all her dreams would eventually come true—if she could actually wrangle those dreams into one coherent concept. But that was a rabbit hole she'd venture down at another time. Tonight, she had plans to make.

With her feet tucked under her as she sat on her golden-yellow couch, she held her tablet in her lap and continued to scroll through pictures of the island where she'd spent her childhood summers. From the time she was three until the summer she'd turned sixteen, she, her sisters, and their father—before his untimely death when Tami was eight years old—had boarded a flight from Boston to Hilton Head Island. From there, they'd hop on the ferry for the forty-five-minute ride out to Daufuskie.

And once on that island with her Grandma Betty, life for Tami had become one adventure after another. Fabulous food; lazy afternoons lying on the dock, just staring up at the brilliant blue sky; and at night there was always music. In addition to having a thick, powerful singing voice, Grandma Betty could play the piano for hours, serenading the girls on sultry summer nights while crickets chirped in the distance and moonlight glistened over the water.

That was, hands down, Tami's fondest memory of her time on the island. Those nights when the family room in the summerhouse was alight with a golden blaze from the table lamps, the patio doors were open to let in the cooling breeze that rolled off the river, and she lay on her back on that burgundy-and-beige Aubusson rug that covered most of the hardwood floor. She was probably about six or seven during her earliest memory of those nights. Lana, who would've been twelve or thirteen then, was already boy crazy and had spent most of her time writing letters to her girlfriends and whatever boy she thought was cute at the time back home, curled up at the end of one of the two walnut-brown couches in the room. Yvonne—who would've been seventeen, already the mature and studious one with her nose in a book—had remained in the family room with them only because Grandma Betty had insisted on their bonding time.

If she closed her eyes, Tami could still see her grandmother's long fingers moving effortlessly over the piano keys, her fingernails polished in one of those nude tones she always wore, rings with huge diamonds and rubies on multiple fingers. Sometimes she'd sing a song, either one of hers or somebody else's from the sixties, her favorite era of music. Other times, she'd hum something distinctly gospel. It didn't matter which; Tami would always lie on her back, one foot planted on the rug, an ankle crossed over her knee. Her arms would be out at her sides, hands on the floor so her fingers could drum to the melody.

A banging sound echoed loudly, jolting her from her thoughts. It took her a moment of blinking and steadying her mind on the here and now to realize it was a knock at her door. She stood and set her tablet on the couch before heading across the room.

"Hey," she said to Gabriel after swinging open the door. "Were we supposed to meet up tonight?" Her brow furrowed as she tried to recall whether she'd totally blanked on their plans.

"Nope," he replied, and then stepped forward. "But it's dinnertime, and I went down to that pizza spot you like. So I'm here to share." As if she couldn't already see the pizza box and the plastic bag on top that looked to be holding two additional containers of food, he lifted his arms to ease the food closer to her face.

As soon as she caught the scent of melted cheese—and that amazing sauce the pizza place used on their pies and as a dipping sauce for their tasty garlic knots—her stomach growled.

"You gonna let me in or nah?" he asked, hiking up one thick brow as he grinned.

Gabriel's smile may have been his most dangerous weapon where women were concerned. It gave way to the tiniest dimples in his cheeks, which were otherwise barely noticeable beneath his low-cut beard. He was bald, with great eyebrows and eyes that laughed right along with his smile.

"When you're bearing such delicious gifts, hell yeah, I'm lettin' you in," she replied, and stepped aside to let him pass.

As she closed and locked the door, Gabriel walked through her small living room to her equally small kitchen.

"You changed that room around again?" he said as she followed him into the kitchen. "I swear, I don't know anybody who needs to have a different furniture setup in their house as frequently as you."

She moved around him to get two glasses out of one cabinet while he opened another to take out two plates. He'd been in her apartment enough times to know where everything was and to have unspoken permission to get things on his own.

"Change is good," was all she said in response to the debate they'd had way too many times. "Besides, Shana's lyin'-ass boyfriend burned a hole in my rug when he was drunk and dropped his cigarette one night. I had to move the couch to cover it."

"You should've made her pay for a new rug," he said, putting a slice of pepperoni—with extra cheese, ham, and onions—onto each plate.

She sighed and held the glasses, one at a time, under the ice maker on the front of the refrigerator to fill them up. "She was packed and gone before I could get a chance," she replied. "Anyway, I'm just glad to have both of them out."

"Until you have to pay your rent on the first of the month."

After grabbing two cans of soda from the case on the floor, she tucked them under her arms and retrieved the glasses. "Don't remind me," she said, and then walked back into the living room.

He looped the handles of the plastic bag on his fingers and then picked up both plates to bring into the living room. The pizza box remained on the kitchen counter. Joining her on the couch, he offered her a plate, and once she accepted, he set the bag on the coffee table.

"Hot wings and fries," he said as he removed the plastic containers from the bag and then opened each one.

"I told you, I'm watching my carbs," she replied with a groan. "And before you say it, I know the pizza crust has carbs. But the fries will only add to it."

"So don't eat them," he said, then reached over to snatch a few and stuff them into his mouth.

That was easier said than done, which was the whole reason she'd brought it up to him again.

"You know if you need any help—financially or otherwise—you can just let me know," he said after they'd been eating in silence for a few moments.

She'd just taken a bite of pizza and now looked over at him. "Huh?"

He smiled when he glanced at her and then reached out to grab the thread of cheese that had obviously been dangling from the corner of her mouth. If it were with any other guy, there probably would've been some embarrassment, but this was just Gabriel. Still, she grabbed her napkin and wiped her mouth; he took one, too, and cleaned his fingers.

"I said, if you need anything, all you have to do is ask."

She fought back confusion. "Why would I ask you for money?"

He folded his slice of pizza and brought it to his mouth before pausing to respond. "Uh, because you're unemployed and your roommate just moved out. It might be a little tough paying bills with no money coming in."

She swallowed. "I get that," she told him. "But I'm really not as irresponsible as everybody seems to think I am. I do have a little bit saved up, so I should be able to scrape by until I get another job. Plus, I'd never ask you—or anybody else, for that matter—for money." She'd work it out. Like she'd been trying to do for the past few years.

That hadn't been the case during college or the years immediately following, when all Tami had seemed to do was make one mistake after another. She could admit that, but she had attempted to soothe the guilt for her bad decisions with the fact that she was young and just figuring out how to be an adult. That excuse could only last for so long, according to her sisters—still, neither of them had ever totally abandoned her. Sure, every time they'd come to her rescue with money for the utility or cable bill in the apartment she'd insisted she needed instead of staying on campus, or filled her refrigerator with groceries, or helped with her car payment because she also hadn't wanted a used car that she was certain would break down on her and cause more financial woes, a lecture had followed their assistance. But neither of them had ever left her hanging; she knew without a doubt that they were there for her no matter what.

This time, though, she'd sworn she wouldn't ask. She couldn't—not with Yvonne shouldering all the responsibilities where their mother was concerned. Although that was and had always been Yvonne's choice. And Tami knew that Lana was trying to have a baby, because she'd let it slip one day when the two of them had gone for coffee after a stressful visit with their mother. No, Tami was through running to her sisters for help, and she wasn't going to start a new habit of leaning on her best friend instead.

Gabriel nodded and continued to chew. "First, I never thought you were irresponsible," he said. "I'm just saying that I'm here if you need me, Tami. That's all."

There was something to his tone—an obvious tinge of irritation, she supposed, at what she'd said. But there was definitely something else that wasn't usually there; she just couldn't pinpoint what it was. And anyway, she didn't like this conversation, so it was best she just change the subject.

"I killed that interview yesterday," she told him. "I thought I was going to be late for it because after that meeting at the lawyer's office, I had lunch with my sisters. But I made it back here just in time. Logged on to Zoom and proceeded to wow the two executives that interviewed me."

"I've never even heard of a record label in Boston," he replied, reaching for one of the sodas to pour into his glass. "And what position did you apply for?"

"Executive assistant," she told him. "And it's a relatively new label. So this is a really, really entry-level position. But at least I'll be in the industry I've always wanted to be in."

He turned to her again, this time with his head tilted. "You never told me you seriously wanted to work in the music industry."

She began picking the pepperoni off her pizza. For some reason, it seemed too salty tonight. "Probably because when I told my family, they didn't take it seriously. Guess I just figured you wouldn't either." She shrugged. "But I actually think it's some kind of fate that I aced that interview right after being told I inherited a house from my grand-mother, who'd been a famous R & B singer."

"Wait, what?" He took a gulp from his glass and then set it down on the table. "Your grandmother was famous? Who was she?"

"You might not have heard of her, since you're so into hip-hop you think no other type of music exists," she said with a shake of her head. "Her name was Betty Butler. And she was amazing. If I close my eyes and let my mind wander back to my childhood and those summers spent with her, I can still hear her singing a cappella." A shiver eased down her spine as she said those words out loud and actually heard Grandma Betty singing in her head. "I don't think I've ever missed her as much as I did today, with my thoughts on the possibility of finally getting a job in music."

"Whoa—first, I know about all types of music; my favorite is just hip-hop. But I think my mother might've had some Betty Butler albums in her collection. She had a deep, throaty voice like Aretha Franklin?"

It warmed her heart to know that he had heard of her grandmother. She'd always been famous and pretty spectacular in Tami's mind, but it was cool to know that others had appreciated her talent too. "Yes! She's been compared to Aretha a lot over the years. Of course, she hated it—said she was better than the Queen of Soul—but on odd days, she could recognize the huge compliment."

"So she passed away? I'm sorry to hear that. When's the funeral?"

She frowned. "They cremated her and had a memorial service quick, fast, and in a hurry. By the time we found out she was gone, it was all over. But yesterday, they read the rest of her will."

"And you inherited her house? Damn, that's amazing."

"Right! That's what I've been trying to tell my sisters, but they're all, 'Let's just hurry up and sell the place,' and 'I don't wanna go to Daufuskie Island just to babysit renovations.' I swear, they're both pains in my ass."

"Hold up," he said. "You and your sisters inherited a house on Daufuskie Island, and now you have to go there to, what—make renovations on it?"

She picked up her pizza sans pepperoni. "We have to oversee the renovations and then decide whether we want to sell it."

"And your sisters want to sell?"

She chewed and nodded. "Of course they do."

"But you, what? You want to keep it? But you live here in the city, and you're not working right now."

"I know," she said—because she *did* know. She'd been weighing the pros and cons of this in her mind just as much as she'd been celebrating her great interview and reminiscing about her grandmother. At this point, all those things seemed somehow interconnected. "But it's our legacy," she continued. "My grandfather's family bought that land after Union occupation, when many of the Gullah people either worked for landowners or made a way to purchase their own. There was only one slave cabin on it at the time, and they fixed it up, painted it blue. And when my granddaddy died, he left that house to my grandmother. She built a bigger house on the property but kept the original house as a nod to the Butler-family legacy. I think she left us both houses and the surrounding property so that we can do the same thing."

"Generational wealth," he said with a nod of his own. "That's what's up."

"Exactly! I know I don't personally have any money to put into this project, but the lawyer said there's an escrow account to take care of the renovations. And since I am unemployed, I don't have anything holding me here at the moment to keep me from going down there and seeing this project through."

Gabriel was quiet for a little longer than she expected, but then he nodded again. "Did you explain why you feel so strongly about this to your sisters? I mean, did you tell them about the connection you feel to your grandmother and her music—and subsequently, this house and all it represents for your family?"

"That sounds so much easier to do than it really is."

A melancholy feeling draped over her as she chewed another bite and glanced over at Gabriel. He still wore the black cargo pants of his security uniform, but he'd taken off the matching shirt before he'd arrived so that he now wore only a white T-shirt. The intricate snow-flake tattoo that he'd gotten on his upper-right biceps in memory of his mother, who'd loved the snow, peeked out from beneath the edge of his sleeve. Tami knew that if she pushed the sleeve up higher, she'd see some of the words from his mother's favorite scripture sketched between the lines of the drawing: *Love is patient.*

"You really do get me," she said after a slightly uncomfortable swallow of her food. The words had that weird silence falling between them again as Gabriel only stared at her. "I mean, my sisters just see it as a thing to do, to get out of the way. Like, I don't know . . ." She paused and then shrugged. "Another item to check off on their to-do list."

To punctuate her words, she made a check-off motion in the air. "Find out Grandma Betty is dead. *Check.* Sell the house she worked so hard to build. *Check. Check.* Make Tami feel like crap. *Check. Check. Check!*"

"You gotta make them see your point, then," he said gently, and dropped a hand to her knee. "People aren't generally mind readers, Tam. If you don't tell them how you feel, how will they know?"

She let out a heavy sigh and, instead of continuing to eat, placed the remaining pizza on her plate so she could slump back on the couch. "They never listen to me—just tell me what I'm doing wrong, how I should fix my life. Act more like them. Be what Mama worked so hard for us to become."

This part of the conversation wasn't new. In the past year since she'd known Gabriel, he'd become an excellent confidant, which was probably why, on several occasions, she'd been able to give her body to him so freely. They had a special friendship that she not only appreciated but also, on some level, needed.

"Or you can just tell them that the only life you want to live is the one that's authentic to you. Stop letting them beat you down with their words and opinions, and stand up for yourself the way you do with everyone else you come across," he said, his hand still on her knee as he looked back at her.

"You don't know them," she replied, hating how whiny those four words sounded. "They're like this indomitable force of strength and tenacity. They're the poster duo for Superwoman, and I've always felt like the incompetent sidekick, running behind them all my life."

Now he sat back on the couch, an action that put him closer to her, the bare parts of his arm touching the bare parts of hers. He angled the other half of his body just enough so that his left hand could come up and cup the side of her face, turning her toward him. "There's nothing incompetent about you. There's resilience and fearlessness. Humor and compassion. Intelligence and beauty. And you don't need a damn superhero title to prove any of that."

His words—spoken with such determination and a tinge of force that sent tiny pricks of arousal scattering along her skin—made her smile. "But I'd look really great in a white catsuit—because black is too damn depressing—and a fly-ass mask with like a burst of color. Turquoise, maybe."

When he grinned, the sizzle of tension that had suddenly dropped over them dissipated, and she felt a wave of relief. "And what would your superpower be?" he asked. "Because you hate running—or any type of physical activity, for that matter."

He wasn't wrong about that. Well, he kind of was. "Not true," she replied. "I like sex."

But she probably shouldn't have said that, because then that strange-ass tension was back, clogging up the air until her next breath came out shakier than she'd anticipated.

With his hand still on her face, Gabriel brushed his thumb over her cheek. "That is true," he said with a slow nod before he dragged his tongue over his lower lip. "And lucky for you, I like sex too."

Her gaze remained fixed on his mouth then. It was a familiar sight; the low timbre his voice had dropped to was a sound she'd heard before too. And because she was used to this happening here and there throughout the course of their relationship, she wasn't alarmed by the arousal swirling in the pit of her stomach. "Two peas in a pod," she whispered, words they'd often used to describe their friends-with-benefits status.

"Yeah," he murmured, and brought his face closer to hers. His usual response for whenever she referred to them that way now fell in a warm breath over her lips seconds before their mouths collided: "Something like that."

Chapter 6

Yvonne

"Contesting a will—even small parts of it—could take months or even years to resolve," Pat Glenn said, reading a text from her husband while sitting in the guest chair across from Yvonne's desk.

Pat was the administrative assistant at Kentrell Middle School and had been ever since Yvonne had come to the school as vice principal five years ago. Over the last three years, as Yvonne had migrated into the role of principal, Pat had become more of a friend, in addition to being a vital resource in the office.

"And Manny also says the fact that this is an out-of-state will could make the process even more tedious and expensive for you and your sisters in the long run," Pat continued before looking up at Yvonne again.

"Well, damn," was Yvonne's response. She sat back, legs crossed at the ankles as she moved just enough to cause a slight swivel in her office chair. "More bills are the last thing I need."

The school year had just ended the previous week, but there were still a few administrative things she, Pat, and some of the other staff members in the building had to finish up before they left for the summer. So they were both dressed down in jeans, T-shirts, and tennis shoes. They'd been there since ten that morning, and it was now almost three o'clock.

"Do you know how long it'll take to renovate the house? I mean, if you're just looking at making a few repairs, slapping on some new paint to give it a fresh look, maybe that's just like a few weeks, and then it can go on the market," Pat said. "When I was talking to Manny about it last night, he said that rich folks are dying to snap up property on the Sea Islands—especially Daufuskie, since it's still largely undeveloped."

In the two days since she and her sisters had sat in Robyn's office to receive the news, Yvonne had done some research as well, so she'd come to the same conclusions regarding real estate on the island. Selling the house could be very lucrative for them, a windfall that Yvonne had been desperately praying for in the past few months since their mother's rehabilitation had suffered one setback after another.

Her mother had been at a church meeting when she'd collapsed a little over two years ago. It was Back to School Night, so Yvonne had been at the school, meeting parents, smiling at her students, and supporting her teachers when she got the call. Lana and Tami had made it to the hospital within moments of her, and the three of them had sat vigil in the waiting room for almost two hours before the first doctor appeared with any news. From there, it'd been an emotional and financial struggle to get their mother situated in her home. Three months ago, the strain had grown deeper, and Yvonne had barely been holding on before the news of Grandma Betty's death came.

Now she was desperately trying to maintain a semblance of hope, no matter how bittersweet it felt.

"I haven't been on that island in twenty-two years," she said, and laced her fingers together on her lap.

"I heard it's beautiful," Pat replied. "My sister-in-law has family in Charleston, and when she visited with them last year, they took a trip out to the island for a couple of days. The whole place is so rich with history, but I imagine it's awe-inspiring to see firsthand."

Yvonne gave a slight shrug. "You know, I never appreciated the historical aspect when I was a child. It was just nice to get away from the city every summer. And after my parents divorced, it was nice to spend that uninterrupted time with my father."

Her father. The first man she'd ever loved and the first man who'd ever broken her heart.

"Well, I can think of worse ways to spend your summer off," Pat added. "I mean, I know you're looking at it like one big headache since you rarely like to travel—"

"I *can't* travel," she interrupted. "Who takes care of my mother while I'm gone?"

Pat nodded. "I know we've had this conversation before, and I totally get your feelings on the situation. Plus, I realize that this particular scenario is different. But . . ."

Yvonne had known that *but* was coming, and she resisted the urge to frown at the only person she'd been able to confide in during the last few years.

"You can't do it all," Pat went on. "And you shouldn't have to. Your mother has three daughters, and sending a check or dropping money sporadically on your Cash App doesn't make up for them not helping you more."

"Girl, you already know I agree with what you're saying. But I've also got to keep it pushin'. I can't sit around and wait for people to act right—especially not my sisters. They are who they are." Even though she struggled to understand how the three of them had been raised in the same house but turned out so drastically different, Yvonne had never been the type to wait for anybody to do anything for her.

"You should hold them more accountable instead of just brushing off their nonsense," Pat continued.

But Yvonne was tired as hell of being a second mother to her younger sisters. She was exhausted from trying to keep her family afloat when the universe seemed to want to tear them apart. This had been going on for far too long, and she was just over it.

"I'm not begging them to do a damn thing for our mother. They're grown; they can make their own decisions." She held up a hand when Pat opened her mouth to say something else. *"But"*—she punctuated the word with a raise of her brows and a curt nod—"I'm not down for any bullshit from either of them this summer. I'm going to go along with this renovation thing, but only on the condition that when we sell this house, we each put up a portion of our proceeds to cover the renovations to Mama's house. This way, I don't have to use the rest of my savings to get it done."

"Oh. Okay, that sounds like a plan. But how do you think they'll react to it? I mean, they really shouldn't need to be told to help their mother, the woman who raised and took care of them." Pat was an only child, and her parents were still happily together. They'd celebrated fifty-one years of marriage earlier this year. She was lucky in that regard.

"I already mentioned it to them after we left the lawyer's office, when we were still trying to figure out what to do," she said. "We've been going back and forth via text in the days since then, but I think we just need to get this started so we can get it finished sooner."

Pat stood as she stuffed her phone into the back pocket of her jeans. "That's probably a good idea. Keep me posted on when you're leaving and if you need to vent—which you probably will—while you're away. You know I'm always here."

"I know," Yvonne replied, and waved as Pat left the office.

Pat had lent her that ear to vent on more occasions than she could count, and she appreciated her friend for that. But she was going to try to get through this summer with her sisters without complaints or headaches—hopefully.

There used to be a time when it wasn't a task to do that, during those summers spent at the summerhouse. That wasn't to say she and her sisters had never had any disagreements or near-physical fights, but back then they'd lived in the same house, so apologies usually came quickly, and then it was back to being all each other had. That's the way they used to see it, like it was them against the world—the Butler sisters against Freda, mostly. Even though Yvonne was usually riding the fence in those cases, since she'd been the only one to figure out how to deal with their mother with minimal fuss—she would just do whatever Freda said without argument. Lana and Tami, on the other hand, had thought that made absolutely no sense. Thinking back on those times, Yvonne realized that was where the now deeply rooted discord between her and her sisters had begun to settle in.

✉

In the past six months, Freda's right hand hadn't been working as well as it had before. The physical therapy she'd started while in the rehab facility five weeks after the stroke had continued on into the following year. A therapist had come to their house to facilitate the sessions until Freda had been forced to retire from her job as a district superintendent and her medical benefits had ceased. The grueling task of monotonous paperwork and repetitive phone calls that came next finally resulted in her being approved for Social Security benefits and, subsequently, Medicare.

With that process taking almost seven months, Yvonne had started paying for the physical therapy sessions out of her own savings account. To her credit, Lana had taken over payments for the speech therapy while they waited for the new medical benefits to come through. Those appointments had been far fewer than the physical therapy, which had started again over the last three weeks.

Her mother dropped the fork she'd been holding with her left hand. "I'm finished," she announced.

Yvonne had cooked a pot of spaghetti after she'd arrived home from school a few hours before. Now she and her mother were sitting at the kitchen table, which had seen more than its share of meals over the forty-two years they'd lived in the house. When they'd all been home, only breakfast was eaten in the kitchen. Dinner and all holiday meals had been in the dining room, but that table mostly held mail separated in piles of medical versus household bills now.

"You ate a lot," she said to her mother. "You must've worked up quite an appetite at therapy this afternoon."

"She gets too smart," was Freda's response as she sat back in her chair.

Alfreda Hanson-Butler's once long and thick dark-brown hair had thinned significantly over the years but still had length, which was now heavily streaked with gray. Yvonne washed it every two weeks, greased her scalp, and styled it in two braids, just like Freda had done for each of her girls when they were young.

"Every time I tell her it hurts, she tells me to keep going," Freda continued. "That's abuse."

In the months immediately following the stroke, her mother's speech had been heavily slurred, and she'd paused constantly to try to get the words to coordinate correctly in her mind. Now, as a result of the speech therapy, her words were 95 percent clear the majority of the time, even if her cognitive skills were beginning to decline. Her neurologist had indicated at the last appointment that this was probably a combination of the stroke and Freda inching toward seventy-two years old.

"Her job is to help you become more proficient in using your right side, Mama. I'm sure that's all she's trying to do."

"Don't defend her. She's getting paid by the state no matter what, so you know she doesn't give a damn if I get better. It's not like when I was going to the private doctors on my other insurance."

She was referring to the insurance she'd paid for out of her paycheck every two weeks—the PPO plan she'd selected, and the doctors she'd researched and approved of. In Freda's mind, the state-run clinics and doctors were barely competent. Yvonne could admit that was sometimes definitely the case, based on the area the provider was in and the appearance of said office. The fact that the proceeds from exorbitant medical charges weren't trickling down to the decor of those locations or the supplies the doctors in those facilities used was often woefully apparent. Still, it was all that was available to Freda at the moment. It was unfortunate that this was the benefit Freda had paid into since she was sixteen years old and had taken her first job. And for a woman who held three degrees in education and had worked her way up from scrubbing bathrooms on the evening shift of a cleaning service to taking meetings with the mayor and on some occasions the governor and other statewide officials involved in the Boston education system, everything the Social Security Administration and Medicare were offering her was a painful slap in the face.

"I know, Mama. I'll give her a call in the morning to make sure we're all on the same page with your treatment and how it's making you feel." At that point, that was all Yvonne could do to appease her mother.

The look Freda tossed her way was a mixture of skepticism and exasperation. "Mm-hmm," Freda murmured, and then turned away from Yvonne. She lifted her left hand slowly, extending her arm across the table until her fingers tentatively touched the glass of fruit punch Yvonne had brought out with the plate of spaghetti.

Yvonne sat up straighter in her chair and started to reach over and assist her mother, but then she thought better of the idea. Freda didn't like feeling helpless; she despised the fact that her body—and the good Lord, because she was certain this was all His fault—had betrayed her. The aneurysm that had led to the stroke and her subsequent collapse in front of the entire usher board at Mt. Moriah Century Baptist Church was a curse He'd wrongfully inflicted on her. After all, she'd done everything she was supposed to in life and exceeded at each turn. She didn't deserve to have fallen like this. Yvonne had watched that anger and bitterness fester in her mother for the last twenty-six months, and it weighed on her shoulders as heavily as the responsibility to take care of the woman she'd once admired.

Freda's fingers eventually wrapped around the glass, but there were still a few moments of pause before Yvonne watched the glass slowly lift from the table. Her mother was right-handed, and that was the side of her body the stroke had attacked, leaving the right half of Freda's face slackened and the limbs on that side less than cooperative on any given day.

Ice cubes rattled in the glass now half-full of the watered-down drink Freda preferred. It was either fruit punch or pink grapefruit juice—half-juice and half-water—when Freda requested a cold drink. Herbal tea instead of coffee, per the doctor's orders, with lemon or honey when she wanted something hot. Eventually, the rim of the glass made it to Freda's thick lips, and she drank slowly.

Her mother was still a strikingly beautiful woman, with her deep-mocha hue, wide-set russet-brown eyes, and high cheekbones. At one time, her hair had been dark brown, and Freda had worn it permed and in chin-length curls that softly framed her face. She'd always been slim—just like Tami—wearing a size 10 for as long as Yvonne could remember. She had dressed stylishly, like Lana, her closet and the two armoires in the basement full of suits, slacks, blouses, and dresses with designer labels. This woman—whose brow was now almost always drawn into a scowl; whose lips never wore warm-hued lipstick anymore; whose ears, neck, and fingers remained free of the gold and silver jewelry that overflowed from the boxes on her dresser—was a shell of whom she had once been. And that broke Yvonne's heart daily.

"It's time for the news," Freda said when she put the glass back on the table and let her left hand fall into her lap.

Freda liked to watch Anderson Cooper in the evenings; *the cute little fella* is what she called him. It was one of the few things her mother seemed to enjoy these days. This was when Yvonne would normally help her mother into the living room, where she'd sit in the weathered recliner until the portion of the news she wanted to see was over, and she would then need help to the breakfast room, which they'd partitioned off from the kitchen in the last few months to serve as her bedroom so that she could avoid the steps.

But before they did any of that tonight, Yvonne needed to talk to her mother.

"Okay, I'll help you in just a second," she said, and then took a drink from her glass of wine. She emptied the glass, needing the liquid courage to say what had to be said and to steel herself for whatever Freda's response would be.

Setting the glass down, she reached for a napkin and wiped her hands one last time before blurting out, "I'm going away for a few weeks." She didn't know specifically if that was the amount of time she'd be gone, but she was reluctant to say *the entire summer*. No, she was hopeful that this endeavor wouldn't take that long. "You remember I told you Grandma Betty passed?"

Freda nodded. "She always did have bad lungs. Just like your daddy. And they both still smoked those nasty cigarettes." The deepened frown on her mother's face expressed just how much she hated that habit.

"Right." It was easier to simply agree with Freda. Their father's death from sarcoidosis, after having been diagnosed with the disease only six months before, had come as a surprise to everyone—even Freda, who by that time had been divorced from Daniel Butler for seven years.

Yvonne, who had been nineteen at the time of her father's death, had read everything she could find about the disease and learned that there were conflicting results regarding its correlation with smoking. She'd finally decided that the studies she'd pored over—and the cigarettes her mother had found so distasteful—didn't really matter, because her father was gone. And now, so was her grandmother, albeit from a different medical condition.

"Grandma Betty left us the summerhouse, and she wanted us to fix it up before selling it. So I'm going back to the island. Lana and

Tami are going too," she blurted out, then held her breath like she was a teenager all over again, waiting for her mother's response.

"Hmph" was the sound that came from Freda first. "Betty always did like to control every damn thing." Freda shook her head. "I swear, that woman thought she was the boss long before Diana Ross claimed the title."

Yvonne almost smiled at the words she hadn't heard her mother say in a very long time. To say the relationship between Freda and her mother-in-law had always been contentious would be an understatement.

"There's a contractor down there waiting for us to get started on the job. I'm gonna call Lana and Tami tonight so we can get the details together on when we'll leave." She'd figured a call would be faster since Lana sometimes took a while to respond to text messages. "Since I'm finished with school for the summer, now's the perfect time to go and deal with this. And Ms. Rosalee said she'd be happy to come and stay with you until I get back."

Her mother rolled her eyes. "Rosalee's a nosy busybody," she snapped. "Always wants to be up in my house, looking around and touching stuff so she can run back to the church and tell everybody what I've got."

Rosalee Patterson had also been Freda's closest friend for as long as Yvonne could remember. The woman had been a godsend during these past couple of years, although Yvonne had been careful not to lean on her generosity too frequently, or Freda would have a conniption. The way she seemed to be on her way to doing now.

"It won't be for that long, Mama. And you know I can't leave you here alone overnight." She hadn't done that since her mother had taken sick. "Your nurse will still come during the day, so if Ms. Rosalee has any appointments or errands of her own, she'll be able to do them. You know she's more than happy to help out, especially since her daughter and the girls moved back to Atlanta with her husband."

Now her mother pursed her lips. "Stupid. Never look back," she said. "There's nothing in the past that'll help you in the future."

That was a piece of advice Freda had frequently given her children.

Finished with providing the details she had about the situation, Yvonne waited a beat for any other comments. She was just about to stand and help her mother into the living room when Freda said, "Yeah, you'd better go on down there. Otherwise, you know your sisters will make a mess of things. Lana's always had her nose in the air, and Tami dreams too much to focus." Her mother pushed back from the table slowly and then reached back to grab her walker. "You go take care of Betty's business, like the boss asked. Woman's intent on being a pain in the ass, even from the grave."

And that was it. Grandma Betty had spoken her wishes, and Freda had given her commands. All that was left for Yvonne to do was what she always did: take care of the things everyone else wanted.

Chapter 7

LANA

"I know I don't have a job or any money to spend on this project," Tami said a few seconds after the three of them were connected on the call.

It was a little after nine on Friday night when Yvonne had called Lana to say she was about to connect Tami so the three of them could discuss the summerhouse situation. That's what it had become in the days since they'd been to the lawyer's office—a situation that needed to be handled. Lana was sick of dealing with situations.

"But I think we're meant to do this," Tami continued. "Together. That's why Grandma Betty put it in her will that way. Remember, she used to always tell us we got more done together than we ever would apart?"

Lana did remember that. It had usually come up whenever their grandmother had given them a task to complete at the house and Tami would find a reason to wander off and do something else. Then Yvonne would send Lana after Tami, and when that took too long, Yvonne would come and find Lana arguing with Tami. A bigger argument would ensue, one that would make Grandma Betty stop what she was doing and come along to break up their discourse.

"I do remember her saying that a lot," Yvonne said. "But—"

"No, just hear me out," Tami interrupted. "Of all the family members that have ever been directly involved in our lives, Grandma Betty was the one who showed us—all of us—the most support."

"That's not true," Lana said. "Daddy was always there for us, even after the divorce. And he intervened with a lot of things that Mama tried to keep us from doing because she didn't like them. So I'd say Daddy was our biggest supporter."

"Of course you'd say that because you had him in your life much longer than I did," Tami said, and Lana clamped her lips shut because her younger sister was right. Tami had been only eight years old when their father died, while Lana had been fourteen.

"And I'm not angry about that," Tami hurried to say. "I mean, not anymore. It's just that I don't want us to mess up this opportunity to return the favor to Grandma Betty. She never asked anything of us, but she gave us everything she had. Even in death."

Both Lana and Yvonne were silent for a few moments. Then Yvonne spoke. "I think we should go down there and fix up the house. We'll use the money from the escrow account so nobody has to come out of their pocket for anything. Well, except our plane tickets. Tami, I'll get yours when I book mine after I hang up."

Tami whispered a relieved "Thank you" to Yvonne. "And I'll pay you back for the plane ticket. I'm really thanking you for agreeing to do this, because I know you'd rather stay here with Mama."

"No, I wouldn't 'rather stay here with Mama,'" Yvonne snapped. "I don't usually have any choice *but* to stay with Mama. But I've got Ms. Rosalee staying with her, so she'll be fine for a few weeks. And hopefully, that's as long as this will take."

"So we're doing this," Lana said. "We're going to the island to fix up this house, and then we're selling this house. Right?" In the last few days, she'd given up on the idea of a quick sale for the house since she'd caught the wavering in Yvonne's texts. Sure, Yvonne still wanted to sell the house, but she'd also been texting them pictures she'd found in some boxes that were in the basement of their mother's home. Pictures of the three of them on the island when they were young. Pictures of them with Grandma Betty at Lana's wedding. And a picture of their grandmother and father on the summerhouse porch, weeks before Daddy had passed away.

That was the one that had pricked Lana's heart and had tears flowing freely. Daniel Butler had been everything to her. He'd been the first man she ever loved, the standard for what she would look for in a husband, and she missed him every hour of every day.

"Because I've got stuff going on," she hurriedly continued before the emotion welling in her gut grew any stronger. "I mean, there's a lot of things I need to focus on here, so this isn't the best time for me to be away." She still hadn't talked to Isaac about his new debt or the fact that she had no idea where they were going to get the money in just a little over a month. With a quick sale of the house no longer a possibility, this entire project was just another link in a chain that was steadily growing heavier around her neck.

"You're not the only one with things going on," Yvonne chimed in. "But we should do this. We *can* do this."

"Yes!" As usual, Tami didn't bother hiding her excitement. "We're doing this, and it's gonna be great, y'all. I've just got this feeling that this is going to be exactly what Grandma Betty wanted . . . and more."

Lana was the first to get off the call since she was obviously the only one not feeling this little adventure they were about to embark on. And truthfully, that was another perplexing thing for her to ponder—she hadn't counted on Yvonne wanting to do this. In fact, Lana would've thought her older sister would have remained firmly on her side after their initial conversation about this, but somewhere between Tuesday and tonight, something had obviously happened to change Yvonne's mind. That meant the sisters were heading to Daufuskie Island for who knew how long, to fix up a house that had once been a big part of their lives. There was really no telling how this was going to end, and that was the last thing Lana needed right now—another situation she couldn't predict or control.

Irritation mixed with anxiety traveled through every inch of her body, settling in the nape of her neck and her forehead, where a pounding headache had taken over.

⊠

Breakfast was Lana's favorite meal of the day—and brunch was even better—because not only could she have her beloved breakfast foods but she could also have them even later in the day and not get remarks like "You're eating eggs and bacon in the middle of the day?" from her sisters or whomever she was with at the time. She'd eat what she wanted, when she wanted, anyway, but comments like that still irked her.

But on Sunday morning, when she rolled out of bed a little after eleven, Isaac surprised her by coming into their bedroom fully dressed, giving her a slow grin.

"Well, good morning, Sleeping Beauty," he said with arms outstretched. He walked over to her and pulled her into a hug.

She fell into the embrace, always eager to feel safe and cherished, something she'd only ever experienced with Isaac. And her father, of course, but that had been so very long ago. "Good morning," she replied with a heavy sigh that had to mirror how off she felt.

Until late in the evening, Lana had spent yesterday in the room she used as a studio, touching up pictures, reorganizing her catalog, and planning what she hoped would be the winning proposal for a photo-book idea that had been percolating in her mind for the past few months. The idea had been for a photo documentary of urban movement from the grins of a child on a playground to the dilapidated buildings in neighborhoods that depicted just as much of an internal breakdown as an external crumbling. Her agent had loved it, but by the time she'd finally fallen into bed at two in the morning, Lana was less than enthused about the shots she'd taken so far, and the outline for the project just wasn't resonating in a way she needed it to.

"I was just coming to wake you," he said, and then pulled back just enough to plant a kiss on her forehead. "Get dressed; we've got reservations at Sid's in forty minutes."

Sid's was an elegant rooftop restaurant nestled in the heart of Back Bay, with sweeping views of the Boston Public Garden. The soul-food-inspired-by-rich-Caribbean-roots establishment served an array of eclectic and flavorful plates, like jerk wings and braised beef short ribs. Isaac especially loved their unique house-recipe cocktails, which included exotic island rums from the West Indies, but Lana's favorite was the fried sweet plantains, which she always had with her beloved breakfast choice of scrambled eggs loaded with American cheese, onions and green peppers, and crispy fried bacon. They also had a terrific apple-and-cinnamon-infused spiced rum that Lana sometimes dreamed about.

Her stomach growled, and Isaac chuckled. "I guess that means you like that idea."

She loved the idea, and an hour later, she was sitting across from him as the early-afternoon sun beamed, staring out at the vibrant floral patterns in the Public Garden.

"You still feeling uneasy about the trip to South Carolina?" Isaac asked as they waited for their food.

Turning her gaze to him, she watched as he wrapped his fingers around his glass and brought the house-made lemonade to his lips for a sip. Isaac wasn't a heavy drinker; when he did drink any type of liquor, it was always late in the day or evening. He had a thing about everything having a time and place that, in the beginning of their relationship, had bordered on compulsive to her—but now, seven years after meeting him, she knew that it was just another part of his personality. Isaac was a generally laid-back man with a quick and infectious smile and a generous heart. He loved his parents, worked hard, and was great in bed—the perfect man for her. At least, that's what she'd thought.

"Yeah," she replied, and attempted to blink away her previous thoughts. "It's going to be weird; I already know that. My sisters and I aren't exactly the DIY types."

Isaac chuckled. "That's probably an understatement," he said and then shrugged. "But I gotta say, I'm really impressed that you all agreed to take this on. It's a big task, and one I know your grandmother probably put a lot of thought into."

She shook her head at that comment because he was right. "Grandma Betty put a lot of thought into a lot of things. I mean, she was just a couple inches shy of being eccentric, with her birdhouse collection mixed in with an extensive music library."

"She was a fascinating woman who lived a full life, from what I knew of her," Isaac continued.

Lana reached for her glass and took a slow sip of the mimosa she'd ordered. "Yes, she was. And she liked you."

His brow furrowed. "You say that like you're surprised by that fact. I'm a pretty likable dude." He grinned and then licked his lips, and her nipples tingled.

Right here, in the middle of the day, sitting in a restaurant full of people, that simple action from her husband had turned her on. She couldn't help but grin back in return; the option to jump over the table and straddle him was obviously out of the question.

"No, I wasn't surprised by how much she liked you. I was, however, totally taken off guard by how dedicated she was to giving us the perfect wedding. She picked everything from the flowers to the menu—and even the nightie I wore on our honeymoon."

"Word?" Isaac asked with raised brows. "Grandma Betty picked that sexy-ass piece of silk that I couldn't wait to rip off you the moment you stepped out of that bathroom?"

That memory brought forth even more salacious thoughts of her husband, and suddenly Lana felt like forgoing brunch in lieu of heading back to their condo for an afternoon of lovemaking. Something that would please her both physically and emotionally, and possibly lead to what she'd been pining for longer than she liked to think about—a baby.

She nodded. "Yup. She said Yvonne was taking her good ole sweet time finding a man to take her focus off her career, and Tami was still exploring, so she had to pour all her money and fanciful wedding ideas on me."

"And you didn't mind one bit," Isaac said.

"I sure didn't," Lana admitted. "I loved every minute of her taking all those details out of my hands. Plus, I knew it would be fantastic. Grandma Betty did not half step in anything she did." She sighed. "But Mama hated how involved I allowed her to be. Now, Freda liked you too—you've got a special touch with the women in my family. But she didn't think we needed all that for a wedding." In fact, her mother had been a bit resistant about a marriage happening at all, but that was just Freda. Ever since the divorce, there'd been no talk of dating or falling in love again for her. Lana had always thought that was a shame.

"Ms. Freda's got her strong opinions, that's for sure."

"Now, *that*"—Lana raised her brow—"is an understatement."

Their meal came, and they ate in companiable silence until Isaac's phone buzzed and he pulled it out of his pants pocket. She didn't watch him as he read the text, just continued eating the last of her plantains, but the moment he slipped the phone back into his pocket and pushed his mostly eaten plate of salmon and summer-vegetable succotash away, she knew something was wrong.

Without a second thought, she said, "Was that about the money you owe?"

His gaze shot up to meet hers. "What?"

She set her fork down on the edge of the plate and relaxed back into her chair. For a second, she stared at him; then she reached for her napkin to wipe her mouth. "The gambling debt," she said, dropping her hands and the napkin into her lap. "I know about the thirty-seven thousand you owe this time."

Now he sat back in his chair, lips going up at the ends as he sighed. "You spying on me now? Going through my phone? Is that what we do now?"

She raised a hand to stop him before his questions led them into an argument she didn't want to have in public. "Your phone was on the island in the kitchen when you were in the bathroom. I was sitting at the island when the text came in, and I glanced at the screen to see if it was a call or message I needed to alert you of right away."

"But you didn't think you needed to alert me of the fact that you'd been reading my messages?"

"I was actually waiting for my husband to tell me he'd been gambling again," she shot back.

A muscle twitched in his jaw, and he looked away. She wondered what he was thinking, what he planned to say next, and more importantly, how this conversation was going to end. For days, she'd wanted to broach the topic with him, to once and for all get this addiction he seemed to have cultivated out in the open and figure out what their next steps were going to be, but she'd been so bombarded with the will, the house, her work, and now travel plans that she'd let it sit in a corner of her mind while she ruminated, the same way she'd done each time this situation had arisen over the last few years.

"Don't say 'again' like that," he said finally, his tone low and solemn. He didn't look at her, either—almost like he couldn't turn his gaze back to meet hers for some reason.

"But that's what it is," she replied. "You gamble and you lose. Then you owe money. Again." Her words sounded cold—harsh, maybe. But they were facts.

"The debt will get paid."

"By me?" she asked. "Again?" She wanted to continue, to tell him to ask for an extension so that she could get this house sold and give him the money to pay it off, but the way he looked when he turned back to her kept her quiet.

"I never asked you to do that." There was a sadness in his eyes, an unexpected hint of pain in his voice.

She sighed. "Like I never asked you to work sixty hours a week to afford us this lifestyle while I pursued my dreams. But you do it because you love me, right?"

Now he dragged his hands down his face. "I'll fix it, baby," he said quietly. "I'll fix it."

But who's going to fix us?

The question hung between them like an elephant in midair.

Lana didn't have the courage to ask it, didn't even want to imagine how the rest of the conversation would go if she did. Her heart was already pounding at the thought, emotion swirling through her chest like a newly formed storm.

Isaac reached across the table, gazing at her with imploring eyes as he waited for her to accept his hand. She did, and welcomed the warmth that spread throughout her palm when his fingers enclosed around hers.

"I'm going to fix this, and then . . . ." He paused. "I'm just going to fix it."

When she opened her mouth to speak, he shook his head again. "No. Don't say anything else, because I know. And like I said, I'll fix it."

Chapter 8

LANA

"Baby." Isaac's gruff voice sounded in her ear, followed by a deep moan as he slid an arm over her waist, his hand instantly moving down between her legs.

It was late—or rather, early, as she could see through one cracked eye the bright-red numbers that shone from the clock on her nightstand. Four a.m. It was Monday already.

"Mmm," she moaned right after him, parting her legs to welcome him.

His hard length was pressed against the crease of her ass, his warm lips on her neck, hot tongue sliding over her skin. She pressed back against him, pulling her bottom lip between her teeth.

"I want you, baby," he whispered. "I *need* you."

Those words, his tone, his touch: this was their love language. Sex—always hot, always delicious, and almost as frequent as it had been in the early stages of their seven-year marriage. This and Isaac's dedication to taking care of her were things she could count on. Things she cherished in her marriage. They were also things she prayed would never cease, especially amid the other dark spot that had eased its way into her otherwise happy home.

"Yesssss," was her response, because there was no other answer. There was no other way to express how she felt for this man.

He'd claimed her heart in their wildly romantic three-month courtship from the day she'd been snapping shots of the regal finback whale during a sightseeing cruise. It had been a last-minute decision to board one of the cruises that tourists loved to take when they visited Boston. She'd finished a tumultuous workweek and completed the assignments in her side hustle's queue—composing résumés on Fiverr—and had needed to get out of her tiny apartment to get some air. While the whole focus of the cruise was to see whales, the moment the finback shot up out of the water and arched through the air, a collective round of gasps from the cruisers had sounded, and she'd lifted her camera, capturing successive shots of the majestic creature. She'd been so busy focusing on the light and her perspective that she'd ignored the mammal crashing back into the sea and the subsequent splash of water it sent over the deck of the boat. An arm around her waist had pulled her back, but not before she and the person who'd grabbed her were soaked. Turning, she'd grinned at yet another breath-snatching sight: a handsome man with an enigmatic smile that immediately gripped her heart.

Isaac pushed her panties down her legs, and while she knew he was also removing his own underwear, she reached for the hem of her nightshirt to pull up and over her head. Tossing it somewhere at the bottom of their bed, she rolled over onto her back and welcomed him when he moved between her legs. She didn't need the light to see his face; she'd dedicated his features to memory. That slit in his left eyebrow, where he'd received stitches at twelve years old because he'd been hit by a hockey stick during practice. The way his brown eyes clouded with passion each time he was about to take her. The slight parting of his lips as his forehead wrinkled when he concentrated on stroking her to a pleasurable end.

She lifted her hands to cup his face and pull him down closer.

"I'm gonna miss you, baby," he told her.

"Hopefully, I won't be gone that long," she replied before nipping at his bottom lip. "A few weeks, tops, and then I'll be back, and we can sell the house and get the mo—"

"Shh." He touched his lips to hers and pressed his tongue into her mouth.

And she shushed because this was more important. Feeling Isaac's hands all over her body, wrapping her arms around his neck and her legs around his waist was exactly where her mind should be. When he pressed his length inside her, she moaned and arched her back as he deepened their kiss.

He felt so good inside her, so familiar and so safe. Just a few of the things that kept her dedicated to him and this marriage. They were both ambitious and tenacious—equally yoked, she would say. Something her parents had never been, hence the reason their marriage had ended in divorce. Lana wasn't going to suffer the same fate. She couldn't. With those thoughts creeping into her senses, she circled her hips faster, urging Isaac's languid strokes to go deeper, to give her every thrust she needed. Her breath hitched, eyes closed, fingernails dug into his back.

He was all she needed. Him, this life they'd built, and hopefully, eventually, a baby. That was her dream, and nothing—not even money—was going to come between them. It couldn't. She wouldn't survive if it did.

"I love you," he whispered, his mouth close to her ear. "I love you, Lana. I love you."

Her body trembled with her release as his words washed over her at exactly the right moment, and tears pricked her eyes.

"I love you," she finally managed to whisper against his ear, just as his body jerked above her and he growled with his climax.

✉

Five hours later, Lana made her way through the sliding glass doors of the airport. She pulled a suitcase in each hand and wore a duffel bag on one shoulder, another one with its straps slung over the suitcase handle, and her purse crisscrossed over her body. She clutched her boarding pass between her fingers as she narrowed her eyes to scan the crowd, looking for her sisters, who'd said they'd meet her at the front door.

Of course, it was a little after nine—the designated time Yvonne had given for them to meet in order to be at their gate by 11:15, even though their plane to Hilton Head didn't begin boarding until 12:05.

The airport wasn't too crowded, but Lana still had to navigate her way around people to keep from dropping everything or slamming one bag or another into someone else. She sent a silent *thank-you* to Isaac for the great morning sex, which had not only left her body limber and sated but had also relaxed her mind to a point where the madness of being in an airport around so many people, carrying so many germs, wasn't sending her into a compulsive frenzy.

"Need some help, ma'am?" A tall, slim guy with wiry gray hair and a quick smile came out of nowhere, pulling one of those big baggage carts behind him.

"No thanks," she replied with a small smile. "I'm good." As if to make her look all the way silly, the strap of the duffel bag slid off her shoulder, yanking her body to the side as it wrapped around her wrist.

"You sure? I can help you get to the ticket counter. Get your bags checked, and then you'll be on your way to security," he continued, stepping away from the cart to grab the handle of her suitcase.

But Lana pulled it away before he could touch it and simultaneously willed her feet not to trip her as the momentum of the bags and her quick movement threatened to send her careening over the dirty airport floor.

"Girl!"

Lana heard Tami yell before she saw her sister heading toward her.

"Why you got all these bags?"

Completely ignoring the bag-cart guy, Tami came to a stop on Lana's other side and pushed her large-framed sunglasses up on top of her head. Yvonne was right behind her, but of course she was looking over at the bag-cart guy.

"Are you paying him to carry your bags when the ticket counter is right over there?" Yvonne asked. She pursed her lips.

"No," Lana replied to her sisters, and then turned her attention back to the bag-cart guy. "I'm good, sir." This time she said it with finality, and he gave her a *No the hell you're not, but if you say so* nod before ambling away with his cart, which probably could've been useful.

Especially since her wrist was screaming from the way that strap had menacingly wrapped itself around it.

"You look like you're leavin' your husband," Tami continued with a quizzical glare as she stepped closer.

Lana's head snapped up, and she frowned. "I've got a one-way ticket to an island I usually only visit once a year and have no idea when I'm coming back. So excuse me if I tried to pack enough clothes. You know, I do like to wear a clean outfit daily."

"You know there's a laundry room with a washer and dryer in the summerhouse," Yvonne clapped back before shaking her head.

Tami came closer and, thankfully, reached out to grab the strap from her wrist. Lana had to bring the suitcase she'd been holding on to with that hand to a standing position before she gladly allowed her sister to take the bag and slip it onto her shoulder instead.

"I packed shorts, tank tops, and sundresses," Tami said as Lana started to readjust the rest of her things. "They're all in my one suitcase. Then I just have my carry-on and my purse."

Even with her signature annoyed look on her face, Yvonne stepped closer and signaled for Lana to release her hold on the other suitcase. Then she took Lana's second duffel bag strap from around that handle.

"You still have one bag too many," Yvonne said to Tami once she had Lana's bag securely on her shoulder. "What's in that carry-on?"

"Oh, these are my shoes," Tami responded as the threesome began walking toward the ticket counter. "I always carry those on with me.

I can buy underwear and clothes if my suitcase gets lost. But not my shoes. I gotta keep them with me in case there's no Steve Madden store wherever I travel."

Yvonne frowned. "You can't keep a job longer than a year. How can you possibly afford a bag of Steve Madden shoes?"

"It's called *budgeting*," Tami replied. "I'm sure you know all about that, with your supersmart self. When I see a pair of shoes I want, I buy them and then spend the next month on a strict diet of ham-and-cheese sandwiches and canned soup."

Yvonne didn't even offer a response to that, and Lana was glad. She hated the thought of anyone overhearing their sarcastic banter as they trucked through the airport. To an outsider, she was certain the relationship between her and her sisters would be construed as dysfunctional at best and possibly toxic at worst, but in her mind it was neither. It was just . . . them. Growing up in a three-bedroom row house with a demanding mother, an over-appeasing-until-he-was-gone father, and a slew of expectations that taught them how to stick together while simultaneously picking each other apart was no easy feat. And when they were finally able to get away from each other, they'd grown deeper into their personalities. Sometimes—*most* times—those personalities didn't mesh well. Lana prayed that wouldn't make this trip even more stressful.

Moments later, after standing in the relatively short line to get to the ticket counter, Lana pulled her bags up first. Tami and Yvonne came right behind her since they each held one of her bags.

"Good morning," she said to the passably attractive man, whose beard could have used a brush or some type of product to make it look a little more appealing. Not that she needed to be concerning herself with another man's appearance. But her eye was always tuned in to details, like she was framing a picture in her mind.

"Hey," was his reply. "ID, and you can put your bags up on the scale one at a time."

Add that he wasn't too cheerful, and her desire to speed this process along was upped a notch.

She hefted the first suitcase onto the scale and then reached into her purse to grab her wallet. She was just passing him her ID when he said, "Sixty-six pounds. That's a seventy-five-dollar charge."

Lana cursed.

"Oh, hell no," Tami chirped, immediately moving around Lana to flip the overweight suitcase onto its side to unzip it. "We're gonna put some of your stuff in this bag right here. Ain't nobody givin' y'all another seventy-five dollars."

She dropped Lana's duffel bag onto the floor and unzipped that too.

"Well, wait, let me figure out what to take out," Lana said. She agreed with what her sister was doing, even if she thought Tami could've lowered her voice a bit.

Yvonne, who'd rolled her eyes the moment Tami had started talking, was most likely thinking the same thing.

"All we gotta do is take a stack of these," Tami continued, snatching up an armful of clothes from the suitcase.

"No, let me just pick out what I want to transfer," Lana argued, and leaned down to the suitcase.

"Girl, we ain't got time for that. Yvonne's head is gonna explode if we don't get to that gate at least an hour before the plane even arrives," Tami snapped.

Then Tami shifted to drop the clothes she was holding into the bag, but Lana wanted to see exactly which pieces were going where. So she reached over to take them out of Tami's arms before they could fall into the bag. But Tami insisted she had it and pulled away with more force than was necessary. There was a brief tug-of-war when Lana grabbed her sister's arm, and the next thing she knew, her clothes went up in the air like someone had tossed a fistful of confetti, falling all over the place. Including onto the computer, where her peach lace thong hung just inches away from Bad Beard Attendant, who stared with a lifted brow.

Chapter 9

YVONNE

"I'm hungry," Tami complained as she folded her arms over her chest.

"And hardheaded and loud," Lana chimed in.

She was still very clearly pissed after the incident at the airport, and Yvonne couldn't say she blamed her. Except their connecting flight had extended their travel time, so the morning's incident had been almost nine hours ago. They'd landed in Hilton Head and hired a rideshare to get them to the ferry Embarkation Center, where they'd had to once again check their luggage with the crew and now waited to board the last ferry at nine o'clock. Also, like at the airport, there was a fifty-pound limit per bag with an accompanying price after the first complimentary suitcase. This had apparently called for another gloating look from Tami, since she'd been the one to lessen the weight of Lana's bag. It had also brought forth another annoyed scowl from Lana, which led to the snappy vibe they were now ensconced in as the sultry evening air began to settle in.

Dealing with her sisters had always been an exhausting endeavor that teenage Yvonne knew shouldn't have been her cross to bear. And yet it was, and she'd done the very best she could because they were two of the people she loved most in this world. That hadn't changed over the years, even if the landscape of their relationship had. She'd been thinking a lot about that relationship these past few days, in addition to so many of her life's decisions that had plagued her over the last twelve months. But for some reason, learning of Grandma Betty's death and the inheritance had cast the tumultuous existence that had developed between her and her sisters since Mama's stroke further into the spotlight.

She sat on the bench with her tired legs extended in front of her and crossed at the ankle. Her one complimentary suitcase had been stored on a cart that would hopefully get boarded on this ferry. If not, she'd have to wait until the first ferry going out tomorrow to receive her suitcase. The strap to her red-and-blue-plaid Vera Bradley tote she'd packed all her important items in—her medications, glasses, jewelry, wallet, Kindle, and laptop—was on her shoulder, the bag tucked close to her on the bench.

She could admit that during the airport incident, she'd shared Lana's mortification, while Tami had shrugged it off as she collected Lana's thong from where it had landed on the edge of the attendant's computer. The attendant had then asked Lana for her number once all their bags had been checked in. Of course, Lana's response had been to flash her left hand in the guy's face, showing off that big-ass diamond-cluster wedding-band set. To which the attendant had only shrugged, as if to say, "And?"

They'd boarded the plane and, for the most part, got on with the next portion of their first travel adventure together in more than ten years. In their adult years, the three of them had rarely booked the same flight when traveling to the island every November. This time, Tami had sat by the window, just like she used to do once she'd turned five and Daddy had felt it was safe enough to sit in the row across from his girls instead of keeping his youngest with him. Lana had sat in the middle because Yvonne had always wanted to be on the end to make sure nobody bothered her sisters. She'd always protected them, no matter what. Maybe that's why she'd come to expect so much from them. Why she wanted them to be better than she was. Smarter, more successful, happier.

Or maybe she'd just been doing what was expected of her, just like she'd done so many times in the past.

"You're going to fall," she recalled her seventeen-year-old self had said as she looked up from the book she'd been reading on a humid summer afternoon. The divorced forty-two-year-old protagonist in the book was just about to sleep with a man half her age because apparently what happened in Jamaica would also stay in Jamaica. But out of her peripheral vision, Yvonne had seen six-year-old Tami walking along the top of the fence like it was a tightrope.

"No, I'm not," Tami had shot back in her ever-precocious tone.

"Yes, you are, and then I'm going to get yelled at for not watching you. So get down!" Yvonne had replied.

"You're not the boss of me," had been Tami's next comeback, just as her left foot wobbled and she had to hold her arms out and do a quick squat to keep herself on the fence.

Tami had been the fearless one. Whatever they'd told her she couldn't do, she did. Yvonne had thought that would come in handy for Tami one day. Tenacity and strength, just like Mama had. How else had a mother of three been able to obtain three degrees while simultaneously becoming one of the highest-paid Black women in the Boston Public School system?

"Just let her fall," Lana had said. She'd been lounging on one of the chairs, flipping through the pages of a fashion magazine in order to prepare for the modeling classes she was set to start in the fall.

With a huff, Yvonne had stuck her bookmark between the pages and slammed her book onto the wide arm of the Adirondack chair she'd been sitting in. "Then not only will I get yelled at," she had said as she stood, "but it'll be just my luck she'll bust her head and we'll all have to wait for the ferry to take her to the big hospital."

"I'm sure ole Ms. Bailey can sew her head up. She's in that raggedy house, delivering babies," Lana had replied.

But Yvonne had already gone down the steps of the back porch. She'd grabbed Tami by the arm and yanked her down. Then Tami had started to cry. The wailing and foot-stomping performance had been so loud and lasted so long that Yvonne had eventually wished she'd taken Lana's advice and let the younger Butler sister fall.

Yvonne had indeed gotten yelled at that day by Daddy, who hated when Tami cried, mostly because he always ended up having to give her something to stop: A chocolate milkshake he'd go into Grandma Betty's big kitchen and make himself. A doll he'd have to travel over to Bluffton or go farther into Savannah to buy in one of the gift shops there. A promise to take her somewhere special—"Just the two of us"—when they got back to the city. Anything to get Tami to wipe away those *crocodile tears*, as Mama had called them, and stop all that ridiculous noise she had liked to make whenever she didn't get her way.

Grandma Betty, on the other hand, had taken Yvonne up to her bedroom later that evening. Her bedroom had huge windows and patio doors that opened straight out back, where the old blue house that Grandpa Riley had been born in still sat to the left. Just beyond that, the water spread out like a slice right through the earth. The other rooms had views of the water too, because Grandma had said that was the way she wanted it—her music room, where she liked to write songs or listen to her albums on the old record player; a huge dressing room; and a guest bathroom all faced the front of the house.

"She'll grow outta that," Grandma Betty had said, patting Yvonne on her knee as she came around to sit next to her on the edge of the bed. "And you'll find something else about your baby sister that nags at you. That's just the way sisters are."

The words had been spoken with a hint of laughter, but Yvonne hadn't felt any humor for the better part of that entire day. She'd had college applications on her mind, the ones Mama had stuffed into her suitcase for her to complete during what was supposed to be her summer vacation. Probably the last summer vacation of her childhood. Mama had wanted early admission to the best schools, so those applications had been completed at the beginning of Yvonne's senior year in high school. These applications had been for the second choices that Mama would accept only if necessary—which, by the tone she'd used when she'd put the list in front of Yvonne, had better not become necessary. Still, Yvonne had been expected to write the essays required for each application as if it were the sole school of her choice. When really, she hadn't even been totally sure she wanted to keep going to school. Her brain had already been so tired from keeping up a straight-A status since she'd been tasked with coloring within the lines.

The sound of Tami's loud "Thank the Lord" yanked Yvonne out of her reverie, and she looked over to see her sister jump up from the bench.

"What?" Tami asked when she looked over her shoulder to see Yvonne staring at her. "I know you're glad to see that ferry pulling up too. I'm hungry and sleepy. Want to get to the house, find some food, and then fall into bed."

Yvonne couldn't disagree with her, so instead of commenting on how unnecessarily loud Tami's voice was while out in public at ten minutes to nine at night, Yvonne just stood up and adjusted her bag on her shoulder. To her left, she noticed Lana had done the same, and the three of them began the walk out of the Embarkation Center and down the long dock to where the ferry waited. To the only place where she'd ever felt truly loved and connected to her sisters—and where she hoped she'd finally be able to figure out what had gone wrong in her life and how she could possibly fix it at this point.

✉

Another hour later and Yvonne was running on fumes. She'd always been an early-to-bed, early-to-rise person, and tonight was no different. Except for that fact that it was ten minutes after ten in the evening by the time they'd walked off the dock onto Daufuskie Island. The deep indigo of night had fallen over the place, crickets chirped in the air, and the old and probably rotting wood planks of the dock creaked beneath her every step.

Her tote bag seemed a million pounds heavier than it had been when she'd first packed it and headed out of her house early that morning. And now her shoulder was sore from carrying it around all day. Her feet hurt, not because her shoes were too small or she'd worn the wrong shoes for traveling, like Lana had done. No, it was because her feet were also tired in the black Crocs she'd worn for ease of slipping in and out of during the security check at the airport. She wore thick, fluffy black socks, which had provided extra comfort for a while, but now her feet just wanted out. They, like the rest of her body, craved a hot shower and a bed. Pronto!

"Hello!" a man's voice called out to them just as they stepped off the dock. "Butler sisters?"

Yvonne was the first to respond. "Yes," she said. "And you are . . . Jeremiah Sinclair?" She hoped it was him, because that's who Robyn had said would meet them at the dock and take them to the summer-house upon their arrival.

"Yes," he said with a nod and a distinct southern accent. He extended a hand to Yvonne. "Yes, ma'am, you can just call me Jeremiah."

The dark-eyed, nicely dressed man gave her a cute smile.

"I'm Yvonne," she told him. "And these are my sisters, Lana and Tami."

Jeremiah released her hand and followed her nod toward Lana, who had come to a stop on her left, and then Tami, who was on her right.

"Hello, Jeremiah," Tami said, her tone much brighter than Yvonne's had been. "It's very nice to meet you."

Jeremiah apparently hadn't been lost to that bright tone, as he'd taken Tami's hand and stared into her eyes. "It's very nice to meet you too, Tami."

"You have a ride for us, Jeremiah?" Yvonne asked, not bothering to give any extra attention to the way he was still holding Tami's hand.

"Ah, yeah . . . I mean, y-yes—yes, I do," he stammered.

"Then why don't you drop my sister's hand and show us to the ride so we can get to the house?" Lana suggested. "We've been traveling all day."

"Right," he said with another nod, and then, as if on second thought, dropped Tami's hand like it was scorching hot. "Yeah, I've got a cart right over here. Are those all your bags?"

He gestured behind them to where the ferry's crew member had just finished stacking their bags on the dock. There'd only been two other people on the ferry with them, and they'd gotten off with their one bag and gone on their merry way—so yeah, the stack of four suitcases and two duffel bags was all theirs.

"Yes, they're ours," Lana replied, and went over to claim her two suitcases and duffel bags.

She stumbled away from the pile, looking exactly like she had when she'd come walking into the airport that morning. And neither Yvonne nor Tami offered to help her this time; they both knew how that *help* had turned out. But Jeremiah was trying to be a gentleman, and he reached for one of Lana's suitcases.

"Let me get that for you, ma'am," he said, and shockingly, Lana released the bag.

Then she tossed a raised-eyebrow look over her shoulder at Yvonne, who almost smiled, since apparently Lana didn't like being *ma'am*ed either. Yvonne retrieved her own suitcase, extending the handle so she could roll it over the dirt ground to the golf cart where she'd seen Jeremiah stack Lana's bag.

"Is that a golf cart?" Tami asked.

"Yeah, it is," Jeremiah replied with a grin as he took Tami's suitcase and added it to the vehicle. "I'm sure you recall that's how we get around here on the island—golf carts or bikes. You can rent both down at Jake Jemison's backyard. He's got a few that he saves for tourists."

Grandma Betty had always had an older gentleman named Pete come to the dock and pick them up for their yearly visits. Ole Pete, as he'd instructed them to call him, owned a noisy, rusted red pickup truck that Yvonne kind of wished would come ambling down the road right about now.

"She already knows that," Yvonne said as she slid onto the back seat of the golf cart. Lana slid onto the seat beside her, as the sisters had figured Tami would want to ride up front with Jeremiah.

The smiles the two of them were still sharing were bright enough to light up the night. It was a little nauseating. Or maybe Yvonne was just hungry too. Who knows. All she was positive of at that moment was that there was a bed at the summerhouse, singing her name.

"I mean, yeah, I did know," Tami said, and then got into the cart. "But every time I come back, it's with the hope that they've done more modernization."

"Nah, my granddaddy says they like ole 'Fuskie just the way it is," Jeremiah said, and started the cart.

Yvonne hadn't heard the place called that in so long she'd forgotten how it sounded to hear natives of the island refer to their home in that way. Unlike when they'd been children, she tended to stay around the summerhouse when she'd visited Grandma Betty as an adult.

"Well, there isn't much they can do about that now," Lana said as they began driving down the dirt road. "I mean, there's already three resorts on the island. Right?"

Jeremiah nodded. His hair was low-cut and wavy. He wore a white dress shirt, the sleeves rolled up to his elbows, with no tie and the top two buttons open. His slacks were dark, shirt just a bit dusty, most likely from the dirt and gravel roads here in comparison to in the city, where she was used to seeing lawyers.

"There are, and they've provided jobs for some of the folk around here, but down in these parts, the motto is, *If it ain't broke, don't fix it*," he replied.

"Well, I wouldn't necessarily call it *broken*," Lana continued as she looked around at the trees they passed; a dilapidated house on the left; and an old, abandoned skeleton of a horse carriage up ahead on the right.

Yvonne knew the sights of the island would be much different in the morning light, but right now, the place was still giving her warm feelings and the sensation of long-buried memories sneaking up to the edges of her mind. It felt different from the other times she'd been back on the island, for some reason that she was too tired to try to figure out.

"Just could use a refresh of sorts," Lana said. "At any rate, I can't wait to get out here with my camera."

Her sister sounded so wistful as she said those words, as if she were already lost in that place of creativity she liked to retreat to whenever possible. Lana had always been the most creative of the sisters, the one with a vision of things that the others never possessed. From the moment Daddy had given her that camera for Christmas the year she'd turned thirteen, Lana had been obsessed. Even though she'd been pretty and shapely enough to become a phenomenal model, the camera had whispered to her. Much to Mama's chagrin, Lana had listened, and worked toward that one solitary goal, regardless of Freda's attempts to reprogram her to find a more suitable career—something with a deeper foundation, a wider path to success. Lana hadn't cared; she knew what her path was, and she'd followed it without ever looking back. Yvonne admired her for that.

"I'll come by tomorrow and bring Deacon, the contractor, with me. Then I'll make the introductions, and we can all sit down and go over the rest of Ms. Betty's plans," Jeremiah said as he eased the cart into a right turn.

Larger live oaks and palmettos jumbled together along both sides came into view just up ahead, and Yvonne gasped. A heaviness settled in her chest as she recalled this particular dirt road—Prospect Road. She knew exactly where it led and what she'd see in just about twenty minutes. Her fingers clutched the material of her tote, and she focused on taking slower, deeper breaths.

"Good, because I've got a feeling this is gonna be a big project," Tami said.

"Oh no," Lana replied with a shake of her head. "Grandma Betty always took good care of her house. And judging from the way it looked when we were here last year, there's not much to do. We can meet with the contractor in the morning—that's good. So we can get this ball rolling."

When they'd first learned about the house and the project, Yvonne hadn't wanted to be on the island any longer than necessary. But Lana's remark had sounded almost desperate, like staying here a second beyond what was required would cause some great catastrophe. It was odd—but then again, it wasn't. None of them had voluntarily come back here after they were seventeen—eighteen, in Tami's case—because she'd taken a gap year from college. Freda had threatened to physically carry her onto campus and deposit her in a dorm the fall of Tami's nineteenth birthday if she didn't get herself registered for classes.

It was only because Grandma Betty had insisted they spend every Thanksgiving together that they'd returned to Daufuskie at all. And even then, for those few days, they all seemed to roam around the house, taking meals when their grandmother mandated it and wishing to be back in the city when she didn't. Nothing had been the same here once they'd grown up, and Yvonne couldn't help but wonder—and possibly hope—if this time would be different.

Chapter 10

Tami

There was no place like the summerhouse. And as tired as she'd been the night before, Tami hadn't been able to sleep in, as she'd originally planned. Excitement had danced in the pit of her stomach the way it used to on Christmas morning. Excitement, anticipation, purpose.

Her room was the smallest of the four on the upper level of the house because she was the baby. At least, that's what Lana had said. But as a toddler, it had been a perfect room, from what she could recall. It was mostly memories of the white eyelet curtains that had hung at the window, the peach comforter on her toddler bed, and the pretty pale-green pillows lined across the back of a toy chest that doubled as a seat. Daddy used to sit on that seat with her on his knee. He'd have one arm around her waist, holding her so she wouldn't fall because she'd always had tons of energy and could barely keep still for more than ten minutes at a time. In his other hand, he'd hold whichever book he was reading to her. A fairy tale—she knew because she'd loved fairy tales since she was a child and knew her daddy was responsible for that.

Her daddy. Whenever she thought of Daniel Butler, she was reminded of strength and steadfastness. Of loyalty and trust and love. He'd believed in her, was proud of everything she'd done and had told her so often. While she'd had no recollection of what it had felt like to live in a house with him and her mother because they'd divorced when she was just a year old, he'd never let her doubt how much he cared for her. And each summer, he came to pick them up and brought them here to his mother's house—his family's home—she'd felt connected to him in a way she knew she'd never experience again.

Sure, there'd been boyfriends—lots of boyfriends, if she let her sisters tell it—but none of them had really understood her. None of them got her in the way her father had. Now, maybe that was a weird comparison to make. Like, what guy should think of her the same way her father had? Weird and gross. But there was part of her that did crave a man who'd look at her with the undeniable love that Daniel had had. A man who'd respect her mind with all its quirkiness—specifically the ADHD diagnosis, which her mother had never acknowledged—and the music that often sat dormant in her soul. He'd love her during her chatty times and when silence was the only comfort she could find. And he wouldn't try to change any part of her, not the way her mother and her sisters insisted on doing.

But those were thoughts for the distant, distant future. She wasn't looking to fall in love tomorrow and dedicate herself to working on a sustainable relationship. There were other things she wanted to do first—namely, get and keep a job that she was passionate about. Which was why the moment she'd stepped out of the shower, she crossed the bedroom to her nightstand and picked up her phone to check her emails. Nothing from 40A Records, the barely five-year-old music company producing some of today's hottest R & B and hip-hop stars. Her interview with them last week had gone extremely well, and she was praying hard that this position would come through for her.

Just like she'd told Gabriel, it was a very entry-level position. She'd probably be answering phones and running errands, but at least she'd be in the music-industry environment, a place she'd only ever imagined herself being when she'd been in this house with Grandma Betty.

Trying not to let "no news" plague her too much, she rubbed her favorite Love-scented lotion from Bath & Body Works over her body and then slipped into a flowing lavender sundress. She redid her hair, pulling it up to the top of her head and securing it with a band again— but instead of smoothing it into a neat bun, she left her puffy curls out. It was a little after nine when she walked out of her bedroom and down the hall that led to the main staircase.

She tucked her phone between her breasts and jumped when it vibrated just as she was about to take the first step on the stairs.

"Hey, you," she said after seeing the familiar name on the screen and swiping up to accept the call. "You slackin' off at the job already today?"

Gabriel's deep chuckle sounded through the phone, and her lips involuntarily spread into a grin. She began walking down the steps.

"Now, you know I'm always focused on the job," he replied.

"Really? How are you focusing if you're on the phone with me? You know I'm an attention grabber," she joked.

"That you definitely are, Tamela. That you are." This was the second time his voice had sounded a little off to her.

The first had been last week, when he'd stopped by her apartment with pizza. The way he'd told her to let him know if she needed any-thing had been odd. Just like now. Though his words weren't that dif-ferent, Tami was confident in her looks and how she appealed to men, even if she couldn't boast the same certainty about other aspects of her life. So when she'd said she was an attention grabber, she'd meant that wholeheartedly, and since Gabriel wasn't blind, he'd conceded to the truth of those words. But it was the way he'd said it, like there was something else to his tone . . . reverence, maybe? Okay, that may have been over the top. She inwardly chastised her dreamy little mind.

"Well, anyway, whatchu up to? Sitting behind that desk, thinking about what you're gonna have for lunch?" One thing she and Gabriel had in common was that they both loved food.

He chuckled again. "Nah, not really. I was just thinkin' 'bout you and wanted to check in to see that you made it there safely. I mean, since you didn't call or text last night."

She hadn't even thought to do that, and when he'd been texting her throughout the day—before she'd boarded and after they'd landed—he hadn't specified that he wanted her to. "It was late when we got in," she said, which was the truth. Something told her that saying she didn't think that was necessary wasn't the right response.

"Yeah, I figured that. But everything's cool? You ain't ready to choke one of your sisters, are you?"

Rolling her eyes as she walked through the foyer, she noted that nothing seemed to have changed since the last time she'd been here. Nothing except for the fact that Grandma Betty was now gone.

"Absolutely not," she replied with a quick shake of her head to clear the gloomy thought. "Even though Lana was pressin' her luck. And all I did was try to help her little stuck-up ass. I swear, she gets on my nerves, acting like I don't know anything."

"You sure that's what she thinks?"

"That's how she acts. Her and Yvonne. They're both always talkin' to me like at any moment, they might need to start talking slower so I'll comprehend. I'm not stupid."

"I don't think they think you are, Tam. Chill."

She didn't want to chill. She was right about the way her sisters talked to her. Gabriel wouldn't know, because he'd never met them. But it was early, and she didn't feel like getting a headache over the Best Butlers—something she'd taken to calling her older sisters behind their backs when she was a little girl.

"This place has hardly changed," she said as she walked into what Grandma Betty had always called *the parlor*.

It looked more like a family room to her, and actually, that was what she, Lana, and Yvonne had called it. The rug was a little worn in some places, but Grandma's piano still sat in the corner, facing the paned windows. Tami walked over to the piano and eased onto the bench.

"Yeah? That's good, right? So this reno might be easy, after all." His tone sounded as hopeful as Lana's had sounded urgent last night.

"Oh, I don't know. I think there's lots of room for refreshing. Possibly adding some modern touches to the Lowcountry style," she said, adjusting the phone between her ear and her shoulder so her hands would be free.

She moved her fingers gingerly over the keys.

"Your fingers are too short to play piano," Freda had said in her testy tone when Tami was ten and had asked if she could take lessons. "And I don't have any extra money to pay for lessons." But there'd been plenty of money to send Lana to that modeling school she hated. And even more money to hire tutors for Yvonne to prep for the SATs, even though her oldest sister was the absolute smartest person Tami had ever known.

"Tam? You still there?"

His voice jerked her away from those irritating memories, and she shook her head. "Yeah. I'm here."

"I was saying you should write down your thoughts on what can be done to refresh the place. That way, you can give them to the contractor."

"Oh, yeah, that's a good idea. I was just going to walk him through each room when he gets here and share my thoughts."

"Which you can still do, but getting those thoughts down on paper is a decent plan too. So he'll have a good understanding of the direction you're trying to go in."

She nodded even though she knew he couldn't see her. "True, true. I'll go back upstairs and get one of my spiral books for that. I'm the only one up right now, so I was just going to walk around and reacclimate myself to the place." She inhaled deeply and exhaled slowly. "It still smells like biscuits and sunshine."

"What does sunshine smell like?" he asked with laughter in his tone.

"Like happiness," she said without a second thought. "It smells like all the happy things, just floating around in the air."

"Yeah, okay. Well, I'mma let you go so you can gather your thoughts before your sisters get up and start working your nerves," he said. "I'll check in with you later, though."

"Okay, and Gabriel?"

"Yeah?"

"Thanks," she said softly, her gaze now focused on the windows and the grassy land surrounding the side of the house.

"For what?"

She shrugged. "For always knowing what to say to keep me grounded. For having such great ideas to, you know . . . keep my mind right."

"There's nothing wrong with your mind, Tami. It's what makes you *you*. And you're perfect, in my book."

The flutter that started in the pit of her stomach and went soaring through her chest was immediate and different and just a little bit frightening.

"That's because you're smarter than that rent-a-cop uniform makes you look, Gabriel Taylor." She hoped she sounded light and aloof like she normally did when she was talking to him—because damn, that was not how she was feeling at that moment.

His laughter was quick and familiar, and it instantly calmed her now-racing heart. "I make this uniform look good! And you know it!" he countered.

Yeah, she did know it. That's why she'd never denied the sexual attraction that buzzed between them. She had never denied it, nor had she ever thought about taking it any further than their periodic sexcapades. And neither had he, so those flutters could take a flying hike. Gabriel was her best friend, her confidant, and lately, her rock. Sure, she could add *sometimes-lover* in there, but she wasn't going to right now. She was already on sensory overload.

"Bye, boy," she said, grinning.

"Bye, girl," he replied.

She disconnected the call and placed the phone on top of the piano. Then she let her fingers glide along the cool ivory keys again. Her eyes closed, and she began to sway to a song she could still hear in Grandma Betty's voice. It was the song she'd won a Grammy for in 1979: "Love of a Lifetime."

✉

By a little after ten, Tami had gone back up to her room, grabbed one of the five spiral notebooks she'd packed in her suitcase and her colored gel pens, and was now sitting in a chair at the kitchen table.

Grandma Betty had loved vibrant colors, something Tami figured she'd inherited from her since Freda's house was a mash-up of dark brown, light brown, medium brown, and white.

"Walls should be white. Fresh and clean. Not some other ridiculous color that you'd want to change with your next thought."

That's what her mother had told her when she was ten and had asked if she could paint her bedroom peach like the bedspread she had at Grandma Betty's house.

Sheer ivory panels stretched along a gold curtain rod to cover the three wide doors that opened out to the back porch. She'd pulled the cords and watched them separate until sunlight poured into the kitchen. Then she'd opened the middle door, letting in the warm dew-scented breeze courtesy of the Intracoastal Waterway about a hundred or so feet from the back of the house.

Across the room, on the wall behind the sink and a stretch of green granite countertops, was whitewashed brick—the most unique and calming feature of the space, in her opinion. With what she thought was her clever smile, she bopped her head and pulled a green pen out of the clear case and scribbled on the first page of her notebook: *Keep the brick wall.*

The table where she sat was close to the doors because Grandma Betty liked to sit in this very spot on rainy mornings and look out on the yard. On clear and bright sunny days like today, she'd take her morning coffee out to the porch to sit at the table in one of the wicker chairs out there. The back porch was just as big as the front, stretching the entire length of the house. But a portion of it that didn't extend out as far as the left side was screened. Above that was the deck outside of Grandma Betty's room.

It was gorgeous back there. A not-so-flat surface of healthy grass traveled down to the wood-planked dock and the stretch of water. Grandma Betty had told her that the dock had been there for hundreds of years, leading out to the boat slip where Grandpa Riley used to sit on the side and fish for hours. Tami didn't like fishing, had never had the patience to wait and wait and then wait some more for a fish to decide if it wanted to take the bait. She much preferred sitting in the kitchen, watching Grandma Betty fry up whatever fish she'd purchased from Mr. Bodine, who lived just down the road and had been fishing since he was five years old. At least then, she'd have her coloring books and crayons to occupy her mind while the fresh fish covered in cracker meal and dipped in hot grease created an aroma that always made her stomach growl with anticipation.

"You daydreaming already, TamTam?" Lana asked as she entered the kitchen, her words nearly cut off by a yawn. Her light tone meant she'd apparently gotten over yesterday's attitude about the flying panties.

Tami hadn't heard that name in forever. It was something Grandma Betty had called her from time to time and that her sisters used too, but only when they'd been here on the island.

"No," she replied. "Taking notes on what renovations need to be done." Well, she hadn't actually written anything that pertained to *renovating* the house—just one of the things she didn't want touched.

Lana opened the refrigerator, so all Tami could see of her sister when she looked over her shoulder were her long deep-brown legs peeking out from beneath the midthigh-length khaki shorts she was wearing. On her feet was a pair of fresh white Converse sneakers. Tami had already peeped the crisp white T-shirt that topped off Lana's attempt at casual. It was an *attempt* because her sister was also wearing a tiered gold necklace that swung past her breasts, gold earrings, and a chunky brown-and-gold bracelet on her left wrist.

"That's a good idea," Lana said, finally backing out of the refrigerator with a gallon of milk tucked under one arm, a carton of eggs in one hand, and several plastic bags with what looked like vegetables and cheese in the other. "We should have a list of things we want done so when this contractor gets here, all we have to do is give him the list and he can get to work."

Tami nodded because, taking Gabriel's suggestion, that's what she'd planned to do. But somehow Lana had made that seem like *her* good idea instead of Tami's. *At any rate,* she thought with a shake of her head, *I'm going to chill. Just like Gabriel advised.* Perhaps if she relaxed a bit with her sisters, they'd be able to do the same with her. After all, it had been months since they'd all stayed under the same roof. No way could they be biting each other's heads off every day this summer. She definitely didn't have the mental bandwidth for that.

"I've already walked around the entire house, but I feel like that was just to reminisce. We should all do a walk-through together and reacclimate ourselves with the space," Tami said. She tapped her pen on the notebook, liking how the green ink brightened up the page.

Colored gel pens were her favorite to write with. The variety and the spice of being able to make a different selection gave her an odd burst of energy. The fact that writing down her plethora of thoughts had been a hobby since she was a little girl only increased her enjoyment of them.

"I need to eat first," Lana said, and moved to the stove.

"Did somebody say 'eat'?" Yvonne asked as she walked into the kitchen. "I didn't have the strength to come down here and find something when we got in last night, so I'm starving now."

"Me too," Lana said. "I'm glad the refrigerator was stocked."

"Robyn said that Sallie came by over the weekend to make sure that everything was in order for us," Tami said. A huge bird flew by, and she turned to look out the window. "The deck looks faded and worn. It should probably be redone." She said that mostly to herself as she looked down at her notebook and wrote, *Use a more weather-resistant product.*

"What are you over there talking about?" Yvonne asked as she came farther into the room and pulled out one of the high-backed chairs at the island.

The bottom portion of the island was painted a shade of green that almost matched the cabinets, something close to an evergreen color. It didn't look as vibrant as Tami recalled it had been when she was younger. In fact, as she surveyed the kitchen again, she wondered if the green was too dark.

She looked away from her sister to write *Green???*, then looked back at Yvonne because she hadn't answered her question. "Just jotting down some things to tell the contractor when he gets here."

"What time is he supposed to be here again?" Yvonne asked. "And is there coffee? I can make some, if y'all haven't already started a pot."

Yvonne eased off the chair she'd just slid onto. She was wearing white jeans today and a white tank top that she'd covered with a short-sleeve denim shirt. On her feet were cheetah-print flats, which Tami thought were more her style than Yvonne's. The fact that her older sister was wearing them made Tami smile; maybe she wasn't as old and crotchety as she'd always acted.

"I don't like coffee," Tami said. "There's orange juice in the refriger-ator, and I saw some tea bags in the cabinet—the kind for hot tea and the ones for iced tea. I was gonna make a pitcher of that for later." But then she'd opened the back door and sat down to take her notes, so she hadn't gone back to make the tea.

"I know you don't," Yvonne replied. "Always said it tasted too bitter, no matter how much sugar and cream you added to it."

Tami scrunched up her face and glanced outside again. "It does."

"I'm making omelets. Anybody want one?" Lana asked as she cracked eggs into a bowl.

"I do," Tami replied. "With lots of cheese, no veggies."

"You need veggies, Tami, to keep your iron up." That was Yvonne, with her mother-hen self. When Tami glanced over her shoulder again, she saw her sister opening a cabinet, in search of coffee grounds, no doubt.

"I don't like them raw," Tami complained. "Maybe some fried onions?"

Lana nodded. "I can do that."

"These cabinets need to be painted," Yvonne said as she closed and opened another one, smiling when she reached in and pulled out a container of coffee. "Put that on your list, Tami. And those rugs in the family room and main living room—they need to come up. Maybe have the wood floors buffed instead. People aren't big on rugs anymore, anyway."

"That's true." Lana nodded and whisked the eggs. "But let's not go overboard. Robyn said there's only fifty thousand in that escrow account. We just need to do enough cosmetic things that'll get us a good return in the sale. I was looking online at more houses in the area, and some of them are going for around 1.5 and up to 2 million. Especially on the Intracoastal Waterway like this one."

"Well, like I said, I don't think we should half step with this. There's a reason Grandma Betty wanted us to come down here and get this house fixed up. And I'm sure she didn't mean for us to do the bare minimum and then run right back to the city," Tami objected.

"Well, just what do you think she meant, Tami? Since you act like you knew her better than we did, when we're the older ones, so we knew her longer," Lana said.

"But you didn't talk to her as much as I did," Tami countered. "And who was the last one to come down here to visit for the whole summer? Me." She huffed. "And for three years straight, I might add, while the two of you were off in college. You never even looked back to her or this island for a summerlong visit after you graduated from high school."

"That's not true," Yvonne interjected as she grabbed the coffeepot and carried it over to the sink. "I talked to Grandma Betty several times a year. Sent her gifts on her birthday and at Christmas. And then we were all here every Thanksgiving, just like she asked."

"That's right," Lana said. "Well, I may not have talked to her that much because I just got busy, and I've never liked talking on the phone. But I did send her cards and things throughout the year. We didn't just walk away from her."

Tami disagreed, and she was just about to say so when Yvonne screeched. She turned in her chair to see what was wrong, and her eyes widened as water shot up into the air like a geyser.

Chapter 11

YVONNE

Yvonne threw her arms up in the air, coffeepot still in one hand as cold water splashed her.

"Dammit!" she yelled, and then tried to look around the spray of water to see where it was coming from.

Well, obviously it was coming from the faucet—so *how* or *why* may have been the better question.

"Oh, shit!" Lana was suddenly next to her, reaching for one of the handles by the faucet and then turning it.

There was a squeaky sound as she did that to no avail; water continued to splash them both.

"What are you two doing? Just turn the faucet off!" Now Tami was approaching, giving a directive that she, for whatever reason, thought they weren't already attempting.

Yvonne tried the other handle even though she'd only turned on the one for cold water. It spun around like it was a toy, and again, nothing happened. "It's broken. How can a whole damn faucet be broken?"

Her answer came when the handle she'd been turning slipped free of her grasp and rolled over the counter. By now, she was basically drenched. She could feel the front of her hair hanging down in her face, her shirts—the denim one she'd left unbuttoned and the tank—were sticking to her chest, and the top half of her pants was wet.

"The whole thing is broke," Lana added.

Tami, now standing between them, pressed her hand to where the water was gushing out like Niagara Falls. But that only made it spray in different directions, all of which still managed to land on them. Yvonne tried to move to the side to get out of the way and at least put the damn coffeepot down, but her foot slipped on the wet floor. The next thing she knew, she was falling.

"Oh, wait, you fell," Tami said, her words—which once again stated the obvious—ending on a chuckle.

"Oh damn," was Lana's follow-up. "Help her, Tam!"

"I'm trying," Tami said as she turned and extended a hand to Yvonne, now lying flat on the floor, the coffeepot having rolled somewhere in the distance.

Yvonne took Tami's hand, trying not to let loose the litany of curses running through her mind, but Tami's hands were wet and, thus, slippery, so instead of being helped up, as her hand slipped from Tami's, her sister lost her battle with the slick floor in those silly rubber flip-flops she was wearing. Tami fell into a heap, just barely missing Yvonne.

Lana burst out laughing while water was still giving her a second shower for the day. On the floor, Tami laughed too, and Yvonne tried her best to scowl.

"It's not . . . funny," she said, her voice breaking with a little chuckle. Then, because the sound of her sisters laughing amid the drenching of the kitchen was something she hadn't had on her to-do list but was still more entertaining than she'd experienced in a long time, she cracked up too.

That's how Jeremiah and the contractor found them when they walked into the kitchen—or at least, Yvonne surmised it was Jeremiah and the contractor, since the first things she saw were feet—one set wearing rubber-soled casual tie-ups and navy-blue slacks, the other in beige steel-toe work boots and light-wash jeans.

"Uh, good mornin', ladies."

Yeah, it was Jeremiah wearing the tie-ups, she realized as her gaze traveled upward and mortification seeped through to her soul, similar to the way the water had soaked through her clothes.

"Oh, mornin'!" Tami yelled as the two of them scrambled to get off the floor.

Yvonne rolled over onto her knees first, swallowing another curse, as that wasn't the best-feeling option. She swore turning forty last year had opened the door for her body to experience every ache and pain imaginable. With purposefully slow movements, she got herself up to a standing position and immediately reached for the edge of the island to keep herself upright.

"Good . . ." Her greeting trailed off as her drenched denim shirt slid from her shoulder when Tami grabbed hold of its hem to help steady herself so she could get up from the floor.

The contractor, who was also wearing a white T-shirt, moved around them in a blur, she guessed—and prayed—to get to the sink and shut off the still-flowing water.

"Here, let me help you," Jeremiah was saying as he came closer to where Tami—in her cute little sundress that hugged her breasts and skirted midthigh—stood. Of course, the dress was now sticking to her younger sister's curvy-and-flat-in-all-the-right-places body.

He draped an arm over Tami's shoulders and walked her around to the other side of the island, which was dry. Yvonne kept her hands on the island and gingerly made her way around to that side too, with Lana right behind her.

"Good morning," Yvonne finally finished in a huff. "As you can see, we've had a little mishap."

"The handles on this faucet and the one in the guest-bathroom sink down here are stripped. But the burst pipe is the bigger issue. I knew it was just a matter of time before that happened." The contractor's voice was a rich baritone that rumbled and fell around the room like a warm blanket.

So she shivered, because what else was she supposed to do now that she was chilled to the bone in wet clothes? Her gaze was fixed on the contractor. The smooth umber skin that stretched over excellently toned arms and biceps. The black hair cut into a fade, with about an inch of cruddy curls on top. The low-cut beard and dark eyes that almost appeared sleepy but were, at the same time, alert and assessing. She was five feet, four inches tall, and even across the space of maybe fifteen to twenty feet, he looked like he'd easily tower over her. The front of his shirt and pants now matched hers, as he'd battled the water, but he finally stood from beneath the sink, where he'd managed to shut it off.

"It's just one of the many things we need to go over today," he said, continuing to talk like he didn't know that she was momentarily stunned by his appearance.

She shouldn't have been stunned by his appearance, though. She'd obviously seen men before, and she'd had a few in her lifetime. Gawking at them like some lovestruck groupie—or like Tami—wasn't normally her thing. Still, her gaze didn't falter as she asked, "'Many things'?"

He met her questioning stare with a nod and replied, "Many."

"That doesn't sound good," Tami said.

Lana sighed. "It sounds expensive."

"Deacon Williams, these are the Butler Sisters—Tami, Yvonne, and Lana," Jeremiah said, then hurriedly dropped his arm from Tami's shoulder when Yvonne turned her attention to him.

"Nice to meet you, ladies," Deacon said, his southern drawl a little heavier than Jeremiah's. "Ms. Betty spoke highly of each one of you, so I've been eager to meet you. Although losing Ms. Betty in order to make this introduction necessary is mighty sad."

"Yes," Tami replied. "Grandma Betty's passing was extremely sad and unexpected. We're all still processing it."

That was true, even if they hadn't formally discussed it. The news of losing their only living grandmother had been shocking, and finding out they'd already missed the opportunity to pay their respects properly had been an even bigger blow. Truth be told, Yvonne's continued ire over that situation was probably what kept her from really feeling the loss of her grandmother. Although she knew she would've opted to respect Grandma Betty's wishes had she known them ahead of time, she still felt a little sting at the knowledge being withheld from them—and she still didn't quite understand why. Robyn hadn't been able to provide an adequate explanation for that, so Yvonne had planned to ask Sallie since she was the one who'd done Grandma Betty's bidding without picking up a phone to call them.

"I've got my tablet with my notes out in the truck," Deacon said, pulling her from those thoughts. "Figured we'd do a walk-around and I'll give you all the details."

"I need to get out of these wet clothes," Lana said with a frown.

"Me too," Tami added. "And then I've got some thoughts on things to be done around the house too."

Deacon nodded at Tami. "Good. I'll just head out to the truck."

"And I guess I'll get this kitchen cleaned up," Yvonne said dryly, since it seemed they were all deciding what to do next.

"I can give you a hand," Jeremiah offered. He'd started to roll up the sleeves of his button-front shirt when Yvonne spoke again.

"That's okay. You go on and have a seat in the parlor." She'd been about to call it *the family room* when the memory of how much Grandma Betty loved saying "pahla," leaving out both *R*s in an exaggerated southern drawl, whenever she referenced the room. A spurt of warmth spread through her at the thought, and before she could help it, she smiled. "I'll go grab some towels and get this cleaned up right quick; then we can get on with the walk-around."

"You're not going to change your clothes?" Lana asked.

"You *need* to change your clothes," Tami added, with a wag of her eyebrows before her gaze fell to Yvonne's chest.

Yvonne glanced down—as she suspected everybody else in the kitchen was doing at that same moment since Tami wasn't exactly subtle—and saw that not only was the white tank top she wore stuck to her skin, but that in its wet state, it was also now terribly transparent, allowing her very hard, very dark nipples to show through the fabric and her thin lacy bra.

"Shit!" she cursed, and grabbed the ends of the denim shirt still hanging partially off her shoulders, thanks to Tami.

Deacon cleared his throat loudly. "Be right back," he said, and then made his way out of the kitchen.

Jeremiah grabbed one of the dish towels that had been hanging on a drawer handle. "I'll start cleaning this up."

And Yvonne promised herself she would die of mortification later. For now, they still had business to tend to.

✉

An hour and a half later, the five of them walked around until they were once again standing at the front of the house. And what a majestic house it was. Even through Yvonne's newly adjusted lens, the house was still a magnificent structure that had borne so much from behind its walls.

The two-story home stood with the same burst of exuberance and flourish that Grandma Betty used to possess. With five gabled windows jutting from the shingled roof and the elegant sweep of the wide porch and elaborate stairway, it was an attention grabber, regardless of how long Deacon's to-do list was. A huge live oak tree stood as if it were guarding the house on the left side of the stairs, with shorter shrubbery around it and on the other side of the stairs. The walkway up to the house had a smooth gravel path, and a fountain that didn't work was about twenty feet away.

"The block-stucco construction was a good way to go, so the bones of the house are still good," Deacon had told them. "It's not a total demolish job, nor do we need to completely gut it to make the changes. But there are some pretty big fixes that need to be made before you can get optimum value."

He'd said that a while ago, when they'd been in the house, standing at the top of the stairs. They'd just completed going from room to room on the second level, and after he'd read off all the items on the list, which seemed never-ending, Lana had sighed. "This is going to cost a fortune. We can't afford to do this."

"We can't afford *not* to do it," Tami had countered. "It's what Grandma Betty wanted."

"Then she should've left us more than fifty thousand to complete this job," Lana had countered right back. "Or better yet, maybe she should've had Deacon get started on some of these jobs before she passed away."

That question had lurked in the back of Yvonne's mind as Deacon moved through the rooms, talking as if he'd done this appraisal long before the previous two weeks after Grandma Betty's death.

"Why didn't she have you start the renovations sooner?" she had asked him, ignoring her sisters and their dispute for the moment. She could—and would—have this discussion at length with them later; she knew that for certain.

Deacon had released a heavy sigh and glanced over at Jeremiah before answering. Was he asking for permission? Did he and Jeremiah know something they didn't? Yvonne wasn't going to like that if that were the case, and she'd known without a doubt that Tami and Lana wouldn't like it either. But for the moment, she'd wanted to try to get what information she could before either of them could react.

"I don't know how much you knew about your grandmother's illness, but she had good days and bad days," he had told them. "I was hired in late March of this year, but I'd been a fan of your grandmother's all my life. My mother was a huge fan too and was always bragging about Ms. Betty having fallen in love and married a been-yah." He had chuckled then, and Yvonne wondered which she liked better: him laughing and using the term for a 'Fuskie native, or giving that solemn look he'd been tossing around during the time they'd been together.

"She had Sallie call my office one day and told me to come over for lunch and to bring my mama with me. I wasn't totally sure what the lunch was going to be about, since I didn't usually take my mother on business meetings, but I wasn't going to question Ms. Betty, nor was I going to pass up the opportunity to get into this beautiful house."

He hadn't been lying about the beauty of the house, which stood amid mature palmetto trees and live oaks. It was the biggest and most prestigious home on this lonely stretch of road. The next house was about a half mile down the road in the opposite direction. There, more houses were clumped together—some that had been built in the past ten or twenty years, and others that were the smaller ones that had been on the island for much longer than Yvonne or even Grandma Betty had been living.

"She talked about the three of you for much of the time we were at lunch and how she wanted to leave each of you something that spoke to how much she loved you," he'd continued. "And to do that, she said she had to get this house in order. I thought she meant we'd start the renovations right then too, so the house would be ready to sell once she passed on, and then the money could go to you. That's how I figured it would go. But no, that's not what she wanted. She told me to make this list, and then she gave me that check with the instructions to put it in an escrow account and hold it there until the three of you were back on the island. So that's what I did." He'd shrugged after that, as if his words had miraculously explained everything.

They had not.

But one thing was as clear as it ever was: Grandma Betty had wanted them back on Daufuskie for another summer. Well, right now Yvonne wanted to get this walk-around over with. She'd always preferred the ripping-the-Band-Aid-off approach; it was best to get all the bad news at one time so she could then regroup and reconfigure what her next steps would be. This situation was no different—they couldn't afford for it to be. All three of them had a life to return to in the city, so whatever needed to be done here needed to be done quickly.

"What are we looking at as far as time?" Lana asked, her tone weary and tinged with irritation as they all stood in front of the house now.

Yvonne listened for Deacon's response but kept her gaze focused on the house, the huge wide-planked porch with four matching rocking chairs and the small table with one plant on top and several others surrounding it in between two of the chairs. The front doors were a dark-oak color, with painted paned windows. Yvonne had always thought it was like walking into the church whenever she came up on the porch and entered through those doors. It had always made her feel like she was special that she not only knew who lived here but knew them well enough to be allowed to sleep in a comfortable bed behind those walls. That the bed had been purchased for her and placed in a room she'd been allowed to assist in designing had filled her heart in a way nothing else had since.

"Ten to twelve weeks at minimum," he said.

"What?" Lana asked. "That's all summer."

Yvonne turned back just in time to see Deacon nod. "Yes, I know. And that's if all the stars align. Meaning, we've got to get the proper permits from Beaufort County and touch base with the Daufuskie Island Historical Foundation to make sure none of what we plan to do disrupts anything historical."

"Right," Tami said. "It's important to not disturb any of the history here. Everything should be preserved for the next generation. I think that's what Grandma Betty would've wanted."

"I agree," Deacon said.

Yvonne wondered how he knew that with such certainty. She could deduce how Tami figured she knew, because what she'd said earlier when it was just the three of them in the kitchen *was* true: she had talked to Grandma Betty the most. And not just in the summers when she'd come down here after Yvonne and Lana had stopped. But because even during the times when they were all here together, Tami had stuck close to Grandma Betty the most. She had always climbed into their grandmother's bed at night instead of falling asleep in her own like the rest of them did. But that had mostly been after Daddy's death. They'd all felt lonely and afraid to an extent then because their future had been so uncertain. Would Mama continue to let them spend the summers with the grandmother she had deemed flighty and irresponsible? Or would their lazy summers filled with hope, great food, and love be taken away, the same way their loving daddy had been?

"Yvonne? You listening?" Tami asked, pulling on Yvonne's arm.

Yvonne had to shake her head to get her thoughts back on the present. "Yes . . . yes. I hear you," she said, and then cleared her throat. "Do you think you could print out that list you have so we can go over it in detail together?" She turned away from the house to look at Deacon, who, along with Jeremiah and Lana, was standing behind her.

When exactly she'd walked away from their group to stand closer to the shrubs in front of the porch, she had no clue.

"Definitely," he said. "Actually, if you give me your email address, I can send it to you now, and you can print it out at your leisure."

She nodded, recalling the small office located on the first floor of the house. Grandma Betty had never liked computers and all the "learnin'" she'd said had come along with them, but she did have one on the pretty antique desk in the office. Along with that, there was one of those multifunctional printers too.

"Of course," she said, and then stepped closer to him to rattle off her email address.

"Great," Jeremiah said. "So we'll leave you be now, let you get settled in. Ms. Janie's having a shrimp boil down at her place later on tonight. She told me to let you know if you wanna stop by. Nothin' formal, just everybody comin' and goin' as they please, getting some good food and chattin' it up a bit."

Deacon grinned. "Yeah, you know how we do down here. Nothin' fancy—just good ole-fashioned fun. Man, I miss this when I'm in the city."

"Oh, you live in the city?" Yvonne asked, not sure why she hadn't considered that.

Sure, you could tell both men were from the South, but there was also a bit of an edge to them. It was in the way they dressed, the way they talked, and she was certain they'd both had to leave the island to attend undergrad, and law school for Jeremiah. Now, Deacon, on the other hand, she'd have to do a little research on. She figured he'd have to have a degree in construction or some other formal study to be running his own company. The DW CONSTRUCTION in hunter-green print on the side of his white work truck had clued her in to him being the owner. That, and the totally boss way he'd walked into the house and taken complete control of the walk-around.

"I'm on and off," he said. "My company's based in Charleston, but I was born here on the island. My mother, sister, and her family still live here."

"Oh, okay. That makes sense," she said. Not that it mattered.

"Yeah, I gotta take a break," Lana said, and then headed toward the back of the house. "I'm gonna take a walk or something. Try to wrap my mind around all this."

Again, Yvonne noted the edge—no, the bitterness—in Lana's tone. There was definitely something bothering her, and Yvonne wasn't totally sure it was just this situation with the house or the loss of their grandmother. Lana was the easygoing one of the trio. She took things as they came, but she was also very intentional about her actions. She'd wanted to take pictures instead of model, and she'd done it, despite Freda's misgivings and hesitance over paying for any of the classes that had come with both of those endeavors. She'd wanted to major in fine arts at MassArt, but Freda had fervently argued that the arts weren't a viable career. Lana had taken all the AP classes she could handle in high school and applied for every scholarship there was until she was rewarded with a full scholarship to the school of her dreams. That had made Freda's case against the school, and Lana's decided career path, a little weaker. And once Lana had graduated, she landed a prestigious internship in Cambridge. After that, she'd returned to Boston a couple of years later, not only with a fine arts degree with a specialty in photography but also with her first gallery showing scheduled and a handsome husband as well.

This version of her sister, who had been so argumentative with Tami yesterday and was both rushed and bothered today, wasn't Lana.

"Fine," Tami said. "I'm still hungry, and I want to take some more notes, so I'm going to fix something to eat and sit out on the back porch for a while."

"Then I'll print out the list and figure out what our next steps will be," Yvonne said. She left off the fact that she was always the one to take charge, even though she knew her sisters wanted to toss out their opinions. In the end, all the big decisions would be on her. Every move they made would rest on her, just as Freda had told her. Just as Yvonne had always hated.

"Cool," Deacon said. "I just sent the email. I'll be at Ms. Janie's tonight if either of you have any questions. But I think we should plan to get started by the end of this week, especially if you want to try and keep that twelve-week schedule."

"And I'm just a phone call away," Jeremiah said. "So just reach out if you need anything or if you have questions. Sallie said she's coming by later this afternoon, but she doesn't know the specifics on the will and such—so those questions, definitely shoot my way. Tami has my number."

He didn't really have to say that last part. The way the two of them had walked side by side during the entire walk-around had sealed their newfound connection. Yvonne had decided it was easier not to fret over how ridiculously quick her sister seemed to move in the love—or rather, lust—department.

Yvonne had never been that fast, or that experienced, in such things. Perhaps because she'd been too busy trying to maintain a mature and responsible facade, which had embedded in her mind that doing something as fanciful as flirting or flourishing in a romantic relationship was a lot harder than it probably should've been.

"Great," she said, and then cleared her throat. "Thanks for coming by. We'll let you know something tonight or tomorrow. I know that time is of the essence, so we won't be drawing this out. The renovations need to be done. We just have to figure out how we're going to pay for whatever isn't covered by the escrow account."

She also had to figure out why she felt compelled to agree with Tami, of all people, that preserving the historical elements was imperative for future generations. But those generations wouldn't be theirs, right? Not if they sold the house.

Chapter 12

LANA

With her camera raised, body still, eyes poised on the stretch of saltwater marshland in the distance, Lana waited for the right moment. A rabbit had wandered into her line of sight. It seemed bigger than any rabbit she'd ever seen in a pet store or even at the zoo when she'd been there on school trips as a child.

Its eyes were wide and dark but alert. Or perhaps *inquisitive* was more like it. Maybe it felt like she did, being surrounded by so much that was familiar and yet still questioning everything around her. The rabbit was also bigger, plumper, around the midsection as it sat back on its haunches, ears sticking straight up. It knew she was there, knew there was an interruption to its ecosystem, its daily routine. She was the interruption.

So she remained perfectly still. She'd already knelt down so that she'd be more level with the beautiful animal, hoping that by doing so, the tall, wispy strands of grass wouldn't block her view. They hadn't, instead adding an extra layer to the picture she was trying to capture. Another texture that would pop through, first on her computer screen and then—once she'd made any necessary adjustments—in print, giving the image life. Every picture should tell a story, and this one she'd already named *Wonder*.

It was indeed a wonder that through all the turmoil going on inside her head, she'd been able to find a semblance of calm, a piece of the normal to latch on to. Every shot was one of a kind, no matter the likeness to something else. It was one moment, one chance, one snap of the camera at just the right moment.

Snap!

She pressed the shutter button, and the camera whirred. She'd set it on high speed so she'd end up with multiple shots, hopefully catching any sudden movements or changes in the shot she'd zoomed in on and adjusted in her lens. When taking live shots like this one, she liked to have options, to be able to study the pictures for every detail before deciding which would be the final one.

Choices and chances: something she knew she'd taken for granted in life. For as long as she could remember, her one focus had been doing what she wanted, in the way she wanted to. Her mother hadn't allowed Yvonne to do that. No, her older sister had been doomed to be Freda's clone, from the order of her birth to the similarities in their looks and personality. While Lana had been the only sister to get Freda's deep-mocha hue, Yvonne had their mother's high cheekbones, take-charge attitude, and smile. Even though neither of them smiled nearly enough.

Seeing Yvonne lying on that floor, giving in to Tami's infectious laugh and Lana's deep belly chuckles, had been a sight Lana hadn't realized how much she'd missed. To be fair, that whole moment—even if it had resulted in each of them being soaked and her sisters landing on the floor—had been as refreshing as the balmy summer air she now breathed. It had made her heart sigh in a way that was foreign but welcome at the same time. And all she'd wanted was to fix something to eat and get started with the work that needed to be done.

Now she was out here, doing what she'd always loved. Some birds flew overhead. Not nearly as high above as she would've preferred, but they made a loud squawking noise that frightened the rabbit and sent it skittering off into the deeper parts of the marsh. She still didn't move, not right away. Instead, she stayed in that squatting position and lowered her camera.

Everything was so still here. She'd always remarked at how slow things tended to move on the island as opposed to in the city, where she'd thrived nine months out of the year, going to school and then modeling or photography class, or whatever other extracurricular activity Freda thought would make her college applications more appealing. From late June to mid-August, she'd enjoyed doing nothing more than waking up in the morning; devouring a huge breakfast Grandma Betty, or the cook she sometimes employed, had prepared; and then spending the rest of the day doing whatever she wanted. That had usually been either walking around the island and taking pictures, lying in the lounger on the back porch and flipping through magazines, or writing letters to her friends back in the city.

In the years since she'd been out of college, Lana had never had as relaxing a vacation as the summers she'd spent here. She hadn't realized how much she missed that until this very moment.

Shaking herself free of the memories, she rose to a standing position. With her camera still in one hand but its strap around her neck, she'd already started to look for another shot. She'd taken a couple of steps, wondering if she should chance going toward the underbrush. Small deer, raccoons, foxes, and bobcats had been known to wander near the wax myrtle and briars, all of which would make a phenomenal set of pictures if she were planning a wildlife exhibit, but she wasn't. And she wasn't in the mood to be scared out of her mind should she actually come face-to-face with a fox or bobcat. She'd seen plenty of deer while on vacations with Isaac's parents at their mountainside cabin and wasn't necessarily afraid of them. In fact, she'd captured plenty of them on camera. But again, she hadn't incorporated animals into any of her shows in the past, and she wasn't about to start now, no matter how much this particular spot seemed to be pulling her in.

All her shows predominantly centered on city life, skyscraper buildings, cars in traffic, the sun rising over the city and setting over Boston Harbor. The whale shots she'd taken the day she'd met Isaac were a memory she'd immortalized in a twenty-four-by-thirty-six print that hung above their bed.

Her phone chimed, and when she eased it out of the back pocket of her jeans, she saw Isaac's name on the screen. It was as if, from miles away, he could sense she'd been thinking of him.

"Hey," she said, sounding a little breathless.

"Hey, baby. How's it going?"

Without a second thought, she let out a heavy sigh. "It's going, I guess. Met with the contractor this morning, and he has a list a mile long of things that need to be done and that Grandma Betty wanted done. It's going to take much longer than I thought."

"Well, you were planning to take the summer to work on your next show, anyway, so maybe just focus on that." Isaac's voice had always been soothing to her. It wasn't deep like Deacon's or raspy and juvenile sounding like Jeremiah's, which was probably why the guy irritated her a little.

"How am I supposed to focus on work when I've got to stay in that house every night with my sisters? You know we don't get along, especially in close proximity for long periods of time," she said.

"But they are your sisters, and you used to stay in that house together before."

"We used to share a bathroom at one point in our lives too, but that doesn't mean we want to go back to doing that," she argued. "Yvonne's her normal I-can-do-all-things-better-than-anybody-else self, and Tami's still in TamiLand, deciding what she does and doesn't want in the house without even consulting us."

He gave a gruff laugh. "You're adults now. I'm sure the three of you can come together and get this done for your grandmother's sake."

"She's gone," she snapped, and then hated how the words left a bitter taste in her mouth. Grandma Betty was gone, and now she and her sisters were here to do whatever it was their grandmother had wanted. Why couldn't she just focus on that? Hadn't she hoped that the differences in their personalities wouldn't cause too much stress? It had occurred to her in that moment that perhaps her quick temper where her sisters were concerned wasn't totally their fault.

"I know that, baby," Isaac continued. "But I also know how much you loved her. I heard it in your voice each time you talked about your summers there. All of you loved her, and she loved each of you. That's why she left this house to you."

Lana shook her head. She didn't want to think too long and hard about the *why* of this thing Grandma Betty had asked of them. "I just know that it came at the right time. We need the money from the sale of this house, and we need it sooner than twelve weeks from now. Did you ask for the extension?" She'd suggested that to him just before he'd taken her to the airport, and he hadn't responded. She hoped for a positive response this time. Maybe then her mood would improve—at least a little.

"I've got that under control," he said, his voice tight. "I told you that before you left."

They had talked about the debt before she'd left, but she still felt so unsettled about how they were going to deal with it this time around.

"It's my problem, Lana. I'll handle it."

"You don't have the money, Isaac. I've checked the balances on all the accounts. The only other account you have in your name only is at the credit union, and I saw that statement when it came to the house last month. You don't have thirty-seven thousand dollars."

He was quiet for so long she thought he might've hung up. If he had, she would've had yet another reason to be annoyed at him and may have used that as an excuse to fly home and cuss him out in person. But she'd refrained from going that route with Isaac. Going off and letting loose with all the thoughts she had about him and his weakness for gambling was something she'd been telling herself she wouldn't do. Because what good was going to come of it? Would saying all those harmful words and reminding him he'd promised to love and trust her make him confess to why he was doing this thing that was threatening their marriage? She wasn't a trained or licensed therapist, but she knew that wasn't how addictions worked.

"You don't have to clean up after me, Lana. I've told you that before."

"And you've also accepted every dime I've given you to pay off whatever bookie or whoever you owe this money to." Some type of insect flew past her face, and she waved it away, almost slapping herself on the forehead in the process. Then she sighed. "You're my husband; of course I'm going to help you."

"Not this time. I got it this time, baby."

She let her head fall back and closed her eyes for a few seconds. "By taking out a second mortgage on the condo?" she asked, unable to hide the irritation in her tone. "I got an email from the bank this morning asking for my business account or profit and loss statements. They need them to properly evaluate our financial situation in order to consider the refinance."

He let out a heavy breath. "Lana, I'm trying to fix this."

"By putting our home in danger?" she yelled. "Are you serious right now? You're willing to risk the home we've spent these past years building together—the place we planned to begin our family—for a gambling debt?"

"I've got to pay them soon," he replied tightly.

"That's why I came all the way down here, still hoping we could get this house sold! If you would just ask for the extension, like another thirty days, I can push harder to get this work done so we can put it on the market."

"I don't want you to rush into that decision, baby. Besides, it's not your decision alone. Your sisters have a say in what happens, and right now at least, Tami is dead set against selling."

She sighed. "Yvonne wants to sell. She doesn't want to be here any more than I do. Tami's just dreamy-eyed about this place like she is about everything else. And she can't even afford to live here now that she's unemployed again. So she might as well jump on the selling bandwagon too, so she won't starve to death."

It sounded harsh, she knew, but Tami worked her nerves almost as much as Isaac did. Why couldn't the two of them get their shit together? They weren't kids anymore; they didn't have the luxury of just doing whatever they wanted when what they wanted to do wasn't taking care of them financially.

"Look, I don't want to argue. I just called to check on you, to make sure you were doing okay. I don't want you to worry about this anymore, baby. I got it," he said. "Trust me. This time I got it."

She wanted to. Damn, she wanted to trust the man she still loved with all her heart, but he'd let her down with his gambling so many times in the past. Not because he didn't treat her right, because Isaac never forgot her birthday or any of their anniversaries—first date, first kiss, first time having sex, getting engaged—he remembered them all, and he gave the best gifts. Christmas in their house looked like they already had children, with all the presents that were always beneath their tree, the bulk of them being from him to her.

And he'd had no problems with his full paycheck going into their joint checking account. She knew exactly how much money he made and when to expect it. Unfortunately, that meant she also saw the times when he managed to get money out of the account before she could wake up and pay bills on his payday. Not so much that they were struggling, but enough that it got him into trouble at the poker table time and time again.

"I want to," she said quietly. "I really do."

"Then do it," he said, his tone urgent. "Trust me to handle my own mistake this time."

"And then what?" she asked, hating that the question had been burning like an iron fist in the center of her chest. "What happens after this time, Isaac? We can't keep taking out mortgages on our condo, and I can't hope for another inheritance to save the day. How do we keep our life together if you keep doing this?"

He was quiet again for quite some time, but she could hear his breathing, so she didn't disconnect the call and didn't speak. He was thinking of what he wanted to say, and she was thinking of how she would react to whatever it was he did say.

"I want to keep our life together," he replied finally. "It's all I want right now, Lana. Just you and me. That's all I want to focus on."

"Then the gambling has to stop," she said without hesitation. "You need to get some help—because I don't know, Isaac."

"What do you mean you 'don't know'?"

"I don't know how to keep doing this with you," she said, hating this admission. She seemed to be saying all the hard things today, and that knowledge made her stomach churn. "I can't keep doing this with you."

The declaration fell like a lead weight over the line. Her fingers trembled as she held the phone to her ear. She couldn't take back her words, and she didn't really know if she wanted to. It was a thought that had been circling in her mind for months, possibly the last year. Definitely since the last time she'd found out he had a huge gambling debt. But it was just another thing she'd told herself not to say, as if somehow, if she remained silent, it would go away. The logical part of her mind knew that wasn't true.

"Don't say that," he whispered, so softly she barely heard him above the sound of another bird screeching in the distance. "Don't say what it sounds like you're saying."

His words tore at her heart, pulled her lids down until she was standing with eyes closed and heart pounding.

"I'm saying there has to be a change, Isaac." And so much more. They both knew she was saying more, but for the life of her, she couldn't bring herself to actually mutter those other words. Opening her eyes again, she whispered, "I've always believed in you—"

"Then keep believing in me," he said hurriedly. "Don't give up on me now. Please, baby. Don't give up on us."

The desperation in his voice pierced straight through her chest like a dagger, and she gasped. She wasn't giving up on them—at least, she didn't think that was what she was doing. She prayed that she was drawing a line, stating her position and giving him the chance to decide which direction he would take with that knowledge.

"I'm trying desperately to save us," she told him. "I need you to come with the same effort."

"I hear you," he said. "I hear everything you're saying—and I've got it, Lana. I can do this. I promise you, I *will* do this."

"Okay," was all she could say next. Of course there were more words, more talking they needed to do to really be in a position to get past this thing that had become a giant hurdle between them, but she couldn't speak them right now. While her mind might've been screaming that she could, her heart was whimpering, just like Isaac, "Please don't." So she didn't. "I've gotta get back to the house." She cleared her throat. "Yvonne wants us all to meet to talk about our next steps in detail before we go to this dinner gathering."

"Oh. You're all going out together?" His tone shifted just barely from that desperate plea to hopefulness.

She touched her free hand to her camera, letting its familiar knobs and grooves comfort her. "Yeah, there's a lady in town that I guess knew Grandma Betty. She told Jeremiah to invite us."

"Jeremiah? That's the young lawyer you said your grandmother hired."

She nodded but then realized he couldn't see her. "Yes. You should see him—he's probably in his late twenties, early thirties at the most. I'm gonna ask Yvonne because I'm sure she's looked him up. He's too busy flirting with Tami, and you know she's snapping up every ounce of attention being tossed her way."

"You sound like that's a bad thing," Isaac said.

She shrugged. "I don't know. Seems fast, and you know how Tami is—she's so impulsive. The last thing she needs is some summer fling to add to all the other drama in her life."

"Well, you should let that be her call," he continued. "You know you don't like people telling you what to do with your life, so be careful about doing the same to others."

Here was a part of Isaac she cherished. He knew about all her family baggage. He was the only one she'd ever confided in about all her hurt and disappointment concerning her family. And he'd always given her level and sound advice whenever she'd poured into him. Sure, he'd made it known that she was his priority and that he'd always have her back, but he'd also never shied away from telling her when she or the way she was thinking might've been wrong or a little diluted by the pain she still carried.

"I know," she replied. "And I'm trying to keep my mouth shut in that regard. Besides, Yvonne's gonna say it for both of us, so really, I've just gotta wait it out. I swear, though, Isaac, it feels like we're teenagers again, all of us in that house last night and then this morning." She didn't tell him about the sink fiasco, even though the thought of it brought a wistful smile to her face. Not the part about the busted pipe, but the part where she and her sisters were laughing together. "It felt like Grandma Betty was right there, smiling the way she used to when we'd arrive for the summer or on Thanksgiving."

"Then that's what you hold on to, baby. That good part right there. Even when things seem really bad—the worst, even—that's when you gotta remember the good and hold on tight, Lana. Hold on tight to the good."

She was still thinking about Isaac's words an hour later, when she was sitting in the parlor across from Yvonne and Tami, awaiting the first of what she knew were going to be many tough discussions between them.

Chapter 13

LANA

"I think we should do all the things on Deacon's list; plus, we should work on the little blue house out back," Tami said, starting the meeting.

She and Lana had each received Yvonne's text telling them they should talk before heading out to Ms. Janie's house. While they weren't expected there for another few hours, Lana knew her older sister well enough to accept that she didn't want to wait until the moments just before they were scheduled to be out together in public. If their history had taught them anything, it was to give each other time and space to be angry enough to want to fight and then calm down.

Judging by the way Tami had kicked things off, there were definitely going to be some disagreements during this discussion.

"His list was already extensive," Lana said, speaking up from where she sat at the end of the floral-patterned couch, which had been there ever since she could remember. It wasn't a pretty couch, with huge burgundy and yellow flowers amid a cream-colored background, but it was still the most comfortable spot in the room. Which was probably why it was always the spot Lana chose to sit in when she was there. "And he didn't sound optimistic about the money in the escrow account being enough to cover it, so how do you suppose we add on to that?"

Her tone was sharp, but after her conversation with Isaac and the feelings it had evoked, this situation was just making things worse.

Tami sat on the floor across from the piano, her legs crossed in front of her the way they used to be in kindergarten. She held the spiral notebook from that morning in her lap as she stared at Lana intently. "You don't understand what this all means, do you? Or can you just not see beyond dollar signs? Don't you and your rich computer-geek husband have enough money?"

Lana sat forward. "What you're not gonna do is bring my husband into this," she said, her tone lethal.

Yvonne lifted both her arms now, flashing a hand in Lana's direction and in Tami's. She was sitting in one of the two chairs on opposite ends of the couch. "Okay, just calm down for a minute. We can discuss this with level heads," she told them. "And that means you don't throw any cheap shots, Tami."

Tami pursed her lips and rolled her eyes skyward the way Lana could recall her doing for most of her childhood.

"Lana's right: Isaac has nothing to do with what's happening here in this house. The decisions that need to be made only concern us, as we're the owners of this property." Yvonne took a slow breath and let her arms drop to her lap. "Now, we're going to take this one step at a time."

Because Yvonne said so. Lana held in those words as she fell back on the couch once again. She rested an elbow on the arm and brought that hand up to rub her temple. These two were already working her nerves.

"I guess what that really means is, 'Tami, shut up, and do what we say,'" Tami snapped. "Just like old times."

"That's not what it means," Yvonne shot back. "You just don't like doing anything anyone else says."

"Because you are not my mother," Tami said.

Yvonne huffed, and Lana watched with amusement, as it was now her turn to deal with Tami's slick-ass mouth without grabbing her by the shoulders and trying to shake some sense into her. Something both

Yvonne and Lana had done on more than one occasion when they were young. Tami was truly the most exasperating person to try to get through to.

"Girl, you don't know how much I thanked the good Lord I wasn't cursed with a child like you," Yvonne said in a tone that was oddly calm for her in this particular situation. "But for the sake of our grandmother, I'm here, and I'm trying to do the right thing."

Wasn't that what Lana was doing too? Trying to abide by Grandma Betty's wishes *and* get this house sold in time to save her marriage?

"Now, before you so rudely jumped to the wrong conclusion, I was going to tell you to speak your piece," Yvonne said to Tami. "Do you think you can do that without all your usual theatrics?"

Instead of looking properly chastised, Tami quirked her lips and then cleared her throat. "I've been looking at houses on the island since we found out we'd be coming here last week. And what I notice about the new builds, and even the look of the resorts that are now trying to take over, is that there's a very modern flair. Like they're trying to bring the outside world onto Daufuskie. But then, when I sit and think about our time here, all the things that made this place special to me—and I think to Grandma Betty, why she decided to live out her retirement here instead of Beverly Hills or some other luxurious place that she certainly could've afforded—it's the basic simplicity. Daufuskie represents what once was, what our people lived through in the harshest of times and what they built through hope and resilience.

"It's that part of us that this world is always trying to bury, to take away and put into a box or a long-lost history book. But what we have here right now, on this day"—she highlighted her words by tapping a finger on her notebook—"is the opportunity to bring all of the things that made us come back to this house—and that house out there, where our great-grandfather used to come in after fishing for enough oysters to sell and take care of his family. We have a chance to put every ounce of our history back into this place and to preserve it for the next generation of Butler sisters, or sons, or even the husbands and wives of those sisters and sons. This is our legacy. And I believe Grandma Betty brought us all back here to preserve it in a way that she couldn't."

Tami should've been an actress. The way her eyes had widened as she spoke, her voice giving just enough inflection at the proper times to have Yvonne's shoulders relaxing and Lana's fingers ceasing to massage her temples. It took everything in her not to clap at the performance. That could possibly be because there was truth to some of her sister's words. Lana could admit that even if the admission didn't change her position.

"Don't you get it?" Tami continued when neither Lana nor Yvonne replied to her comments. "This is our opportunity to create generational wealth—if either of you even know what that is."

Yvonne sighed. "We know what it is, Tami. And it's not like we don't already have generational wealth in the family. Mama's house will pass to the three of us."

"You sure about that?" Tami asked. "Mama acts like she can barely tolerate being in the same room with me for any length of time. I would think I'm the last person she'd want to give anything to."

"And you don't contribute to that at all with your constant back-talking and complaining?" Yvonne asked.

This turn in the conversation had Lana back to rubbing her temple again. It was probably too optimistic to think they'd never broach this subject while staying here.

"The fact that I have an opinion other than Mama's doesn't qualify as backtalking," Tami snapped. "But I guess since you're her protégé, you wouldn't think so. But I swear, if you'd take ten minutes to think for yourself instead of mimicking everything Mama has said and done her whole life, you might just start to live a little."

"Okay, I'm not going to take much more of this from you," Yvonne told her. "If you have something to say about the renovations and this house, then we'll hear it and consider it. As for your opinions about my life, you can keep that shit to yourself."

"Oh, I can keep my opinions to myself, when all you ever do is toss your opinions out as if they were law!" Now Tami was shouting, and Yvonne looked as if she were ready to reach out and touch her.

Lana figured it was her turn to keep the peace, the role she thought she'd given up a long time ago.

"Calm down, Tami, damn!" she yelled at her. "You came to this meeting already on ten, and we're just trying to have a mature discussion. We both hear what you're saying, and I don't think we disagree on the point of bringing this house back to its former glory."

Tami rolled her eyes. "You just want to sell it once we've done that."

"It's the option that makes the most sense," Lana said, trying to project the calm demeanor she'd advised Tami to take but that she didn't feel herself. "We all have lives back in the city. What are we going to do, renovate this house and then leave it sitting empty?"

"We could rent it out," Tami replied, her eyes going wide again. She had such pretty whiskey-brown eyes that captured her every emotion, whether extreme happiness or debilitating sadness.

And because of them, Tami had never been able to hide her feelings. Not that she'd ever tried. If there was one thing you could count on about Tami, it was to tell you exactly how she felt, in the moment that she felt it. A tiny part of Lana had always envied her sister for the ability to say things without a care about how anyone else took them. While that could seem rude or insensitive sometimes, Lana could only imagine how freeing it was to not carry around so many bottled-up thoughts and emotions.

"I don't want to be a landlord," Yvonne said. "It's time consuming, and I've already got my hands full with my full-time job and Mama. Speaking of which, don't forget about the agreement we all made to split the proceeds from the sale of this house, but that you two will also put up at least fifteen percent of your proceeds to go toward fixing up Mama's house so she'll be more comfortable."

That was another discussion Lana didn't want to have. Quite simply put, she didn't want to talk about any of this shit. What she wanted to do was go upstairs and lock herself in her bedroom. There, she could at least sit in the dark while her mind continued to war over her marriage.

"So we can fix up Mama's house and make it more of a shrine to her, but we can't save Grandma Betty's house?" Tami was back to her snappish mood.

Lana hadn't missed the dramatics her younger sister could perform, but she couldn't help leaning a little on Tami's side with that last comment. Yvonne was always hyperfocused on their mother—like almost to the point of being obsessed with making Freda happy. Whereas Lana had given up on that effort a long time ago.

"That's not what I said," Yvonne told her.

"Okay," Lana said, holding up a hand. "So let's get this straight: Tami wants to fix up the house and keep it in the family. Yvonne wants to sell it and dictate how we spend our portion from the sale."

"And what do you want, Ms. High and Mighty?" Yvonne asked. "You've been walkin' around here acting like we're upsetting your very busy schedule all day long. Snapping at Deacon each time he said something, and then stomping off to go take your pictures just like you used to do when you were young and didn't get your way."

Now Lana turned to glare at Yvonne. After this morning's waterfall in the kitchen, she'd pulled her wet hair up into a high ponytail that swung down to the nape of her neck. Her normal hairstyle—the one she'd been wearing since college—was down to her shoulders in big fluffy curls. And that wasn't a bad style, especially not on Yvonne's cute, round face. But it was almost just like Mama's, only a little longer, which was probably why Yvonne kept it that way.

Freda had never allowed them to cut their hair. When they were younger, she would wash it on Friday nights, then give them big chunky plaits until it dried. On Saturday afternoons, she'd take it out to press with the hot comb, which burned Lana's ears and neck every damn time. They all had long, thick black hair, and by the time each of them had gotten into middle school, they'd expressed the urge to change the style. Glossy tight curls that came from those ridiculous pink sponge rollers weren't exactly hip, and Lana could recall being teased on more than one occasion. All the other girls their age had been getting perms and wearing their hair in smooth and silky wraps or stylish rod and bump curls.

"Don't get me mixed up with you and Tami," Lana said with a dry chuckle. "I never needed either of you—or your mother, for that matter—to give me my way. I always knew where I stood as the middle and the darkest child. I did whatever I needed to do to keep myself happy, thank you very much."

"Oh boy, there she goes with the 'I'm the dark middle child, so nobody wants to play with me' routine," Tami snapped.

"Girl, if you don't stop with all your nonsense," Lana said to Tami. "You were too young for me or Yvonne to consider playing with."

"And too spoiled," Yvonne chimed in.

Lana looked at Yvonne and pointed a finger before she nodded. "That part."

"Hold up, I wasn't the one Mama spoiled," Tami countered. "Not by a long shot."

"Mama didn't spoil anybody," Yvonne said evenly. "She didn't believe in giving children too much."

"Didn't believe in giving us anything but directives. 'Do this.' 'Do that.'" Lana would never forget those directives, especially the ones aimed directly at her.

Don't stay on the phone too long with those fast-tail girls. And stop talking about those nasty boys. They only want one thing, and that thing ain't gonna pay none of your bills or put a roof over your head after you've given him what he wants. And make sure you put some lotion on. Can't stand you out here lookin' all ashy. Next thing you know, the ladies down at the church'll be sayin' how I must can't afford lotion since your daddy left.

Lana's teeth clenched at the sting those memories brought back.

"She was such a pain in my ass," Tami continued as she looked down at her notebook. "I could never do anything right in her eyes."

"Is that why you tried so hard to do everything wrong?" Yvonne asked, and Tami's head shot up.

"Stop it!" Lana snapped before the two of them could go at it again. "This isn't getting us anywhere. We need to make a decision on this house, *this* situation and in *this* moment. The past is in the past." Those words were much easier spoken than believed, but something had to be said or else they'd sit here all night, reminiscing about how horrible a mother Freda Butler was—or, in Yvonne's case, trying their damnedest to defend the indefensible. There were so many things their mother had said and done that had undoubtedly shaped the women each of them had ultimately become, but there was nothing any of them could do about that now.

"Fine," Yvonne said. "The first decision is already made: we're fixin' up this house."

"Right," Lana replied. "Now, I don't watch a lot of those home improvement shows, and Isaac and I own a condo that was brand new when we moved in five years ago, so there's been no desire to make any changes." And no extra money, either, if the desire had been there. "But I'm just guessing that all that stuff Deacon was talking about doing isn't going to be covered by that fifty thousand dollars."

"Most definitely not," Tami said. "But that's why I told Jeremiah we wouldn't mind pitching in to help with some of the work if that'll cut the costs. I mean, since we're here, it doesn't make sense that we walk along the beach and go into town for shopping sprees while they're working on the house. We can just pull up our sleeves and get to work too."

Yvonne frowned. "Like we did this morning with the sink?"

Lana couldn't help it—the moment she said those words, the visual of her sisters on that wet floor laughing had her chuckling once more.

Tami laughed next, shaking her head as she looked at Yvonne. "Oh no, we definitely need to keep you away from any plumbing work."

Just when Lana thought her older sister would keep the frown she'd been wearing, Yvonne's lips spread into a wide grin. A warm and pretty smile, with that tiny dimple in her left cheek that Lana wished her sister would display more often.

"I don't know," Yvonne started to say.

"Oh, come on, y'all—we can do this!" Tami looked excited again as she stared from one sister to the other. "We have to do this. Despite our differences, we're still family, and we can't change that. Remember Grandma Betty used to say that all the time?"

Lana nodded. "Yeah, she did. Every time she caught us arguing, she'd come right in the room and say, 'Y'all might as well stop all this yip yappin' and get on with your day. You can't choose your family, and there ain't no receipts to return 'em.'"

"Oh my goodness, you sounded just like her saying that," Yvonne said.

"You sure did. Your voice is husky just like hers was. Like you'd smoked just as many cigarettes as she had," Tami added.

They all knew that wasn't true; Lana had suffered from asthma really bad when she was growing up, so smoking or anything else that would further compromise her breathing wasn't an option. But now that she thought about it, her voice was a little on the deep side like their grandmother's. For some reason, having that connection to her made Lana feel better. Which was probably why she added, "Okay, I'll agree to doing some minimal things to chip in on the work. But I want to keep a close eye on the budget and the schedule. This has to be done as soon as possible, y'all, so we can get back to our lives."

"I agree," Yvonne said. "And I know we don't need to get into all the details right this moment, but at some point, we do need to talk about the changes to the house that are necessary for Mama's recuperation. Neither of you are there every day to see her continued struggles. So all I'm sayin' is, the least you can do is chip in to make it a little better, even if you're not going to come around more."

When Tami opened her mouth to say something, Lana shook her head and held up a hand to stop her.

"You're right, but we're gonna take this one step at a time," Lana said. "So let's go down this list again, and then we'll talk to Deacon tonight. See if we can get started in the next few days, like he said."

Yvonne nodded and then stood. "That works for me. But I need a cup of coffee before we get into more details."

"Works for me too," Tami said, with a glance down at her notebook again. "But I need a stronger drink."

"You stay drinking in the afternoon," Lana said as she got up to follow Yvonne out of the room. "I saw some wine coolers in the refrigerator this morning. I'll bring you one of those."

"It's five o'clock somewhere," Tami called out as Lana left, and Lana just grinned because she knew her little sister would never change.

Chapter 14

YVONNE

Ms. Janie's house was an old wooden structure that looked to have been added on to, by the discoloration on one half of the dwelling. It was what would've been called a ranch-style home in the city, with a long front porch and no railing—just the evenly spaced beams that held the flat-shingled roof above. There were folding chairs up and down the porch, most of them occupied by people holding paper plates loaded with food on their laps as they ate and talked.

Well, the talking kind of quieted down as Yvonne and her sisters approached. Sometime after their discussion about the renovations, Tami had gone for a walk down to Mr. Jemison's backyard, where she'd rented a golf cart.

"We gotta be able to get around while we're here," Tami had told them when Yvonne and Lana had come out onto the front porch at the time they'd designated to leave for the gathering.

"Good thinking," Lana had told Tami as she climbed into the front seat beside her.

Yvonne had eased onto the back seat and tried not to think about how different this felt from when they used to come here. Of course, there hadn't been many cars on the island then, either, but riding in a golf cart, or on the bikes her father had purchased for each of them to keep at Grandma's house, just hit different when you were a child than it did as a grown woman. Back in the city, she drove a Lexus RX, and as the sun had already set, on a day that had turned overcast in the late afternoon, she'd wished for the leather interior of her car, which would've surely kept her dry should an unexpected rain shower hit.

Yvonne didn't recognize any of the faces that were now staring at them as they made their way up the four wooden stairs. But she did say "Good evening" as she stepped onto the porch. She said it once as she looked to the left and then again as she turned her head to the right, figuring she'd covered speaking to them all. There were a few waves in return and some nods, but mostly just these looks, which she couldn't quite explain.

Right behind her, she heard Tami speaking in the same way she had, but Lana remained silent. As odd as it may sound, Lana had always been shy when she was on the island. Where she was a social butterfly back in the city, she would get down here each summer and act like she didn't have two words for anyone other than Grandma Betty, Daddy, or whoever was working at their grandmother's house at the time. It seemed that no matter how much time had passed, her sister hadn't gotten over that.

"Hey, you made it," Jeremiah said, coming from across the room to greet them the second they stepped into the house.

The living room was a wide space, with a matching couch, love seat, and chair. There were wood end tables with lamps on each, dark-brown rugs on the floor, and heavy cream-colored curtains at the windows. Every available seat was taken by more people holding more plates and enjoying the meal and conversation. She had no idea where Jeremiah had come from, but Tami's exuberant "Hey" meant that she, at least, was happy to see him.

Yvonne didn't really dislike him—she supposed he was doing his job. She just wondered why—out of all the lawyers she could've hired—Grandma had chosen this very young, albeit attractive, guy to assist them with something as important as her estate.

"Come on out to the back porch," Jeremiah said. "Ms. Janie's out there, and she wanted me to bring you to her as soon as you arrived."

"Why do I feel like we're being summoned?" Lana asked.

She stood closer to Yvonne's left side, while Tami had already broken their line of three to stand next to Jeremiah. That girl could go any way the wind blew.

"Nah, it's nothing like that," Jeremiah said. "She's just been looking forward to seeing you. Sallie's out there too."

"I thought she was supposed to come by today," Yvonne said.

Jeremiah looked at her and asked, "She didn't?"

"Nope," Tami replied.

"Hmm, well, I guess that's no nevermind—you'll see her in just a few minutes." Jeremiah led them through the rest of the house.

There were people everywhere, either sitting or standing, all of them talking and eating and having a good time. Jeremiah had been right: this was definitely an informal gathering, where all these people seemed to know and have a rapport with each other. She felt out of place, and she figured her sisters did too. Even Tami, who, although she was clinging to Jeremiah at the moment, had often felt left out when they were young. It was because of the age gap between them, just like Lana had said earlier. Yvonne was eleven years older than Tami, and Lana was six years older than Tami was, so for the most part, she had grown up in a space of her own. She was also the only one of them who'd grown up in the house without their father—an experience Yvonne knew Tami despised her and Lana for having.

"Ms. Janie," she heard Jeremiah say after they'd walked through the kitchen with its old linoleum—that's right, after all these years, that's what it was, and despite it looking faded in some spots, the floor seemed to still be in good shape. "Here they are: the Butler sisters."

They'd traveled out the back door and onto another long porch. At the end of this one was a rocking chair, where a heavyset woman with silver hair in six fat plaits sat, her chubby hands in her lap. In the chairs immediately next to her were two women, one with a riot of brown and black curls, the other wearing a short Afro.

"Well, I'll be . . ." Ms. Janie's words trailed off as she stared at them. "Come closer," she said with a wave of her hand. "I ain't got my glasses on, so I can't see too good from all the way ovah here."

Yvonne moved first, feeling her sisters flank her sides and follow.

"Good evening, ma'am," she said, and extended a hand once she was close enough for the woman to accept. "Thank you so much for inviting us here tonight."

Ms. Janie took Yvonne's hand and pulled her down for a hug. Startled by the motion, Yvonne tried to both keep from toppling over the woman and keep from being suffocated as Ms. Janie wrapped her arms around her in a tight-ass embrace. It didn't help that her face was smushed into the woman's ample bosom, because she hadn't been expecting a hug and thus hadn't aimed herself correctly.

"It's so good to see Betty's babies," Ms. Janie was saying as Yvonne continued to struggle for breath. "I ain't seen you gurls in a long, long time."

When she was finally released, Yvonne took two steps back from the woman and pasted on a smile.

"You the oldest one, right?" Ms. Janie asked.

"Yes, ma'am. I'm Yvonne. And this is my sister Lana." Yvonne had to yank Lana's arm to get her to move closer to the woman.

Ms. Janie's arms were already outstretched for Lana, who barely croaked a "Hello" before she was pulled into the older woman's embrace.

Ms. Janie wore a burgundy dress that stretched over her belly and her bulky knees, which were spread wide. Luckily, the material was flexible enough to come down over those knees and keep hidden all that was between Ms. Janie's legs, or this greeting would've been made much worse.

Tami just walked right into the embrace, probably figuring she didn't have a choice anyway. "Hi, I'm Tami," she said, before her next breath came out in a whoosh when Ms. Janie folded her arms around her and pounded her on the back.

"Such pretty gurls. Ain't they, Cora?" Ms. Janie said as she looked at the three of them standing side by side again. "Betty sure did brag on y'all and all that fancy stuff y'all did in the city."

"She sure did." The woman who Yvonne supposed was Cora—because she'd given a slow nod in answer to Ms. Janie's question about them being pretty—sat to Ms. Janie's right. She was the woman with the short Afro, who had a slim build and wore a black-and-white maxi dress and flat black sandals.

"Well, I'm Sallie." The woman who was probably closer to Yvonne's age—or possibly older—with the big curly hairdo stood from beside Ms. Janie. "My mama was Ms. Odessa, and she used to be good friends with Ms. Betty. I guess the two of them are reunited in heaven now." Sallie didn't extend her hand, but she made eye contact with each of them, so Yvonne only nodded in her direction.

"You're the one who cremated our grandmother and had her memorial service without thinking to call to let us know?" Tami asked, and the air around them seemed to shift from stuffy summer night to heat from hell rising up.

Sallie tilted her head slightly as she stared at Tami. "I did what I was told," she replied. "That's how we behave around here."

"What's that supposed to mean?" Lana asked, and Yvonne waited for Sallie's response. This could only get worse.

"It means, when we get explicit instructions, we follow them," Sallie said. "Just like I'm sure you plan to do with the rest of Ms. Betty's wishes."

"I don't think it's any of your business what we do with our house," Yvonne said, with the sweetest smile she could muster because she—like her sisters, she was sure—didn't like this chick. "But since you're talking about following instructions, we expected you at the house earlier today to give us any other information our grandmother may have given you."

"You didn't go over to de house to make sure things was straight for dem, Sallie?" Ms. Janie asked.

"Yes, ma'am, I did. I went just as soon as Jeremiah told me they were coming. The food's in the refrigerator, and all the linen were cleaned. As for anything else your grandmother instructed me to do, there was nothing. The cremation and memorial-service instructions had been in writing for my mother, but since she passed before Ms. Betty, I had to handle it. So I did."

"I'd like to see those papers," Yvonne told her. "When you get a moment to bring them over, please do."

"You want me to fix you a plate, Jeremiah?" Cora asked as she jumped up out of her seat like she had to hurry up and ask that specific question at that exact moment.

And before Jeremiah could get out a reply, the shorter woman looped her arm through his and practically dragged him down the porch steps toward the rows of three tables that were out in the yard.

"I'm going to eat too," Sallie said, giving Yvonne another curt nod before she left.

Lana mouthed "What the hell?" to Yvonne as they both watched the woman walk away, and Yvonne could only shake her head.

"Don't pay her no mind," Ms. Janie said. "You two come on and take a seat next to me. Sallie gets her panties in a bunch over the silliest things. Always has." Ms. Janie clasped her fingers over her wide girth. "But it's been a mighty long time since y'all was on the island. I won't have nobody startin' no mess between y'all."

What the hell? played in Yvonne's mind now. Hadn't they just come here for a meal? What happened to *It's just an informal get-together?* This felt oddly like an inquisition, or like they'd walked right into a firing squad.

"Betty knows she was wrong for not tellin' you gurls she was sick. I told her she shoulda said something, but you know how stubborn she was," Ms. Janie said.

"Grandma was sick?" Lana asked. "She seemed well when we were here back in November—and then I talked to her in May for her birthday, and she sounded just fine then too."

"Me too," Yvonne said. But Yvonne had known that her grandmother had a compromised immune system. Freda had mentioned it to her one day when they'd somehow gotten onto the subject of Grandma Betty and Daniel.

It was just another thing that Freda had used against the Butler family, telling Yvonne that neither of them had taken good care of themselves, with some type of ailment befalling them both. Yvonne had told her mother, in as even a tone as she could muster, that people didn't choose to be sick, but Freda had only sucked her teeth at that, swearing that neither Yvonne's father nor his mother had done anything to take care of themselves. Karma truly was a bitch, considering Freda's current medical condition.

Tami, who had pulled up one of the folding chairs to sit closer to Yvonne, leaned over and asked Ms. Janie, "When exactly did she get sick, and how?"

"Oh, she'd had that cough for a while now. Back around Christmas, I think. You know, Cab—he used to go out to the house to check on her all the time, and he used to tell us how she was doing. We'd see her on Sundays at church, but she never stayed long after. Never sat with the ladies like everybody else. But you know, that was how Betty was."

What Yvonne suspected she meant was that since Betty was a famous singer, she didn't spend a lot of time wandering around town with everyone else, which wouldn't be totally wrong. During the summers they were here, Grandma Betty would be off from touring or recording. She always said it was her family time, and the record company better respect it. But the other nine months out of the year, she traveled all over the world, doing shows, interviews, and most recently making guest appearances on a few of those reality singing competitions. But hanging out at something like this here on Daufuskie wouldn't have been something Grandma Betty would've done.

"Who's Cab?" Lana asked.

"Oh, he was married to Odessa, Sallie's daddy, for some years. Then those two just couldn't get along no more, so they broke up. For a good while, Betty was the only one woman in 'Fuskie still speaking to Cab. Everybody had to help poor Dessa 'cause she was so broken after he left." The way Ms. Janie twisted her lips and narrowed her eyes said she either hadn't believed Ms. Odessa was heartbroken or she hadn't agreed with the woman being heartbroken. Either way, Yvonne continued to be intrigued by the entire conversation.

"Wait, Grandma Betty was the only one speaking to Sallie's father?" Yvonne asked.

"Yep." Ms. Janie nodded. "But he and Sallie ain't nevah got along good either. Cab's a funny kinda fella. Got an eye for the womens, though."

"Did he have an eye for Grandma Betty?" Tami asked.

Ms. Janie shook her head. "If he did, Betty put him in his place long ago. She ain't want no man since her Riley died. Not one to keep, no way. But anyhow, I wanna hear all about what you girls are gonna do to that house. Such a gorgeous house—from the outside, 'cause you know Betty ain't do no invitin'."

That was definitely true. For as big as the house was, Yvonne couldn't remember one time when her grandmother had hosted a party or even just a little get-together—outside of their Thanksgiving dinners. Her father was an only child, and thus, they were the only grandchildren. As far as Yvonne knew, they were the only ones to have ever stayed at that house, hence the reason the bedrooms had been decorated specifically for them.

"Just because she was an entertainer by trade," Yvonne said, more so to herself than as any contribution to the conversation. "Didn't mean she had to do the entertaining when she was at home."

Ms. Janie threw her head back and laughed. Her skin was a smooth mahogany tone, and her laugh was a hearty sound. "You got that right," she told Yvonne. "You got that exactly right."

A couple of hours later, as she sat on an old swing that hung from an even older tree, Yvonne was still turning over some of the things Ms. Janie had told them about their grandmother. Spanish moss drooped down from the branches like shingles in what had looked like a picturesque setting as she'd approached. In fact, she was certain she'd seen a replica of this grassy knoll beneath a tree on one of those postcards that had been at the airport.

Across the yard, the get-together was still in full swing, with what seemed like even more people coming into the backyard to get plates of food from the three tables that were heavy with trays, bowls, and pots. She'd had some of what Ms. Janie had called her famous *tada salad* and a nice pile of poppin' fried shrimp while she and Lana had sat at one of the tables a little earlier. Tami had somehow wrangled Jeremiah from Cora's clutches long enough to get him to walk her down to the creek. She'd told Yvonne and Lana she was going to try to get more information from him about Grandma Betty's illness and when she'd prepared her will, because each of them had been thoroughly perplexed by some of the things Ms. Janie had said, along with the frigid treatment they were getting from Cora and Sallie.

Now, that one had really been a shock, because the way Robyn had talked about her when they'd met in her office, Yvonne had assumed that Sallie was an ally. She'd been the one on the island to handle their grandmother's arrangements, so Yvonne had figured she would be another source of help. But tonight had proved her wrong on that front. Sallie definitely had a chip on her shoulder, but Yvonne had no clue why. Tami's general response to Sallie and Cora was, "Fuck 'em!" to which Lana had partially agreed. But Yvonne had shared her concerns with her sisters that something was going on, something she didn't think they could just brush off with those simple two words.

"You're lookin' pretty as a picture out here tonight," Deacon said in that deep drawl that sent a quick and succinct jolt of lust between her legs.

Crap! She'd been hoping her initial reaction to him was just that: a first-time—and hopefully, only-time—reaction to seeing a man this big and sexy up close in this particular setting. But no, she was feeling it again, and it was annoying her just as much as it had the first time.

"Good evening, Deacon," she said, and then cleared her throat before adding, "Thank you."

He tipped his head toward her, and she could almost imagine him wearing a big-brimmed cowboy hat, making that same gesture. She didn't think she was a cowboy type of woman—but there was something about the way Deacon wore those jeans that weren't too tight but weren't baggy, either, and the button-front white shirt he'd changed into that put in her mind one of those sexy men she'd seen at the Black Cowboy Festival years ago.

"Why're you out here alone?" He pushed his hands into his front pants pockets and stood with his legs partially spread just a few feet away from her. Like he knew that his every movement was tormenting her but was too smug to stop it.

"Just thinking." And she'd wanted to say that she would like to keep doing that alone, but he took another step closer, and then another, until he was behind her.

She knew exactly what he was going to do, and it took every ounce of "save her pride" for her not to jump up and get the hell out of the way before he touched her.

The tips of his fingers grazed her upper back first, and he gave her a light push. She had to lift her feet from where she had them planted on the grass to keep herself still before the swing moved a small distance. He hadn't given her a big push, but once she extended her legs in front of her, she picked up momentum.

"Thinking about the boyfriend you left in the city?" he asked after he gave her another push, harder this time.

She shook her head as the warm summer's breeze fanned over her face. "If you wanted to know if I had a boyfriend, all you had to do was ask the question, Mr. Williams," she said. "And if pushing me on this swing is your way of flirting, you can probably stop."

He didn't stop, but chuckled before pushing her again when she was close enough. "When I flirt with you, you'll know it, Ms. Butler. And I thought that was asking if you had a boyfriend."

Now she laughed—because why not? He was easy to be around, which was just another thing that gave her pause. Yvonne wasn't an easily intimidated woman. She'd been taught to be sure of what she wanted and to go get it without any reservations. So being coy around guys had never really been her thing. When she'd wanted to lose her virginity, Troy Belham had been right there with his sexy Method Man glare, eager body, and a box of condoms he kept in the glove compartment of his car. That had been a good-enough time—so good she'd worked through most of that box with Troy the fall of their junior year in high school. After that, it had been SAT prep, tutors just to make sure she was as smart as she could possibly be, and then finally, the SATs and college applications. Between all the studying and keeping up with her extracurricular activities and the last summer visit to Grandma Betty's, Yvonne had been too busy to return any of Troy's calls or notice the attention of any other guy.

By the time she'd gotten settled in college, she'd also become well versed in taking care of her own pleasure, and thus, the need for an actual guy in her life had become almost moot. While every now and then, as an adult, she could admit to feeling like there was no substitute for the real thing, she was basically the epitome of "I can do *all* things." Because she could—she was a success in her field; she took care of her mother; she ran an entire household; and at least three times a month, she maintained a basically healthy libido with the assistance of her wide array of sex toys.

"The question should've been, 'Hey, Yvonne, do you have a boyfriend?' To which I would've then responded, 'No, Deacon, I do not, but I'm also not looking for one.'" She spoke in a lighter version of her usual tone and hoped he didn't get all offended by her shutting him down, because she was fairly certain his pushing her on this swing was flirting. Like, really, it was cute and romantic—didn't that equal flirting?

"Okay," he replied. "I guess I could've said that, but I like being my own man. Saying what I wanna say, the way I wanna say it."

Why did that send a shiver down her spine? Not the creepy let-me-get-the-hell-away-from-this-dude type of shiver, but that sexually aware one that had her squirming just a little in the swing's seat. Obviously, she had to be careful about the squirming or else she'd slip out of the swing and land flat on her face in the grass. Another embarrassing moment in front of this man was another thing not on her to-do list.

"Well, it's been said now, Mr. Williams."

"I like it better when you call me Deacon."

Had she called him by his first name today? She couldn't remember saying it out loud, at least. But she was certain the name had rolled through her mind more than a dozen times throughout the day, and sadly, it wasn't just because she and her sisters had been talking about the renovations.

"Oh, we decided to move forward with the renovations," she said, because it had just popped into her mind, and it would change the slightly uncomfortable conversation they'd been having. "We want to get started right away, and Tami suggested we help with some of the work so we don't go too far over budget. Well, Lana plans to not let you take us over budget at all."

"What's your plan?" he asked.

"Huh? I just told you what the plan is."

"No, you just told me that 'we've' decided to go through with the renovations, and Tami wants to help with the work, and Lana's concerned about the budget. I'm asking about *you*. What do you plan to do while you're here this summer, Yvonne?"

Mmm, her name sounded kinda good in his voice. She cleared her throat. "I plan to keep my sisters from strangling each other, and to keep my hands to myself as well." She gave a little laugh. That plan sounded much more optimistic than she felt.

"Y'all don't get along? Really? I couldn't tell. You seemed like a united front earlier today."

"That's because we are a united front when in the face of anyone else. But alone, we're a little combustible, like I guess all siblings are."

"Nope, not me and my sister. We get along fantastically."

She peered over her shoulder just after he pushed her. "You're not serious."

He shrugged. "I am serious. Because I learned early on to just let her have the last word."

"Whether she's right or wrong?"

"Yup," he replied. "For one, I'm her younger brother, not her father. I let my dad handle all the rules with her, and my mom does all the bossiness. As for me, I just let her play with my dump trucks when she wanted to; hid her Barbie doll when our dog, Big Red, chewed its head off; and covertly threatened any guy who even glanced at her."

She grinned at the last part, because it was sweet, and the previous parts, because they were sweet too. "So you figured out how to work around her early on."

"That's what you have to do with people," he said. "Once you get a good idea for who they are and how they are, you can decide how you're going to deal with them. It doesn't have to be hard, and it doesn't have to be a battle. If you don't like them, don't deal with them. But if they're family and you *have* to deal with them, then you have to figure out how."

She grew quiet as she let his words settle in. She'd always thought she had figured out how to handle her sisters, since she was the oldest and their mother had put her in charge all the time. It was a given without her even having to focus too hard on it. Except in these last few years since her mother's stroke, she'd begun to rethink the relationship between her and her sisters and their mother. It all seemed so toxic now, so draining, and while she hadn't been ready to make that a verbal admission, his words had her thinking that might be coming really soon.

"I just want to get through this summer without feeling any more stressed than I already am," she said finally as the swing slowed because she'd stopped lifting her legs up and down and he'd begun pushing her slower.

She was about to get up when he touched his hands to her shoulders and held them there until the swing came to a complete stop, his voice stopping her.

"I can help you with that," he said, his tone as soft as a voice that deep could get.

Before she could respond, he let his hands fall from her shoulders and came around to stand in front of her. "Now, *that* was flirting," he said, and winked before he reached for her hand to pull her up.

She felt like she should tell him again that she wasn't looking for a boyfriend and that she didn't want him flirting with her. But then he said, "My mama makes the best Tummy-Yum Bread Pudding. C'mon over here and taste a slice."

Bread pudding was one of her favorites, and she never turned it down. *Ever.* So she'd let the flirting slide this time, as long as it ended with dessert. "Okay," she said, and allowed him to pull her across the yard.

140

Chapter 15

TAMI

Jeremiah was a smooth one. In addition to his almost-too-handsome face, he was also really smart and extremely easy to be around. From his laughter, to the way he listened intently to everything Tami said and then followed up with questions that proved he'd been listening to her—and, not to be forgotten, that sexy little cleft in his chin—he was the complete package, topped with college degrees and his own law office, the main one in Savannah and then a smaller version on the island.

Her mother would be pleased. Finally.

And for that reason alone, Tami had decided he wasn't for her.

"That's because she's your girlfriend," Tami said as she started up the steps to the front porch of the summerhouse. They'd been having a conversation about Cora and the dirty looks she'd continued to give Tami throughout the night.

"Ah, man, how many times I gotta say she's not my girlfriend?" Jeremiah said from beside her.

They'd walked from Ms. Janie's house to his golf cart. When he'd asked to take her home, she'd given Lana the keys to their cart and agreed.

"But she used to be," she continued, and dropped down into one of the rocking chairs.

He sat down, his lips twisted to the side, and he huffed. "Okay, yes, she used to be. But that's been over for a few months now. She's gotta move on."

"Easier said than done," Tami said with a shake of her head.

"You speaking from experience?"

"Absolutely," she admitted. Because why not? They weren't in that sometimes awkward getting-to-know-you stage that new lovers initiate. She didn't have to worry about whether her replies pleased him or not. "It's not easy to get over somebody you cared about and perhaps saw a future with. And just because the other person feels like they're over it doesn't make it better. Like, what's she supposed to do with all those feelings she had?"

"Wow," he said, dropping his hands to the arms of the rocking chair. He leaned back until the chair started moving. "So you're on her side, and you don't even know what happened."

She shrugged. "Not on anybody's side. Just sayin' that I can relate to what she's feeling. And with that said, I'll also note that being able to relate to her on some level doesn't excuse her being an evil bitch to me all night just because she probably thought I wanted you in *that* way."

Now he blew out a breath. "I'm really sorry about that. I don't know why she kept making all those ridiculous remarks to you."

"Because she doesn't like you smiling at me, I guess." Even though Tami sensed there might be a little more to it than that because of the look Cora had given them when she and her sisters had first approached Ms. Janie. That look had made Tami feel like Cora and Sallie had already discussed her and her sisters and decided not to like them. It felt like a really childish thing for two grown women to do, but it wasn't a totally foreign concept. But as long as the two of them kept their sour attitudes to themselves, Tami could ignore the hell out of them.

"This sounds too much like high school," he said.

She chuckled and then groaned. "You're right. Let's stop it right now."

They both laughed then.

"You've got a nice laugh," he said. "That's not something I usually notice about a woman."

"Oh really? Let me guess, you're more of a butt-and-breast type of guy?" she jokingly asked. Jeremiah really did feel like a friend or brother to her. Of course, she'd already received warnings about flirting with him from Yvonne, and knowing looks from Lana. Her sisters truly did believe they still had to monitor her actions and tell her right from wrong. In this case, though, the warning hadn't been necessary; she hadn't been feeling any type of way about Jeremiah from day one, except for friendly.

With a start, she realized the "friendly" way she'd felt about Jeremiah was a stark contrast to the "friend zone," where Gabriel resided. But now was neither the time nor the place to contemplate that revelation.

He rubbed a finger over his chin. "Well, I can't lie—I peeped those out too."

"Oh, shut up. I don't even want to hear what you think of my butt or my breasts. We'll just leave it at the laugh." And with that, she chuckled again. "I like to laugh," she admitted. "But I don't think I do it as much when I'm in the city as I used to do when I was here."

"You think that's because of your grandmother or the island?"

"My grandmother meant the world to me. She was one of the only people who ever understood me. Her and my dad, actually." She rubbed her flattened palms up and down her thighs.

"What about your sisters and your mother?"

Tami shook her head quickly. "I do *not* want to talk about them," she said. "Tell me more about my grandmother and how you ended up working for her."

When he didn't respond right away, she shifted, pulling one leg up to tuck under the other and propping an elbow up on the arm of her rocking chair.

"Nothing much to tell." He shook his head and then glanced over at her. "My family knew who she was and knew she lived on the island. My grandmother wasn't as close to her as Ms. Odessa or Ms. Janie. But there's not that many permanent residents left on 'Fuskie now, so you know that saying about everybody knowing everybody."

"Yeah, I can see that, especially here. What is there, like an estimated four hundred permanent residents on the whole island?"

He nodded. "Yeah, give or take. The development of the resorts has added to that number over the years. The staff they've brought in to work there year-round. But still, there aren't that many lawyers, doctors—you know, the professional types—on the island. And mostly, the people here are used to hopping on a boat and heading over to the city for those types of services."

"But you opened an office here. Why do that if people are used to coming to the city?"

He shrugged. "This is my home. I'm always gonna do what I can for my family here. When I'm on the island, I don't just help with law stuff. I help my grandfather and my father down at the dock, pulling in the shrimp baskets they've set for years before I was even born."

"See, that's what I'm talkin' 'bout right there—the way you're set in your career and intent on giving back to your community. That's what I want to do. I want to have a grip on how I'm going forward and still be able to reach back and help my people," she said. Now she propped her chin up on her hand, feeling a little drowsy as she stared over at him.

There was a light on in the foyer, and it glowed through the first two windows, but the other lights on the first floor were out. Lana and Yvonne had no doubt already gone upstairs to bed. But one of them— most likely, Yvonne—had left the porch light on for Tami, like she was a teenager coming home late from a date. She was actually grateful for that light at the moment since it had allowed her to see Jeremiah's warm brown eyes when he'd spoken so earnestly of helping his family.

"You aren't doing that now? I mean, you're here, doing this for your grandmother, and it'll undoubtedly help the community. It's a job for Deacon and his staff. Which, he's actually going to bring on a few more local guys to help down at the docks when the supplies that have to be shipped over arrive."

"Oh, I didn't realize that." She shook her head. "I mean, I did know that supplies would have to be shipped here since there are no warehouses or furniture stores or stuff like that here on the island. But he's going to hire extra people."

Jeremiah nodded. "Couple of my cousins, and he's got some family too. Plus, Mr. Jake's twin boys said they'd come down to help when they finished at the general store and on weekends."

"Well, I guess this is a pretty big job, just like Deacon said."

"It is," he added. "But what do you do in the city that's got you sounding unhappy with yourself?"

"Oh, I'm not unhappy." At least, she told herself that every morning when she looked in the mirror. That, plus the affirmations that were printed on the spiral notebooks she'd ordered online gave her the daily boost she needed to keep the smile in place and a measure of optimism moving through her mind. But that wasn't something she was going to share with him. "I'm good with who and what I am. I just know that I could be doing more."

He narrowed his eyes at her and then gave her a half grin. "Ooookay, well, what are you doing back in the city that makes you 'good'?"

"At the moment, I'm in between jobs," she said, and then waved a hand before he could speak again. "I quit my last job as a manager at a day care center because I was unaware that the term *manager* included me taking over in the infant room when a teacher throws up and has to leave. I did not sit through a billion lectures, write millions of papers, and study for an infinite amount of tests and exams in college to change poopy baby diapers." She wrinkled her nose at the memory.

He chuckled. "You're cute when you do that."

"That baby with poop up her back wasn't cute, and five minutes after I managed to get her and the table where I'd been changing her cleaned up, I felt like I was going to throw up, just like the teacher who'd left early."

He laughed harder. "I guess childcare isn't your calling, then."

"It most definitely is not," she said, and was finally able to at least smile along with him. "It's the third job I've had and lost in two and a half years. My sisters and my mother all believe I'm a habitual failure."

Why she was telling this guy whom she'd just met yesterday some of her personal business, she had no idea. Perhaps because he'd asked, and because he was still interested in talking to her even after she'd told him she could relate to the woman whose heart he'd broken.

"How old are you?" he asked.

"Twenty-nine," she replied. "How old are you?"

"I'm thirty."

She tossed her hands up in the air as if in surrender, and let them fall back into her lap with a loud slap. "See, you're only a year older than me, and you've got your life all together."

"Nah, I ain't say all that," he said. "I've got an undergrad degree in criminal justice from Jackson State, and then I came back home to get a law degree from USC Law. Yes, but I partied my way through both those schools and barely passed the bar since I was completely hungover the morning I walked into that room to take the exam. So I'm far from the one who never hits some bumps in the road."

"'Bumps.'" She shook her head. "Try *potholes* for me. I go to these interviews and give them my best. They hire me; then I get on the job, and it's not what I thought it would be. Not what I want to be doing with my life."

"I've always wanted to be a lawyer, from the time I used to watch *Perry Mason* reruns with my Paw Paw. I knew exactly what I wanted to do with my career, and I mostly coasted along until I got there." He leaned forward, rested his elbows on his knees, and turned his head so he could look at her. "But once I got there and I sat across the table from my first client, telling them that I would take care of everything, I sobered up real quick. I started out as a public defender, and so I had a man's freedom in my hands. My focus shifted from 'This is the job I've always dreamed of' to 'I can't mess this up because somebody's depending on me.'" He sighed.

"Did you win that first case?"

"Nope," he replied quickly. "It was a DUI, numerous traffic citations, and a driving-while-uninsured charge, and he was found guilty. Luckily, the judge took into account that he was under the influence of medications given during oral surgery he'd had performed that morning and decided not to impose any jail time. He did get a ton of fines, though, and the conviction will remain on his record for at least three years until his probation is completed and he can apply for an expungement."

He shook his head at what she figured was the memory of that time. "But my point is, that case inspired me and it rejuvenated me. I've been working steadily and enjoying every case since then, because like I said, I'd always known this is exactly what I want to do with my life. Maybe you haven't found exactly what you want to do yet, and that's why you keep hitting these bumps in the road."

She let her head fall back on the chair and stared up to the porch ceiling. "Makes sense," she said. "I guess it also makes sense for me to take my tired bones to bed."

"Is that your way of kicking me off your porch because I've talked too much?"

She turned her head only to look at him again. "Of course not. You're welcome to sit on this porch for as long as you want. I"—she slapped her palm to her chest—"am going into that house to get into my bed."

He grinned.

"Yvonne said Deacon's gonna be here first thing tomorrow morning to start talking about demo work we can get started on before his crew arrives. So I gotta be bright-eyed and bushy-tailed for that."

"What?" he asked.

She did a double take. "What? Don't tell me you've never heard of that saying."

"Nah, I have. I was asking what you just thought about that had you smiling like that?"

Lifting a hand to her face, she touched her lips; she *had* been smiling. "Hmph." She shook her head. "Grandma Betty used to say that to me at night. It would be after I'd been out playing all day. Swimming with Daddy or riding my bike all over the island, looking for anything and nothing. Or following her around the house, nagging her to tell me stories about her travels and all the great people she used to meet. Then we'd have dinner, and after dinner, she'd go into the parlor and play the piano. I never wanted her to stop, always asked for another song even after Lana and Yvonne had gone up to bed and Daddy had gone off to do whatever. I just wanted to keep listening to the music. She'd finally make me go upstairs, and then she'd tuck me in and say, 'I'll see you first thing in the mornin', all bright-eyed and bushy-tailed.' I'd get a kiss after that and a long snuggle, because I loved her snuggles."

He sighed. "That's a great memory."

"It is," she said, and watched him stand.

He came over to her and reached down to take her hands, pulling her up from her chair. "I've got business in Savannah for the next couple of days. I'll be back this weekend, but if you or your sisters need me, just call."

She nodded. "Will do."

They stood like that, just holding hands and looking at each other, before he finally sighed. "Well, good night, Tami."

"Good night, Jeremiah."

He held her hands a second longer, giving them a little squeeze before he released them, and turned to walk off the porch. She watched him all the way down the walkway to his cart before she turned and went inside the house.

$$\boxtimes$$

Twenty minutes later, she was freshly showered and dressed in boxer shorts and a tank as she climbed into bed. And just like any other night, she lay on her back—lights out, eyes closed—but didn't fall asleep. She never went to sleep as soon as she got into bed. Not even when she was bone-tired. Instead, it always took at least thirty to forty minutes for her mind to finally calm down enough to welcome sleep.

Tonight, it seemed to be taking longer. So long that amid all the thoughts from today and tonight circling through her mind, she remembered that Gabriel had texted her while they'd been at Ms. Janie's place. She rolled over and reached out to the nightstand to grab her phone. The screen lighting up like a beacon in the dark room alerted her to the time—1:53. Too late to call him, even though she knew there was a strong likelihood that he'd be awake.

Gabriel was a night owl. He hated early-morning wake-up calls or good-morning texts, but he wouldn't be overly upset by a late-night one. Still, after reading his message again, she realized she didn't have to call him—she could just respond by text, and then he wouldn't have more slick words to say about her ignoring his messages when they talked again.

GABRIEL: How's it going? You being good?
HER: It's going and you know I'm always good. ☺

It wasn't until after she'd already hit "Send" that she grinned, because she could just hear him challenging her *always good* comment. How many times had he told her she brought out the bad in him? And how many times had she countered that with the fact that she couldn't exacerbate what wasn't already there? That thought had her smiling even harder. She missed him already, and that was weird because, one, she hadn't been gone that long, and two, they weren't the type of friends who missed each other. Well, up until this moment, they hadn't actually had to be, since she hadn't had any extra money to travel anywhere, and Gabriel just wasn't a big fan of traveling. At least, that's what she thought since he never went anywhere.

The buzzing of her phone gave her a little jolt as she read his response.

GABRIEL: Now you know that's a lie. And it's too late for you to be up texting. Go to sleep.

HER: Not fair, you're awake.

GABRIEL: I'm off tomorrow so I can sleep as late as I want. You're in a house that's about to undergo renovations. Work crews will probably be there at the crack of dawn.

Not tomorrow, but she hadn't had a chance to tell him the details of what they'd decided to do and the tentative timeline.

HER: I do have to be up early.

GABRIEL: So go to sleep.

That was what she'd told Jeremiah she was coming in the house to do. But then sleep hadn't found her, and she'd started texting Gabriel. She didn't feel any sleepier now than she had when she'd reached for her phone. She refused to believe that this had anything to do with Gabriel. And to prove that point to herself, she replied:

HER: I am. Good night.

GABRIEL: good night

Tami put the phone back on the table and plopped down in the bed. She pulled the blankets up to her neck and tried like hell to get to sleep, but that still didn't work. Eventually, she climbed out of bed and walked a familiar path out of her room and down the hallway to the primary suite, Grandma Betty's room.

It was a familiar trek down the long hallway until she stopped in front of the closed door. She didn't recall who'd closed the door after their walk-through earlier in the day, but now she simply stared down at the knob like it was a foreign object. The mixture of hesitation and anticipation that swept through her was weird and probably unnecessary. She'd been in this room hundreds of times before—hours earlier, to be exact. But at this moment, for some reason, standing here felt different.

It felt like an intrusion.

With a shake of her head, she told herself that didn't make any sense. Grandma Betty was gone, and in the next couple of days, complete strangers would be in this house and in this room. So what if she—who was definitely not a stranger—walked in here tonight? And did what? Why had she come down the hall to this room tonight?

When she was younger, especially in those years immediately following Daddy's death, she'd always walked this path; given a brief, quiet knock; and waited for Grandma Betty's "Come in" before she entered. It never took long for her grandmother to respond, no matter what time it was, like maybe she'd been waiting for Tami to appear. She lifted her hand then, letting her knuckles glide over the ridges of the wood door as if she were going to knock. But she didn't. There was no one on the other side to answer this time. The thought had her lowering her head and closing her eyes to the tears that instantly welled.

Then, as if her mind knew exactly what her heart needed, a song popped into her mind, and she began to hum. It was one of Grandma Betty's songs, an up-tempo one that had been in the top ten on the Billboard list for seventeen weeks in 1979. Maybe it was odd that she'd remember that song while standing at this door in the middle of the night, but maybe it wasn't.

She let her hand ease down until her fingers closed around the knob, and she turned it, then pushed the door open. Her feet moved across the carpeted floor as fast as they used to when she was younger, until she stood at the foot of the bed. Pillows were still stacked neatly; the cream-colored comforter, which she could see only because of the slashes of moonlight that filtered through the windows, was still smoothed over the mattress. It was a huge four-poster bed made of heavy oak. Tami had always thought it looked regal, like the queen slept here. Betty Butler was the queen of Tami's life.

And this was the bed Tami was going to sleep in tonight. Just as she had so many nights before.

She walked around to the other side of the bed—the left side, because Grandma Betty always slept on the right. And she was just about to climb up into the bed when her foot smacked into something on the floor.

"Dammit!" The word shot out of her mouth as she hopped back and lifted her foot into her hand. When tears sprang to her eyes this time, it was because it felt like her toe might fall off after it finished throbbing from whatever she'd just kicked. "Shoot. Shoot! Dammit!" she continued before finally leaning against the bed and closing her eyes, hoping to will the pain away.

It didn't, but then curiosity got the best of her, and she stepped back away from the bed to look down at the culprit. It was a box.

She reached over to the nightstand and turned on the lamp. Soft, golden light bathed the space now, and she could see it was a light-brown box with swirling green vines and huge bright-white magnolias printed over it. The damn thing was also heavy as hell as she picked it up and set it onto the bed. Then she climbed onto the king-size bed that, as a girl, she'd thought was too high off the floor. As an adult standing at five feet, two inches, it was still too damn high off the floor. So there'd been a moment of getting onto the bed and then settling herself back so that her feet no longer touched the floor.

Without preamble, she opened the box, and her heart thudded at the hundreds of envelopes she saw inside. Yellowed and tattered envelopes, some with postmarks and stamps, others plain but for the scrawling, teacherly handwriting she recognized as Grandma Betty's. If Yvonne were here, she'd most likely say something about privacy. Lana would agree with Yvonne, but her eyes would still be wide with curiosity. Tami would still do exactly what she had just done—pick up an envelope, open it, and pull out a letter. Because if there's one thing she knew for certain, it was that people didn't leave their private stuff out for anybody to trip over and read. Now, of course, these were different circumstances, and for the life of her, she'd never recalled seeing this box in Grandma Betty's room before, which likely meant it was private to her grandmother. But now it was here, which also meant that Grandma Betty had probably left it out for someone to see.

For Tami to see, because this had always been Tami's side of the bed.

With a smile and a swipe of the back of her hand over the fresh tears that had fallen, Tami settled back against the pillows and began to read:

> *Miami is always beautiful but oh how I miss my girls. Can't wait 'til this tour is over so I can get back to the island and their pretty faces. Daniel was such a sweet blessing to me. A surprise really because Riley and I were happy running around that big ole house by ourselves. But then the good Lord blessed us with the most darling boy. And that boy turned right around and blessed me with the most heavenly girls. My heart bursts with joy each time I settle my eyes on them.*

And Tami's heart burst with grief as she read each word with Grandma Betty's voice in her head.

Chapter 16

LANA

Two weeks later, the summerhouse was filled with noise. There were people in every room of the house, either covering the furniture that would stay with tarps, tearing out wallpaper, removing windows, pulling up floors, banging on something or other, walking, talking, singing—because Tami had insisted on blaring Motown hits throughout the house during the workday—and just otherwise giving Lana a headache.

Seriously, she'd had a headache for the last twelve days, and no amount of Tylenol was getting rid of it. She was on her way to take another two tablets when somebody yelled, "Look out!" and instead of taking that to mean *Get the hell out of the way*, she froze.

Terrible choice.

A huge bag fell to the floor just a couple of feet in front of her. The bag exploded, and white dust filled the air. Lana started to choke, using one arm to wave away whatever it was she was now ingesting, and bringing up her other hand to cover her mouth.

"Oh shit! Oh shit! Oh shit!" that same voice now chanted, getting closer.

"Dammit, Frankie, what the hell are you doing?" Deacon appeared in front of her, putting his hands on her shoulders and easing her back. "You okay, Lana?"

She was shaking her head now and coughing, which she figured meant she was not okay, but she didn't bother saying that. Now her head was throbbing, and her chest was burning from the dust.

"What happened?" Yvonne came running into the part of the foyer that was just about to turn into the doorway to the kitchen. "Is she hurt?"

Lana answered for herself this time. "No, I'm not hurt."

"But she could've been," Deacon said, cutting his eyes at Frank, who now stood a few feet to Lana's left.

"Sorry 'bout that," Frank said, rubbing both hands down the back of his head. His gray eyes were wide with what she figured was the same shock hers were probably displaying. "Really sorry, Ms. Lana."

Frank was a senior in high school who lived down by the docks. He'd been so excited to get this summer gig that he couldn't help telling Lana most of his life story, which was probably why she resisted the urge to yell at him.

"I'm okay, Frank. Really. It didn't touch me, and I guess I should've heeded your warning when you said to look out," she said.

"You should've been wearing your hard hat," Yvonne scolded.

"And goggles and a mask," Deacon added.

With a frown, Lana looked from one to the other. "Okay, Mom and Dad."

"Don't get smart," Yvonne replied. "We have safety discussions every morning. You know that because you lead them sometimes."

"And I forgot this time," she said. "I went outside for some air and to make a couple of phone calls; then I just came back in to get some water and some pain pills."

That had Yvonne's worried-turned-irritated voice reverting right back to worry. "Why? You still have a headache?" she asked.

Lana nodded.

"Maybe you should stop taking those over-the-counter pills and see a doctor. It's been a couple of weeks now."

"It's a headache, Yvonne, not a stroke." The minute those words left her lips, Lana knew they were a mistake.

Yvonne's frozen stare confirmed it, and Lana cursed.

"I just need to get some medicine and sit down for a while," she said. "That's all, Yvonne. It's not a big deal."

"But it could be," Yvonne said, her tone noticeably softer. And laced with a hint of fear.

"You could be on the ferry to the mainland in an hour," Deacon said. "I can call my mother and get a number for one of those urgent-care places."

"I don't need to see a doctor. I just need those Tylenol that I bought last week when we went into town, a glass of ice water, and a chair that's preferably far away from all this noise," she said, and started to walk toward the kitchen again.

Deacon put an arm out to stop her. "Not without a helmet, glasses, and a mask," he said. "So how 'bout this: you turn yourself around and head back out to the front porch, where I don't think there's danger of anything falling on you, and I'll go into the kitchen and get you that glass of water."

Yvonne wrapped an arm around Lana's shoulders before she could say something to, one, tell Deacon she was capable of getting her own water, and two, get Yvonne to stop coddling her.

"Yes, Deacon, that's a great idea. Thank you," Yvonne said, and turned Lana toward the front door.

"I just came from the front porch," she complained as they walked until they were right back on the front porch again.

"Take some deep breaths," Yvonne said, walking them all the way to the other end of the porch, where there was no construction crew. "Get some fresh air into your lungs to cover up for that mess you've ingested."

Lana gave a short cough and then did what her sister suggested. "What was that, anyway?"

Yvonne shook her head. "It looked like another one of those bags of cement mix. You know, the ones Deacon was yelling about not needing to be in the house yesterday."

Lana rolled her eyes. "So I guess he was right about that."

"Yeah, I guess so." Yvonne shrugged. "Here, sit down right here."

There were no chairs out here on the porch anymore. Tami had driven Deacon's work truck across town to Pete Lyon's back porch, where the older gentleman painted everything from fences to old trash cans, which he made look like the grassy scene down by the marsh Lana had become accustomed to visiting. Ole Pete, as he'd told them to call him every time he'd picked them up from the docks for their Thanksgiving visits, was going to paint all the rocking chairs a brilliant cobalt blue at Tami's direction.

Yvonne's hands were on Lana's shoulders again, this time easing her down until her butt plopped onto the planked porch. Yvonne followed.

"Now, tell me what's going on with you. What are you stressing about that's giving you headaches that won't go away?" Yvonne asked her.

"I'm not stressed," she said.

"You were always bad at lying," Yvonne said with a shake of her head. "Remember that time Tami spilled that jar of spaghetti sauce, and you tried to help her clean it up? You swept up all the glass, and Tami used the whole roll of paper towels trying to wipe up all the sauce from the kitchen counters, the floor, and the cabinets where it had splashed."

Yvonne lifted her palms to her forehead and tried not to laugh for fear of causing more pain. "And then she didn't want Mama to see all the paper towels she'd used, so she stuffed them in the trash can and then lit a match, trying to burn the evidence," she said.

"And you, being the only one in the room with an ounce of sense, found the fire extinguisher and put out the fire before the whole house burned down," Yvonne said, a mixture of irritation and humor in her tone.

"By the time Mama came home, there was no trace of the spaghetti sauce or the burned paper towels," Lana said.

"But that smell was still in the house. Even after you opened all the kitchen windows in the middle of January," Yvonne continued.

"Mama was pissed!"

"And the first thing she said was, 'Who did it?' Tami ran out of that kitchen so fast. And you immediately confessed."

Lana nodded, lifting her head as the memory played as if it had just happened yesterday instead of twenty-five years ago. "I told her I'd broken the jar of sauce and tried to clean it up and burned the paper towels so she wouldn't find out."

"I was standing in the doorway, watching every second of that terrible lie. Your eyes were blinking a mile a minute—a sure sign that you weren't telling the truth," Yvonne said.

"Only because I've got these big ole Diana Ross eyes," Lana said. That's what Mama had called them, and while Lana didn't hate Diana or the Supremes' songs, she wasn't a fan either.

"Not true," Yvonne said. "All that blinking would've been noticed on anybody. You looked like you'd just had those drops in your eyes they give you when they dilate them at the optometrist's office."

Lana didn't respond.

"I know it was pretty dusty in the house, but just now, out here in the fresh air, you were just blinking like that again." Yvonne reached for Lana's hand and twined her fingers through her sister's. "Tell me what's going on."

"It's nothing," she said. It was a knee-jerk response.

It had been a really long time since she'd confided anything in Yvonne. A long time since they'd felt like anything other than people who shared the same parents. At one point, though, when they'd been two little girls with bushy ponytails and then two teenagers with pretty smiles, they'd been thick as thieves. Since Yvonne was five years older than Lana, Yvonne had, of course, been Lana's protector, but she'd also been her encourager, the one Lana had looked up to and tried so hard to be like. Especially since Yvonne had been the one to hold all their mother's positive attention, even after Tami had been born. But no matter what Lana did, even if she knew she'd done and said exactly the same thing Yvonne would have, it never had the same effect with Freda. The woman only saw Yvonne when she looked at her daughters, and Lana had hated her for that. She still did.

"It's nothing worth talking about," was her follow-up to the statement. "I mean, there's no sense talking something to death. It's not going to change the situation."

"How do you know?" Yvonne asked. "Sometimes a new set of ears can hear something different. Can pick up on a possibility that you hadn't considered."

"Can save the day?" Lana snapped. "I don't need you to come riding in on your 'take care of my baby sisters' white horse, Yvonne."

If Yvonne was bruised by Lana's harsh words, she didn't show it, and she didn't release Lana's hand. "I haven't been too good at that lately, anyway, so you don't have to worry about it."

Now Lana felt like crap, on top of the headache.

"It was never your job to take care of us," Lana told her. "You had too much on your shoulders at too young an age."

And because Lana had known that, she hadn't hated Yvonne when she was younger, like she did their mother. Yvonne was Freda's favorite because that's the way Freda had raised her to be. Their mother would talk to Yvonne in a totally different tone than she did Lana and Tami. She'd take Yvonne to the grocery store with her and leave Lana home with her father. Then, when Daniel had left, she'd leave Lana at home to watch Tami while she and Yvonne shopped for groceries and whatever else they needed in the house. Then, whenever Freda had late meetings at work or parent-teacher conferences, Yvonne would be in charge again, fixing dinner and making sure Lana and Tami got their baths before bed.

"And you've got a lot on your shoulders now," Yvonne replied. "I'm not trying to get in your business or even swoop in and help take your problems away. I'm just sitting here telling you I'll listen if you want to talk."

Yvonne sounded sincere. But did Lana want to talk? Did she want to tell her judgmental sister about her marital problems?

Before she could answer her own question, she looked up to see Deacon coming out of the house. He looked down one side of the porch and then to the side where they were sitting, and began walking their way.

"Maybe we should talk about him instead," she whispered, and then nudged Yvonne to look up.

"Here's your water," Deacon said when he was close enough to crouch and hand her the glass.

"Thank you," she said, and accepted the glass.

"You sure you don't wanna go to the doctor? I can call my mother right now. I'm sure she has that clinic's number memorized, as much as she has my sister riding over so she can make a visit," he said.

"No. I'll be okay," she replied. "Just probably need to lay down for a while."

He didn't look convinced, if that arch of his thick brow was any indication. Deacon was a very good-looking man, with broad shoulders and a wide chest. Construction was definitely the job for him; she doubted she'd ever seen a man who looked better in raggedy jeans, dusty work boots, and tight T-shirts. Yes, indeed, he was good looking, and so was her big sister. The one who'd suddenly gone silent beside her.

"Well, then, I'll get back to work. But you don't come back inside without a hat, goggles, and—"

"A mask," she finished for him. "I know the rules, Deacon. And I'll follow them from now on."

He grinned. "You'd better."

"Oh, she will," Yvonne piped in, as if just remembering she could be part of the conversation.

When Deacon stood and turned to walk away, Lana said, "A man who looks like that should be waking up in some woman's bed every morning."

Yvonne didn't miss a beat. "He probably is."

Lana shook her head. "Tami said he's single."

"How would she know?" Yvonne asked.

"She asked him, of course." Lana took a sip from her water and chuckled. "You know that girl ain't got no filter. Especially when it comes to men."

"Men lie," was Yvonne's unbothered response.

"And that's a fact," Lana said with a nod and another chuckle. "Even after you marry them."

"Girl, let Mama tell it—they lie, *especially* after you marry them."

"Is that why you never married?" It had been something Lana had wondered every now and then, when she let herself think fondly of her sister instead of being thoroughly irritated by the woman Freda had created.

Yvonne eased her fingers from Lana's. Then she pulled her legs up until she could wrap her arms around them and lean her chin on her knees. In that moment, Yvonne—the smarter, better-at-every-damn-thing sister—looked more vulnerable than Lana had ever seen her before. Her hair was in the high ponytail she'd been wearing daily now, laced through the opening at the back of the Celtics snapback she wore pulled down low over her brow. Today's outfit was baggy green sweatpants, a black T-shirt, and black Vans on her feet. Her face was makeup-free, which was always the case except for when she was going to work or to some other type of professional meeting. But since they'd been on the island, the only product she'd seen Yvonne put on her face was this peach lip gloss that Lana low-key wanted to borrow.

"Marriage isn't for everybody," Yvonne said.

"Girl, you are spittin' facts tuhday!" For just a second, Lana thought her comments might be giving something away—but then, she just didn't care.

Yvonne had been the one she'd run out of the bathroom in the middle of the night to wake up and whisper in her ear when she'd gotten her period. Her big sister had also been the one to go back into that bathroom with her and wipe her face because Lana had cried the moment she'd seen that stain in her panties. Then Yvonne had pulled out the box of sanitary napkins from the cabinet under the sink and had begun the explanation of how and when to use them, cleanliness, and the most important part of that bit of coming of age—how to *not* get pregnant.

"And marriages don't always last," Yvonne continued.

Now Lana was silent. And so was Yvonne. They sat like that for what felt like endless moments. It was hot outside, and as Lana stared down at her glass, she swore she could see the ice cubes already starting to melt. That made her take another sip.

"Do you want to fix it?" Yvonne asked suddenly.

"Do I want to fix what?"

Yvonne turned her head so she could look over at Lana, who was already staring at her. "Whatever's going wrong in your marriage. Do you want to fix it?"

Lana blinked, and then she blinked again. Then she sucked in a breath and released it slowly before responding, "I don't know."

Chapter 17

TAMI

"This is what you call *subtle*?" Lana asked, her face scrunched into a frown.

To be fair, Lana's face was often frowning, especially anytime she was inside the house. And it was such a shame, because she was easily the most beautiful woman Tami had ever seen. Lana's deep-mocha skin had always been flawless, just like her body: perfect C-cup breasts, which still seemed to be high and perky; what she knew from hanging around Gabriel and his friends would be called a fine "apple" ass; and a slim waist. At five feet, seven inches tall, when Lana put on heels and makeup, she was a goddess.

Albeit a grumpy-ass goddess, who was currently driving Tami to drink.

"I think it's pretty and fun," Tami replied, and moved over to the wall, unrolling the paper she had in her hand in the process. "And I never said I was getting something subtle."

"*I* said subtle," Yvonne chimed in, because it just wasn't a normal day of summerhouse renovations if the older Butler sisters weren't ganging up on her.

"Well, I'm the one who was up bright and early this morning to be on that first ferry," Tami said, and then lifted her arms to press the wallpaper against the wall. "And I'm the one who stayed in town, riding around with Hitch and Frank while they picked up one thing after another, saving the wallpaper store—the one place I needed to go—for last. You see it's almost six o'clock, and I just got back forty minutes ago."

"Yeah, that's not subtle," Yvonne said as if she hadn't heard a word Tami had spoken.

"It's actually kinda loud," Lana added.

Tami looked at the floral pattern in pretty, cheerful pastels. Some of the roses were much bigger than the others, but they were all lovely blush and cream colors amid the multicolored background.

"It's called Romantic Pink-Teal Watercolor-Chic Floral Pattern," Tami said, and smoothed her hand over the paper once more.

"That's a lot of name," Yvonne said.

"And it's a little ugly," Lana countered.

Tami shot them both a seething glare over her shoulder. "Y'all just hate me." She turned and attempted to walk to the other side of the powder room, where the window was, but she'd unraveled too much of the wallpaper off its roll, and she tripped over it. Cursing, she tried to bunch it up under her arms.

"We don't hate you," Yvonne said, and started toward her. "Come here, let me help you get that back on the roll."

"I can do it myself," Tami said, hating the pouty sound of her voice. "I was just trying to get this powder room done so it would be one less thing on our list to do." She was still trying to wrap the excess paper around one arm when the roll slipped from her other hand and traveled across the floor.

Now the watercolors stretched out like a red carpet from where Tami stood by the vanity, past the toilet and the doorway that Yvonne had just come through, and out into the hallway, where Lana was standing. Nobody said a word as they watched it travel.

Then Lana sighed and picked it up. Yvonne reached for the end of the paper currently wrapped around Tami's arm.

"Stop taking everything so personally," Yvonne told her. "We can not like the wallpaper you selected without it meaning we don't like you."

From in the hallway, Lana yelled, "But for the record, I'm not enjoying chasing a runaway roll of wallpaper, and that's solely your fault for standing there whining like a babyface!"

Tami grimaced. She'd always hated when Lana called her that, which probably explained why her sister had chosen that moment to say it. *I'm not a babyface* was on the tip of her tongue, but she clamped her lips shut and returned her attention to helping Yvonne straighten out the paper she was still holding.

"I thought these colors would complement the kitchen since I agreed with y'all's suggestion to lighten that up a bit, going with a soft sage green over the deep hunter that was in there," she said.

They'd ripped all the cabinets out of the kitchen earlier that week, so now it was just down to the studs. Which left no counter space for them, but the sink, refrigerator, and stove hadn't been taken out yet. Those would go the first of next week. Deacon had to charter special ferries equipped with space that could haul out big pieces of furniture, so the demolition and removal was a slower process than it would've been had they been on the mainland.

"I see what you're saying," Yvonne said in that part-conciliatory, part-condescending tone she'd perfected. "But it might be a little too busy for this small space."

"Or . . . ," Tami countered, and started to step toward the door, where Lana stood with the roll in hand. "It'll give it just the punch of vibrancy this house needs."

"I thought that, in addition to trying to preserve the legacy, we were going to pay close attention to maintain the historic Lowcountry design of this house," Yvonne said.

Tami nodded. "That's why I went with these pastels. Did you know there was a Pastel Society of South Carolina? They promote public awareness of the pastel as a fine-art medium. That should be right up your alley, Lana, with your big ole degree in the fine arts."

"The question is, why do *you* know that?" Lana asked, frowning again.

"I know it," Tami said, and then looked down at the paper she held once more, "because I've been reading up on South Carolina and Daufuskie. The history, the culture, the style. It's all been ruminating in my mind. And I'm gonna hang this wallpaper."

With determined steps, she moved past where Lana was still standing, giving her a quizzical glance. She didn't even turn back to see how Yvonne was looking—her guess would be irritated and on her way to pissed because Tami was about to do something she disagreed with. She didn't care and she didn't stop. Instead, she stomped all the way down the hall toward the foyer, where most of the supplies were being stored until they were ready to use. There was another stockpile of stuff on the back deck, but Tami knew the primer-sizing product and the adhesive that Hitch had instructed her to get at the wallpaper store were down here. So were the spatula-like things and the tarps to cover the floors. Cursing because she should've left the roll of paper upstairs, she stuffed it under her arm and picked up all the other things she would need, and then she headed toward the back of the house again.

She was shocked to see Yvonne and Lana still standing outside of the powder room. As she approached, Lana put her hands on her hips and said, "I hope you've got everything we need to get this done."

Narrowing her gaze at her sister, Tami replied, "I do. At least, I have everything Hitch said I would need."

"Then let's get started. I'm hungry, and Ms. Janie sent us a pot of beef stew to heat up for dinner," Yvonne said as she reached for the bucket in Tami's right hand that held the spatulas, sponges, and ruler.

"It's too hot to eat beef stew," Tami complained. She'd seen that huge glass bowl covered in aluminum foil sitting on the stove when she'd gone into the kitchen to get a bottle of water after her trip into town. "Plus, we'll have to dig dishes out of the box to heat it up."

"Well, we've gotta eat," Yvonne said.

"We sure do," Lana added. "Plus, it's been forever since I've had beef stew. Don't even begin to know how to fix it myself, but I remember how hearty and good it tastes."

"Mama used to make it on Sundays in the winter," Yvonne said, still going through the bucket and pulling out everything to sit along the floor just outside the powder-room door. "And she'd bake corn bread to go with it. Y'all remember that?"

"Yesssss," Lana said. "That sweet, warm corn bread, once you dip it into the stew." She rubbed her stomach and closed her eyes, looking like she was having more of an orgasmic experience than a memory about some home-cooked food.

"I didn't like all those big ole cooked carrots in it, but otherwise, the stew was good." Tami picked up the tub of primer and the one of adhesive and walked them into the bathroom. "But I haven't eaten since a chili dog I had around noon when I was in town, so I guess I'm eating beef stew for dinner too."

In the next few moments, Tami had moved into the powder room, with Yvonne right behind her. Lana came in after them but stopped in the doorway to scroll through her phone. "The directions say we need to remove all the fixtures and heat registers first."

"I think Frank was in here yesterday, doing that," Yvonne said.

"Yep!" Tami yelled back to them. "He did, and he filled up any holes with that joint-compound stuff, so we're good to go."

"And Deacon knows we're doing this?" Yvonne asked.

Tami looked over her shoulder at her sister. "I told him this was a small assignment and that I could handle it. Now that the *I* has become a *we*, I'm feeling even more confident. This is going to be amazing."

"It's gonna be something," Lana added as she continued scrolling on her phone.

✉

Three hours later, there were two strips of paper on the wall behind the powder-room door. They were crooked and had clumps of adhesive around the edges, but they were hanging.

"It doesn't seem as loud as I originally thought," Yvonne said as she tilted her head and looked at it.

They were all squeezed into the small space, the door closed so they could see their progress.

Lana was leaning against the vanity. "It's still a lot of flowers, but I guess that works in a powder room. But I think this should be an accent wall. Then we get Deacon and his crew to paint the other wall, pulling one of the paler colors from the paper."

"*We* can paint it!" Tami said, unable to hold back her excitement. She was feeling particularly proud of the partial wall they'd completed and even more jubilant that her sisters seemed to like the paper she'd selected now. "This looks good over here, so I'm sure we can handle paint."

"It's crooked, Tami," Lana said. "That's why I'm thinking we should just let Deacon and his crew do the rest."

Tami sighed. "No, we can finish this." Then she tilted her head. "And it's not *that* crooked."

Yvonne reached out and cupped her hands around Tami's face; then she moved her head so that it was straight.

Tami sighed and then gave in to a small grin. "Okay, it's crooked. But we can fix it."

Lana shook her head. "If you say so." She stepped away from the vanity and then grabbed the edge of the last strip they'd hung and tried to pull it away from the wall.

Because it was still wet, it came up almost painlessly, and they were able to hang it straighter this time. It was on the next round that things got a little sticky. Yvonne marked off the paper in the correct places while Tami held it against the wall. Lana did the cutting and moved the excess paper to the side of the vanity that was out of their tiny amount of workspace. Then Tami handed the paper to be hung off to Yvonne, and she turned to scoop a bunch of the adhesive out of the two-gallon jug they'd purchased. She smeared it on the wall the way she'd done twice before, and then she turned to Yvonne to grab the paper from her.

"I gotta pee," Lana said. "Move over there while I go."

"What? You're just gonna pee while we're all in here?" Yvonne asked as Lana put her hands on Yvonne's shoulders and eased her forward so she could get past her to the toilet.

"It's a bathroom, isn't it? Besides, Tami never gave any of us any bathroom privacy when we were living with Mama," Lana said. "And it's not like we're outside and I said I was gonna take a squat."

"Oh, like you used to always do when we were swimming in the creek," Tami said. She was bent over, putting more primer at the very end near the baseboard because that's where the other paper had kept popping up before.

"Oh, no, babyface, that was you," Lana said. "Oh shoot, is there toilet paper in here?" she asked just as Tami heard her stream begin.

"Wait, I think it's in the bottom of the vanity," Yvonne said. But when she attempted to move toward the vanity, her butt bumped against Tami's, and Tami lost her balance, falling into the wall.

Her left shoulder, arm, and her entire right hand pressed against the wet primer, and she screeched, "Dammit, Yvonne!"

"What?" Yvonne asked, and turned to see what had happened.

Tami was turning then too, showing her sisters the gooey mess on her arm and hand.

"Oh well. Wait a minute—let me get this toilet paper, and then we'll find some towels or something to get you cleaned up," Yvonne said.

She got the toilet paper out of the vanity and then turned, tossing it to Tami. "Here, take this, and I'll run out real quick to find some of those work towels. I think there're some in the hallway."

"Wait!" Lana yelled. "Don't open that door while I'm sitting on the toilet."

"Here," Tami said. "Take this toilet paper and get your butt up."

She tried to toss the toilet paper that Yvonne had just thrown to her to Lana, but some of it stuck to her hand while the rest of the roll clumsily fell forward.

"Girl, how am I supposed to get that?" Lana asked.

She leaned forward to attempt to pick up the roll just as Yvonne opened the door.

And Frank was on the other side.

"Oh, hey, I was looking for you ladies to—"

Frank's words were cut off by Lana's yell.

"Yvonne! I told you not to open that door!"

Tami was still trying to get the toilet paper off her hand, but she snickered at the confused look on Frank's face—a look that quickly turned to interest in Lana's bare ass.

"Oh shit!" Yvonne said, as if finally realizing what was happening. Then she slammed the door in Frank's face and turned back to see Lana finally grabbing the roll of toilet paper. "Sorry." But the apology was drowned out by the chuckles that followed.

"Not sorry!" Lana said after she ripped off the toilet paper she needed and then threw the roll at Yvonne.

✉

"It's been forever since we had a pajama party," Tami said at midnight, when they were all sitting on the floor in the formal living room.

It was one of the only rooms in the house where they weren't pulling up floors, taking down wallpaper, or moving out furniture. The three of them, along with Deacon, had decided to keep the furniture, paint the walls, buy new curtains, and polish the original wood floors. But for now, the furniture was all covered with tarps; the books that had been on the built-in shelves were packed into boxes; and all Grandma Betty's knickknacks, lamps, and other stuff had been stored in plastic bins that they needed to decide what to do with.

After they'd all showered and changed into their pajamas, they'd come back downstairs. Yvonne had gone into the kitchen to heat up the beef stew and bread Ms. Janie had sent while Lana spread out one of the tarps on the living-room floor.

"Damn, that was some good eats," Lana said as she lay back on the floor, one hand over her stomach, the other arm dropping over her forehead. "I haven't eaten sweet tada bread since the last time I was here and Grandma had hired that girl from down the road to cook for us. Y'all remember her? What was her name?"

Tami had just finished the iced tea she'd been drinking. She set it aside on the part of the floor closest to her that wasn't covered by the tarp. "Her name was Charity. She was just a little older than me and trying to earn some extra money to pay for culinary school. Jeremiah told me she came back here and opened up a little restaurant. It's along the road close to one of those resorts so she could get the tourist traffic. We should check it out one day."

Yvonne nodded from where she sat across from Lana and Tami. "We should definitely support her. Grandma would've liked that."

"I think so too," Tami said.

They fell silent, each of them in their own thoughts. Tami's had drifted temporarily to the fact that she still hadn't heard back from that record company about the job. It'd been three weeks since the interview, but she'd been trying to remain optimistic. Which had been Gabriel's advice, but since she had other stuff going on, she figured she could follow along for a while. The house was the next thought, and what other work they needed to do. They hadn't yet touched the blue house out back because Yvonne and Lana had decided they would get the summerhouse finished first. Tami figured that was so that if they ran out of money on the renovations here, they'd have an excuse to tell her to forget about her plans for the blue house. But Tami wasn't going to do that, no matter what they said.

Yvonne spoke finally, her voice somber. "We should talk about Mama."

By the way she looked down and picked at a nonexistent piece of lint on her pajama pants, Tami could tell that even her sister knew what she'd just said was putting a damper on the otherwise amiable last few hours they'd shared. It wasn't easy being with her sisters—never had been. But she couldn't forget that there'd also been some really good times. Tami knew that, and she cherished them, especially in the years that they'd become so distant.

"How's she doing?" Lana asked, rolling over onto her side and propping up an elbow and resting her head on her hand. "Last time I talked to her, she was complaining about the doctors lying to her."

Yvonne pursed her lips and nodded. "Yeah, she doesn't like many of the doctors she had to choose on the Medicare plan."

"But she doesn't have a choice, does she?" Tami answered. "They're the only doctors she can go to, right?"

"No, not really. I mean, there are several providers on the Plan C portion of Medicare, but I don't know if it'll be any different. She just doesn't like the fact that she's on Medicare," Yvonne said.

"Something else for her to be unhappy about," Tami said. "I swear, for a woman who always had so much, she never seemed happy with anything."

"That's not entirely true," Yvonne said. "She was happy when we were little. Don't you remember, Lana? She used to love Christmas and all the gifts Daddy used to buy us and her. We used to sing Christmas carols while riding around the neighborhoods, looking at the lights on all the houses."

"I remember," Lana said. "But it seems like so long ago. I don't think I remember her smiling much by the time I graduated from elementary."

"She never smiled around me," Tami said. "Not at Christmas or any other holiday. Not at any of my graduations, even though she knew how hard I worked to get to each one of those milestones." She sighed. "The doctor I see now, she said being on some form of medication—even if it had been a really light dose when I was younger—might've made my school experience a little less traumatizing."

"You felt like you were traumatized because you had to go to school?" Lana asked.

Tami shook her head. "No, that's not what I'm saying. But school was hard for me; I know you two knew that. Mama used to make you sit at the table with me every night, trying to get me to understand my homework."

"And you still struggled," Yvonne said. "I remember those nights. I used to feel so sorry for you because I knew you were trying really hard. I knew you were doing the best you could."

"Me too," Lana said. "That's why I used to just write the answers on most of her math homework."

Yvonne looked shocked by the admission.

"Mama didn't want to admit that I had a problem. Swore the school system and doctors were always quick to medicate the Black kids. But she just didn't want to say it out loud that I wasn't perfect," Tami said, the heaviness in her chest threatening to choke her. "My therapist said I should've talked to Mama about this a long time ago—the two of you as well, but I didn't want to. Didn't want to rehash all that pain."

"That doesn't sound like you at all," Lana said, and Tami tossed her an annoyed glare. "I mean, you never were one to hold your tongue. Especially when something pissed you off."

Tami shook her head. "Not when it was Mama. You know there was no backtalking in Mama's house, and no opinion that was better than hers."

"I don't know if that's fair, Tami," Yvonne said.

"Oh boy, here she comes. I was thinking for just a minute that maybe you were ready to have an honest discussion about her," Tami said.

"If an honest discussion includes you taking some responsibility for your actions for once," Yvonne rebutted.

"C'mon, y'all, are we really going to do this now? It's late," Lana said, pulling herself up to a sitting position.

"All I wanted to discuss was our mother's health," Yvonne countered. "She's been struggling since the stroke. The neurologists think she's starting to experience more of the residual effects from the type of stroke she had. That means in some ways her mind is deteriorating, and that has her strength and overall health declining. That's why she needs everything to be on one level so she'll be able to get around easier."

"But you moved her down into that back room off the kitchen, right?" Lana asked. "And there's a little bathroom downstairs."

"There's no tub or shower in that bathroom, Lana. And Mama hates being in the room off the kitchen. She's always saying it smells like food and makes her nauseous and that it's her pantry, not a bedroom." Yvonne ran a hand down her hair, which she'd released from the ponytail.

She would most likely wrap it tonight before putting on her silk scarf; that and the perm she was still getting was how she kept it so straight every day. Tami didn't dislike the style—she'd just loved when she used to see Yvonne's hair in its natural state: thick, black, 3c curls that used to frame her sister's pretty brown sugar–toned face before she learned how to blow-dry it straight and bump curl the ends.

"What about senior housing?" Lana asked. "Isaac's grandmother lives in a really nice building, and she participates in all types of activities with the other residents."

"I don't know if that would work for her; she'd probably need something more like assisted living, and I've heard horrific things about those facilities. If Mama doesn't like the state doctors, she's certainly not going to like being in some state-run assisted-living facility." Yvonne shook her head. "Besides, she doesn't want to leave her house. Says she worked too hard for too many years to get her house paid off to just toss it all away now."

"How do you stand it?" Tami asked.

"Stand what?" was Yvonne's response.

Tami crossed her arms over her chest. "Living with her. How could you move back into that house with her after being out on your own for so long?" It was something she'd wondered about for the last couple of years.

Yvonne frowned. "How could I not?" she asked. "After the stroke and her time at the rehab hospital, they said she couldn't come home to an empty house. There was no money for a full-time nurse, and neither of you offered to stay with her. So what other choice did I have?"

"Who's with her now?" Lana asked.

Tami hadn't even thought about that in the time they'd been here. And a small part of her felt really bad about that fact.

"I told y'all, I got Ms. Rosalee to stay with her," Yvonne replied. "She's always asking what she can do, and she comes and sits with Mama sometimes when I have late meetings and things like that. She's been giving me text updates every few days since I've been gone."

Tami lifted a brow. "Does she sit with Mama when you go out on dates?"

Yvonne's lips pursed. "I don't go on dates."

Lana huffed. "That explains a lot."

"What the hell is that supposed to mean?" Yvonne shot to her feet and yelled.

Taking her time to stand, Lana shook her head. "I'm just saying you look exhausted, Yvonne. I mean, you did each time we met at Robyn's office. Since you've been here, you're starting to get some light back in your eyes."

"Especially whenever Deacon's around," Tami said in a singsongy voice. She picked up her glass before she stood and started toward the kitchen.

"First of all, I don't need a man to put any light in my eyes, for your information," Yvonne said, hot on Tami's heels.

"Whatever you say," Tami chided.

"And second—no, I don't date, and that shouldn't be a surprise because I barely dated when I was younger. But the bigger issue is how the hell you think I'm supposed to work, take care of our mother, and entertain a man!" Yvonne had stopped by the island, one hand on her hip now.

Lana came into the kitchen behind her, leaning against the other side of the island while Tami put her glass in the sink. She'd have to remember to wash it first thing tomorrow morning or Yvonne would have a cow.

When she turned to face her sisters, she shrugged. "I don't know what you want me to say about that. I came to the hospital every day after Mama had the stroke, and the first chance she got, she asked me how I could be there so much. Said I must've lost another job if I had so much free time on my hands. So I didn't go back."

"She's your mother, Tami. Regardless of anything else," Yvonne told her.

Tami shook her head. "Not my mental health. I don't have to put myself in a position to endure her abuse anymore. I have a choice."

"Well, what about *my* choice?" Yvonne yelled. And Yvonne *never* yelled. "How come the two of you got to choose how involved you wanted to be in Mama's health crisis, but I didn't?"

"I don't think you considered a choice, Yvonne," Lana said quietly. "You never did. You just did whatever Mama wanted, said what pleased her, acted how she told you. There was never any pushback from you."

"She's my mother! Pushback would've been disrespectful." Yvonne sounded incredulous, her eyes were wide, and her hands had started to shake.

Lana went to her and took her hands. "You're a whole person, separate and apart from Alfreda Butler. She may have given birth to you, but you have your own mind, your own opinions."

"Standing up for yourself is not disrespectful," Tami said, trying to keep her tone as level as Lana's.

"Is that what you call yourself doing, Tami? All these years of going against everything anybody ever tried to tell you, tried to help you with. You were just standing up for yourself when you went out there and did the exact opposite, falling on your face every damn time, messing up every chance you could get."

"Really, Yvonne? Is that what you think? Is it really me messing up just because I do something you don't approve of? Damn, Yvonne! I get so tired of you complaining about everything I do, judging me according to one high-ass standard you and Mama set without any regard for who I am or what I might want for my life.

"That's why I don't come to the house to sit with Mama or go to any appointments with her. If you're the only one who ever does anything right in her eyes, then you should be the only one she has to deal with. Lord forbid I force her to see me and all my failures," Tami finished.

Yvonne was speechless. Her eyes had gone even wider with shock, and she yanked her hands away from Lana's hold, clenching her fingers as rage seemed to bubble inside her. "You know what? You're absolutely right. Why should you help take care of the woman who gave birth to you, who kept a roof over your head after your precious father left us? Why should you give a damn about anybody other than yourself?"

Yvonne stormed out of the kitchen before Tami could respond, and when Tami looked to Lana to give her the answer, her other sister just shook her head.

"I'm done with this tonight," Lana said. "This shit is never going to be right between us, no matter who dies or how many houses we fix up."

Chapter 18

YVONNE

Now *she* was the one with the headache.

Yvonne sighed as she came out of the en suite bathroom and walked over to her nightstand. When she was home in the city, she always brought a glass of water upstairs to her room in case she got thirsty in the middle of the night. She *always* got thirsty in the middle of the night. In the weeks she'd been here on the island, she'd done the same, but since they'd packed away most of the dishes, she'd been bringing a bottled water upstairs with her instead. After opening the drawer, she pulled out the makeup bag she used to carry her medications. She sat on the side of the bed and put the bag beside her, dragging the zipper open slowly.

This was her morning routine—at least, it had been for the past year. She got out of bed, went to use the bathroom, washed her hands, and afterward, sat on the closed toilet seat to say her morning prayers. Then, after thanking the Lord for all the ways she'd been blessed, she reached for her medication bag. She had the steps memorized now, and even though she was in a different location—a different state, actually— this morning, she was about to do the same thing.

Because what else was she going to do? Not take care of herself? Not do the things that the doctors said she needed to do to remain as healthy as possible? The questions were a moot point; she knew she didn't really have a choice.

Not in this, nor in anything else.

If she didn't take care of herself, who would take care of her mother?

The throbbing stretched across her forehead, traveling behind her ears and down the back of her head. Stress headaches. She'd had them since she was a teenager, although she hadn't known what they were called back then. All she'd known was that her head was hurting, so she'd take some aspirin and go on about her business. It wasn't until her sophomore year in college when she'd felt dizzy after class that she'd gone to the nurse, who subsequently suggested she see her primary care doctor. That was the first doctor to tell her something more was wrong than just a normal headache. He'd explained other measures for her to relieve stress and recommended a specific over-the-counter medication instead of the generic aspirin she'd been taking since she'd lived with her mother.

For years, that had been all that was medically wrong with her. The hypertension diagnosis came when she was in her early thirties, right after she'd finished her master's degree and begun applying for school principal jobs. Another pill had been prescribed for that. Then, last year at her annual exam, her doctor had informed her that she had type 2 diabetes.

Part of her had wanted to crawl into a corner and cry, because the last thing she'd wanted was to have to take more pills—and worse, the daily insulin shots. But that part wasn't allowed to breathe, as she still had responsibilities. She had her job and all the people in that school who depended on her to do it well. And she had her mother, who depended on her for . . . well, everything.

As she pulled the alcohol swabs and the insulin pen from her bag, she sighed. Now she had another thing to add to her list. Her sisters were depending on her to see this renovation through to completion. They needed her here to do her part in helping to get this house ready for sale. But they didn't need or want her for anything else. Tami had barely spoken to her in the last few days since their blowup after the impromptu pajama party, and anytime Lana wasn't helping them with some task around the house, she was closed off in her room, doing who knew what.

She'd thought they could at least get through this renovation without alienating each other all over again, but she'd obviously been wrong.

Stress wasn't kind to Yvonne. It manifested in not only the headaches but also in blood-pressure spikes and changes in her eating habits, which in turn messed with her daily blood-sugar numbers. And that would require more insulin and possibly other serious consequences. Closing her eyes to the thought, and the way she often felt helpless to fight against any of these circumstances, she whispered another prayer—this one for strength—because so often, she didn't know how she would make it through a day on her own.

When that was done, she took a deep breath and began the process of taking care of herself first. She opened one of the alcohol swabs and then set it down while she removed the cap of her insulin pen. She swabbed the rubber stopper at the tip of the pen and then attached the needle. Tears sprang to her eyes as she moved through each step. Her vision was blurry as she checked the name and expiration date on the pen and then performed the test shot, waiting until she saw the drops of insulin spring from the needle tip.

By then, warm tears slid down her cheeks, and she sniffled, willing her hands not to tremble. Clearing her throat, she set her dosage on the dial at the opposite end of the pen and then opened the second alcohol swab. She pulled up the T-shirt she'd slept in and swabbed a spot on her stomach a few fingers away from her navel. Then she grabbed the pen in one hand and gripped the wet spot of her stomach in the other, quickly performing the injection before dropping the pen back to the bed.

Then she just sat there and cried.

Not because the injection hurt—she'd become used to that recurring pain in the last twelve months, just as she was used to the tips of her fingers feeling raw where she had to stick three times a day to check her glucose levels. No, the reason she cried this morning was totally different. It was a helpless cry, a cry of pity that Yvonne forced herself not to indulge in too often. But after these last few days, and especially after last night's call, she couldn't help it.

"Hello? Vonni?"

Her mother's voice had come through low and slow a little after ten when Yvonne's phone had rung.

"Hey, Mama. Is everything okay?" She'd sat straight up in her bed when she saw the name on the phone screen.

"No, but I guess it is what it is," Freda had said in a gruff voice.

Breathing a sigh of relief because her mother didn't sound any different than normal—thus, she believed there wasn't a real emergency—Yvonne had dropped a hand to her lap and held the phone to her ear with the other one. "What are you doing up so late? Where's Ms. Rosalee?"

"She's in there sleepin' on the couch. I told her she couldn't lay upstairs in your bed or mine."

Yvonne had rolled her eyes at that. She'd given Ms. Rosalee permission to sleep in her bed, but of course the woman would've done whatever Freda said. Everybody seemed to do what her mother told them to do. Except for her sisters.

"Mama, she could've slept in my bed. I told her I didn't mind. I want her to be comfortable while I'm down here."

"Well, what about me?" Freda had asked. "You know I don't feel comfortable with strangers in the house, but you left me here with her anyway."

"Ms. Rosalee is not a stranger. You've known her for more than forty years," Yvonne had said, trying not to sound as tired and exasperated as she felt. "And don't forget, you told me I needed to come down here."

Her mother hadn't responded to that comment, just continued with what was on her mind. "Anyway, I was calling to see how things are going. You keeping things in line down . . . t-there?"

That last word had been stammered after a pause, which had, unfortunately, been happening more frequently when Freda talked recently.

"We're doing okay. I told you when I talked to you the other day that me, Tami, and Lana put new wallpaper up in the powder room."

There had been some shuffling on the other end and then the sound of Freda grumbling before she finally said, "Who has a powder room? It's a *bathroom*. Betty was always actin' so bougie. That's when she was bothering to tell the truth at all."

Yvonne had refrained from saying Grandma Betty had been the one to call Freda bougie. In reality, both women had been a bit over the top in the clothes they wore and the money they spent. Of course, Grandma Betty, with her fortune from singing, could afford to be a little more extravagant than Freda, but Yvonne had never thought that jealousy was the true source of contention between them. Still, Freda had never made it a secret that she didn't like Betty Butler, and after a time, she'd made it known that she didn't like her son very much either.

Yvonne had closed her eyes to the memory of the two years before her parents divorced—the year Freda was pregnant and the year after she'd had Tami. Not long after Tami's first birthday, her father had packed up and moved out of their house.

"It turned out really nice," Yvonne had said. "Tami's got a good eye for decorating. She's really working close with the crew to get things done, and she's doing a lot of research."

"Figures she'd be good at something that isn't paying her a dime," Freda had said.

"Well, in the end, this is going to pay off for her. She's really invested in the finished product," Yvonne had told her mother, but wondered why she hadn't said those words to Tami. Surely her sister would have liked to hear something positive from her, considering she'd made it known that she always thought Yvonne was judging her.

"Just make sure you're keeping an eye on her and on Lana," Freda had said. "I don't . . . I don't . . ." Her mother had paused, and Yvonne thought she heard her curse quietly before she continued. "Last time I talked to her, she didn't sound right."

Yvonne had thought something was going on with Lana too, and after their conversation last week, she knew it had to do with her marriage. She wasn't telling Freda that, though.

"I bet it's that husband of hers," Freda had said, and Yvonne wondered if the woman could read her mind. "I never trusted him."

Her mother didn't trust any men, and she'd told Yvonne that so many times over the years. And considering her earlier comment about Grandma Betty never telling the truth, it seemed Freda didn't trust a lot of women either.

"Lana's okay, Mama," she'd lied. Although this was what she and Freda did often—talked about her sisters and what they needed in their lives as if their words were the law that her sisters should follow—Yvonne hadn't felt like doing it that night. Not when Lana and Tami were right down the hall. And if she'd had anything to say to them about their life, she could just go to their room and say it, since they were now in closer proximity than they'd been in years. "We're all doing fine, and we're gonna be done in about eight more weeks."

"Eight weeks? You're going to be down there *all* summer?" Freda had asked.

"Probably. That's how long the contractor said it would take to get the house back together." She knew she'd told her mother this when she'd spoken to her a few days after arriving on the island. But in addition to everything else that was going on with Freda's health, her short-term memory had been failing as well.

"Hmph. I bet that was Betty's plan all along." Freda had coughed. "She hated that you girls grew up and stopped coming down there for the summers. Couldn't just be satisfied with the Thanksgivings she guilted you girls down there. Noooo, Betty wanted you living down there with her, said that family should be together. Like, what the hell was I?" She'd coughed again but continued. "Called me one day and cussed me out because she swore I'd told you girls something to keep you away. But I didn't. I never said a bad word about her lying ass or her trifling son."

And she'd been right: her mother had never spoken an ill word about either of them, not to Yvonne or her sisters. Now, she didn't speak any complimentary words about them, either, but she certainly didn't bad-mouth them. It was no secret that her mother didn't like Grandma Betty or their father, but it hadn't always been that way. Yvonne wished she could remember exactly when that had changed.

"Mama, it's late. You should be asleep."

"I should be doing whatever I want," Freda had snapped. "Now, I want you to make sure Tami doesn't get into any trouble while she's down there. And find out if she has enough money in the bank. Lana has money, I'm sure. Even if she's not making anything on those pictures she's so hell-bent on taking, Isaac has a good, stable job. I can't believe he let her out of his sight to come down there. The way that man dotes on her is sickening sometimes."

"She's a grown woman, Mama. And this was family business. I doubt she would let him tell her she couldn't come."

"You know Lana would do anything for that man. You see how fast she up and married him just because he proposed. And now she's sitting in that house, letting him take care of her." Freda didn't hide her distaste for Lana's life choices either.

"She fell in love and married the man of her dreams," Yvonne had said, defending Lana. "I don't see anything wrong with that. And she's a professional photographer, Mama. Her pictures have been shown in several art galleries."

"But are they making any money?"

"Well, that's none of my business."

"It's my business because I'm her mother, and I know it's not. Otherwise, she wouldn't be living in some little condo; she'd have herself a big house." Freda had huffed. "But I am tired. Just wanted to call and make sure you knew to keep an eye on your sisters. You know you're the one I trust to take care of everything, Vonni. You're the only one that never let me down."

So by the time Yvonne had finally gotten off that call last night and lain down to go to sleep, all the ways she'd let herself down had been floating through her mind.

When had she decided that her life would only consist of her job? Hadn't there been a time when she'd imagined the life that Lana had? Not the photography part, because Yvonne truly had felt her calling was with children—whether teaching them or helping to guide them through the educational system—but the other parts that Lana had seemed to effortlessly claim. Meeting a kind and caring man who would propose marriage and build a home with her—that's the part she'd missed . . . or rather, she'd pushed aside in lieu of career achievements. And now what? She had certifications and degrees, a decent savings account, financial retirement plans, and a title she was proud to hold in her industry. What she no longer had was her own town house—which she'd sold when she moved back home with her mother after the stroke—or her own life, for that matter. Not that she'd done much socializing before Freda's health crisis, but since that day, Yvonne had done zero socializing. She hadn't been on a date in almost three years. Hadn't gone out with coworkers or even some of the women from the church that she'd grown up with. All she did was work and take care of Freda.

And she was tired of it.

That admission had come sometime during the early-morning hours, when she was still wide awake. She'd been feeling unsettled and uncertain for the past year but hadn't really wanted to let her mind circle enough to find the culprit for those feelings.

But during those hours when sleep hadn't found her, some long-overdue answers *had*. Now, at a little after seven in the morning, as she got up to start her day, she had to figure out what to do with those answers.

Or rather, here she was, falling apart instead of thinking about last night's revelations or starting her day.

It was Saturday, so there wouldn't be a full crew working at the house. At least, that's what Deacon had told her last night. They needed to do some demolition on the back part of the house, removing some parts of a corner of the foundation where the plumbers needed to dig down to get to the pipes. She'd planned to work on cleaning up in Grandma Betty's room. They were going to save that room for last to refresh but she, Lana, and Tami had agreed that they would go through all her personal things together.

She used the edge of her shirt to wipe her face and then cleaned up the things she'd used from the medication bag. After dropping the trash in the small brass can beside the nightstand, she grabbed the bottle of water and dug into the bag again to pull out a bottle of pills. She took the first and then the second pill, drinking the rest of her water and then dropping the bottle into the trash too. She was just about to grab the bag and put it back into the drawer so she could go take her shower when her phone buzzed with a notification.

It wasn't a ring, so she knew it wasn't her mother. Freda did not text. Lifting the phone and removing it from the charger, she swiped the screen to see what the notification was. It was a text from Deacon.

DEACON: I'd like to feed you dinner tonight

Yvonne stared at that message for she didn't know how long. What she did know was that he couldn't be serious. Like, really, this must be a misdial or mistext or whatever it was called. In the past few weeks, she and Deacon had shared a few meals—if you counted sandwiches that had been ordered from the café at one of the resorts, which one of his staff members had gone to pick up, or leftovers of whatever food Ms. Janie had sent them since the woman was intent on feeding them like they were children. Not that Yvonne was complaining. With the kitchen in such disarray, it would've been hard for them to cook anything, and the way her diet needed to be set up, home-cooked food was better for her. Ms. Janie's food, however, still made it a struggle to maintain her weight and keep a close eye on her sugar intake. That bread pudding she'd had from Deacon's mother a few weeks back had sent her sugar skyrocketing. But she knew she could indulge here and there; she just couldn't make a habit of it.

And none of that mattered, because Deacon couldn't be asking her out to dinner. She'd told him to stop flirting with her weeks ago. And to her knowledge, he'd listened, because all they'd been doing since then had been working on the house. Except this text had come on the weekend, way earlier than normal work hours. Still, he could text her at any time about work; they'd already established that, which was why he had her phone number in the first place.

The ringing phone had her ready to jump out of her skin a few minutes later as she was still standing by the nightstand staring at it.

When Deacon's name popped up on the screen, she cursed.

"Good morning," she answered, trying not to sound like she was as perplexed as she felt.

"Mornin'," he replied. "Figured I should call, since tone and clarity can be misconstrued via text."

"Uh, yes—yes, it can," she answered.

"I'm asking you out to dinner," he said. "I mean, it's not actually *out*. It's dinner at my mother's, but I want you to come with me."

Shit. That was worse than him asking to take her out to dinner. Wasn't it?

"Yvonne? You still there?"

"Uh, yes, yeah, I'm here." Acting like a goofball. She shook her head, forcing herself to get it together. "You want me to come over to your mother's for dinner? Tonight? Why?"

He chuckled. "Yes. Yes. And because you need to eat dinner, right?"

"I do, but I've been eating dinner right here with my sisters," she said.

"I know, but tonight I'd like you to eat dinner with me," he said. "And my family. If you want, I can ask your sisters if it's okay for you to go."

She smiled. "Don't be funny."

His response was to chuckle some more. "Look, it's dinner. Good food, nice people, a walk by the water. I know you like that."

She did like it, and he knew because he'd mentioned seeing her go for her daily walks along the shore every day. It was relaxing and gave her time to think of something other than all the worries in her life, so she'd made a point to take that walk every day. It was also good for her health, but she hadn't told anybody that.

"I can walk along the water here," she said.

"You can, but then I won't be there to hold your hand and share pleasant conversation with you."

"I don't need you to hold my hand and share pleasant conversation."

"Sure you do," he said. "You're just not ready to admit it. But before you launch into a whole spiel about me not flirting or what you do and don't need, just say yes. My mother's feelings will be hurt if I have to hang up this phone and tell her you declined."

She closed her eyes. "Ohhhh, that's so low," she said, finding herself enjoying this conversation a little more than she probably should've.

"I know," he said. "Did it work?"

There really was no reason for her to say no. It was just dinner, and she'd had meals with him before. If it was with his family, that was cool too. That didn't have to mean anything in particular. Just like she'd gone to dinner at Ms. Janie's, she could go to dinner at Deacon's mother's house. It would be fine. She hoped.

"Yeah, you knew it was going to work. I'm not here to be pissing off people who have fond memories of my family. I've gotta be respectful," she said.

"Such a good southern girl," he said.

"Except I'm really from the north," she shot back.

This was how their daily banter went—easy, light, sometimes funny, most times professional. Spending these past weeks in his company on a daily basis had been more pleasant than she would've thought having to deal with construction workers in and out of her personal space could've been. Then again, she'd already known that Deacon wasn't like other guys she'd met in the past. For one, she actually talked to him and didn't feel awkward or like she was forcing herself to get through the conversations.

"What time should I be ready?" she asked when she felt like she was sinking too deep into her thoughts about this again.

"Six, but I'm on my way to you now, so I can be there with the crew and the plumbers just in case something comes up."

"Is something supposed to come up?" she asked. "I thought they were just going to dig up that side of the house near the old oak so that the plumbers can look at the pipes."

"That's right, but you never know when you start digging things up. So I just want to be there in case decisions have to be made on the spot. You can come down and watch too."

"Uh, no, I don't think so. I think I'll go and catch the ferry into town for a bit. I need to get some things."

"Good. That'll be nice, since you haven't gone over since you've been here."

He was right—she hadn't. When she'd come here during those summers as a child, she'd never liked boarding the ferry to go into town either. This was her time away from the city and the hustle and bustle of people. Coming to Daufuskie had really been a vacation, from so many things that had weighed heavily on her. Even though this time was fraught with the grief of losing her grandmother and the stress over getting these renovations done and what to do with the house when they were done, there was still calm here for her. There was still a peace that she'd never gotten anyplace else. But she would go into town today because now she needed to get something to wear for tonight.

Chapter 19

YVONNE

It wasn't a date—she'd told herself that a kazillion times throughout the day. It was just a dinner that she wanted to look nice for, and she'd only packed jeans, capris, and shorts for this trip. That was why she'd gone over to Bluffton for a quick shopping trip, and that's also why she hadn't told either of her sisters what she was doing. Answering questions about this non-date wasn't something she wanted to do either.

By the time she'd returned late in the afternoon, Tami was sitting on the front steps, her spiral notebook on her lap, a pen in her right hand. Yvonne saw white buds in her ears and figured she was probably listening to music. Tami loved listening to music, dancing, and singing in her slightly off-key voice. It was one of the things Yvonne had always thought brought Tami closer to Grandma Betty than the rest of them.

Dropping her bags onto one of the steps below, Yvonne sat a couple of feet away from Tami. When Tami didn't look up or otherwise acknowledge her in any way, Yvonne reached out to tap her shoulder.

Now Tami's head came up. She'd pulled her natural hair into two Afro puffs that made her look like she was seven years old again. The sight had a smile ghosting Yvonne's lips. Her denim shorts were very short, her toenails painted a bright lime green in the white flip-flops on her feet. She had on a tank top that was almost the same shade of green as her toenails, and her eyes, when they landed on Yvonne, were guarded.

"Can we talk?" Yvonne asked, knowing that if Tami couldn't hear her, she could at least read her lips.

On a sigh, Tami reached over to her other side and picked up her phone. She swiped something across the screen—probably turning off whatever she was listening to—and then she pulled one of the buds out of her left ear since that was the side of her where Yvonne sat.

"I want to apologize for the other day," Yvonne began without preamble. During the forty-five-minute ride to the mainland, she'd thought about the fact that she'd been able to walk out of the house and not say a word to either of her sisters about where she was going.

Sure, she hadn't wanted to discuss the non-date with them, but she hadn't even left a note just in case one of them had a need to find her for something. They wouldn't need her—they never did. That was her logic, but a small part of her had acknowledged that she might be the cause of why they acted like they didn't need her.

"You shared something that I know wasn't easy for you, and I don't think I gave you the consideration that I should've," she continued before looking away from her sister.

Her gaze went forward to the fountain—or at least, the bowl of the fountain. The actual marble statue of the little girl pouring the water from a flower jug had been removed and taken to an antique shop in Bluffton for restoration. The landscape looked odd without the little girl standing there like a guard at the door of the summerhouse, and Yvonne felt an emptiness that she hadn't experienced before.

"I knew school was hard for you," she said after what seemed like endless moments. "I knew Mama was being extremely hard on you."

"Then why didn't you stand up for me more?" Tami asked.

Yvonne leaned forward, resting her elbows on her knees and bringing her hands together to clasp in front of her. She took a deep breath and released it slowly. "There were days that I tried to explain to Mama that it took you a little longer to get exactly what the teacher was asking you to do. And other times, when I'd try to explain why you'd forgotten to dust the tables in the living room or clean the baseboards in the kitchen."

"I never heard you say those things to her."

Shaking her head, Yvonne continued. "Because I didn't say them in front of you. I didn't want to appear disrespectful to Mama when she was disciplining you."

"Berating me," Tami said, her tone edgy.

Yvonne looked back over her shoulder at Tami. "Okay, she was berating you."

"And it seemed like it was always me. No matter what anybody else did in that house, I always got yelled at the worst. No matter how hard I tried, I wasn't good enough for her."

There was a sadness in Tami's voice that Yvonne had never heard before. Tami might've been the youngest of the Butler sisters, but Yvonne had always thought she was the strongest and the most resilient. She could stand in that kitchen, with tears rolling down her cheeks, while Mama disciplined—no, *berated* her—for one thing or another one minute, and a few hours later, Yvonne would see her lying on her stomach on the floor in the bedroom, playing with her dolls or coloring in one of the billions of coloring books she had. And while she did either of those things, her head would be bopping to the side, joy glittering in her eyes as she talked to the dolls or hummed some song while she colored. Like the words Freda had said to her a while before had simply dissipated in the air. It was that capability that Yvonne suspected irritated their mother more than anything else Tami ever did.

"You never acted like it bothered you," Yvonne said. "Never cried longer than the few minutes after a beating or a lecture. You just moved on."

"Until the next time," Tami said. "It's how I coped with the situation. I realize now that I developed several ways to cope with things at home that didn't make me feel loved or accepted, just like I eventually began adapting to things in school to mask my deficiencies there. I copied off Melissa Anderson's paper a lot in the sixth grade. In eighth grade, I started raising my hand first and asking a question—that way, Mr. Rubin wouldn't call on me in that moment that I didn't know the answer to something and then embarrass me because I didn't know."

"Oh, Tami," Yvonne said, and reached out a hand to grip her sister's.

When Tami didn't pull away but let Yvonne twine her fingers with hers, Yvonne sighed. "I wish I had all the training I eventually received in spotting children with learning or mental disabilities that I do now back then. I wish I'd been able to say to Mama that there was something wrong with you and that didn't mean that the something was a bad thing. But I was her child too."

"I know," Tami said, and nodded. "You were just so much better at doing what she said than me or Lana were."

"It was easier that way," Yvonne admitted. "If I just did what she said, she wouldn't look at me like I'd disappointed her. I guess I needed that approval." That empty part of her that had appeared at the sight of the missing statue started to form a pit in the center of her stomach as she wondered if she could continue to live for Freda's approval.

"We all wanted her approval," Tami said. "But only you got it." She shrugged. "After a while I think Lana just stopped caring and just did and said what she wanted. And for some reason, Mama didn't put up much of a fight with her."

"That was odd," Yvonne said, recalling the day Freda had told Lana she wouldn't be going to photography classes. Lana had calmly told her mother that was fine but that she would drop out of the modeling classes as well since that wasn't a career that could provide a stable and respectable living for her either. But for Freda, modeling would've been a spotlight for Lana to fill. A way for people to say, "Wow, look at Freda's daughter out there, looking amazing." And there was money to be made in modeling, even if it may have been only temporary—Freda had known that too. Before she could give in, though, one of the mentors at the modeling school had taken note of Lana's passion for photography and had called Freda to ask if she could continue to work with Lana free of charge.

"Yeah, a lot of things Mama did was odd," Tami said. "Like, did you notice how she never talked about Grandma Betty or Daddy? How, to her, neither of them existed even though she and Daddy were still co-parenting."

This wasn't the first time Yvonne had noted that fact. It was the first time she'd noted it in at least twenty years, though, and it was the second time today that it had crossed her mind. Freda had acted differently starting the year she'd gotten pregnant with Tami—or at least, that's when Yvonne thought she'd first noticed the change.

"I thought I was the only one who'd figured that out," Tami said with a little chuckle.

"Anyway," Yvonne said, still holding on to her sister's hand, "I wanted you to know that I'm sorry for not being there for you when we were young, and I guess in the years that followed. I also wanted to say that I think you're doing a great job here with the house. You've really taken charge of most of the decisions that need to be made, especially decor-wise, and I'm really proud of you."

Saying the words felt like a weight lifting from Yvonne's shoulders, but watching how Tami's face lit up after she'd spoken them was an unexplainable pleasure. Tami was a beautiful young lady, with pretty brown eyes, a pert little nose, and the prettiest smile. Watching the genuine happiness play out on those features now almost brought Yvonne to tears.

"You really mean that?" Tami asked.

"I do." Yvonne smiled. "Have you ever thought about going into interior design? I mean, I'm sure there're people out there that will appreciate that teal-watercolor-rosebud paper you insisted on for the powder room."

"Guuuurrrl, stop," Tami said, waving her free hand at Yvonne. "You know that room is the bomb now!"

Yvonne chuckled. "Yeah, you're right—now that Deacon and his crew have added that cheerful melon-colored paint you picked out, it is coming together."

"That's right," Tami said, holding her free arm over her head and moving the top half of her body like she was in a club, dancing. "I did that! I did that! You know it!"

Yvonne continued smiling. "You're a mess, girl," she said, then immediately followed it with, "And I wouldn't have you any other way."

Tami lowered her arm then and leaned in to wrap both her arms around Yvonne. "Thanks, sis. Your words mean a lot to me."

A few hours later, while Yvonne sat on the porch, waiting for Deacon to pick her up, she thought back to Tami's words and how poignant they were. If Yvonne's words had meant a lot to her, imagine how Tami would've felt if Freda had found it within herself to say something nice to Tami—or any of her other daughters, for that matter. And what if Lana could put into words whatever was going on between her and Isaac? Would talking about it make that situation better? The safer and more taxing question was, would saying the words Yvonne knew she needed to say to other people in her life lessen some of the stress and turbulence she felt brewing in her soul? Would it bring her and her sisters closer?

There was no more time to contemplate any of that as she watched Deacon's work truck pull to a stop in the driveway. His was one of very few vehicles on the island, and she suspected it was allowed because it was related to his work. It didn't bother her as much as it probably did others that there weren't many cars on the island. For her, it was part of Daufuskie's appeal. The portion of the island that had managed to remain untouched by the world, the dirt roads and mature trees, the scent of salt water floating on the warm summer's breeze—all those things made this place unique and homey in a way she doubted could be captured anywhere else.

"Well, you're looking awfully pretty for this to not be a date," Deacon said as he took the steps.

She'd stood from the rocking chair and met him at the top step, smoothing the material of the straight, white off-the-shoulder sundress she was wearing. Her thought in selecting that dress had been that it was simple enough with just that touch of dressy in the length, which stretched to her ankles. She'd paired it with a long gold chain with a whimsical crescent-moon piece and a gold cuff on her left wrist. Her Fitbit was always on her right wrist. The straw purse she carried was just big enough to hold a smaller pouch, where she kept her glucometer and test strips, along with her phone, lip gloss, and keys.

"I can say the same about you for this to be just dinner at your mama's house," she replied.

He looked as he always did: too damn fine. His deep skin tone was accented by the cream-colored button-front shirt he was wearing, with khaki slacks and crisp white tennis shoes that were a sharp contrast to the work boots she usually saw him in.

"Now, you know my mama would curse a blue streak if I came to dinner dressed in my work clothes." He chuckled, and butterflies took flight in the pit of her stomach.

She flattened a hand over the area, in shock over the sensation, and tried to keep her smile affixed.

He reached for her free hand and clasped it gently in his. "But seriously, you look really nice."

She hadn't styled her hair in any particular way, just washed and blow-dried it before adding a thin brown headband and letting it hang straight to her shoulders. Same for her face—she only wore mascara and her favorite peach lip gloss.

"Thank you," she said. "And you look really nice too."

With the hand that had been unsuccessfully trying to tame the butterflies, she reached out and tweaked the collar of his shirt. "I like you in something other than work clothes."

He grinned. "So my work clothes suck, huh?"

They started down the steps. "No, they definitely don't suck," she said, and prayed that the way she'd practically drooled over him in those rugged jeans or sweatpants—*especially* the sweatpants—T-shirts, and work boots on a daily basis wasn't noticeable in her tone.

The smug grin he gave her just before he released her hand and opened the passenger-side door said he'd noticed.

He turned on the radio as they rode the twenty minutes of curving dirt road until they arrived at his mother's house, so there was no more talking. But the moment he came around and opened the door for her, he took her hand and helped her out of the truck. She was about to say she could handle it herself, but she kind of liked this chivalrous side of him.

"Now, my sister, Emory—she talks a lot. And really fast too, but you might be used to that since you're from up north." He was still holding her hand after he closed the door and started walking her toward a lovely pale-gray house with a yellow golf cart parked in front of one of the windows. She kind of liked how comfortable it felt to walk hand in hand with him, even if a bit of nerves had begun to bubble up now that they were actually at his parents' house.

"You know you're not funny, right?" she asked with a smile. "I do not talk fast."

He shook his head. "Yeah, you do. And you've got that distinct Boston accent. I'm gettin' used to it now, but your summers on the island sure didn't do anything to curb that."

She was about to give him another snarky reply, but she had to stop walking and just take in the scenery. The house was old—she knew that because of the structure of it, similar to that one-level layout of Ms. Janie's. But it was obvious that some work had been done here, no doubt by Deacon. The roof was definitely newer, with shingles that looked more like those found in the city than what she'd seen on some of the other Daufuskie houses. And the siding was probably newer as well, but shutters on the windows and the door, all painted in a cheerful shade of light blue, were all Daufuskie. She'd seen doors and windows in this shade on other homes and had wondered if they'd all simply bought an abundance of this color paint at one time.

"Why blue?" she asked. "I guess I never really noticed it before when I was on the island, but I've seen it around a lot on this trip, so I was just wondering. It's really pretty. Reminds me of robin's-egg Easter candies."

"Oh, yeah, that. See, the color's called Heaven Blue, and the Gullah people who originated here on the island painted their doors and shutters this color to keep the haints—or evil spirits—from entering the house."

She scrunched her nose as she looked away from the house to him. "You serious?"

"As a heart attack," he replied. "And my mama still believes in it. Her great-grandfather was one of the freed slaves who'd worked the plantations here on the island. After the war, the cotton industry started to slow down, so he and some others who'd stuck around trying to make a way here on their own started oystering. Your great-great-grandfather used to do the same, right?"

Yvonne nodded, having heard a similar story about her family's origin on the island from Grandma Betty, who'd gotten all the details from Grandpa Riley before he'd passed away. "Yeah, that's true. Grandma Betty used to say how much she hated oysters, so whenever she was here on the island with Grandpa Riley, he'd only cook other seafood that he could catch for her. But there's so much about the Gullah culture that seems to be forgotten." Or that she didn't really know herself. In that moment, she felt like that was a horrible shame and something she needed to remedy.

"Not here on 'Fuskie," he said. "At least, that's what my mama would say if you mentioned that to her. This is her way of life, and she's not trading it for the world."

"How does she feel about you trading it for life in the city?"

They'd started walking toward the house again now, and Deacon was still holding her hand. She didn't know why she hadn't pulled away.

"I don't guess she feels any kind of way, considering how much I come back. My goal was never to leave the island and forget all my heritage. I wanted to make something of myself so I could bring more of our culture to the forefront. So when those big-resort people came sniffing around here, I went to school and got my degrees; then I came right back and started pitching to them ways they could make their resorts reflect more of our culture here instead of trying to bring their whitewashed world down to us."

"Oh, I bet that didn't go over too well," she said as he let her go up the three planked steps first.

"Not with everybody, but I've had a few contracts with them here and there. Mostly for some private cabins that are situated behind the main resort property. Several of them have the Heaven Blue doors and shutters, but in a much more modern-looking cabin. Still, they've hired some of the women from down here to cook in their kitchens."

"I bet they did. How else are they going to live up to the authentic Gullah cuisine they have advertised in their brochures?" she said.

"You two out here, just a-chatterin'." A boisterous woman with a wide smile and Deacon's dreamy eyes pulled the front door open and stepped out onto the porch. "Dinner's gettin' cold."

"We're right on time, Mama," Deacon said, looking at the watch on his wrist.

"'On time' is late in my house, Deacon Paul Williams, and you know dat. Who's this pretty one?"

"Hello," Yvonne said, stepping forward and extending her hand. "I'm Yvonne Butler. I'm . . ." She didn't get to finish the rest because—like Ms. Janie—Deacon's mother pushed her outstretched hand out of the way and stepped forward to fold Yvonne into a hug.

It wasn't nearly as forceful or uncomfortable as the hug from Ms. Janie, but it was still a very friendly one coming from a person she'd just met.

"You gotta be kiddin'," the woman said, pulling back but keeping her hands on Yvonne's shoulders.

They were just about the same height, but she was a little thinner than Yvonne's 152 pounds—and deceptively a hell of a lot stronger.

"This can't be Ms. Betty's grandbaby."

"It is, Mama, and you're gonna crush her if you hug her like that again." Deacon spoke evenly as he grinned. "Yvonne, this is my mother, Jolene."

Jolene was already shaking her head. "Folks 'round 'Fuskie just call me Mama Jo," she said, and grabbed Yvonne's hand. "And a good hug ain't nevah hurt nobody."

Yvonne could probably argue that, but she didn't. If nothing else, the woman's cheerful welcome was working to ease some of the jitters she'd started to feel. Not all of them, because this still felt like she was being presented to the family as more than a friend, but she was trying like hell not to let that overwhelm her.

An hour later, Yvonne was full from crab patties and butter beans. Mama Jo had also prepared what she called Sea Island Okra Gumbo, but since Yvonne had never liked okra, she'd passed on that part of the meal. She'd also passed on the carrot cake for dessert, asking if she could instead take a few pieces home to share with her sisters later. To that, Mama Jo had been elated. They were sitting in the small living room now: she and Deacon were on one couch; Emory, his sister, was across from them in a chair; and Mama Jo and Deacon's father—Paul Sr., they called him, even though Deacon wasn't a junior—sat on another couch.

"We're gonna miss Ms. Betty around here," Emory said. "She was our only star for the longest time."

Mama Jo nodded. "She sure was. I remember back in the sixties, we was listenin' to Smokey Robinson and the Temptations on those old battery-powered radios while the oil lamps glowed in the living room." She paused and gave them a serious glance with a nod. "Electricity and telephones and stuff took a while to trickle out here to us. But even when it came, not all of us could afford it right away."

Yvonne felt a pang of sadness at the fact that even when it had seemed like the world was moving forward, there'd been people—those who'd eventually become *her* people—down here, still left behind.

"We heard Ms. Betty's songs, but when Mr. Riley came back from one of his trips—you know he used to go around, trying to sell those things he carved from the old tree trunks in back of their house. Well, when he'd come home from one of those trips, he had Ms. Betty with him, lookin' like one of those shiny new dolls that used to be in the window at the stores over in Bluffton," Mama Jo continued.

Paul Sr. nodded. "Yup. Me and some other young fellas was helpin' him down at the docks one day and asked all kinds of questions 'bout how he was able to get such a good-lookin' woman, seeing as he could barely see good without his big ole glasses." He laughed.

The way Deacon clenched her hand said he didn't find what his father said that funny. "I think we're gonna head out now," he hurriedly said.

But Yvonne wasn't bothered by Paul Sr.'s words. To the contrary, she was intrigued to hear another side of the story of how her grandparents came to be. Of course, Grandma Betty had shared the story when they were younger, leaving Tami with a starry-eyed gaze and Lana with wedding dreams floating in her mind. But for Yvonne, it had been all about the times the two of them were together, the feelings she could still see in her grandmother's eyes as she spoke about the love of her life and how many times she'd wondered if she'd ever feel that for herself.

"Oh, well, no, wait a minute," Mama Jo said before getting up from her seat. "I've got something for Yvonne."

Deacon passed his mother a baleful look, and Emory sucked her teeth. His sister wasn't as tall as Deacon, and her skin was a few shades lighter, but she had her father's smile and her mother's sandy-brown hair. "I don't know why you're acting like that. You knew she was going to be excited. If you'd bring more of your girlfriends home to meet her, she wouldn't have to act like this was such a monumentous occasion."

"I'm not his girlfriend," Yvonne quickly replied, and Emory's brow went up.

"This here used to belong to your grandmother," Mama Jo said when she came back into the room. She walked over to Yvonne and put the multicolored beaded purse in her hands. "When Mr. Cab and Ms. Dessa had a second wedding, they wanted everybody to dress up like we were fancy. I was just a young girl then, barely sixteen, so I only had a couple of dresses that I wore to church. But I'd saved up some nickels that I made sewing for people. So I was on the ferry one day, heading over to Bluffton to find me some fancy things, and who did I look up to see on the same ferry but Ms. Betty."

Yvonne had been running her fingers over the beads, which seemed to shimmer in the lamplight. It looked like something her grandmother would carry, and the thought had unexpected tears springing to Yvonne's eyes. "Grandma Betty always told us she hated riding on the ferry and going into town. That's why she had all the things she needed shipped over here."

Mama Jo shook her head. "Not back then. Ms. Betty shopped a lot, and she would get right on that ferry at the drop of a dime. You know, during the times she was here with Mr. Riley and not going around the world touring." She sat back down, and Paul Sr. put his arm across the back of the couch behind her. "Anyway, Ms. Betty wondered why I was traveling all by myself, and when I told her my mama was busy with cookin' and my sister was busy with runnin' 'round after her man, Ms. Betty just chuckled. Then she said she'd keep an eye on me. And shoot, I didn't mind. I got to spend the day with a star." Mama Jo's eyes lit up. "We shopped all afternoon and talked. I believe that was the start of our friendship, although she was a lot closer to Ms. Dessa than anybody else on the island. But that day, Ms. Betty said she had the perfect purse to go with the dress I bought. So when we got off the ferry, I went up to that big ole pretty house with her."

"And you're just returning her purse after all this time. Dang, Mama, that's rude," Emory said and grinned.

Deacon rubbed a finger over his forehead, and Paul Sr. chuckled. Yvonne remained silent as that wave of sadness she'd just experienced passed, and instead she found herself kind of agreeing with Emory. Not that she was offended in any way. To the contrary, she was mostly amused by this easy, laid-back family vibe she'd been getting from them the past couple of hours.

"I just forgot about it, I guess, and I think Ms. Betty did too. Or she probably had so many purses and things, she just didn't worry about it. Your daddy, Daniel, he was around my age. I think he might've been a year older than me. And one time, Ms. Betty had even suggested to him that he take me out, but I already had my eyes set on Paul Sr., so that wasn't happenin'."

"You got that right it wasn't happenin'," Paul Sr. said. "I would've put my foot up his—"

"That's it," Deacon said, cutting his father off. "We're leaving."

Now Yvonne bit back a grin as Deacon hurried to take her hand and help her to her feet. "It's okay. I understand, Mr. Paul," she said, because she couldn't bring herself to call this man Paul Sr. when there was no logical reason for the name. "I totally understand you protecting what's yours."

When the older man stood, he pushed Deacon out of the way and pulled Yvonne in for a hug. "That's 'cause you're a smart girl," he said. "Just like my Jolene."

Mama Jo hugged her next. "You come on back whenever you feel like it. And don't be afraid to call me if you need something. I know Deacon's up there working on the house, so if you just need to get away to some quiet, or you need me to fix you and your sisters something to eat, just give me a call."

The offer of some quiet stood out way more than the offer to fix food, which Yvonne knew Tami would disagree with if she were here. "Thank you," Yvonne said. "Thanks so much for your kindness. Everyone here has always been so kind to us." And that was true: everyone on the island—with the exception of Sallie and Cora, whose attitudes Yvonne still didn't get—had been more than sweet and generous with them since their arrival. She liked how that felt, this sense of community coming together to take care of their own . . . or the descendants of one of their own.

"That's what we do here," Mama Jo said. "We take care of our own. Now, Deacon, you get her on home. She's looking a little tired now."

She was feeling tired; traveling back and forth on the ferry had been a lot, and then she'd just had a very heavy meal. A hot shower and her bed were definitely calling to her.

"We didn't get a chance to take our walk," Deacon said when they once again stood on the front porch at the summerhouse.

"No," she said with a sigh. "We didn't. But I'll walk in the morning after breakfast."

He grasped both her hands and leaned his butt against the railing of the porch, pulling her closer to him. She didn't know what it was about this man and her hands, but she could never seem to pull away from him. Even now, when she knew she was standing way too close to him, she made no move to get away.

"Is that an invitation for me to join you?" he asked, his voice going lower.

She narrowed her eyes, not nearly as averse to the suggestion as she probably should be. "I don't think that's what I said."

He grinned. "You're making this really hard."

"Making what hard? This wasn't a date, remember?" It seemed as if she was much better at reminding him of this than keeping herself convinced of the fact. Tonight had definitely felt like a date, one of the most enjoyable ones she could recall, and part of her desperately wanted a repeat. That part needed to meet the more realistic part of her that said getting romantically involved with this guy was a mistake. She wasn't interested in a long-distance romance; they both deserved better than that.

"You're right: this wasn't a real date," he conceded. "But I'm trying to work up to one, if you'd stop blocking me every time I try to shoot my shot."

Laughing, she shook her head. "That's not what I'm doing."

"It is, and you're damn good at it," he told her. "Good thing my ego can take it."

"I like you, Deacon," she said, opting for honesty because she was too tired for anything else. "But there's no need in us working up to a date when I'm gonna be heading back to the city soon."

"In eight weeks," he said with a nod. "The plumbers may've hit a snag earlier today, but they're supposed to get back to me with a definite solution on Monday."

Her brow furrowed. "A snag? What? Nobody told me that. Why didn't you call me?"

"Tami was here, and we talked about solutions and the timeline." He brought her hands up to kiss the backs of them. "Don't worry until we know if there's something to worry about."

"Tami handled it?"

He nodded. "Yeah. She's really good at this, you know."

"I do know. I told her that earlier today."

"Good," he said. "From what I've learned about her in the month since y'all have been here, she likes to act like she doesn't need anybody's approval, but she appreciates the validation. Just like everybody else, I guess."

"She does," Yvonne said. "And unfortunately, she didn't get enough of it during her childhood. So thank you for seeing her and appreciating her."

"That's absolutely no problem at all. If she wasn't anxiously waiting to hear back from that job she interviewed for before coming down here, I'd offer her a job at my company. It'd be great to have an in-house designer."

"Wow, you think she's that good? I mean, I just mentioned being a designer to her this afternoon, but you really believe she could do it?"

"Definitely," he said. "And if she takes your suggestion, I'm gonna need you to make sure she comes to see me first before taking a job anywhere else."

Yvonne smiled. "Will do, sir."

"But back to what I was saying about shooting my shot with you."

She eased a hand from his and touched her fingers to his lips. "Don't," she said. "Really, Deacon, as much I wish this were a different time and place so I could finally let myself explore a real relationship, this is not the best time."

He kissed her fingers, and Yvonne hurriedly pulled them back. Once again, the smirk that covered his face told her he knew why she'd pulled away so quickly: because she was feeling exactly what he was.

"Besides our location, tell me your other reasons for turning me down," he said. His tone was so gentle, not at all hurt or defensive—just curious, she guessed.

"Because I'm my mother's sole caretaker, and that takes up all of my spare time," she said.

And because I might be on my way to needing a caretaker at some point in my life as well. Even though she knew that was a horribly negative thought to have. She was doing a good job maintaining her diabetes and high blood pressure, so there was no reason to think that might change. Then again, there was every reason to believe it might. Having both conditions put her in risk groups for certain other, more serious conditions that she didn't want to ponder right now.

He nodded. "Yeah, you told me she had a stroke a few years ago, and I get that. I'd do anything for my parents too. But you still deserve a life of your own. You know, some time to take walks with good-looking men, maybe go to fancy restaurants, or possibly even go away to foreign places to see new things."

Yvonne couldn't help it—she grinned because, despite everything going on around her, this man made her feel giddy and excited. And other things she hadn't thought she'd ever feel. "And I'm sure you have a specific good-looking man in mind for me to do all those things with."

He smirked. "Well, I mean, I'll just say you don't have to look that far. Like, he could be standing right in front of you if you'd just open your eyes."

But Yvonne's eyes were wide open. She did see Deacon and all his physical fineness. She also saw what she thought was a good man who loved his family, was devoted to his people, and took pride in his work. At another time in her life, he would've been perfect. Now . . . well, she wished he could be perfect now too.

"You get these lines in your forehead when you're starting to worry over something," he said, and then leaned in to softly kiss the lines he was presumably referring to. "Go to bed, Yvonne. Get a good rest, and I'll meet you back here in the morning for that walk."

He didn't wait for her to respond but instead gently released the hand he was still holding and eased away. She watched him walk toward the steps and then to his truck, stood on the porch until the headlights from the vehicle were no longer visible. And then she sighed. Not that weary kind of sigh that went along with the weight of the world on her shoulders. But a dreamy kind of sigh, the one she thought might go with a woman falling for a man.

Chapter 20

TAMI

"Think positive."

Why did those words sound better coming from his mouth? How many times had she told herself the exact same thing today? Yesterday? Last week?

"No news could mean good news . . . eventually," Gabriel continued when Tami still hadn't responded.

"Or no news could mean this is why they needed an executive assistant, because there's nobody there to send out that form-rejection email response." She knew she was being a Negative Nancy, and that was so unlike her. But it was also a natural reaction to waiting almost four weeks to hear back from a job interview. "It's just that I want this so much. I've never wanted anything else like this."

"Even me? Because I distinctly recall one night about six months ago when you sent that 'I want you, I need you' booty-call text."

Laughter exploded from her, and she fell back against the pillows in her bed. "One time," she said through loud guffaws. "And in my defense, I was drunk from those weak-ass Jell-O shots Shana had made."

He was chuckling now too. "They were strong enough to get you drunk."

"Only after I had like twenty of them," she countered, turning her lips up at the memory.

"Well, you were sober enough to jump me two seconds after I got to your room and rode us both into oblivion."

Her pussy twitched at that part of the memory. With any other guy she'd slept with, that comment might've seemed weird—or at the very least, uncomfortable, since she rarely participated in sex talk during or after with any of her previous lovers. But Gabriel was no other guy. He never had been.

"Yes, I definitely did," she said, remembering bits and pieces of that night. Mostly, the pieces that included Gabriel filling her so completely, in more ways than just the physical.

That had been the first time she'd felt that way about him. The first time she'd wondered if the friendship—which had started with her locking herself out of her apartment and him being the one to come up from the management office with the spare key—could be something more. By morning she'd let those thoughts fade with the night. Especially since Gabriel had a date with the new clerk at Walgreens that next evening. He'd sent Tami a text that afternoon, long after he'd left her apartment—when she'd still been telling herself that destroying their unique friendship by entertaining the idea of something more serious with him was ludicrous—asking if he should still go. He'd said he really wasn't feeling the woman like that and didn't want to waste her time. And Tami had responded by telling him to take a chance. "You never know where this one date might lead," she'd said. Because even if she was too mixed up in the head to figure out what she did and didn't want from him, she still wanted to see him happy.

"I could come down to that island of yours," he said, his gruff voice pulling her from the memory. "Bring some Jell-O and help you relieve some of the stress you're carrying because of that job."

Why did that sound better than any other proposition a guy had ever made to her?

"You're a goof," she replied, and let her hand fall to her stomach. Her tank top had risen up when she lay down, so her fingers brushed the bare skin of her midriff, sending an odd chill up her spine.

"Nah," he said. "I'm serious. All you have to do is say the word, and I'll be there. I kinda hate that I'm too far away to help you get through this."

He sounded so serious, so sincere.

"You've been helping me through one crisis after another in the year that I've known you. Aren't you tired yet?"

"Nope. I like being here for you. And I like knowing you're here for me."

"That's right, because the majority of the booty-call texts between us have been initiated by you." She was trying to keep this suddenly heavy conversation light. Trying to maintain the uncomplicated rapport they'd both come to count on.

"Because I'm obviously the one who accepts how good we are together," he said.

"Gabriel—" she started, but he cut her off.

"Ah, c'mon, Tam, don't do that."

"Don't do what?"

"Don't say my name like you're getting ready to start some bullshit."

"Whoa, wait a minute. You don't know what I was getting ready to say."

"Bet I do," he said, and then, before waiting for her to respond, he continued, "We're just friends with benefits. Remember, we decided that's what we were going to be." She suspected the high-pitched tone he was using was supposed to be mimicking hers, but Tami wasn't amused.

"If you know the truth, then why are we having this conversation?"

"Because you know that truth has long since changed. I haven't been with another woman in six months," he told her. "And unless you've been lying to me—which I know you haven't 'cause that's not who you are—you haven't been with anybody else either."

"First," she said, feeling her mouth go dry but forging on anyway, "that's not true; you went out with that Walgreens clerk right after my drunken booty call."

"I went out with her, but I didn't sleep with her. I haven't slept with another woman since your drunken booty call."

"Oh." That statement hit her unexpectedly. "Well, that's not true, either, because you and I slept together that night of my interview when you brought over the pizza."

"*You*, Tami. I've slept with you and only you in the last six months."

She knew that's what he'd meant; she just didn't like the spurt of joy that had soared through her at his admission. She sighed. "I can't talk about this right now," she said. "It's out of the blue, and it's uncomfortable, and I have so much other stuff going on. I've got to get through these renovations with my sisters. Lana's acting weird. Yvonne's probably sleeping with the contractor. No, I take that back—Yvonne's not bold enough to sleep with the guy, but I know she likes him and he likes her." And that wasn't the line of conversation she wanted to circle back to with him. "We might have plumbing problems, although I hope not, because Lana will lose her shit and Yvonne might just say to hell with it and put the house on the market as is."

She paused long enough to move her hand from her midriff and rub her fingers over her now-throbbing forehead.

"Stop," he said, with more bass than he normally used when talking to her. At another time, she might've thought that was a little sexy. Tonight, it was just more confusing. "Just stop and take a breath. I'm not asking you for a commitment tonight, Tami. I'm just saying I think we need to stop skirting around this thing that we both know is growing stronger between us."

She sighed again, this time closing her eyes. She should say something, do something, decide something. But she couldn't.

"Look, I'm sorry," he said when she remained silent. "I'm sorry if me bringing this up has upset you. That's the last thing I want." He sighed, frustration clear in the sound, and she felt awful for being the cause of it. "But I want to be with you, and I've tried to go along with your 'friends with benefits' only mantra, but I don't want to do that anymore. And I just thought it was time I just said it."

"And what if I don't want the same thing? Do I lose my best friend?" she asked, hating how her heart had started to thump wildly in her chest while she waited for a response.

"I . . . ," he started, but she shook her head and cut him off.

"No. No. Don't answer that. Just . . . don't." She kept her eyes closed, like it would somehow make the painfully irritating conversation go away. "Can we just talk about this when I get back? That may not be a fair thing for me to ask, but I can't . . . I just need to . . ." She didn't know what she needed to do. All she knew was that she didn't want to lose him, and she didn't want to commit to something that she wasn't sure she could handle.

"Tami, baby, listen to me," he said. "We can stop talking about it. I don't like hearing you sound so off-balance. Just . . . if you could just breathe. Tackle one thing at a time. How are your plans for the kitchen coming along? Did Deacon go for the change in the style of cabinets you wanted?"

And just like that, Gabriel had done what he was somehow always able to do with her—calm her, assuage her, see her.

The remainder of their conversation consisted of talk about cabinets, floor types, and backsplash. Gabriel had started watching the shows on HGTV that Tami told him she watched, so he knew all the jargon and had even added some suggestions of his own. Not that she was taking any of his suggestions, because they were stark, modern ideas that she didn't think would fit in with the almost-rustic vibe she considered their Lowcountry theme to be. But by the time they said good night, they were on an even keel again. She wasn't feeling overwhelmed or afraid—she only felt happy to have such a good friend.

☒

Hours later, Tami tossed and turned in bed, her dreams causing as much anxiety as the reality she lived in.

She'd spent years hating this woman, hours wondering what she could have possibly done in a former life to be cursed with the life she'd been given. The youngest child of parents who'd divorced a year after she was born. A tumultuous childhood partially due to a delayed diagnosis of ADHD, years of therapy to just get her to a point where she wasn't being suffocated by depression every day. And now this.

She still held the phone in her hand, unable to throw it out of the window or put it back to her ear to hear the rest of what Yvonne had said. She'd checked out of the conversation right after her sister had said, "Mama's had a stroke. She's at Gaithersburg Memorial."

Everything had stopped at that moment. Whatever she'd been doing, she'd forgotten. She breathed—she knew because she could feel the rise and fall of her chest, could hear the quickened beat of her heart. Her eyes blinked because warm tears rolled down her cheeks. And she wanted to scream with the deceiving pain that ripped through her chest.

Her mother, Alfreda Hanson-Butler, the woman who could do no wrong. The esteemed multidegree-holding superintendent of the Lehigh County School system. The strongest and smartest Black woman Tami knew, coming before only her sister Yvonne.

She'd had a stroke.

Was she going to die?

Would her mother know if Tami came to the hospital or not?

Would she survive if her mother passed away?

She couldn't breathe now, could still hear the incessant thumping of her heart, but it sounded so far away, like she was in a dark tunnel and running so fast, just running and leaving everything behind. Leaving this pain that had snuck up on her so fast and ripped through her chest like a sharp, familiar blade.

Familiar. This felt all too familiar. It felt like the night she'd been called to the hospital because her father had died.

Daddy had been gone for twenty-one years, and she'd continued to live this life with just one parent. The parent who'd never loved her like her father had. Who most likely hadn't loved her at all. What was she going to do if her mother died? Who would she be then: the orphan who hadn't been enough to keep her father in the house with his family, or the daughter who'd never been good enough for her mother?

A loud crackle of thunder jerked Tami awake, and she shot up in bed. Through barely open eyes, she saw the bright slash of lightning as it ripped through the sky and brightened her room momentarily.

Sometime after she'd fallen asleep, it had begun to rain. When she'd been out today, she'd seen Ms. Janie on her way back from some meeting she'd had at the church. Cora, with her sourpuss face, had been with her, but Tami had stopped to talk to both of them anyway. Ms. Janie had mentioned that rain was coming even though it had been a bright sunny day. Well, it seemed that along with being a great cook, Ms. Janie could also predict the weather.

Rain pelted the windows as Tami sighed and dropped her head. Residuals from the dream still weighed heavily on her mind. Why was it the best dreams—like the one where she had her legs wrapped around Michael B. Jordan's waist and was screaming his name like a banshee in heat—never stuck with her after awaking, but the worst ones hung around like ghosts haunting an old mansion? She rubbed at her eyes, hoping to scrub away the urge to cry all over again. Like she had the night she found out her mother had had that stroke. She'd cried and cried for almost an hour over the woman who'd never given her anything but heartache. Then she'd washed her face, gotten dressed, and taken her ass to the hospital. And Freda had lived.

She lived and breathed only to keep taunting Tami with her disapproving gazes and hurtful words. But Freda wasn't here now. She'd never been at the summerhouse when Tami had been there. When Grandma Betty had been here. Her grandmother was gone now, and Tami hadn't cried for hours. Not since she'd been here, and not when she'd received the call over a month ago.

Yes, she'd been heartbroken, and she'd shed some tears, but what she'd done not even an hour after hearing of her grandmother's death was pull up one of her old albums on her phone and listen to it. That had been her comfort. It had been her reminder of something Grandma Betty had said to her after her father's death: "I'll never leave you, Tami. You don't have to worry about that, because you'll always carry me here and here." Her grandmother had tapped her jeweled fingers over Tami's heart and then her ears that sunny morning at the church.

So the loss of her hadn't hit her like the loss of her father had, or like the almost loss of her mother had, because Grandma Betty was still with her.

Another long roar of thunder was followed by a fierce crackle of lightning, and Tami jumped again. But this time, she threw off the blankets and hopped out of bed. She didn't even stop to put on her slippers—just ran for the door, opened it, and darted down the hall.

She knew exactly where she was going and exactly why she was going there. Her hand was on the knob of the bedroom door, and she immediately turned it before pushing the door open. Then she was across the room and hopping onto the bed and under the covers before the next rumble of thunder came.

"What the . . ." Yvonne rolled over, slamming a pillow into Tami's face.

"Hey! Stop it! Stop it! It's just me!" Tami yelled with her arms up, covering her face.

"What . . . Tami?"

"Yeah," Tami said, and then pushed away the pillow Yvonne held just inches from her face. "It's me."

"What are you doing in here? What time is it?" Her sister turned to look at the lighted screen of the digital clock on her nightstand.

"I don't know," Tami said. "But it's thundering and lightning, and you know I don't like storms."

Yvonne pushed the pillow she'd been using as a weapon back behind her head and lay on it. "It's three o'clock in the morning, Tam. And you're twenty-nine years old, not nine."

"And the sky is blue, and the Yankees are a better team than the Red Sox—tell me something else I don't already know." Tami turned on her left side and pulled the covers up to her neck. "We can go back to sleep now."

Yvonne sighed. "Really? With your grown ass sleeping in the bed with me?"

"Mm-hmm. Night night," Tami murmured.

Behind her, Yvonne sighed again, but she didn't say good night in return. She suspected her sister just pouted as she lay there, attempting to go back to sleep. But that wasn't going to happen anytime soon because there was another clap of thunder and, seconds later, another round of footsteps coming down the hall.

"Scoot over," Lana mumbled when she came into the room on Yvonne's side of the bed.

"What? You've got to be kidding me? Both of you are still afraid of thunderstorms?" Yvonne asked as she huffed and puffed and scooted her ass over to the middle of the bed so Lana could get in.

"And thundersnow," Lana said. "Basically, anything with thunder wrecks my nerves. I can't stand it."

"Me either," Tami added.

"You're both goofballs, and I hate being in the middle." Yvonne groaned.

Tami chuckled. "You always hated it."

"Yup, you sure did," Lana said. "But you were the big sister, so you had to be in the middle so you could comfort both of us."

"I wanted to stuff both of you in the closet so I could get some sleep. You never stopped talking when you got into my bed," Yvonne complained, but Tami could hear the hint of laughter in her voice.

That had Tami turning over on her back and flattening her arms over the covers. "You remember that night it was storming out, and Mama had some late meeting thing at school? We were all in your bed, eating popcorn and drinking Kool-Aid, knowing Mama would've killed us if she knew we had food and drinks in the bedroom."

Lana turned onto her back too, and giggled. "Yes! That was so much fun. It felt dangerous. I was so scared."

"That didn't stop you from eating most of the popcorn," Yvonne said.

"Well, it was caramel. Y'all know that's my favorite," Lana said.

"Not mine," Tami added. "It always stuck to my teeth. I liked the white cheddar cheese better."

"Do you two see what you're doing?" Yvonne asked. "You're doing the exact opposite of going back to sleep."

Tami lifted up slightly and looked over Yvonne to Lana. "Do you think that's what we're doing, Lana?"

Lana lifted up too, glancing over at Tami. "Maybe." She shrugged and then said, "Probably."

Tami giggled. "Definitely."

Yvonne groaned. "I hate you both."

The three of them laughed, and it felt like that first day they'd been in this house, when the kitchen sink had exploded all over them. That unmitigated enjoyment of each other. With all their flaws and misconceptions, in that moment, they'd just been happy together. Just like tonight.

After a few moments, after Tami had sobered, she bit down on her bottom lip for a second, wondering if what she was about to do was the right thing. It could spoil the great moment between them. Cause one or both of them to get angry about her keeping it from them. Then there'd be an argument, because she had every right to keep it from them since usually everything she did or said, they had a problem with. Why should she put herself through that unnecessarily? Especially since it wasn't that big of a deal. But it was something that she hadn't told them, and it had been nagging at her for weeks now.

So, with a heavy sigh, she just blurted it out. "I found a box of letters in Grandma Betty's room."

"What?" Yvonne asked.

"When?" Lana's question came right behind Yvonne's.

"A couple of weeks ago," Tami said, her fingers clenching the sheets in front of her. "I couldn't sleep, so I went to her bedroom like I used to do when we were here and the two of you were busy doing whatever you did that you never wanted me to be a part of."

"Like sleeping," Yvonne muttered.

Lana chuckled. "Did you read the letters? What did they say? Were they love letters?"

"Oh. My. Goodness. You did not read freaky letters Grandma Betty got from her admirers? Or worse, Grandpa Riley." Yvonne sounded properly mortified, and Tami couldn't help but laugh.

"No, girl. Ewwww. I wouldn't have read those," she said, and then after a brief silence, continued. "Yeah, I would've definitely read those."

Lana was still laughing. "I know you would've."

"But no, it was nothing like that. There were some notes she'd written to herself, I guess, talking about how important it was for us to be here with her every summer and how much we meant to her." She'd read those notes repeatedly because they'd solidified the connection she'd always felt with her grandmother and had bolstered her desire to do everything in her power to keep this house in their family.

"But most of the ones I read were letters she'd received from fans, I guess, and a few from Grandpa, I think when he was away on his sales trips or while she was away on tours and stuff." Tami sighed. After the conversation she'd had with Gabriel tonight, her grandparents' love seemed enviable.

Tami had never seen her parents happy together, and by the time she was born, her grandfather had already passed away, so she'd never seen firsthand what a healthy, loving romantic relationship looked like. So how could she ever have one of her own?

"But there was one that seemed odd," she said. "It was from Ms. Odessa."

"Why would Ms. Odessa, who lived right down the road, write Grandma Betty a letter?" Lana asked.

"Well, Mama Jo—that's Deacon's mother—she said that it took a while for things to trickle down to the island. Like electricity and phones and stuff like that. So maybe the letter was written when there weren't any phones," Yvonne said.

"But couldn't they have just walked to each other's house, met at the halfway point in the road? I don't know. It just seems peculiar that they'd be writing each other letters," Lana said.

"When did you get so close to Deacon's mother that you started calling her Mama Jo?" Tami asked, extremely interested in what seemed like a new development between Yvonne and their contractor.

"That's a good question," Lana added.

Yvonne moved, pulling on the pillows so that a little more of the four that were on the bed were in the middle beneath her. "I went to dinner at his mother's house tonight. And before you ask more questions, the food was delicious. I brought you both back some carrot cake. He has a sister who's really nice, a daddy who's just as handsome as Deacon is—and no, I'm not sleeping with him."

"You could've just started with that last part," Lana said.

"Really." Tami sighed. "Because you should probably just go ahead and sleep with the man. Put y'all both out of y'all's sexually frustrated misery."

"What?" Yvonne nudged Tami. "I am not sexually frustrated."

"Gurl, you are wound tighter than a violin cord," Lana said.

"I know, right!" Tami couldn't help but chime in. "And it's not like you didn't bring your little toys with you, but I swear they must not be working, because you be staring at Deacon like you want to sop him up with a biscuit all day long."

Lana laughed so loud and long Tami thought Yvonne was going to push both of them out of the bed.

"First of all, little girl, you are still nosy as hell. How did you know what was packed in my bag? And second, I do not stare at him all day long. I get just as much work done around here as the two of you do." Yvonne's ire was clouded by the laughter tingeing her voice.

"Noooo," Lana cut in, still a little out of breath from her laughing fest. "You definitely be eyeing that guy. But it's cool, because I've seen him watching you the same way. And what's wrong with that? You're both consenting adults. I say go for it."

"I say that too," Tami added.

"What you didn't say was how you knew what was in my suitcase," Yvonne continued.

Tami chuckled. "I have the right to remain silent and not incriminate myself."

Their chatter went on for another hour or so, and by seven o'clock, Yvonne's ridiculously early alarm was going off, and the three of them jumped out of bed, getting the day started way too early.

Chapter 21

LANA

"Termites!" Lana screeched. "This house has freakin' termites!"

Deacon stared at her for a moment—his brows raised, eyes wide—before he shook his head and held up both hands. "I'm not gonna tell you to calm down, because I've learned from my sister that it's not the best thing to say to a woman."

When Lana's, Yvonne's, and Tami's brows raised, he cleared his throat.

"Shit. What I meant was, you're entitled to your feelings, and I respect them." He lowered his hands and then turned away from all three of them.

"See," he said when he stopped walking near the corner of the house, where it looked like someone had run one of those golf carts into it, creating a crumbling hole of wood and cracked siding. "Tami was here on Saturday when Hitch, Jamie, and Frank dug up this trench, and then because of what they saw down below—"

"Termites," Tami said with a nod.

"Wait, you've known we've had termites for two days, and you just didn't think that was something you should mention to us?" Lana asked, shooting her gaze at Tami now.

"Is this the problem you told me you were getting a solution to the other night? Because right now I'm not hearing a solution—I'm just seeing a huge hole in the house and an even bigger hole in the ground, which we conveniently managed to avoid during our walk yesterday," Yvonne said.

"Ladies," Deacon said in a stern tone that had all of them clapping their mouths shut. Then, because he was probably thinking better of that too, he ran a hand down his face. "Yes, there's a termite problem. We believe it's isolated in this area of the house."

"How do you know that? You haven't ripped up any more parts of the house without telling us, have you? Are there more holes in the ground around the estate?" Lana asked.

Deacon shot her a glare, then relaxed his shoulders. "Look, me and the guys spent this morning going around the entire house, checking small portions to see if there was any evidence of further infestation. We didn't find any, but just to be sure, we called the professionals, and they're coming out first thing tomorrow morning to further assess." He stepped away from the house and slipped his hands into the front pockets of his jeans. "What I can tell you today is that the plumbing work that we knew from the start was needed is going to run us roughly twelve thousand. Now, we only had eight in the budget for this, but we're moving the laundry room upstairs, so we have to run piping up there now."

Lana swore and rubbed her fingers over her temples. She hadn't had a headache in a couple of days, but she still felt like crap and desperately wanted to go home.

"How much do you think the termite termination is going to cost?" Yvonne asked. "Because I'm presuming we're not moving forward with anything else until that's done."

"A really rough estimate, I'd say about nine thousand, just because we'd want to thoroughly fumigate this area of the house and the ground. Then we have to replace the structure here and here." He pointed to the gutted-out portions of the house. "Replace the siding—we were already painting the entire house, so that's no extra charge over here. The biggest issue is going to be the time setback while we wait for this to get done to finish up the plumbing. Hitch and I've been working on revising the schedule so we can get some of the final touches on some of the other rooms done while we wait. Paint the main living room and the parlor and the foyer. The wainscoting you wanted in the dining room is in, so we can get that installed. I think the new drapes are in too, so they can be hung. So what I'm saying is, there's stuff we can do to try and keep as much moving as possible while we take care of this issue."

"Okay, that sounds doable," Tami said. "I wanted to talk to you about Grandma Betty's room and changing out the fixtures in her private bathroom."

"What! Are you serious?" Lana asked. "You're just going to start talking about doing something else when we haven't figured out how we're going to come up with the money to do all of this? Termite treatment definitely wasn't in our budget."

"No, it wasn't, Lana." Yvonne started coming over to stand next to her. Lana knew that tone: her older sister was about to start consoling her, and the last thing she wanted was to be consoled. She wanted this damn renovation to be over with.

She was tired of waking up every morning to banging, and she was tired of eating every single thing that Ms. Janie—or now, Mama Jo—was sending over for them. She was annoyed at not having a Starbucks down the block, where she could just take a ten-minute walk to get a venti caramel macchiato with extra caramel. She missed rolling over and feeling Isaac's warm body throughout the night. Missed her chair by the window in their bedroom where she could sit and stare out at the city.

"We can talk about the budget," Yvonne continued. "But I think right now, the important thing is to keep the guys working on what they can. We don't want to get any further behind than this is already going to put us."

"How can you say that?" Lana asked, knowing she sounded like she was overreacting. The way her sisters and Deacon were looking at her made that perfectly clear. But she wasn't. This was exactly what she'd been afraid would happen: extra expenses—and once they started, they'd become like an avalanche, burying the three of them instead of rescuing Lana and her marriage the way she'd prayed this house would. "I told you this would happen. I told you we were getting in over our heads and we should've just sold this house from the start."

"And *we* decided that we were going to try and do what Grandma Betty wanted," Tami countered.

"That's what *you* want, Tami. You don't know what the hell Grandma Betty wanted, with her cryptic will and these ridiculous instructions she's fed everybody." Lana wanted to just run upstairs and pack her bags, but she knew that wasn't possible. Just as she knew her yelling and being so disagreeable today wasn't going to change a damn thing. They were too far into this renovation to turn back now. They'd have to see it through to the end, even if it ended up breaking each one of them.

"Okay," Yvonne said, putting a hand on Lana's shoulder. "I'm not afraid to tell you to calm down." Her sister was speaking in her motherly tone now, and it irked Lana, but she didn't say anything in response. "We're going to head back into the house, get us a cup of tea, and sit down and talk about this rationally. And we'll figure it out, Lana. You know we always figure things out."

"No," she said quietly. "*You* always figure things out, Yvonne. That's your job. We just decide if we're going to follow along or not."

It was unfair and she knew it, and she wanted to take the words back just as soon as they'd tumbled out of her mouth, but she couldn't.

Yvonne dropped her hand from Lana's shoulder. "I'm going to the house. You coming, Tami?"

"Right behind you," Tami said.

"Good," Yvonne replied. "Deacon, you and your crew move on with your work. Let me know what time the termite people will arrive tomorrow. I want to be here."

"I'll be here too," Tami said.

Then the two of them walked away without looking back or waiting for Lana to follow.

When they were gone, she let her head fall back. "Dammit!" she cursed.

"At the risk of angering you any further, I'm going to just say that the cup of tea might do you good," Deacon said quietly. "You look like you're really struggling with something right now. Maybe your sisters can help you with whatever it is."

She shook her head. "You don't know anything about me or what I'm going through. And you don't really know my sisters." The instant the words were out, she wanted to yank them back or at least dial her ire back so the words didn't hold such a sour tinge to them.

He shrugged. "Maybe not, but a blind man can see you're upset. Too upset for this to just be about some termites."

He was right: this wasn't just about the termites, but she wasn't interested in this man romantically, like Yvonne was, so she didn't need to give him a list of reasons why she felt like her life was being tossed around in the funnel of a tornado. "We don't have the extra money for this, Deacon, and you know it. And Tami still wants to do work on the blue house over there. How's all that going to happen?"

"My mama always said if you have faith the size of a mustard seed . . ."

Lana nodded. "You can move mountains. Yeah, I know the scripture. Grandma Betty used to recite it to us too." And she'd listened to it, had fallen on that concept more times than she could recall.

When her mother had insisted she wouldn't support Lana's change to photography, Lana didn't have a clue how she was going to make it happen, but she'd had faith that the Lord wouldn't give her a dream without providing the tools to assist it in coming to fruition. Why couldn't she have that faith now? Why couldn't she just lean on His word the way she had before? Because she'd also prayed for her husband to get himself together, and that hadn't happened.

"Listen, this is more than just a job to me. I didn't know Ms. Betty well, but my mama adored her, looked up to the woman as if she were her second mother, so I heard a lot about her in my house growing up. I remember seeing you girls here some summers, and I know how happy that made Ms. Betty. So doing this"—he motioned toward the house—"is like a gift to me. A gift Ms. Betty gave me when she asked me to be the one to do these renovations, and a gift back to her by making it everything she ever wanted this house to be. I'm going to do whatever I can to make that happen, Lana. You can trust me on that."

She tilted her head and gave him a wry chuckle. "Does that trust come with a check?"

✉

Half an hour later, Lana found her sisters sitting on the front porch, both in folding chairs because the rocking chairs weren't back yet. There was an empty third chair to Yvonne's left, as if they'd been expecting her.

"I went to lay down for a few minutes to get my mind together," she said as she walked up to them and took the seat.

"You needed to," Tami quipped, and Yvonne glared at her.

Lana ignored her younger sister because, well, she was right.

She took a deep breath and released it slowly. "It always smelled so peaceful here."

"How do you smell peace?" Tami asked, her nose crinkled as if she were really trying to figure that out.

"You know what I mean. Like it doesn't smell like car exhaust or overflowing garbage from a dumpster," she said.

"Or chicken boxes and fries from Lenny's," Yvonne added.

"Guuurrrll, don't you bring up those chicken boxes. That was our go-to after school every day," Lana said, remembering that scent even as they talked about it.

"The fries used to be so greasy you could see right through the box," Yvonne said.

"And taste it on those two slices of bread they always put in the bottom of the box," Lana said.

"*Gross.*" Tami sang the word.

"Oh, that's right—you were the pizza queen. Always coming home with that sauce on your clothes that we had to scrub out before putting them in the washer so they wouldn't stain," Lana said, and Yvonne nodded.

"That's right. That sauce was so sweet it was nasty. But you loved it," Yvonne said.

"I sure did, especially with extra cheese, sausage, and crushed hot peppers." Tami rubbed her stomach. "I could go for a slice right now."

"Not me," Yvonne said, shaking her head. "There's so many things I can't eat anymore."

"Why not?" Tami asked. "You on some kind of diet?"

Lana looked at Yvonne too. "You don't even need a diet, Yvonne. What are you, like a size 8 or 10? For your height, that's just fine."

Yvonne looked away from them and then back before she sighed. "It's not just about my weight. It's about my medical condition."

"Shit," Tami whispered. "Girl, are you dying?"

Lana tossed her a glare. "If she was, that'd be the worst question to ask."

"No," Yvonne said with a slow grin. "At least, I'm doing everything I possibly can to put that off for as long as I can."

"Then what is it, Yvonne?" Lana asked. She suddenly knew this was serious.

"I have type 2 diabetes and high blood pressure. So I watch the things I eat now, and I take medication, and needles every day." She wiggled her fingers.

Lana reached out and grabbed one of her hands, turning it over so she could inspect. "Yvonne," she whispered when she saw the two bruised spots at the tips of Yvonne's fingers, "why didn't you tell us? How long has this been going on?"

Yvonne slid her hand away. "It's nothing. I mean, I know it's something, but I've just been dealing with it. Doesn't matter how long," she said.

"It does matter if we could've been doing something to help you," Tami said.

"How? You're never around," Yvonne said, and the words fell around them like weights.

They weren't around—she was right about that. Because she and Tami didn't want to deal with their mother or how Yvonne acted when she was around Freda, they'd both chosen to stay away for as long as they could.

"We have to do better," Lana said. "It's as simple as that. We can't have you getting sick too, or . . . or . . ." She sucked in a breath, hoping to keep the tears that were filling her eyes at bay. "We just gotta do better."

"Well, you can start by not freaking out every time Deacon tells us something about the house. That stress can't be good for Yvonne. The less butting heads we do on this project, the better. Let her find some of that peace you were just smelling while she's down here," Tami said.

"I know you're not talking about not stressing her when *your* unemployed behind is the one doing the most stressing," Lana replied.

"I'll have you know, I'm waiting to hear from an interview I went on before I left the city," Tami countered.

Lana threw up her hands. "Do you hear yourself? That was over a month ago. You think there's still a chance you're going to get that job? Grow up, Tami."

Tami stood then. "Oh yeah, let me grow up so I can be just like you, Lana. I can have the husband and the fancy condo, the nice cars and the big bucks in the bank accounts. You and Isaac have so much—why don't you just fork up the extra money we need to fix the house? Then we can get it sold faster, and you can be on your merry way."

Lana was speechless. And apparently motionless at her sister's words. Was that really what Tami thought of her? Was that how she saw Lana's life? Full of fancy cars and money? If so, she was sadly mistaken.

"I can't do that," Lana said slowly.

"And why the hell not? It would be an investment, Lana. You could get your money back when we sell the house." Tami stood with one hand on her hip now, her lips turned up as she waited for Lana's response.

Lana looked away from Tami, who was bubbling with attitude and indignation, and she stared at Yvonne. Her older sister was just sitting there, her gaze locked on Lana as if she were waiting for the answer too. But Lana could see the fatigue in Yvonne's eyes now and the slight slump of her shoulders. Hadn't she just been the one telling Tami to stop stressing their sister? The sister who'd taken the weight off them where their mother was concerned all their lives? Even when they were younger because, since Yvonne was the good one, Lana and Tami could be the not-so-good ones. As long as Freda had her favorite by her side.

"We don't have the money," Lana said finally. "Because Isaac keeps gambling it all away."

Chapter 22

YVONNE

Late Friday afternoon, Yvonne sat on the dock, her bare feet dangling over the edge. She wore jean capris and a sky-blue T-shirt; her natural-colored sandals sat on the planks beside her. Across the water, she could see boats in the distance—private vessels, charters, and supply boats either coming back to the island for drop-offs or going over to Bluffton for pickups. The sun was just settling over the horizon, casting the lower half of the sky in layers of hot orange and poppin' golds. A slight turn of her head, and she could see a bit more of the coastal area, silhouettes of old oaks and palms, and wisps of sweetgrass blowing in the cool breeze now coming off the water to usher in the night.

With her hands in her lap, she tilted her head back and inhaled a deep breath. A smile lifted her lips as she released the breath and welcomed the peace that Lana had spoken of days ago. Her sister had been right: There was a sort of peace in the air here. A stillness that Yvonne had never experienced anywhere else, and surprisingly, she was drawn to it. Somewhere deep inside her craved it and wondered if it was something she could have forever.

"Need some company?"

She startled at Deacon's voice as it broke through the contemplation that had been skirting around her mind all day. Opening her eyes, she kept her head angled back and glanced to the right, where he was standing. "Sure," she said, and watched as he lowered his tall body down to settle beside her.

Still in his work clothes, he smelled like sawdust and sweat. Not in a funky kind of way, but definitely in that I've-been-working-hard-labor-for-hours-thank-the-heavens-for-good-deodorant type of way. There were smudges of whatever white substance he'd worked with today across his forehead, and his hands, although she could tell he'd washed them, still had some grit around the nail beds and definitely a bit of ash on the knuckles—all things that might've been a put-off if she were back in the city, but here on this island, after watching him and his crew work all day, she could admit still made him damn sexy.

"It's beautiful out here," she said after a few moments of silence.

"A unique and undisturbed beauty is a hard find," he replied.

"That's the truth. Especially when you find yourself locked into one place where the view is always the same and never as rewarding." Those words just tumbled free, and she didn't really regret them. She'd given up wondering why she felt so at ease with Deacon that she could talk about things that she'd never spoken to anyone before. She knew the reason. It wouldn't make a difference in the long run, but she knew, and for now she decided just to go with the flow.

"Nobody ever said you have to stay in one place," he said. "That's why they invented planes, boats, trains. You know, all those forms of traveling."

She tossed him a wry grin. "I swear, I don't know who told you you were funny."

He grinned, just as she'd expected he would, just as she enjoyed seeing. "I don't know why you keep tryin' to deny my skills."

"What skills?" She chuckled. "As a contractor? Because that's something I can vouch for."

"Nah, my skills for being able to make you smile." He reached over and took her hand then.

She let her fingers slide easily into his grasp, noting the calluses on the inside of his palms and pressing her palm to them. It was a symbol that he was real—his work hands, the bulging biceps she'd seen flexing as he lifted something or cut something. This man who was sitting beside her was the realest man she'd ever met. He wasn't the figment of her imagination that she often conjured when enjoying her toys, and he wasn't like the few she'd allowed into her personal space temporarily.

"Well," she said, "I guess I can give you that one."

"Thank you very much," he said, and then surprised her by leaning in to give her a gentle kiss on her forehead.

He hadn't kissed her since almost a week ago, when they'd returned from the dinner at his mother's house. Probably because he and his crew had been so busy with trying to keep things going at the house. Or, as she'd thought a few days ago, maybe he wasn't going to kiss her again, since she'd basically shut down the possibility of anything romantic happening between them. But hell, this moment right here seemed as romantic as any scene Yvonne had watched in a movie, and she wasn't complaining.

"How're you holding up?" he asked after they'd fallen into another comfortable silence. "I mean, I know it's been a little tense between you and your sisters since we found out about those extra expenses."

She shook her head. "I told you the other day to go ahead and get it done."

"You did," he replied. "But you've also been busying yourself around the house every day this week until I've only seen you in flashes. So I haven't really had a moment to talk to you. That's why I stuck around after the crew went home tonight."

"Oh." She didn't know what else to say.

"Tami's been full speed ahead with ideas and implementing the ones she knows how. She's also pretty eager to learn more. But she hasn't been as talkative as usual. And Lana . . ." He paused and then gave a shrug. "She's been pretty much how she's been since the beginning, but sadder, I think."

"Wow, you've been paying a lot of attention to the Butler sisters."

He nodded. "That's nothing new. I mean, I never got the chance to be this up close and personal with you before, but I noticed y'all some of those summers you were here. I especially noticed you."

Now that took her off guard, and she couldn't help but stare at him quizzically. "Really? You noticed me?"

His brow furrowed, and he moved his head back a little as if he were as startled as she'd been by his comment. "What? Why do you seem so shocked that I'd notice you?"

"Because I wasn't anything to notice back then. I mean, Lana was the stunning one, with her long, thick hair she mostly wore in braids, and equally long legs—and she definitely developed as if she were the oldest sister," Yvonne said, remembering the envy she'd once had over her sister's body and looks.

Everybody loved Lana's skin tone, even though she'd always seen it as a reason her sisters didn't get along with her. But Yvonne distinctly remembered hearing some of the women at their church remark on how she had that "pretty, dark chocolate–brown skin," and then there'd been a few of the guys on the neighborhood basketball courts, where she and Lana would sometimes walk past on their way to the store for Mama when they were teenagers, who'd call Yvonne the "cute redbone," but Lana was the "sexy Nubian queen."

"Yeah," he said with another nod, his face going back to normal. "Lana was cool, but I always found myself staring at you longer. One time you came to the church, and your father was with you. Ms. Betty didn't come, but Mr. Daniel brought y'all into the church house and sat in the second pew like y'all were every-Sunday parishioners. But that was fine with me 'cause that meant I could look right in your face. Since my mama always made me and Emory sit right up front on those side pews so if we dared to doze off during the service, everybody in that place would see us and somebody would most likely come by and shake us awake."

She laughed at that because Mama had done that to them plenty of times when they'd fallen asleep during service.

"You had this long dress on, so I couldn't see your legs that day." He was grinning now as he stared out at the water like he could see the long-ago scene playing out in front of him. "I'd seen your bare legs like a day or so before when you were swimming in the creek with Lana and a couple other girls."

"So you were a creeper teenage boy, huh?" she asked, but there was no animosity in her tone.

"Not at all." He grinned. "But I was a normal, horny twenty-four-seven teenage boy." They both laughed at that. "But for real, though, the dress was kinda plain, like a pink or real light-orange color, I think. And it had those thin straps at your shoulders. I kept looking at your shoulders for a long time because they looked so soft and creamy. Then, when I felt things getting a little too happy in my dress pants, I quickly pulled my gaze up to your face."

"For real?" she asked, but continued to laugh. "How could you sit in church and have those thoughts?"

Now he had that faux frown that made him look like an adorable child. "Are you serious? I was fifteen, Yvonne, and you were like a goddess or something. Coming onto the island for what felt like three of the shortest months of the year and then staying up in that big ole house like you were every bit a princess most of the time." He sighed. "But when I looked at your face that day, I was like, 'Man, I'm done for.' I couldn't get you out of my mind after that."

"Why didn't you ever say anything to me? I don't think I even noticed you back then."

He shook his head. "You and Lana really acted like you didn't notice any of us on the island. And me and the fellas, we talked about y'all all summer long, but none of us were bold enough to approach you."

"'Bold'? What was there to be afraid of? We were just girls, and I'm sure you were talking to other girls throughout the year that lived here," she said.

"They weren't Ms. Betty's granddaughters. Nobody was trying to get swatted on the back of the head for thinking they were good enough for one of her granddaughters. The way your grandmother talked about y'all and all the fine work y'all were doing in school and extracurricular activities, it was like there wasn't anybody on Daufuskie or even the planet that was good enough for y'all. And then your father was built like a linebacker, so we were all like, nah, we'll look but we ain't even crazy enough to try and touch."

She used her free hand to swat at his arm then. "Now, I didn't say anything about touching."

He grinned. "I dreamed about touching you." His thumb ran over the back of her hand as he looked down at it and then back up to her. "Like this, I mean. Not the other way."

She smiled. "Yeah, right."

More chuckling ensued, and Yvonne found herself letting her head rest on his shoulder. "I wish my childhood had been different. I wish my life now was different."

He waited a beat before saying, "Your life can be whatever you make it, Yvonne."

She sighed, feeling the hope in those words and letting it settle over her.

"Right after we arrived here—and Tami talked so passionately about not only wanting to fix this house up but fixing up the blue house too—I did something."

He somehow knew to remain silent and wait for her to continue, and she appreciated him even more for that.

"I called the HR department at the school system, and I asked for the steps to taking out a loan from my 401(k). I know of a few teachers and other administrators that I've met over the years who did that to get the down payment on their homes or to take care of other really big expenses. So I applied for an additional fifty thousand dollars to be used if we went over budget here. I wanted to make sure we did all the renovations, even on the blue house."

"Did you do that to ensure you'd get the best price once you sell the house?" he asked.

She looked up from his shoulder and shook her head. "No. I did it because I wanted Tami to feel everything that Grandma Betty felt when she was here. I wanted her to feel like she'd accomplished something and that our family legacy would stand."

He squeezed her hand and then lifted it to his lips, where he placed a soft kiss over her knuckles. "Does that mean you don't want to sell the house now?" he asked as he lowered her hand again.

"I don't know," she admitted. "I really was just thinking about fulfilling Grandma Betty and Tami's wishes."

"You like fixing things for other people, don't you? Especially for your sisters?" he asked.

He had no idea how true that statement was. Yvonne had spent the last three days trying to figure out if the money she'd borrowed from her 401(k) would be enough to cover the additional renovation expenses and take care of Isaac's debt. Once Lana had told them about his gambling habit and the trouble they were in the other day, all the weirdness they'd been seeing in her had made sense. Lana wasn't sure if Isaac had requested the extension like she'd told him to, and now she was afraid for Isaac's life and their future. She had insisted he hadn't said they were actually in physical danger, but Yvonne had a feeling that who he owed and how much he owed this time was bigger and worse than anything they'd gone through before. The fact that Isaac had been so desperate that he'd tried to refinance their condo without talking to

Lana first had been a big clue. Yvonne hadn't said anything to Lana or Tami about the money yet, but she planned to talk to them this weekend about their options.

"I've always felt responsible for my sisters, if that's what you mean."

"And your mother too?"

She shook her head. "Not necessarily responsible for her but definitely indebted. Like, she's my mother, and you only get one. It's my duty to take care of the woman who brought me into this world. Wouldn't you do the same for your mother or father?"

He nodded. "Without a doubt. I've got a savings account reserved just for their care, should the need ever arise."

With a heavy sigh, she replied, "I should've thought of that." Another thing she should've thought of was taking out that 401(k) loan to get the money to pay for the renovations to Mama's house. And actually, that had been the default plan she'd go to if she depleted her savings for the costs. But a huge part of her had wanted her sisters to step up—for once in their lives—to be there for Freda in the same way that Yvonne had been.

"But my parents would never expect me to give up every aspect of my life for them," he continued. "It seems like maybe that's what you've done for your mother."

"Honestly, I don't know what I've done. All I know is that I'm not happy. I don't even know what happy would look like for me, because I've never thought about it. I've only ever thought about my career." Because Mama had made it seem like that was the most important thing.

Even after Freda'd had children, she'd remained hyperfocused on building her career, making a name for herself that stood separate and apart from mother and wife. For a long time, Yvonne had thought that might've been what finally broke up her parents. Her father had worked in the education field as well, as a college professor, which was why he always had summers off to spend with them on the island. But Mama never shared in those trips, and perhaps after a while, that just built a wall between them. At any rate, watching the dysfunction and demise of her parents' marriage hadn't given Yvonne any grand ideas about love. So what else was there to be happy about other than her work?

"Is your career still fulfilling?"

His phone buzzed loudly in the otherwise quiet area, giving her a minute to think about his question.

He cursed. "This is a text from Hitch. We've got a problem with the appliance order for the kitchen. We're expecting delivery first thing Monday morning, so I've gotta go take care of this."

She nodded. "Absolutely. Go, go, I understand. I'm just gonna sit here awhile longer with my thoughts."

With the hand that had been holding hers, he brushed his knuckles over her cheek. "Do me a favor?"

"What?" she asked.

"Toss in a few happy thoughts while you're out here."

The warmth that spread through her at his words had lingered long after he was gone and had put her in a mood to prepare a nice dinner for her and her sisters.

Well, as nice as she could, with her sparse supplies. In fact, she ended up driving over to Charity's café and picking up a delicious-looking seafood salad, grilled salmon, and asparagus. At a bakery not too far down the road—and run by a lady named Mattie, who had an autographed picture of Grandma Betty on the wall behind the counter—she bought a beautiful lemon-meringue pie for dessert.

The dinner was delicious, and her sisters were appreciative of Yvonne's efforts, but their behavior was still off. Yvonne figured that telling them about the extra $50,000 she had might be something to lift their spirits, but then she felt the urge to do something else. Something that wouldn't remind them of their current problems but would perhaps bring back memories of their good times together.

"Hey," she said, once they'd finished cleaning up the dishes they were using on repeat so as to not disturb the rest of the dishes that had been packed away. "Let's go up and get into our pajamas and then meet back in the parlor in ten minutes."

Lana frowned. "If it's for dessert, I'm full. I think I'm just going to go to bed now."

"It's only eight thirty," Tami replied with a shrug. "We can use my friend Gabriel's Netflix login to watch a movie."

Although she'd made the suggestion, Tami didn't seem thrilled by it, but Yvonne was taking the suggestion alone as a good sign.

"Just do it," she said, draping the dish towel through the oven handle before heading out of the kitchen.

Yvonne hurried upstairs to change and get back down in the parlor before her sisters. The couches had been moved out, since they'd ordered new furniture for the space. Nothing was staying except the piano, and that was only staying depending on whether or not they sold the house. If the house *was* sold, Tami wanted the piano, even though she definitely couldn't keep it in her tiny apartment. But the new floors had been installed because the original hardwood was too badly scarred. There was a stack of folded tarps, along with a box of what looked like leftover wood slats, piled in one corner. Yvonne made sure the surface was stable and placed the record player that she'd brought down from Grandma Betty's music room on top of the box. Then she plugged the cord into the socket and took out the records she'd tucked under her arm. The dust jackets were worn and a little faded, but they'd brought so many memories tumbling back into Yvonne's mind when she'd seen them on the shelf in the music room.

Grandma Betty had an extensive music collection full of original vinyl albums and 45 records. There were even some eight-track cassettes tucked into a glass case in one corner of the room. The music room was the only room that they hadn't decided what to do with yet. It was partly because none of them really wanted to disturb the part of the house that was filled with so much of their grandmother's spirit. But tonight, Yvonne had gone in there because she knew this was exactly what they needed at this moment.

She'd brought down a 45 that was especially meaningful to them even though she knew for certain she hadn't heard the song in years. Just pulling the small record out of the original black-and-white jacket had her heart thumping. The round yellow adapter was still inside the center hole of the record, and she placed it onto the turntable portion of the record player. Then she moved the arm, placing the needle at the beginning of the record.

There was that fuzzy, staticky sound for the first few seconds as the needle moved over the record. Then the guitar started the intro that would be recognized for generations after its original 1964 recording, and seconds later, David Ruffin's voice blasted throughout the room: "I've got sunshine on a cloudy day."

Tami and Lana both walked in at that exact moment. Yvonne moved away from the record player and stood in the center of the new dark-wood floors. She'd traded her sandals for thick, purple fuzzy socks that didn't match her green pajama pants and T-shirt, so she slid a little as she made her way to where she needed to be. Tami acted first, squealing as she ran across the floor to stand to Yvonne's left. The black-and-white-striped boxer shorts and white tank top she wore were a contrast to Yvonne's colorful ensemble, but she loved Tami's Wonder Woman slippers.

"I remember Daddy used to play this for us, and we'd all get up and hold hands in a circle, dancing with him because we were *his girls!*" Tami continued to squeal as she took Yvonne's hand and they started to dance.

Yvonne laughed. "I know. I was thinking about him earlier today, and tonight it just seemed like the time to spend with him," she said, and then looked over to where Lana was still standing in the doorway, hands at her side like she was somehow frozen to that spot.

"C'mon, Lana, you know our circle was never complete without you," Yvonne said.

She extended her free hand to her sister just as Tami started crooning, "My girl, my girl, my girl!" in her very off-key voice.

"We can't let her sing The Temptations like that," Yvonne continued. She and Lana had always been the better singers, even though Tami loved to sing the most and the loudest.

"Oh, don't hate 'cause y'all can't hang with me," Tami said, and launched into the next verse.

Lana's face broke into a frown then, but she started walking toward them, shaking her head. "Girl, Grandma Betty didn't teach you a thing about singing, did she?"

Lana wore hot-pink silk pajama pants and a matching top, with black slippers on her feet. She came closer to them and grabbed Yvonne's and Tami's hands to make their circle complete.

They danced and sang the entire song, laughing and holding tight to each other's hands just like they used to do when they were here with Daddy. And when that song went off, Tami rushed over to the record player.

"What else did you bring down?" She picked up the stack of albums and flipped through them. "Oh yesss, hunty! Yes! This was my jam, but Lana hated it."

Which meant Tami was definitely putting that one on next. Yvonne only shook her head because she knew exactly what record was about to play. Lana must have too, since she rolled her eyes and moved to her place in the center of their circle this time. And right after Tami ran over to join them, they were each ready to extend that arm with their hands up, palms facing forward as they sang in unison, "Stop—in the name of love."

Lana was always Diana Ross—and not just because Mama had declared she had the singer's eyes, but also because Lana really was the best vocalist of their trio. And while Lana had claimed she despised this song and any of the others that Grandma Betty had used to play by the Supremes or the Boss, she absolutely got into her role, moving her hips and stepping in front of Yvonne and Tami just like she was the leader of the singing group.

They were all laughing and out of breath by the time that record ended, and Tami, now insisting she was the DJ for the evening, ran over to the record player again. But this time, while they waited for her to put on the next record, the distinct sound of breaking glass caught their attention.

Chapter 23

LANA

Lana grabbed one of the extender sticks that had been added to the paintbrush a few days ago when the parlor had been painted. Tami had moved away from the record player and found one of the spatula-scraper thingies, which she now held in her hand like a knife. Yvonne had found a loose wood plank and was ready to wield it like a baseball bat.

There'd been a second loud crash, and as she looked at her sisters, Lana knew their hearts were racing right along with hers.

"There's somebody in the kitchen," Tami whispered.

"No shit, Sherlock," Lana snapped.

"Shh," Yvonne chastised.

The three of them stood close, taking baby steps that would lead them out of the parlor. Lana suspected they probably looked like the Three Stooges, with their ridiculous weapons, going off to fight who in the hell knew who—but they weren't backing down, that was for damn sure. Something else crashed, and then there was a thump and a curse.

Shit! There really was someone in the house.

But they were on an island. Were there break-ins here, like in the city? Did they even have a police force? Someone to help them if there was a gun-toting murderer in their kitchen? Because if the intruder had a gun, they definitely didn't stand a chance with their weapons.

Oh, Lord, please don't let this intruder have a gun. Maybe it was just someone looking for a meal, and that's why they came in through the kitchen. If that were the case, they could feed that someone and get them the hell out of the house.

"Maybe they left," Tami said as they continued walking through the foyer but hadn't heard another sound from the kitchen.

Yvonne shook her head. "I don't think so."

"We've gotta check it out anyway," Lana said. "They definitely broke something trying to get in here. Probably the window."

"Oh no, not the new windows and doors we just had installed," Tami moaned. "That's gonna cost us more money to replace."

"If we're alive to replace it," Yvonne said.

Lana groaned. "Please, let's not talk dying into the atmosphere."

Then they heard footsteps—quick, approaching footsteps—and they stopped. Lana had turned off the lights in the kitchen and the part of the foyer closest to the back of the house when they'd finished dinner. She hated wasting electricity, especially since the three of them were each currently paying two utility bills—their own in the city and part of the one here at the summerhouse. So when a dark, shadowy figure stepped out of the kitchen and turned, heading directly toward them, they all screamed.

Then they charged, weapons held high, as they were hell-bent on taking down the intruder if it was the last thing they did.

"Wait! Hold the hell up!" the intruder—a man—yelled. "Wait a damn minute! Lana!"

She'd already swung her stick, hitting the man in the shoulder or somewhere—she just knew it had connected. And Tami had jumped on him, wrapping her legs around his waist as she smacked him on the head with the spatula. Yvonne had gone for his legs, swinging the wood plank until he groaned.

"Dammit! Lana! Get your sisters!"

Lana stopped midstrike, her arms still held high, as she'd been about to swing on the intruder again when she heard her name. Had he said it before? Wait a minute, was that . . . "Isaac?"

"Where?" Yvonne asked.

"Get off me!" he yelled before something else crashed to the floor.

Yvonne found the light switch, and the end of the foyer was illuminated.

Lana gasped. "Isaac."

He had his hands around Tami's wrists now, holding them both tightly as he pushed her back to the wall. "Stop hitting me with that thing!" he yelled into Tami's face.

Isaac's eyes were wild, face pulled into a grimace. Tami's mouth formed a big O as she pulled her hand back slowly and let her legs fall to the floor.

When she was standing on her own, Isaac backed away from her. "Fuck!" he yelled, and then dragged a hand down his face. "What the hell is wrong with you three? I thought something had happened to you." He glanced toward Lana. "Hell, all of you."

"Us?" Yvonne asked. "What's wrong with you, breaking into people's houses in the dark of night? We're the ones who belong here, not you."

"Yeah, you know, we could've shot your ass if we'd been packin' some real heat," Tami chimed in.

"What are you doing here?" Lana asked, watching her husband carefully. He didn't look like himself. Beads of sweat lined his forehead, and he was heaving like he'd either run a marathon or he really was afraid something had happened to her.

He wore dark jeans, a black hoodie, and black tennis shoes. Definitely not an outfit one should wear when they were planning to break into someone's house. But surely Isaac hadn't planned to break in here. Why would he do that? She didn't have any answers; her thoughts were too scrambled.

"You ever heard of a front door?" Yvonne asked when neither Lana nor Isaac had said anything else.

"I tried the front door," he said with a sigh. "I pressed that bell like twenty times before it dawned on me that it must not be working. Then I knocked on the door, but when I didn't see any lights on downstairs, I figured y'all were probably upstairs in bed. But then I could hear music, so I came around to see if you were out back on the deck. Then, when I didn't see any of you, I got worried." He pinched the bridge of his nose and sighed heavily. "I wanted to see my wife."

He said those last words as if they'd needed to be strongly pronounced. But it wasn't like everybody didn't already know who he was.

"Why didn't you just call me?" Lana asked him.

"I did," he told her. "Where's your phone?" He looked her up and down, probably surveying her pajamas and the lack of any place to carry her phone.

It was her turn to say, "Oh. It's upstairs on the charger."

He nodded and attempted a weak smile. "So you couldn't hear that ringing either."

"Still doesn't make breaking and entering the best idea," Tami said. "Sorry about that bruise you're gonna have on your forehead tomorrow."

Isaac reached up and rubbed his forehead where Tami had smacked him with the spatula. He shook his head. "It's nice to see you too, Tami."

"Oh, don't be like that, brother-in-law," Tami said, waving a hand at Isaac. "You're partially responsible for the welcome you received."

"She's right about that," Yvonne said as she finally propped her wood plank against a wall.

"You still haven't told me why you're here," Lana said. She was fairly certain she should've gone over to hug her husband, whom she hadn't seen in just about six weeks now. Or he should've run over to hug her.

Well, the fact that she'd been beating him with a stick and her sister had been latched on to him like a rabid animal might have had something to do with the stalled greeting.

Isaac walked over to where she was still standing and pulled her into the hug she'd just been thinking about. "Hey, baby," he whispered in her ear as he held her tight.

Lana hugged her husband back, inhaled the scent of his cologne, and realized just how much she'd missed him. She buried her face in his neck and closed her eyes, holding on even tighter.

He was the one to pull back from the hug first, but he didn't completely release her. Instead, he lowered his mouth to hers for a desperate kiss. She wasn't normally one for PDAs—even when the public was just her sisters—but it had been over a month since she'd seen her man. She opened her mouth to his tongue, and a little moan escaped because, yeah, she'd really missed him. But when the kiss was broken, she still stared him directly in the eyes and said, "What are you doing here?"

"Let's go to your room, baby. So we can talk," Isaac said.

Lana's heart thumped wildly, her stomach churning in the way it had been recently whenever she thought about Isaac's precarious situation. Peering around him, she could see that Yvonne had moved to stand next to Tami, who had both hands on her hips. They were staring at Lana and Isaac, and Lana knew why.

"If it's about the gambling," she said, "they already know. So just say what you have to say."

Six weeks ago, she never would've said that to him. Never would've aired the dirty laundry of her marriage in front of her sisters. Because the last thing she wanted was for them to judge her any more than they already had. But when she'd told them about Isaac's gambling earlier that week, their reaction hadn't been what she'd expected. Her sisters had actually turned out to be very supportive.

"Lana, this is private," he said. "And it's urgent."

At that last part, she tilted her head. "What's so urgent that you came running all the way down here? What happened?"

"I do not want to talk about this in front of them," Isaac said.

"We'll go into the kitchen, Lana," Yvonne said. "Close enough that if you need us, we'll be here, but still giving you some privacy."

Isaac turned to look at Yvonne, who was giving him an empathetic stare, while Tami made that motion of her fingers to her eyes and then his to let him know she was keeping an eye on him. Isaac sighed when they were in the other room; then he turned to her.

His hair was low-cut; his lips, which were usually easy to spread into a wide, infectious grin, were drawn into a tight line. "Baby, look, I need you to sign these papers," he said, reaching into his back pocket and pulling out an envelope. He handed it to her. "I need you to sign them tonight, and I'll be on the first ferry out of here tomorrow morning to take them right to the bank."

"What?" She took the envelope and opened it. "What's this? And you know I'm not signing anything without reading it first."

"It's the refinance papers," he said. And when she glanced up at him again, he rubbed his hand down the back of his head.

"I thought we talked about this," she said through clenched teeth.

"We did, but listen . . ."

She was shaking her head as she turned away from him to pace. "I told you I didn't want you putting our home on the line for this, Isaac. Dammit! Tami suggested we take out a home equity loan, but we'd have to make sure we didn't need to turn in receipts for any work done, or the bank didn't require direct payments to be made to the vendors." On a turn in her pacing, she glanced back at the family room, where the good time she'd been having moments ago with her sisters had faded.

"I've been thinking about it the last few days, and a personal loan might be better all around. I didn't want to create another bill for us—especially not now—but that might be the best option," she continued.

His hand was on her arm when she walked closer to him again, and he grasped her lightly. "Baby."

Something in his tone had her looking up to focus on his face. His eyes were wide and etched with sadness—or was that . . . fear? A muscle clenched in his jaw. But it was when he dropped his gaze from her momentarily that Lana's heart sank. "You're scaring me, Isaac."

He returned his gaze to her. Then he had both hands on her arms, pulling her close to him. "I messed up, Lana. I messed up so bad, baby. But I'm trying to fix it. *This* is gonna fix it." He nodded down at the papers still scrunched in her hands.

"Something happened, didn't it?"

Isaac dropped his hands from her and stepped back. "Look, I'm gonna fix it. Just like I told you I would, and then it'll never happen again. I swear to you, it'll never happen again."

Her limbs felt heavy, feet frozen to the spot where she stood, but blood pumped fiercely through her veins, filling her with that boiling heat of anger as she asked, "What happened?"

"They know who you are," he said, rubbing both hands down his face now. "Fuck! Lana, they know who you are!"

"What . . . what does that mean?" she asked, even though the pounding of her heart and the trickle of fear down her spine said she already knew. The fear that shot through her like a blast of light must have somehow shown on her face, because Isaac immediately closed the distance between them.

"No. No. No! I won't let anything happen to you. I'm not gonna let anything happen to you!" He was back in her face, his hands smoothing down the sides of her hair, moving down to cup her chin. "That's why I'm here now. I begged for an extension since I had to gather more paperwork for the loan officers, and they gave me an additional three weeks. But then . . . the moment they mentioned you, I knew time was up, and I couldn't risk waiting another second. Just sign the papers, baby, and I'll take care of this—and I'll pay off the second mortgage by the end of the year. This won't happen again, Lana. I swear. I swear."

But she was already backing away from him again. Tears stung her eyes as her fingers crumpled the papers. She'd never known whom Isaac owed his money to. At one point she'd assumed it was casinos—but then, once she'd seen a note he'd written on a sticky pad with the address and time of a private poker game, she'd tossed out that idea. So was it the men he played poker with whom he owed? Or loan sharks? Were they threatening to hurt Isaac *and* her if he didn't pay up?

The first tears fell, and then it was like the release of a dam. Her chest heaved, and Isaac's face collapsed as he walked toward her.

"I'm so sorry, Lana. But I promise you this won't touch you. I promise they won't get near you." He'd just reached for her when she took another step back.

"What about our baby?" She wasn't even sure if she'd said those words aloud, hadn't muttered that last word to another soul since she'd taken her fifth pregnancy test last weekend.

Isaac's eyes widened. "Did you just say . . . our . . . baby?"

"She sure the hell did." Tami spoke up from where she stood in the doorway to the kitchen before Yvonne clamped a hand over her mouth.

Chapter 24

LANA

With his arm wrapped securely around her waist, Isaac led Lana into the kitchen. The new table-and-chair set hadn't arrived, so they'd been using an old card table and folding chairs that had been stored in the blue house. He pulled out a chair, and she sat down slowly, afraid that any sudden movement might somehow trigger another unwanted surprise tonight.

Her head was throbbing. She hadn't had a headache in days now, but a call to her GYN back in the city on Monday had confirmed it was a normal early-pregnancy symptom. Her doctor had referred her to an obstetrician, but Lana hadn't made that call yet. She hadn't even decided how or when she was going to tell her husband or her family. Well, that was taken care of now.

She propped her elbows on the table and then rested her head in her hands. Her arms and legs were still trembling as Isaac's words played back in her mind.

"They know who you are." "I won't let them touch you."

"Who are they, Isaac?" she asked without looking up.

She could hear a chair sliding across the floor and felt Isaac next to her when he put one hand at her back and the other on her knee. "Baby—"

She shook her head. "Tell me. I have a right to know." And she probably should've asked before. At this moment, she felt like there were so many things she should've done before now, so many things she should've said.

In the distance she heard movement, and then, "I'm going to put on some water for some tea. You'll feel better after tea."

That was Yvonne. She'd shifted into her caretaker role, and for the first time in her life, Lana welcomed it. Grandma Betty used to think tea was a cure-all. She used to boil water and fix herself a cup of chamomile tea every night before she went to bed. Of course, they all knew she also put a generous helping of brandy into that tea as well, but Lana was certain Yvonne wasn't going to do that to hers. Not after the announcement she'd inadvertently made.

"Thanks," Lana murmured to her sister, but didn't speak again to Isaac.

He cleared his throat. "His name is Jimmy, and he works for an, uh . . ." He paused, but she still didn't look at him. "He owns the bar where we play the private poker games in the back. And he also makes loans."

Her chest hurt, and she shook her head again, tears dropping from her eyes onto the table. Isaac's hand moved to her back as he leaned in, his mouth close to her ear. "I can't begin to apologize enough, Lana. It's a problem, I know that now, and I remember every word you said when we talked about it before. I just need you to know that I love—"

"Stop!" She lifted her head and turned until her face was aligned with his. "Just stop it! Don't tell me you love me when you knew what you were doing was wrong and that it could hurt our marriage. Our . . . family." That last word had her gasping, and a sob broke free.

Isaac dropped his head and waited a beat before looking up at her again. "I know," was all he said next. "I know."

"Then why the hell did you do it? Why, Isaac? You make good money. I make good money, between the résumé writing and my photography. We're not wanting for anything. Except . . ." She sighed and slid an arm from the table so she could touch her palm to her still-flat stomach.

Isaac covered her hand, his gaze focused on them, on her stomach. "I know. I know, baby."

"Then tell me what we're supposed to do now. You came here, breaking through windows, thrusting paperwork in my face, because what? You think they'll hurt me if you don't pay your debt?"

"No. I'd never let them hurt you," he said. "I told you that."

"It doesn't matter what you tell me, Isaac. None of that shit matters anymore! All that matters to me is this baby." She shrugged. "That's all."

He nodded. "That's what matters to me too. You, us, our family— that's what we always talked about."

"But you're fucking it up," she said, her voice shaking. "And I don't understand why."

"I don't understand it, either, Lana," he replied, his voice raised, tone frustrated. "I don't know why I keep doing it when I know the consequences. I hated every time you gave me money to cover debts. I don't even know how you knew I owed. I felt like such a loser—and not just when I got up from the poker table, but every night I lay beside you, knowing what I was doing, I felt like a loser."

"Then why didn't you stop?" Lana asked, again because she was still waiting for his answer to that question.

"Because he can't," Tami said.

Both Lana and Isaac turned to see her standing near the island. She had mugs lined up and was placing tea bags in each of them. Apparently, they all needed a cup of tea tonight.

"Tami," Yvonne scolded, "let them talk."

"I was," Tami said. "But I know how he feels." She looked over at Isaac. "Lana's going to keep asking him a question he doesn't have an answer to right now because that's how addictions work. He knows what he's doing is wrong, but he just can't stop. Won't stop—until *he* decides that's what he *has* to do."

All eyes were on Tami now as Lana frowned. "Why would you say you understand? What kind of addiction do you have?"

Her sister shook her head. "I didn't have an addiction, but in my support group that my therapist got me into, there are people struggling with different issues. Some have drug or sex addictions, others have compulsions or other symptoms of mental disorders that make them feel helpless to stop certain things." She took a breath and then looked from Lana to Yvonne and then to Isaac. "I used to believe that I couldn't stop messing up. No matter what I did, I was going to make the wrong decision and disappoint the people I loved the most. That kept my anxiety ramped up, and that only exacerbated my ADHD. I was a complete mess." She shrugged. "I still am, on most days. But what I know for certain is that things got better once I decided I needed to play an active part in making them better."

She finished with the tea bags and folded her arms over her chest as she faced the table now. "When Isaac decides this isn't what he wants his life to be anymore and that he needs help getting to a better place, then he'll be able to pull back the layers to see why he felt so compelled to gamble even when he knew he was in over his head. You asking him repeatedly to answer a question he doesn't have an answer to at this moment is pointless."

Lana was silent. She didn't know what to say. Not to Isaac at this point or to her sister, who continued to surprise her. These past weeks that they'd been back at the summerhouse, Tami had been different. Still the same sometimes, like her ability to always be the first to laugh and to have fun in the midst of turmoil. Like tonight, when she'd run straight into the family room and started to sing. She had a natural exuberance that made her personality sparkle. But besides that, she'd been doing a great job with the renovations. And now, apparently, she was a therapist as well.

"I don't want this to continue," Isaac said when he turned back to Lana. "I want to do better, for you and for our child."

Looking into his eyes now, Lana felt a little bad that this discussion had ended up taking place in front of her sisters. But then again, she didn't. Yvonne and Tami had been here for her in the past month, even when they didn't know what they were supporting her through. Having them close had been both a distraction from her problems and a comfort as good memories from their past came pouring in. Sure, they'd struggled through some things—who didn't? But this was how it always ended with them. One. Two. Three. Each of them standing together like one, two, three.

Yvonne walked over to the table with two mugs in her hands. She walked around them so she could set the first mug in front of where Lana sat, and then extended her arm to put the second one in front of Isaac. "I'm going to say something, and then I'm going to drag Tami out of here so you two can have some privacy."

When Isaac looked at her with a raised brow, Yvonne only smiled and shook her head. "You know how sisters are," she told him. "We might not be together all the time, but we're a united front when we need to be."

Lana almost smiled. She'd been thinking something similar.

"I can loan you the money to pay these loan sharks off," Yvonne said, and now both Isaac's brows were raised.

Lana sat back in her chair, shaking her head.

Yvonne held up a hand before either of them could speak. "Just hear me out," she said. "When we found out about this house and the land coming to us, I wasn't sure what I wanted to do about it. I mean, I thought, let's just sell it and do something else with our proceeds. But then we came down here, and Tami was so passionate about making this place what Grandma Betty always wanted it to be that I started thinking. Tami was closest to her, so she'd be the one to know what our grandmother wanted." Yvonne clasped her hands on the back of the folding chair in front of her.

"Lana, you're the planner and the detail person, so you were gonna watch the budget like a hawk; we all knew that." A smile ghosted her lips, and Lana sighed. "But I agreed with you. I didn't think we'd have enough money in that escrow account to take care of all the renovations. So I took out a loan from my 401(k)."

"Yvonne, no," Lana said on another sigh. "No."

"Oh my goodness," Tami added.

"That's why I told Deacon to go ahead and call those termite people, and it's why I'm offering to loan you the money you need to pay this fool. Because if he comes after my sister, he's gonna have to get through me first," Yvonne said with a curt nod to Isaac.

"And me," Tami added. "But next time, I'll have something better than a spatula."

Yvonne rolled her eyes at Tami, and Lana brought her hands up to wipe her face. "I can't let you do that, Yvonne."

"I'm not offering it to you," Yvonne said to her. "Isaac, you're the only brother we've got. You're our family, and family—not just sisters—stick together too. You take this money, pay that man, and then you and I will work out a payment plan for you to pay me back."

Lana saw that muscle twitch in Isaac's jaw again. He was agitated and worried. And she was fed up.

"If you take this money from my sister and pay this man, it's still not enough," she said, and all eyes immediately fell to her. "I told you once that I couldn't keep doing this; now I'm telling you for the last time: I *won't* keep doing this." She was crying again, and that was annoying her on a totally different level. Because crying wasn't something she did often. "I heard what Tami just said, and I'm sure there's some truth to it—but for me, as your wife, I'm telling you to either get some help and work through this or I'm leaving, and we can figure out a co-parenting plan instead."

She knew she sounded harsh, knew that her sisters were shocked, especially since it seemed that Yvonne had just given them a solution to the problem. But Lana knew the problem was much bigger than this particular debt. And as she locked gazes with Isaac, she was certain he knew it too.

"What Tami said actually made a lot of sense," he said finally. "And I'd thought about that on that long ferry ride over here. I'm gonna get help. The job has some type of therapy program, and I'm gonna look into it. I told you I want to fix this, Lana. I'm not playing about that. I want my family." He reached for Lana's hands again, bringing both of them to his lips, where he kissed each before looking over to Yvonne. "Thank you," he said, and when she nodded at him, he said it again, his voice cracking a bit. "Thank you."

"Can we talk about the fact that I'm gonna be an auntie now?" Tami asked, clapping her hands while she smiled brightly.

Yvonne shook her head. "No, girl. We're going to bed and leaving these two alone . . ." Then she walked around the table and turned back to add, "To clean up this kitchen."

Chapter 25

TAMI

With shaking gloved hands, a dirt-smudged face, and sweat rolling down her back, Tami ended the call and let out a squeal of delight. She pumped a fist in the air and then danced around in circles until she almost toppled over onto the pile of trash that needed to be hauled out of the little blue house. It was late afternoon, and she'd been working in the house alone, while Deacon, Yvonne, and the rest of the crew continued with projects over at the summerhouse. But next week was the beginning of August, and if they wanted everything finished by the end of summer, she needed to get started over here now.

Still, the timeline didn't stop her from continuing her celebration. With her lips spread into a huge smile, she jogged out of the house, stopping on the rugged front porch. She had to call Gabriel.

Staring down at her phone, she kept trying to swipe over the screen to get the call going, but the big work gloves she was wearing hindered the process. How she'd been able to swipe to answer the call that had just come in about ten minutes ago and wasn't able to make a call now, she wasn't sure, but she wasn't going to let that kill her joy either. So she pulled the gloves off and dropped them to the tattered planks below, then made the call.

"Come on, come on," she said, and she wanted to dance around some more but considered the possibly unstable foundation she was on at the moment and just continued to grin. "Pick up! Pick up!"

"Hey, beautiful," he finally answered.

"I got the job!" she yelled. "They just called me, and I got the job!"

His deep, rumbling laughter filled her with even more glee, and she thought her heart would jump right out of her chest. "Congratulations, babe! That's what's up!"

"I'm so excited I can hardly breathe!" she told him. "They said there was a big launch they had to get moving—that's why they hadn't called back sooner. And then they expressed that this is the reason they need someone in the position, so that important things won't have to take a back seat while current staff is juggling two and three jobs. The salary isn't fantastic, but I knew that going in. It's just the opportunity, you know; I'll be at a record company, learning more about the industry, getting hands-on experience. I just can't believe it! I can't believe I really got the job!"

When she finally stopped talking, she was out of breath, heart still racing, eyes stinging with happy tears.

"You deserve this, Tam. It's the opportunity you've been waiting for, and you deserve it," Gabriel said. "I'm so proud of you."

That's when she stopped near one of the beams barely holding up the dilapidated porch roof. She leaned on it regardless of the fact that it might fall and take her ass out with it. This was too good of a moment for that to happen—she hoped. Her head tilted until it was also leaning on the beam, and she closed her eyes, replaying the last words he'd just said.

"Thank you," she said in a much calmer voice. "Thanks for listening to me go on and on about this job and my dreams. About my two-steps-away-from-being-broke status, the jobs I had and hated, my family, this renovation . . . everything. I feel like I've been dumping so much on you for so long and I just—I just appreciate you always listening."

"Always, Tami," he said without hesitation. "I'm gonna be here whether you're laughing or crying, happy or sad."

"A part of me wants to say thank you again because I feel like I don't deserve that type of dedication or unmitigated support from you—or anyone else, I guess." She blinked and stared out at the majestic house across the yard, with workers coming and going, painters standing on ladders, landscapers digging up weeds, and the sounds of banging and clanking mixing with the screech of birds and the warm summer breeze.

"But another part of me knows that this is exactly what I deserve. The job of my dreams and . . . the guy that I never dared to dream about." It was an admission that had been haunting her daily since Gabriel had expressed his desire to be in a real relationship with her. She was afraid of that, afraid that a commitment to being his woman would taint the friendship that she'd come to cherish. She'd also been afraid to take a chance on herself all these years, to go out and get the job that she wanted instead of trying to walk the path that others wanted for her. But look at God.

"You deserve everything that makes your heart happy and your voice sing with the excitement I hear in it right now. Damn, I wish I was there to hug you and take you out to dinner to celebrate. When are you coming home?"

She sighed. "Oh, yes, I wish I was there right now because you'd definitely be making reservations at Del Frisco's for us tonight."

He laughed again and she joined in. "Wooow, so it's like that. You're ready to break a brotha's pockets for this celebration, huh?"

"Absolutely! This is a special occasion."

"You're right, you're right. And I'd make those reservations in a heartbeat. In fact, the first night you're home, it's a date."

Butterflies danced in her stomach at the sound of that, and she couldn't help but giggle. "Okay," she said softly. "It's a date."

Fifteen minutes later, she'd hung up with Gabriel and was running across the yard to get to the summerhouse. She almost plowed into one of the landscapers pushing a wheelbarrow full of fresh dirt, but then she laughed and yelled, "Sorry 'bout that!" when he scowled.

She ran up the new steps leading to the new deck, the teak pre-finished composite tiles she'd selected gleaming in the sunlight. The kitchen was still a minor mess, with the backsplash just being installed and the appliance shipment still on the mainland. Her goal was to find her sisters—one or both of them, it didn't matter. The news was burning in her throat to spill again.

"Have you seen Yvonne?" she asked Frank, who was coming down the foyer when she stepped out of the kitchen.

"Upstairs, in the primary bedroom with Deacon," he said with a nod.

"Great! Thanks!" Then she was off again, maneuvering around more of the crew and a weird piece of plastic that seemed to be hanging from the ceiling in the upstairs hallway for a reason she didn't know and couldn't be bothered to stop and figure out at the moment.

She bolted into the room only to come to a quick stop when she saw them in the sitting area near the big window. Grandma Betty used to have a hot-pink love seat in that area, with a purple shag rug. The Tiffany lamp and the huge ottoman had an array of the same bright colors, and the small shelf that had sat in one corner boasted a collection of books as vibrant and eclectic as her grandmother's style had been in that small space. Now Tami knew exactly where she'd gotten her decorating sense from as a flash of her apartment and her bright-yellow couch had her connecting instantly to Grandma's space.

But all those things had been moved out now. New floors were being installed in here at the end of the week, so Yvonne and Deacon were standing in an empty space. That didn't seem to matter to them, because with the way they were looking at each other, they didn't have room for anything else. For a moment, Tami just stared at them.

The sun was streaming in through the window, giving Yvonne's skin a sun-kissed glow. She looked extra cute today in her light-blue denim capris and green Celtics T-shirt—the one NBA team they could agree on supporting. Her hair was in that damn ponytail again, but at least she'd added a green headband and gold stud earrings. Deacon was his usual fine self, in work boots, jeans, and a gray T-shirt. As he lifted a hand to run a finger along the line of Yvonne's jaw, Tami resisted the urge to release a huge *Aawwwww*. She'd never seen her big sister with a guy before, and she had definitely never seen that look on Yvonne's face as she stared up at Deacon. It didn't matter what he was saying to her—that look said it all. Yvonne was falling for him, and Deacon had clearly fallen for her. And that, combined with the news about Lana's baby and her news about the job, had Tami's heart overflowing with joy.

She took a deep breath and then resumed her giddy excitement, yelling, "Hey, y'all, I've got some news!" to let them know she was there before she made her way farther into the room.

As expected, Yvonne almost jumped out of her skin, trying to move away from Deacon like Tami was the police coming to arrest her for liking a man. Deacon, to his credit, hadn't reacted at all like he was caught doing something wrong. And just as quickly as Yvonne had moved a couple of steps away from him, he'd casually ended up right beside her when he asked, "What's up? You found the hidden treasure in the old blue house?" he joked.

"Ha ha," Tami replied. "If I had, I'd be on the next ferry back to town so I can do some real shopping."

Deacon laughed. "I bet you would."

"Oh, she definitely would," Yvonne added with a grin. "What's going on?"

Normally, Tami would've thought of some grand way to make this announcement, but to hell with it—she was too damn excited for that. "I got the job!" she blurted out. "The job I applied for at the record company and interviewed for just before we came down here. I got it, Yvonne! I got it!"

Seven weeks ago, Tami would've been on edge about sharing this news with Yvonne. She would've been bracing herself for her sister's litany about the job somehow being beneath her; after all, she was a college graduate and should be looking for something with more growth and earning potential. All of which would make Tami feel like a disappointment, even in the midst of an accomplishment. And she'd get off the phone with irritating thoughts about not being good enough or working hard enough and never being able to please the people who had at one point meant the most to her.

But today, Yvonne's smile came quickly, and she hurried to close the space between them, enfolding Tami in a warm hug. "Oh, Tam, I'm so happy for you! I know how much you wanted this. So, so happy for you."

The tears that had sprung to Tami's eyes when she'd been talking to Gabriel a few moments ago were back as she embraced her sister, closing her eyes to the feeling of Yvonne's arms around her and the sincere sound of her sister's words.

Still, when they broke apart, she asked, "Really?"

Yvonne nodded. "Really. Look, I know I got on you about telling Deacon about the job and not me, but I understand why you didn't. And now, being back in this house and seeing how you've immediately bonded with all that you were when you were here as a child, I believe in my heart that this is the job for you." She shook her head. "Not that you need my approval in any way," she insisted. "But I think I forgot how much of Grandma's music was in you. How you used to hang on her every word about touring, recording, and anything else in the industry. While me and Lana were just excited to have a beautiful grandmother whose face was on album covers."

Tami chuckled. "Yeah, y'all did use to go home and brag to everybody who'd listen about our famous grandmother."

"Congratulations, Tami," Deacon said, coming in to give her a hug.

She hugged him back and whispered, "Thanks."

Then she released a heavy sigh. "I've got to find Lana to tell her, but I'm just so happy about this."

"As you should be," Yvonne said. "Hey, when you find Lana, tell her we're going down to Charity's café for a celebration dinner tonight."

"Oh yes!" Tami said, doing her happy dance again. "I love me a celebration dinner! Especially when it's celebrating me." She was grinning again as she ran out of the room.

✉

At a little past eight that evening, the Butler sisters walked onto the porch of the summerhouse.

"I never used to like oxtails, but whatever Charity's recipe is, that food was amazing," Tami said as she plopped down into one of the folding chairs. They still hadn't put the newly painted rocking chairs on the porch because they were waiting until the outside of the house was painted. But Mr. Pete had done a wonderful job on the fresh and bright chairs that were now sitting under one of the tents Deacon's crew had erected in the yard to cover some of their tools whenever there was inclement weather. Some of them brought tools and supplies over on the ferry every day, but since the sisters were staying at the house, Deacon had felt that they could safely leave a few things on-site to cut down on transport.

"Well, I should hope it was, considering you ate my entire plate," Yvonne said as she leaned against the railing.

It was a nice evening; the humidity had decreased significantly, and now the evening breeze was just cool enough to be relaxing. She wished she could open her window and sleep under the breeze tonight, but the central air was running to keep the entire house cool when the temperatures were high during the day, so she wouldn't tamper with the thermostat tonight.

"No, I just had a little taste," Tami said, knowing that wasn't the total truth.

From where she'd taken a seat in another folding chair across from Tami, Lana shook her head. "Girl, you know you ate her entire plate of food. She had to make a whole other order."

Yvonne chuckled. "And I ordered something different too, 'cause I didn't want you deciding you wanted seconds."

"It was just so good," Tami said, remembering. "Something about that gravy. And then that peach cobbler. If I didn't have this new job, I'd move down here just to enjoy the food."

Lana sat back and rested her hands on her still very flat stomach. "The smells were bothering me too much to really enjoy my food. But the fish and pinto beans weren't bad."

"Do you have morning sickness all day?" Tami asked as she looked at Lana, wondering how her svelte sister was going to look with a baby bump.

Lana shook her head. "Not all day—and it's usually not the most popular nausea or vomiting. Headaches and fatigue have been my biggest issues so far. But tonight, all the different smells were making my stomach turn a bit."

"I was gonna say, you don't seem to be bothered when we eat in the house," Yvonne said, concern already lacing her tone.

"I don't. That's why I think it was being in the café with all the different foods and scents. Here, I'm pretty used to the scent of sawdust or wood or paint, so that doesn't bother me. And the food we heat up doesn't either. Maybe I'll just have to enjoy Charity's to-go for my remaining time here," Lana said.

"That's fine with me," Tami said. "We can order, and I'll go pick it up."

"Works for me. That, coupled with the food Ms. Janie and Mama Jo are constantly sending over here, and we'll be straight for the next few weeks," Yvonne said.

"Yeah, just three more weeks and we'll be finished. Can you imagine how everything is going to look?" Lana asked.

"I think it's going to be grand and majestic. The big white house at the end of Pinetree Road." Tami loved the thought of how beautiful the finished houses would look against the backdrop of the Intracoastal Waterway. It would be just like one of those paintings she'd seen online when researching the island.

"I know we haven't brought this up in a while," Yvonne said. "Figured we were all trying to wait until the renovations were done to really decide . . . but what are your thoughts on selling the place now?"

Tami had been dreading this conversation, because she feared that even with Yvonne falling for Deacon, she would still side with Lana— who Tami figured would certainly still want to sell to have extra money to put aside for the baby now.

None of them had time to answer, as the sound of another golf cart making its way up the driveway caught their attention.

"Who's that at this hour?" Lana asked, looking over her shoulder so she could see down the driveway.

Yvonne had turned to look as well, while Tami stood from her chair and walked a few steps until she was standing at the top of the stairs. "It looks like Sallie."

And she was right: Sallie Henderson stepped out of the front seat of the cart and then leaned in to the back seat to pull out a box. She wore a long white dress that looked more like a sack but Tami knew was called a kaftan. While she preferred more formfitting clothes herself, she knew some women liked the comfort of a loose dress. Sallie was apparently one of them.

Chunky gold bangles were on both Sallie's wrists, a chandelier-type gold necklace around her neck. Her curly hair was left to its usual wild frame around her mocha-hued face. And she frowned. Just like she had each time Tami had seen her since they'd been on the island. Neither she, Lana, nor Yvonne had figured out why the woman had had a change of heart toward them—or if her carrying out Grandma Betty's will and stocking the house before their arrival had been, as she'd said, her following the directions she was given. And not from any type of personal obligation. Truthfully, Tami knew that she and her sisters had decided that whatever the woman's issue was, it was hers and not theirs to deal with.

"Good evening," Sallie said in a crisp tone. "I think it's time we talk."

She'd walked up onto the porch by then, holding the box—Tami could now see it was a hatbox—under her left arm. Glancing to her right, Tami saw that Yvonne had pushed away from the railing and was now standing with one hand on her hip. Lana rose from her seat to stand beside Yvonne.

Yvonne spoke next. "Good evening, Sallie. Let's go inside. I'll put on some tea."

Oh shit, this wasn't gonna be good. Tami could tell by the frost in Sallie's tone and that cool resignation Yvonne tended to get when she was about to back somebody into a corner with the slick mouth she kept reserved for just these types of circumstances. Yvonne walked toward the door, using her key to enter, and Sallie followed. Tami glanced at Lana, who raised her brows, acknowledging that she'd come to the same conclusion about what was about to go down.

When the four of them were seated in the kitchen, water waiting to boil on the stove, Sallie flattened her palms on top of the hatbox, which she'd set on the table in front of her.

Instead of waiting for her to speak this time, which Sallie clearly looked like she was ready to do, Yvonne went first.

"I suspect you're here because you have something you want to get off your chest," Yvonne said, her hands flat on the top of the card table as well. "And that's fine. We'll listen while you say your piece, but understand that if you're here to start some nonsense, you can just turn around and leave. You've seemed to have a problem with us since we stepped foot on this island, and we haven't said or done anything to provoke it. I'm not going to let you bring that type of drama into our house."

"This should've been my house," Sallie rebutted quickly.

Yvonne lifted an eyebrow. "Excuse me?"

Tami sat up straighter in her chair, and Lana's lips thinned as she continued to glare at Sallie.

Sallie tilted her head and gave Yvonne a look that said *You heard what I said.* To that, Yvonne responded with a steady gaze, eyebrow still up as she waited for Sallie to clarify her statement.

"My mama didn't ever want me to say anything after I found out," Sallie continued. "She was dying, and she asked me to keep my mouth shut and be grateful for the life I had. And I tried to do what I was told, tried to honor my mama in life and after her death. But I can't." She clapped her lips shut and then let out a loud exhale. "I can't watch the three of you walk around this island like you're the grand princesses of Daufuskie, coming back to grace us with your presence like you used to do every summer."

Had they seen Sallie during their summers here? Tami couldn't recall, most likely because Sallie looked to be closer to Yvonne's and Lana's age, not hers. If her older sisters had seen or known Sallie, none of them would've noticed Tami much. Whenever Yvonne and Lana went out during their summer visits, they didn't take Tami with them. Which was fine with Tami because she'd had her father—or even better, those were the times she'd have Grandma Betty all to herself.

But one thing Tami did recall from their summers on the island was how, when her sisters sat out on the front porch, boys and girls their age all seemed to hang around out front. A few of the girls would come up and sit with Yvonne and Lana, but the boys always just lurked, grinning and acting goofy because they were too shy or awkward to come and talk to them. She used to hear Lana and Yvonne talking some nights when they'd come into the house about which ones they thought were cute and which ones were just too immature. Never—not once—did she recall her sisters mentioning Sallie.

"But it should've been me," Sallie said. "I should've been a Butler. I *am* a Butler!"

"What the hell are you talking about?" Yvonne asked.

"You wanna know what I'm talking about?" Sallie asked what seemed like a ridiculous question, because of course they all wanted to know what the hell she was ranting about.

In response—since neither Yvonne, Lana, nor Tami replied—Sallie ripped the top from that floral hatbox and dropped it to the floor.

"Oh, wow," Tami whispered as she looked at what was inside.

Stacks and stacks of letters. It made her think of the box she had upstairs in her room, the one she'd found that night she'd gone to Grandma Betty's room to sit when she couldn't sleep. But that box wasn't a hatbox. It was square and the color of a tree trunk. And there'd been over a hundred letters in that box. Staring at the one Sallie was now digging through, it looked like there could be the same number of envelopes in that one too.

"Here!" Sallie said, picking up an envelope and holding it triumphantly.

Again, the Butler sisters remained silent.

Sallie pursed her lips and then removed the letter from the envelope before reading:

> *You've been a dear friend since the first day I stepped onto this island. We've grown close over the years so I know this is your heart's deepest desire and that you would give anything for this opportunity. Well, I'm not asking you for anything in return, but I'd like to give you this baby to love and raise as your own.*

The teakettle began whistling the moment Sallie ended that sentence. And it was a good thing too, because nobody knew what to say. Well, Tami did, and she said it: "Get the hell outta here!" She shook her head. "Are you saying my grandmother gave your mother a baby? Gave *you* to your mother?"

"How old are you?" Lana asked while Yvonne got up from the table and went to turn off the teakettle.

Tami watched as her sister turned off the fire and moved the tea-kettle to another burner. Then, instead of getting tea bags, mugs, and sugar, Yvonne turned right around and came to sit back at the table.

"I need you to just say what you came here to say, Sallie. Because this"—Yvonne waved her hand in front of the box—"is . . . more than I feel like dealing with tonight."

Sallie set the letter on the table beside the box and crossed her arms over her chest. "I'm saying that thirty-four years ago, Daniel Butler was on this island for the summer. At the same time, a woman named Trudy was visiting. Daniel and Trudy had a fling that resulted in Trudy finding out she was pregnant, and a year later, Trudy returned to the island and left her baby on Ms. Betty's porch with a note."

Tears welled in Sallie's eyes as she shook her head. "Seems all the business was done via letter back then. What a difference a real conversation could've made."

"Hold the hell up! Are you saying our daddy is your daddy too?" Tami's head was spinning, her heart slamming in her chest.

"No fucking way," Lana said. "No. Just no."

Yvonne was quiet another beat before she reached for the letter Sallie had put down on the table.

Sallie didn't try to stop her; she just continued. "I'm thirty-three. My mother, Odessa, the only mother I've ever known, tried to have children the first fifteen years of her marriage. I didn't learn all of this until she got sick. When Mama knew she wasn't going to make it after that second round of chemo, she told me to go through her papers and find the insurance stuff. I found these letters instead."

"Ms. Janie said your father was in love with my grandmother and that your mother knew but never said anything," Yvonne said as she placed the letter on the table. "Is this some sort of cruel way to get back at us for whatever may have happened between them years ago?"

Sallie frowned. "You don't believe that."

"Well, shit, I don't know what to believe right about now," Tami said, because it was the truth. How had the day taken such a drastic turn?

One minute she was flying high after landing the job of her dreams; the next, she was bonding with her sisters over some damn great food in a way she hadn't done in years and now this. She brought her hands to her face and scrubbed them down, hoping that when she let them fall to the table again, nobody would be sitting there and this would have all been a bad dream. Well, not the part about the job and the good food.

"What do you want?" Lana asked. "Why are you really here, telling us this tonight?"

Now Sallie grimaced. "I want the truth out, once and for all. There's been years of lies circling around this island. More people knew about this than you can imagine, and nobody bothered to tell me. I didn't talk to my mama much about it after she told me to keep my mouth shut. Didn't want to upset her more than was necessary, not in her condition." She took a deep breath and released it on a heavy sigh. "But I asked my father, and he told me the truth. Said he was tired of lying too. Had been lying for too many years about too many things."

Tami heard her voice catch on those last words and, for just a second, let herself really hear Sallie's voice.

"I don't want this house," Sallie said with a shake of her head. "I don't want anything of Ms. Betty's. That doesn't mean that it shouldn't have been mine, just the same. I had a right to know who my parents were, just like you have a right to know who your . . . *our* father was. I just wanted the people that it affected most to finally know the truth."

"This isn't enough proof," Yvonne said. "Where's your real mother? Have you talked to her?"

Sallie shook her head. "All I know is her first name: Trudy. Nobody else knew anything more. My birth certificate says Odessa and Cabell Henderson are my parents. Says I was born right here on 'Fuskie." She shrugged. "They were good to me. I was loved and well taken care of. I guess if I'd grown up someplace else, anyplace else, everything would've been just fine. But no, I grew up here and had to watch every summer as he brought you three down here to stay in this house, wear those pretty new clothes, and be treated like royalty. While he ignored me."

"How do you know he knew?" Lana asked finally, even though disbelief still swam through her mind.

Tami suspected the three of them felt the same. This woman was sitting at the card table in her grandmother's kitchen, telling them that their father had been a liar and a cheat. That their grandmother had known this, and nobody had said a word. She swallowed and considered getting up to fix herself a cup of tea. But then she'd have to find Grandma Betty's brandy to add to it, because tonight desperately called for something stronger.

"I'm sure Ms. Janie also told you that my father liked his drink. Between him being in love with another woman thirteen years older than him and staying drunk most of the time because he couldn't have her, his marriage to my mama became nothing but an arrangement. There was no talk of a divorce; he continued to pay the bills and take care of me, but that was it. He loved someone else and that was that." She looked down at her hands and then back up to them after a few seconds. "He told me that the last time he tried to convince Ms. Betty that they should be together—I was six—and your . . . our . . ." She sighed. "Daniel was here with you and Lana. Ms. Betty turned him away again, told him he had to go home and be a husband to my mama and a father to me. Daddy was drunk and heartbroken, said Daniel should take responsibility and be a father to his own child. Daniel walked in on the argument." She shrugged, then reached up shaking fingers to quickly swipe at the tears that had finally fallen from her eyes.

"So he knew before I was born," Tami whispered.

"I think I'm gonna be sick," Lana said, and stood from the table before rushing out of the room.

Yvonne rose slowly. "I'm going to go take care of my sister," she said. Then she pushed the incriminating letter across the table until it was once again in front of Sallie. "I don't know what else to say about this tonight."

Sallie shook her head. "I don't need you—any of you—to say anything. I just thought it was time the truth was out."

There was a moment of silence before Yvonne gave a curt nod. Leaving Tami there to sit and stare at this woman who now claimed to be her sister.

"So your parents just stayed married even though everyone knew your father was in love with my grandmother?" Tami asked. She was determined to get more answers, even if Yvonne chose to be the immature one and run away this time.

Sallie had stared after Yvonne and Lana for a few seconds before replying. "Yes. People from that generation weren't big on divorces. It was easier to agree to accept certain things and let go of others, I guess. My mother seemed content as long as my father continued to handle his financial responsibilities."

While Tami's mother had never seemed content a day in her life. "I know you understand that this is a lot for us to take in."

Sallie's fluffy curls moved as she nodded. "Just as tough as it was for me to find out when I did. And believe me, I don't wish this feeling on anyone. I told myself to let it all die with Ms. Betty. But then y'all inherited this place, and instead of selling it and staying away from 'Fuskie, you came back here." She laced her fingers together and then nervously pulled them apart. "I probably could've continued to keep the secret if I never had to see you. But when you showed up, it was just like all the years you've always come down, with everybody falling all over y'all like you were royalty, and them same people choosing to forget that I belonged in this house too."

"You mean all the people on the island who knew?" Tami asked.

"That's right. So many of them knew. Especially all the old folks. 'Fuskie's too small to keep a secret like that, and nobody ever saw my mama pregnant. They knew," Sallie said.

And for that, Tami's heart broke for her. Because despite how horrible Freda was the majority of the time to Tami, there'd never been any doubt that she was her mother. And even for the short time she'd had Daniel in her life, he'd shown Tami all the love and devotion a father should have. She'd had her biological parents, with all their flaws, and her sisters, with their different personalities, while Sallie had a lie.

They sat in silence for a few minutes before Sallie stood to leave.

"I want to know the full story. Do you think your father would talk to us?"

Sallie picked up her box, hugging it close to her chest. The corner of her mouth lifted in a small smile, and for just a second, just a quick flash, that smile resembled Daniel Butler's.

"Even though she's dead and gone, that man would still do anything for Ms. Betty," Sallie replied. "If her granddaughters have questions, I have no doubt he'll answer."

Chapter 26

LANA

"I love you too," Lana said into the phone as she lay in bed the next morning. Isaac had called to tell her that Jimmy had been paid in full.

It was Friday, one week after Isaac had come to the island and broken into the summerhouse. After her pregnancy announcement and Yvonne's generous offer, he'd stayed with her the remainder of the weekend and was on the first ferry to start his trip back to Boston on Monday morning. When his flight had landed, he'd called her to say that Yvonne had wired the money to their account. And Lana had found her sister in the backyard, wearing goggles and gloves and attempting to use the table saw—with Deacon supervising, of course. She'd hugged and thanked Yvonne again before leaving what she and everybody else in that house knew was a budding romance alone.

Now the debt that had been looming over her marriage was paid. In addition to that news, Isaac had also called to tell Lana that his first therapy appointment was on Tuesday. With a sigh, she dropped the phone to her bed after they ended the call and let her hand fall to her stomach.

There was a baby growing there. Her and Isaac's baby. A smile ghosted her lips, and she closed her eyes. How long had she waited for this day? How many times had she prayed for her and Isaac to start a family? How many times had she hoped that having a child would save their marriage?

With that last question, her eyes popped open, and she stared at the ceiling. Sunlight was already streaming through the sheer curtains at her bedroom windows, giving the room a bright, golden glow. Birds were up and chirping, and she suspected her sisters would be stirring in their own rooms as well.

Her sisters. Yvonne and Tami.

And Sallie?

Another heavy sigh followed, and she continued to rub her hand over her stomach. How could a mother just drop her child off and walk away? How could a father see his child three months out of the year and not claim her? And how the hell were they supposed to deal with this information now?

Had their father, Daniel Rutherford Butler, lied to them? Obviously, that would've been a lie by omission, because never once in all the years her father had been in her life had Lana ever thought to ask him if he had other children. Daddy was an English professor at the local community college, but he was there every day when she came home from preschool. And when she was in the first grade and had started learning to read, he would sit at the kitchen table and help her make letters into words. Lana was seven when they divorced, but Daddy still came to see her and her sisters two nights out of the week and took them to stay at the new house they'd helped him pick out every other weekend. The summers were his and Grandma Betty's because that had always been their tradition, and Mama had agreed because she always worked year-round, so it was easier to have them out of her way for a few months than add the expense of summer camps to entertain them.

Sallie was a year younger than Lana and four years older than Tami. What had Sallie done all year? Did Grandma Betty check on her, make sure she was getting everything she needed the way Lana knew her grandmother always did with them? As she grew older, she could recall Mama being so upset anytime Grandma Betty would call their house and ask her about them. She'd always yell, "They're your son's children too—ask him how they're doing. You don't have to call me."

But Grandma Betty still called, and Mama only seemed to get angrier and angrier when she did. This was all after the divorce, after Tami had been born. After, Sallie said, Mr. Cab had told Daddy that Sallie was his child.

Her stomach roiled, and Lana hurriedly pushed the covers back, jumped out of the bed, and ran into the bathroom. Forty minutes later, her stomach had basically settled to a low threat, and she'd brushed her teeth twice, showered, and dressed for the day. She unwrapped her hair and combed it down, swiped some gloss over her lips so she didn't look totally like the walking dead, and went downstairs to the kitchen.

She was first to arrive, which was what she'd hoped. Each morning, both her sisters came into the kitchen for coffee or orange juice and whatever pastry or quick breakfast item they had on hand. This morning, Lana wanted them to sit and have a full breakfast. She needed food in her stomach, not just something sweet and quick, and they—the three of them—needed to talk.

"Mornin'," Yvonne said when she walked in just as Lana retrieved a box of buttermilk biscuits Mama Jo had sent via Deacon yesterday from the refrigerator.

"Good morning," Lana replied, and grabbed the plate of ham slices too. She took them both to the island, the only counter space they had at the moment.

The marble countertops they'd finally decided on and ordered were set to be delivered next week. In the meantime, all the other counters had been taken out except the island, because Yvonne had insisted they needed some space to operate in here. And she was right. As much as Lana hated to admit it, her big sister was right about a lot of things.

"I need coffee this morning," Yvonne said as she moved to the box where they'd started keeping items that would normally go into a cabinet. "You want some?"

"No, thanks," Lana said. Then she added, "Caffeine," when Yvonne gave her a quizzical look.

Yvonne's face softened, her lightly glossed lips going up into a smile. "That's right—my little niece or nephew doesn't need all that caffeine," she said, and then put the canister of coffee she'd retrieved down on the island and reached for both of Lana's hands. "I almost forgot we still had happy news to celebrate. I'm so excited for you, Little Sis."

Lana gave a tiny chuckle at the nickname Yvonne had used for her often. When Tami was born, Yvonne had stopped using it, but Lana had understood why.

After a few seconds, Yvonne dropped her hands and pulled Lana into a hug. "I'm so happy for you and Isaac. You're gonna make wonderful parents."

Wrapping her arms around her sister, Lana held on in a way she hadn't in years. Well, it had been years since they'd felt at ease enough with each other to share an embrace, to open their hearts.

"Thanks, sis," Lana said when they pulled apart. "I'm so nervous." It was her first time admitting that out loud.

"Really? Why?" Yvonne asked as she moved to the coffee maker they'd run an extension cord over to the socket near the refrigerator to power. "You've never been nervous about doing anything."

That's what she'd thought. Lana knew she'd always put up a decisive and unshakable facade, but that was the furthest from what she was feeling right now or had for a long time. She found a knife in the plastic bin they were keeping the silverware they used on a daily basis in. "Girl, this is uncharted territory for me. I mean, Isaac and I have been talking about starting a family for a while, but that's as far as the thoughts went—and now there's actually a baby growing inside of me, and I'm still trippin' over that."

"I guess I can imagine that. It's new, but it's also exciting." Yvonne moved over to the sink to put water in the pot.

"Exciting and scary as hell. I don't know how to carry a baby. I drink Starbucks every day, sometimes three times a day. Those hot, gooey Cinnabons with the caramel and pecans is still my favorite dessert of all time. I like sleeping all night and taking naps whenever I can. I hated gym, so you know exercise and all that take-care-of-your-body stuff has been out the window for me."

"And yet, of the three of us, you're the one who's always had the most amazing body," Yvonne said.

She shrugged. "High metabolism, I guess."

Yvonne chuckled. "Lucky you."

"Well, I'm certainly feeling lucky now, with this news." Then she thought about what she'd said as she sliced the biscuits open, placing the two sides on a plate. "No, you know what? I'm blessed. We all are."

"Yeah, you're definitely blessed to be having a baby with the man you love," Yvonne said, pushing the button to start the coffeepot.

"I think we're all blessed to have gotten to this point in our lives. Remember Janel Lang? She used to hang out at the rec center with us sometimes after school."

Yvonne took a seat at the island and nodded. "Oh yeah. Her brother was the one who used to always say, 'Damn, girl, your ass is phat!' every time you walked past him on the basketball court."

Lana nodded and grinned. "Until I dunked on his ass, and then he stopped speaking to me altogether."

"And that right there was a blessing," Yvonne said, and they both laughed.

"Right," Lana said, and then put ham slices on the biscuits and walked the plate over to the microwave. "But Janel died last year of complications from lupus. And when I went to my ten-year high school reunion, two of my other classmates had passed too. So when I say we're all blessed, I mean it. We're still here, despite all the ups and downs we go through."

Yvonne nodded. "You're right."

"And so was Sallie," Tami said, coming into the kitchen with a box in one hand, a small stack of envelopes in the other.

The mood in the room immediately shifted. Lana felt it, and by the immediate frown that covered Yvonne's face, she did too.

"Good morning," Lana said. "Yvonne's brewing coffee, and I've got ham biscuits in the microwave. Let's sit down and eat."

Tami had already set the box on the island, but when she looked up at Lana, she raised a brow. "Oookay," she said. "And then we're gonna talk about this new-sister thing, right? Because it's a pretty big thing, and we can't actually just shrug it off."

"No, you're right—we can't shrug it off," Lana said. "But I and your niece or nephew need to eat first."

That made Tami smile. "That's right—you do need to feed Auntie's baby."

Seeing both her sisters excited about this pregnancy was something Lana had never really imagined. Just like she'd started to tell Yvonne, she and Isaac had been discussing having a baby for a while, but this pregnancy couldn't have come as more of a shock to her.

"I still can't believe you're pregnant," Tami said as if she'd been reading Lana's mind.

Lana removed the plate from the microwave and set it on the island between her and her sisters. "Well, that makes two of us," she said.

"What do you mean? I thought you said you and Isaac had been planning to start a family," Yvonne said. She poured herself a cup of coffee and then looked to Tami to see if she wanted one.

Tami nodded and went to the box to find her mug. "I'll get you some orange juice," she said to Lana.

"Thanks," Lana replied as she sat on the stool at the island. "Yeah, we were planning, discussing, but I'd actually begun to worry that we weren't really moving forward with that discussion. I mean, with the gambling and all that stress."

"I still can't believe straitlaced Isaac with his goofy self is out here gambling like he's a pro," Tami said, setting the glass of orange juice in front of Lana.

"He wasn't a pro," Lana said with a shake of her head. "And that was the problem." They'd talked about Isaac and his gambling and the toll it had taken on their marriage at length the day she finally admitted to them what was going on, so Tami's comment didn't really surprise or agitate her. "But I'd started to feel like his focus was more on that than starting a family, and I was so worried about all that stuff that the family thing wasn't at the top of my list of priorities. I think I'm about four to six weeks along now, but I'm not totally sure."

"Well, we're excited either way," Tami said when she sat across from them and reached for a napkin. "I've never thought about having a baby myself, but I always thought it would be a joyous occasion. I guess it's not for everyone."

Lana knew they weren't going to be able to put this off for long, no matter how much she was beginning to think Yvonne wanted them to. "That probably depends on the circumstances," she said.

Tami had taken a bite of her biscuit and was now nodding as she reached for the stack of letters she'd brought in with her. "I'm guessing the circumstances around Sallie's birth were anything but that," she said while she chewed and attempted to pass the letters to Yvonne.

But Yvonne sipped her coffee and didn't even look at the letters. So Lana reached for them. She set them beside her on the table and took a bite of her biscuit. "That's the box of Grandma's letters you told us about." That night of the thunderstorm, when they'd all been huddled together in Yvonne's bed, she'd told them about the letters, but after Tami had said she hadn't read any love letters, they'd all kind of lost interest.

Tami wiped her mouth after she finished chewing and nodded. "I hadn't read all of them, just a few. And then I started feeling creepy about it, so I stopped. But after all that Sallie said last night about communicating with letters instead of just having a conversation, I wondered if Grandma had communicated anything about a baby too. So I stayed up half the night, trying to get through them all."

Yvonne took a bite from her biscuit, still acting disinterested. Lana opened the first envelope because, unlike her big sister, she *did* want to know what they said.

I won't come back.

That's all that was written on the first piece of paper she'd pulled from the envelope.

"There's more," Tami said with a nod toward the envelope.

Lana reached inside and pulled out another sheet of paper. "She signed over all her parental rights," she said, frowning. "Her name was Gertrude Jones, and she just gave up her child."

"I know," Tami said. "Sad, right? I mean, I guess it's better than keeping the child and not being able to take care of her or abusing her or whatever. But still, sad."

Lana moved on to the next envelope. "A letter from Ms. Odessa," she said as she read it. "Shit," she muttered when she was finished. Then she picked up her glass and took a long drink. "It was like a transaction."

"No." Tami shook her head. "An agreement. Grandma gave Ms. Odessa a baby, and they agreed to keep it a secret. No lawyers, no documents—just a verbal agreement."

"And just like that, our half sister grows up thinking she's someone else's child," Lana said, feeling a wave of unexpected sadness.

For a moment the three of them were silent. Then Yvonne spoke. "I don't know how to feel about this. I sat at that table last night, listening to her, watching her, and I just don't know." She picked up her mug again and brought it to her lips, but this time Lana noticed that her fingers trembled.

"I think Mama knew," Lana said, because there was no use holding it back. Not that she'd even considered that in the first place. She'd known that they needed to talk about this, and she'd planned to do it over breakfast, but it would've been really nice if they could've just continued to talk about being happy about her pregnancy. "I think Daddy told her when he found out."

Yvonne shook her head. "No, she would've put him out the moment she found out about this. You know what she used to always tell us about men—not to trust them. They could be good in bed but useless for anything else, which is why we should focus on our personal success making us happy."

"Yeah, well, how's that working out for her?" Tami asked snidely.

Before Yvonne could reply and the two of them could start their usual bickering, Lana continued, "Not if she was already pregnant with Tami."

They were silent again.

"Mama was so angry after Tami was born," Lana said finally. "She worked even more, and Daddy tried even harder to give us everything—his time, attention, love."

"That would explain why she hates me, I guess. Although I'm not the 'other' child; I was hers too." Tami's voice wavered, and Lana reached across the island until she extended her hand.

Clutching her younger sister's fingers between her own, Lana said, "She didn't hate you, Tami."

"I couldn't tell," Tami said with tears forming. "I mean, I could never do anything right in her eyes. No matter how hard I tried."

"None of us could," Lana told her. "That wasn't just you."

"So we're going with the idea that Daddy didn't know about this child until she was, what? Five or six years old? Then he finds out and still ignores her and his responsibilities?" Yvonne asked. "And on top of that, our mother learns about his infidelity and this outside baby—then, instead of leaving him, she has her baby and prolongs the inevitable for another year before she's finally had enough? Then everybody just goes on with their life after the divorce as if all of this is normal?"

Lana shook her head. "But wasn't it, though?" she asked. "I mean, remember we went to Aunt Esterene's funeral when you were in high school, and in the obituary, there were two mothers listed?"

Yvonne nodded. "And Mama explained to us that Aunt Gail had raised Aunt Esterene as her daughter but that Aunt Mabel was really her mother, and she'd given her sister her baby because she'd already had six kids and couldn't afford to raise any more."

"Right," Lana said. She'd been in middle school then, but she recalled being flabbergasted by that for weeks after the funeral.

"All I knew was that Aunt Esterene used to bake the best yeast rolls," Tami said. "So I cried my little eyes out at that funeral."

Lana grinned. "Yeah, you did. Then you ate so many yeast rolls at the repast that you got a stomachache, and we had to take you upstairs and stay in Aunt Gail's bedroom with you in case you needed to throw up."

They all grinned at that but then went silent again.

"She said she doesn't want the house," Tami said.

"Good, because she can't have it," Yvonne declared. "It's already in our names; she would have to take us to court to lay any claim to it. Then I'd request a DNA test, and this could go on and on."

Lana nodded. "You're right."

"Maybe she really did just want us to know," Tami said. "And now we do."

"And now we do," Lana replied.

"I told her we'd meet her at her father's house—well, Mr. Cab's house—today at noon," Tami continued.

"You did what?" Yvonne spoke in that dangerously low tone that sounded just like Mama's.

Tami pursed her lips. "There's no running from this, Yvonne. Just because you got up and walked out of the room last night didn't mean we didn't wake up this morning with a new sister."

"I didn't wake up with anything," Yvonne snapped.

"And denial doesn't make it go away either," Tami continued. "So I decided last night—without the two of you—that the three of us would go over to Mr. Cab's house, where we can all sit down and talk about this."

"Talk about what, Tami? Because you can't make those decisions for me."

Lana held up a hand to intervene. "I don't think the intention was to make decisions for us," she said. "It was to present a united front—you know, like we always try to do, regardless of our disagreements behind closed doors. If she's really our sister, don't you think we all deserve to know the truth?"

Yvonne ran her hands down her hair and closed her eyes. She breathed slowly, as if she were trying to relax. Tami tossed a knowing look in Lana's direction, and Lana shrugged.

"We all know how big this is, Yvonne. Just like we all know it's not going to go away just because we don't want to face it. Don't you think that's what Daddy and Mama—and hell, even Grandma Betty—tried to do all these years? And look, Sallie still waltzed in here last night, finally being the one bold enough to just release the secret."

It was another few seconds before Yvonne opened her eyes. "Fine. I'll go and I'll listen. But don't expect anything else from me. Don't expect me to open my arms and heart to this woman, who has barely spoken a kind word to us since we've been here."

"She wasn't unkind last night," Tami said, and Lana nudged her. "What? She wasn't."

Yvonne rolled her eyes. "I'll be ready at noon," she said before, once again, leaving her sisters alone in the kitchen.

Chapter 27

YVONNE

Cabell "Cab" Henderson was a single man in his midseventies. Yvonne knew his age after Tami's rundown of her solo conversation with Sallie the night before. His house was medium size in comparison to the other older homes on the island. It had white siding and a sloped metal roof, a black door and matching window shutters. The house was situated between two huge old oak trees that were partially covered in Spanish moss.

They'd driven their golf cart over, following the directions that Sallie had given Tami. All the while, Yvonne still wondered what she was doing and why.

Part of her understood full well why Tami wanted answers. Tami had always wanted to know everything about everything. When they were young, her inquisitiveness could be irritating, but now, looking back, Yvonne could recognize it as Tami's way of working through things. Because her brain didn't process things like everyone else's, she had to gather information in her way for it to make sense. And what way made sense to Yvonne?

To go with the flow and let all her questions, doubts, and recriminations marinate until she felt like she was slogging through the thick mess she called a life.

"This place is picture-perfect," Tami said wistfully as she stepped out of the cart and stared ahead.

"Yeah, it is lovely," Lana added when she came around the cart to stand next to Tami. "Wish I'd brought my camera with me."

With a hand held against her brow, Tami shielded the sun from her eyes. "What are you going to do with all the pictures you've taken on the island? They're not what you normally sell in the galleries."

"No, they're not," Lana replied. She was wearing large-frame sunglasses and a floppy-brim sun hat that, coupled with the navy-blue halter-top maxi dress, made her look like she should be headed to the beach instead of into a stranger's house.

But was this man really a stranger? When she finally exited the cart and followed her sisters across the yard and up the front steps of the porch, Yvonne had an eerie feeling that this man knew more about them and their family than she or her sisters could ever imagine.

Sallie opened the door before Tami could knock. There was a hint of a smile to her lips as she muttered, "Good afternoon," and then stepped to the side to let them in.

Yvonne was last, meeting Sallie's gaze momentarily before she decided to look away. After a restless night of sleep, a tumultuous morning with her sisters, and more minutes spent contemplating the situation than she wanted to give, she was no closer to resolving this in her mind. Or her spirit. Like, what was she really supposed to do with all this newfound information? What did her sisters expect her to do? Turn against the parents who'd raised them, had given them the very best they could, and embrace this woman and the wildly painful but uncomfortably possible story she'd told them?

The interior of the house was just as neat as the outside, with thick-planked dark-wood floors, white beadboard walls, heavy oak furniture, and light. Plenty of light spilled in from windows with the shades pulled all the way up. It made the place feel airy and homey at the same time. Pictures were on every wall—some big, some small, most in weathered frames with panes so old they were pricked with tiny dots that could never be wiped away. Black-and-white pictures, mostly of men posing near the docks or in what looked like fields. A few with people sitting in big rocking chairs on wide porches, and then, like a beacon blaring life into the otherwise dim arrangement of memories, there was an eight-by-ten color photo of Betty Butler.

Lana walked up to the photo first, lifting her shaking fingers to the edge of the gold-rimmed frame, which appeared in much better condition than the others. "Grandma Betty sure was beautiful," Lana whispered.

Tami had stepped up right beside Lana, staring at the picture as if it were the first time she'd ever seen it. Yvonne knew that it wasn't. Grandma Betty had been as proud of her looks as she had her voice, so there'd been plenty of pictures of her in her office and the music room, and more in boxes stored in her bedroom closet. This one had to have been taken in the sixties, because she wore that high bouffant style, her hair a glossy black that made her cinnamon-hued skin glow. Heavy eyeliner gave her eyes a catlike quality, or perhaps it was just the bewitching way in which she seemed to be staring at the camera.

Yvonne couldn't help the tears that filled her eyes as she stared at the woman who'd brought them all to this island time and time again. The woman who'd given birth to their father and had orchestrated the events that would lead to this very moment.

"Is this why you brought us here?" Yvonne asked. "Is this why you were so adamant that we come back to this island to fix up your house?"

"It is!" Tami said, and whirled around to face her.

Yvonne hadn't even realized she'd spoken the question out loud.

"We've all been wondering why she put those stipulations in her will. Why we had to be the ones to come back and oversee the renovations," Tami continued. "This has to be the reason why."

Glancing at her younger sister, Yvonne could see that she'd lost her battle with holding her tears at bay. They ran down her cheeks, even as her eyes held an excited glow. When Lana turned around next, Yvonne almost sighed because she, too, was crying.

"Really, y'all," Yvonne said, her voice cracking as she blinked furiously to keep the tears from coming. "We came all the way to this man's house just to cry. We could've done this back at the summerhouse. Or at home again, like we did when we first found out she was gone."

"But you just would've grieved her again once you got to 'Fuskie," a deep, raspy voice said. "Her presence was strong here, and I suspect it always will be."

The sisters all turned their attention to the man who'd entered the dining-room area of the house. He had a deep-mahogany complexion; his low-cut beard was snowy white, while the hair on top of his head was a salt-and-pepper sprinkle. As he stepped closer to them, Yvonne noticed his broad shoulders and fit upper body in the white dress shirt he wore. The sleeves were rolled midway up his arms, one of which he stretched out when he was closer to Tami.

"You're Tamela," he said, his narrow eyes resting on her. "The baby that Betty said couldn't hold a note but had music in her heart."

More tears spilled from Tami's eyes as she accepted his hand to shake it vigorously. "Yes. Yes!" she said with a quick nod. "That's exactly what she used to tell me."

He grinned. "You have her smile," he told her.

Tami beamed and then reached up to swipe the back of her hand over her cheeks, wiping away her tears.

"And you're Alana." He reached for Lana's hand in the same way he'd done Tami's, and Lana accepted it. "From the time you could walk, Betty said you should be in pictures, but then you grew up and decided you'd rather control the camera than be in front of it. Pretty, talented, *and* smart."

"Thank you, sir," Lana replied, her tears now lighted by a smile as well.

Yvonne couldn't find a smile. Not at how easily her sisters had accepted this man's greeting or to cover over the heavy grief that had now washed over her. But when he came to a stop in front of her, she did meet his gaze.

"Betty's serious baby girl. The one who'd learned to walk and talk just so she could hold the weight of her family's woes on her shoulders. Oh, how she'd prayed the light and love that lived inside you would someday break free."

"My name is Yvonne," she said as if it had to be noted. He'd said everyone else's name but hers, and she didn't like it. Nor did she like how the words he did speak had pierced through her heart like an arrow hitting a bull's-eye.

His look sobered for a moment, but still, he reached out a hand to her. She glanced down at it and could feel the expectant gazes of her sisters shooting at her from the side. Without another thought, she accepted his hand and then brought her eyes up to meet his again.

"I'm Cab Henderson," he said. "It's my pleasure and honor to meet you, Yvonne."

There was a smoothness to his tone, something she suspected had won the hearts of Ms. Odessa and plenty of other women back in the day. But not Grandma Betty's. Yvonne wondered why.

She pulled her hand from his grasp. "Thank you for having us today," she said. "We won't take up much of your time."

He chuckled. "Well, now, these days I don't have much more than time."

Sallie spoke up. "I made tea."

Yvonne hadn't even noticed she'd left the room or when she'd returned, she'd been so engrossed in the pictures, and then in this man. She should've been paying more attention to the whirlwind of emotions that were roaring through her, since she was obviously the sister who'd have to keep her mind right during this little visit. Not that this was anything new.

"Let's take it in the living room, Sallie," Cab said, and then walked ahead of them to lead the way.

Lana came to stand beside Yvonne and took her hand. "It's going to be okay," she assured her.

But Yvonne wasn't convinced. She had a feeling that none of them were going to walk out of that house feeling the same way they had when they walked in, and she couldn't explain why that scared the hell out of her.

"I loved your grandmother with my whole heart," Cab said after Sallie had served them each a cup of tea that smelled and tasted heavenly. "But she never loved me more than she would have a brother or a very close friend."

"Because she was so much older than you?" Tami asked.

Cab gave a wry laugh. "No. No, I don't think that was it." He dragged a hand over his jaw and settled back on the hunter-green couch.

Sallie sat beside him, her hands folded in her lap, her gaze resting on the man she called her father.

"You know those songs where Betty used to sing about the love of her life? The love that made her life complete? Or the love that would sustain her until the ends of her days?" He sounded thoughtful.

Tami sat at the edge of the armchair she'd taken because it was closer to the side of the couch where Cab was situated. "Oh yes," she said, flattening a hand over her chest. "I loved her songs and used to dream about the lyrics all through high school. Our music just didn't have that soulful feel like music in Grandma Betty's time."

Cab rested an elbow on the arm of the couch but pointed a finger at Tami as he said, "You've got that right." Bringing that same finger back to his face, he rubbed it along the line of his jaw. "Betty could sing those lyrics like nobody else because she felt them deep down in her soul. She loved ole Riley's goofy behind from the moment she saw him until the day she stood by his rust-colored coffin and said goodbye to his earthly form. And then she loved every memory of him just as fiercely.

I couldn't compete with a ghost," he muttered. "Not with everything in my arsenal, I couldn't compete."

Sallie reached out a hand to grasp his free one. And when he looked over at her, they both smiled at each other. It was like Sallie understood this man who'd been married to her mother's love of another woman. That seemed odd to Yvonne—but then, on another level, impactful.

"That's why you and Odessa took the baby," Yvonne said quietly. "Because both of you loved Grandma Betty. You were in love with her and would do anything she asked you to do, and Ms. Odessa loved her as a friend and the woman who could make her once-unattainable wish come true."

The words just tumbled free, the muted sense of understanding seeping through the pain and grief that now threatened to suffocate her.

"And we loved Sallie," he said with a slow nod toward Yvonne. "From the day we carried her home in that basket, we loved this little girl like she'd been born from us." His brow lifted and he continued. "Now, just because Betty gave us this beautiful blessing, don't you go to thinking that she just forgot about her, because she didn't. Every month she put money in an account for Sallie to have when she was an adult. And she always checked in with me and Odessa to see what, if anything, Sallie needed. She made the decision to watch this granddaughter grow up from a distance, the same way she had to watch the three of you living in the city. She didn't like any of it, but she always said she did what she had to do."

He lifted the hands he and Sallie had clasped and kissed the back of hers. "I'm blessed and grateful to have known and loved such a classy and compassionate woman. And I thank the Lord every day that even though she couldn't give me her heart, she gave me this lovely child, who has grown into a beautiful woman, inside and out. Smart, loyal, and not a bad singer either." He gave Sallie a wink. "Before you leave the island, you should come to church one Sunday. Hear my baby girl sing like her grandmother used to."

Those words had Tami gasping and crying again.

"You can sing like Grandma?" Lana asked.

"And Daddy," Tami added. "Remember, he used to sing us to sleep—and how, at Christmas, we always begged him to sing that Nat King Cole song because he did it so well?"

Sallie looked over at them, her eyes a little watery now too. "I can sing," she said. "Always thought the gift just came from the Lord, and so that's where I used it."

"We'll come to church on Sunday," Lana said.

"Yes," Tami agreed. "We certainly will."

Yvonne almost chastised her sisters for making another decision for her, but she kept her mouth shut. She was suddenly too tired—or too overwhelmed. She couldn't tell which to tell the difference. Instead, she mustered what she hoped was a cordial-enough smile and was about to say that they had to leave, when her phone rang.

"It's mine," she said, and pulled the device out of the back pocket of her shorts. "I'll be right back."

Chapter 28

YVONNE

"What the hell is going on?" Yvonne asked moments after she'd stalked through the front door of the summerhouse, heading straight to the kitchen. "Is Mercury in retrograde or something?" she asked no one in particular.

"Wait, you said Mama fell and that she's in the hospital. But I thought Ms. Rosalee was staying with Mama to help her. How did she fall?" Lana asked, following behind her.

She recognized that this wasn't the time to stress Lana, and these past weeks had definitely been stressful. But she couldn't *not* tell them what was going on. Dealing with one big-ass secret at a time was enough. Besides, Yvonne had been more than ready to get the hell out of Cab Henderson's house and away from the way everything about Sallie seemed to remind her more and more of their father. She was trying her best not to be pissed at the father she'd loved and respected, not to rush to judgment about a decision she could never imagine making herself.

"Ms. Rosalee walked Mama into the bathroom to get her shower. She said she left the new soap Mama had ordered online in the living room. So she told Mama to sit on the toilet seat and that she'd be right back to help her into the shower. But Mama didn't wait," Yvonne said.

"When did she get so bad that she couldn't step into the shower on her own?" Lana asked.

Yvonne resisted the urge to sigh in frustration. "In the last few months, she's been losing function of her hand, arm, and leg on the right side. It happens on and off, but that was another reason the doctors thought it would be better if she had everything she needed on one level and why I wanted to get the work done on the house. It needs to be handicap accessible. With a new shower, she could just walk in; she wouldn't have to lift her leg to get inside the tub." Yvonne went to the refrigerator, thinking that she needed something to drink. But then she walked right past it, toward the back doors that had just been repaired.

She stared out into the afternoon sunlight, her heart slamming in her chest. How was she supposed to handle all this? Pain radiated from the back of her neck, across the line of her shoulders, as the weight of everything that had been going on these past few weeks—hell, the past few years—seemed to bear down heavier than ever before.

"Is she going to be okay?" Tami asked in a low voice from somewhere behind her.

Yvonne nodded, even though she wasn't sure exactly what *okay* for Freda would look like after this. "Ms. Rosalee said she's alert. She said she didn't think she hit her head but that when she found her, the way she was lying on the floor, with her side crumpled against the edge of the tub, she couldn't tell what might've been hurt. But then, when the paramedics arrived, Mama told them it was her arm and ankle. The ankle is broken, and they may need to operate to fix the break."

"So she's gonna be even more immobile," Lana said, and Yvonne turned to them before nodding.

"I'm gonna go up and pack, see if I can make the next ferry," she said.

"What? You're leaving?" Tami asked. "What about the rest of the renovations?"

Yvonne paused and stared at her. "I'm not staying here while Mama may be going into surgery."

"But you said she was going to be okay," Tami countered.

"And I believe that to be true, but that doesn't mean I want to be hundreds of miles away while she's in the hospital."

"But Ms. Rosalee's there, so she's not alone. And we're almost done. Don't you want to see this through to the end and then—"

"No, Tami. I want to go home and make sure Mama is all right."

Tami blinked. "What about Sallie?"

"What about her?" Yvonne asked. "It's not *her* mother in the hospital."

The room fell silent.

"I think what she's asking is, aren't we going to try and get to know Sallie? After today's meeting with her and Cab, it just seems like we should. But how would we do that if you're not here?" Lana asked.

The storm of emotions that had been steadily brewing inside her burst free with a searing gaze Yvonne aimed at Lana. "You're kidding, right? I mean, I know it's her norm to be ridiculous about anything regarding responsibility—but you too, Lana?"

"Hold up," Tami started, but Lana put up a hand to halt her words.

"Stop. Take a breath and just listen, Yvonne. There's a lot going on; we all realize that. But I think we should just focus on the things that we can control at the moment. Like, we can decide how to move forward with Sallie and finish up these renovations. Ms. Rosalee is with Mama, and she can keep us posted. If things become more serious with Mama—"

"No, you stop right there," Yvonne said, crossing her arms over her chest. "You two really want me to stay here and ignore what just happened so that I can have a conversation with a woman who's spent the last few weeks staring daggers at us instead of just telling us what she knew the moment we got here?"

"Maybe that's not as easy as you make it seem, Yvonne," Tami said. "Lord knows, everybody doesn't always have the right answers, like you seem to think you do."

"I'm not gonna do this with you right now, Tami. I'm just not." Because Yvonne couldn't explain the conflicting emotions surrounding this particular part of her newly drama-filled life. She clenched her fingers and recalled how she'd been running on fumes that morning after tossing and turning in bed most of the night. She had no idea how she felt about her father having this other child or the fact that her grandmother had kept this secret all these years. That, on top of the incessant pull toward this island and the people she'd met here that she hadn't been able to quash. She'd awakened that morning with a headache, and she was certain the saltiness of that ham on the biscuit they'd had for breakfast hadn't helped. That biscuit was a problem too, adding to the carbs she didn't need. There were just so many things rolling through her mind at the moment, so much that she felt dizzy with it all, like at any moment she was either going to scream or collapse beneath the pressure. She couldn't take another thing. Not one more damn thing.

"You don't have to go running every time she calls your name," Tami said, and Yvonne felt those threadbare bits of patience she'd had a death grip on break.

"It's my mother!" she yelled, closing the distance between her and Tami. "What else am I supposed to do?"

"She knew, Yvonne! Didn't you hear what Sallie said? Mama knew about her, and she never said a damn word!" Tami roared. "Not. One. Word!"

Okay, so they were really stuck on this thing with Sallie. "What woman wants to tell people that her husband had a baby outside of their marriage?" Yvonne asked.

"What woman takes her anger at her husband having a baby outside of their marriage out on their youngest child?" Tami retorted. "That's the thing I'm struggling with right now."

"Look," Lana said, stepping between them and waiting until Tami turned and walked a few steps away from where Yvonne stood, chest heaving. "Ms. Rosalee is there with Mama now. She said Mama's stable, right? Now, we left Mr. Cab's house so that we could talk about this, and we have. So maybe you don't have to run back right at this moment. Maybe we can get a cup of coffee or whatever and go sit on the front porch to just be for a few minutes. We all need that to figure out what we're going to do about Sallie."

"Sallie, Sallie, Sallie!" Yvonne yelled. "How am I supposed to focus on Sallie when my mother is hurt?" She turned away, rubbing her hands over her face. It didn't stop the rampant beating of her heart or the throbbing in her temples. Her skin felt hot all over, and that dizziness she'd been trying to ignore almost had her swaying on her feet. "Okay," she said, trying desperately to find some control, to keep from completely buckling under all the pressure. She turned back to face her sisters. "So Daddy had an affair with some woman who was also vacationing on the island. That woman got pregnant but didn't tell him. Then she came back to the island and dropped the baby off here, on Grandma's doorstep. Only for Grandma to turn around and give that baby to the man who was in love with her and his wife. If that isn't the wildest shit I've ever heard." She sighed. "But truth is often stranger than fiction. So what now? What the hell am I supposed to do with all that information? It has nothing to do with me or my life in the city."

"It has everything to do with our family," Tami said. "This legacy we've been here this summer trying to preserve. Sallie's a part of that. You said it yourself when you saw Grandma's picture hanging on Mr. Cab's wall—this is why she brought us here. To not only fix up the house but to fix the mess that had been made of our family."

Because those words sounded too damn close to the truth, Yvonne gasped, and then she bit back a sob. "So what? Are we splitting the proceeds of this house in fours now? When only our names are on the deeds? I thought we just decided that wasn't going to happen," she said.

"It's not just about the house, Yvonne," Lana added.

"No, dammit! None of this is just about the house. It never has been. The three of us coming together to do anything was never going to work. Because just like always, you're leaving me holding the larger share of the responsibility." This was spiraling out of control—*she* was spiraling, and she was deathly afraid she wouldn't be able to stop it. She wouldn't be able to remain the sister with all the answers, the epitome of calm, cool, and collected. She wouldn't be able to be everything she'd ever known how to be.

"What are you even talking about now?" Tami asked.

"You know what I'm talking about," Yvonne snapped. "I put out the extra money to keep this renovation moving. I've been taking care of Mama while the two of you have been living your life. Now I've gotta go back and take care of Mama again while you two sit here and have tea with your new sister."

"Yvonne," Lana said, "that's not what we're saying. And it's unfair of you to throw that shit about the money back in our faces. We didn't ask you to take out a loan for the renovations or to help Isaac."

She shook her head. "No, you didn't ask me, but I did it because I'm always the fixer. I've always been the one to do whatever was necessary to keep this family going. And I'm tired, Lana. I'm fuckin' tired!"

"Then don't do it!" Lana yelled back. "There's no law saying you've got to be the fixer, Yvonne. You picked up that mantle a long time ago, and you've been waving it like a sympathy flag in our faces for as long as I can remember. That's what I'm tired of. Take responsibility for the shit you decided to do, and stop playing the damn martyr."

"I take responsibility for me and my mother," she said. "What about you, Lana? Can you say the same?"

"Why should I say the same when you're always so fast to jump up and do *all* the things? You don't let us decide what, if anything, we want to do to help Mama because you're always there doing it."

"Because y'all never did. All y'all did was complain about this and complain about that."

"We complained about her mistreatment of us," Tami countered. "Just like every other child in the world. That didn't mean we didn't love her just like you did."

"Well, you have a funny way of showing it," Yvonne shot back.

Tami waved a hand in dismissal. "Why try to show someone something they don't want to see? All Mama ever wanted to see was you. And now, the way you keep saying '*my* mother' like she didn't give birth to two other children, is proof of that."

Yvonne didn't reply.

Tami fumed, her fists clenched at her sides, and Lana rubbed her temples.

It was a pointless conversation. Nothing was ever going to change. "I'm leaving," Yvonne said. "Y'all can do whatever you want—or rather, just keep doing what you always do."

✉

"I told you I can be there in a few hours," Deacon said over the phone.

"And I told you, it's okay. I'm fine." Yvonne wasn't fine, but he didn't need to know that. Nobody needed to know how broken she felt at that moment. How utterly helpless and confused she was as she sat in the waiting room, alone.

Grandma Betty used to say that people couldn't be expected to act a certain way when they didn't have all the information. And that seemed to make sense; she couldn't expect her sisters to react differently toward her if she didn't tell them everything that was going on with her. So she had. She'd told them about her health struggles and how stressful it had been dealing with their mother alone, and what had they done at the very next sign of trouble? The exact same thing they'd always done: left her holding the bag.

It had taken her all day to travel from Daufuskie back to Boston, and by the time she'd arrived at close to nine on Saturday night, the doctors had just decided to take Freda into surgery. So she was sitting in the waiting room alone because she'd sent Ms. Rosalee home with instructions to get some rest and not come back until tomorrow morning. Yvonne was ready to settle in at the hospital for the night.

"It's okay to not be fine," he said.

She gave a wry smile, which she knew he couldn't see. "You've told me that before."

"Because it's true." He chuckled. "Have you at least eaten something?"

A couple of days ago, Deacon had walked into the kitchen while she'd been doing her finger stick to check her glucose level. There'd been nothing else to do in that situation but tell him about her diagnosis, even though she was certain he knew the meaning behind what she'd been doing. Admittedly, he hadn't reacted in the way she'd thought he would. Then again, her issues with her condition where Deacon was concerned weren't based solely on his reaction.

"I grabbed a salad from the hospital cafeteria before it closed," she said. "Like I said, I'm fine. I'll text you when she's out of surgery."

"You can *call* me if you just need to talk before then," he said. And before she could reply, he continued. "But I'll look forward to the text as well."

She was smiling again when she thanked him for his concern and disconnected the call. Then she settled in to wait for the four-hour surgery to be completed.

✉

"Yvonne. Wake up."

She heard the familiar voice and jumped, her eyes popping open. Yvonne hadn't realized she'd fallen asleep until she heard her name being called and now felt a hand on her shoulder.

"Hey," Lana said with a small smile.

"Hey," Yvonne replied, blinking rapidly as she tried to completely wake up. "What are you doing here?"

She sat up straighter in the chair as Lana took a seat to her left. Isaac was standing on the other side of her, and he leaned in and gave Yvonne a half hug as she spoke. Then he went to his wife's other side to take a seat.

"I left the island right after you did," Lana said.

"Yeah," Tami added, coming into the waiting room with a guy Yvonne suspected was the best friend she'd mentioned to her and Lana the night they were chatting and reminiscing during the thunderstorm. "If you would've waited a minute instead of stalking off, we could've all gotten on the ferry together."

Shock didn't begin to describe how Yvonne felt seeing her sisters here. But that wasn't the most prevalent feeling she was experiencing right now. Her chest filled with pride, mixed with contentment, and she once again fought the urge to cry.

"You didn't act like you wanted to come," Yvonne said as Tami dropped down into the chair beside her and rested a hand on Yvonne's knee.

"We didn't," Lana said. "And that was our fault. You're not in this alone." Lana reached for Yvonne's hand and held it tightly.

"Nope," Tami said. "I can be here for you, respect Mama, and still feel a way about how she treated me at the same time."

Where Yvonne would've normally had a response to that—a wordy one that would probably have ended in Tami rolling her eyes—tonight, she simply accepted Tami's hand when she enfolded it with Yvonne's free one and said, "Thanks for coming."

They sat there like that, the three of them holding hands, while they waited for the nurse or a doctor to come out and give them news about Freda. It seemed a little like déjà vu, carrying them back to the time they'd sat in the waiting room, waiting for news after Freda's stroke. But this time was noticeably different. She and her sisters had spent weeks together in the summerhouse, reliving memories from a time when they were both on each other's nerves and happy. The happiest, Yvonne would venture to say, they'd ever been together.

Admittedly, when they'd first learned about the terms of Grandma Betty's will, they'd each been confused. Well—Tami, not so much. But Yvonne knew for a fact that she'd struggled with understanding why her grandmother hadn't just willed them the house and then let them do whatever they wanted to with it. Or, if she'd wanted the house to remain as a shrine to the Butler family on Daufuskie, why she hadn't gifted it to the Historical Foundation. Making them come back to the island had seemed so pointless, an unnecessary infringement on their time and their wishes.

But it had ended up being so much more than that. And no, they weren't finished with the house—but sitting here, in this moment, with her sisters' hands in hers as they presented what Lana had called their *united front*, Yvonne realized that going back to Daufuskie had done way more than any of them had ever expected. It had brought them together in a way she knew they never would have come to on their own in the city. It had given them the space to air all their feelings and hurt and to be forced to deal with it. If nothing else came from this summer, Yvonne vowed to hold tight to that and, as she gripped her sisters' hands tighter, to them.

Forty minutes later, the doctor came through the electronically controlled double doors and headed toward them.

"Her neurologist saw her when she was admitted, and he'll be back sometime tomorrow to evaluate her again," Dr. Solomon, the orthopedic surgeon, said as he stood directly across from the sisters.

Isaac stood with an arm around Lana. And Gabriel, who'd introduced himself to Yvonne with a smile and a warm handshake a little while ago, stood right next to Tami. It was good to see her sisters supported and loved, because both of these men definitely had love in their eyes for them.

"I'll also be watching her closely for the next few days," the doctor continued. "I want to make sure there's no swelling before I send her to the rehab facility."

Yvonne nodded as waves of relief washed over her. "I understand," she said.

"Can we see her now?" Lana asked.

"Keep an eye on those doors over there; the nurse will come out and get you when she's completely awake," he said. "And I know we talked about this before during one of her other visits, but if at all possible, I'd really like you to think about making things more accessible for her. There are some programs I can refer you to that will help with the costs, if need be. I know your mother wasn't amenable to hearing about those options, but this fall could've been a lot worse. Not that a broken ankle and sprained wrist aren't bad enough."

Yvonne nodded again. "I understand," she said. "And I'm going to take care of it."

He gave them a curt nod before accepting their second round of *thank-you*s and then left them alone.

"She hated that last rehab facility," Yvonne said. "I'll have to look for another one that'll accept her insurance."

"We shouldn't dismiss those programs that he mentioned either," Tami said. "Mama has worked since she was sixteen years old, paid her taxes and all that. So she's earned every service the state can offer her."

"I agree," Lana added. "She has earned it. Probably paid more than her share."

Yvonne wholeheartedly agreed with her sisters. But she also knew their mother. "Which one of us is gonna tell her that she's accepting all the assistance that she can get?" she asked.

Moments later, after the three sisters had silently stared at each other, Tami was the first to speak. "Well, I guess that'd be me, since she always expects me to say something she doesn't like, anyway."

For a millisecond, Yvonne considered telling Tami she'd do it so that Tami wouldn't have to endure what would undoubtedly become an argument between her and Freda. But then she paused and recalled what Lana had said back on the island. Had she really never given her sisters a chance to step up and deal with Freda in the way they needed to? What would happen if she didn't intervene this time? If she let Tami say her piece and then let Freda either decline or accept the help?

Before she could come up with an answer, Tami broke the line they'd been standing in and walked toward the double doors. Apparently, Tami was through waiting for the nurse to come and get them.

"She's got a point," Lana said with a grin and then followed Tami. Yvonne shrugged and followed her sisters.

It was probably divine intervention that had kept them from getting booted out of the hospital when Tami walked right past the nurses' station to the recovery-room door. But then, as they stood there, Lana reached out, grabbing Tami and Yvonne by the hand to stop them from going in.

"I want to say something before we go in there," Lana said.

"Make it quick 'cause I have to pee, but I want to see Mama first," Tami said.

"Yes, ma'am," Lana replied, and then rolled her eyes. "You never could hold your bladder when you were anxious about something."

Tami's reply was to shrug, but Lana rubbed her thumb over both their hands.

"Listen, Yvonne, Tami and I talked after you left, and we realize we haven't been doing our part. Regardless of what feelings we each have about our upbringing, we're not going to turn our back on Mama or you." She paused and looked over at Tami before returning her gaze to Yvonne.

"It was never our intention to turn our backs on either of you, but it was our way of coping with all the feelings we'd let bottle up over the years," Lana continued.

"She's right," Tami added. "Sallie said something very interesting last night, and I kept going back to it as I read Grandma's letters. Remember, she said that if they'd just had a conversation instead of writing letters back then, maybe that situation could've turned out differently? Well, maybe if we would've just sat down and had an honest conversation about everything we were feeling with Mama, our relationships could've been different."

Yvonne wasn't certain about that—not back then. Throughout the night, she'd been thinking so much about their time on the island these past weeks and how healing and fortifying it now seemed with them back in the city. She truly felt that timing had been everything for them in this scenario.

Another thing she could admit was that Freda was obstinate and didn't always accept her responsibility in a situation. Yvonne knew, because she'd tried on multiple occasions when they were growing up, but Freda had insisted that one, both, or all of her daughters were at fault instead. Or, as her favorite response to Yvonne whenever she'd questioned something about her mother's parenting was, "So I guess you think I'm a bad mother." A statement to which no fifteen-year-old—at least not Yvonne at fifteen—was going to answer yes.

"Look, I know I was probably just as unbearable as Mama was at times," she admitted with a heavy sigh. "And for that, I apologize. I felt like I never had a choice in how I acted or what I did, just like the two of you. The difference was, both of you found your own way and moved in that direction regardless of what Mama said. Me, on the other hand . . ." She shrugged. "But I'm not gonna stand here and blame Mama for every one of my decisions. They were mine, and that's that. I can choose to make better decisions now, ones that reflect how *I* feel and what *I* want." She'd thought about that throughout the night as well.

"You're right about having the ability to make your own decisions," Lana said. "But you know what else was right? 'Mothers love their daughters, even if they show it poorly.' Remember that from that old movie you used to watch all the time?"

Yvonne smiled. "I do. It's from *Hope Floats*."

Tami scrunched her face and tilted her head. "I think I've seen that. But it's not a favorite."

"Yeah, I know, you're more a fan of musicals. You don't have to remind us," Yvonne said, and grinned.

Lana chuckled too, and then continued. "What we're trying to say, Yvonne, is that we're here. We're always going to be here."

Tami nodded. "Right. Because we're sisters. I know sometimes people say that blood isn't the only family, and they're correct. But in this instance, we are blood—so to me, that only strengthens our bond. We're devoted to each other, forever."

Now Yvonne's eyes were welling with tears. When she glanced at Lana, she saw the same. Tami, however, had her confident grin lighting her pretty brown eyes.

"I didn't know how this summer was going to turn out," Yvonne said to them. "I figured we'd probably do our best not to kill each other on that island. And I know we still haven't finished the house or figured out what we're going to do with it, but I can say this: I'm glad we went. Glad we had that time in the house together to get back to what we were before: sisters who can argue over any damn thing."

They all broke out into laughter.

"But who come through in a clutch," Lana added.

"Whether that be with money or just general support," Tami said.

Yvonne nodded as the first tear fell. "Exactly. And still love each other just as fiercely," she said softly and squeezed Lana's hand.

Chapter 29

YVONNE

Just as they'd been for the past couple of days, a myriad of thoughts had rolled through her mind in the last twenty-four hours, and she'd experienced so many feelings and revelations. And that morning, all Yvonne wanted to do was stay in bed, tucked under the warmth of the sheets and duvet in the bedroom she'd occupied for the past two years. But that hadn't felt as comfortable as it had before.

She'd tossed and turned until she thought she was going to flip right out of the bed to land on the floor. Since that wasn't a smart option, she'd finally climbed out of the bed. After noticing it was later than when she usually awakened, she hurried into the bathroom to take her medications. But when she returned, she didn't lie in that bed again. No, she crossed the room to the desk she'd had pushed against the wall when she was a teenager. Pulling out the chair, she took a seat and leaned forward to rest her elbows on her knees.

What was she doing here?

The quick answer was that she'd rushed back to Boston to take care of her mother. Something she'd done before. Something she'd always done. And just like before, Lana and Tami had also come back to take care of their mother. Tami had even offered to spend the night at the hospital so Lana could go home and sleep in her own bed and Yvonne could do the same.

"Are you sure?" Yvonne had asked, her tone as skeptical as she felt when she'd glanced back at the bed to see Freda still asleep.

The doctor had said she would be out of it for quite a while, but they'd wanted to see her anyway.

"Positive," Tami told her. "She's probably going to sleep through the rest of the night. So I'll sit in here a little while longer, and then I'll head out to the waiting room to bunk there in case something changes. Y'all can come relieve me in the morning."

Lana had frowned. "But what about your guy out there? Did you forget he was waiting for you?"

"Oh, Gabriel?" Tami had asked, a quick smile covering her face. "He's not my . . . Well, hmm, maybe I guess he is my guy." Then she shrugged. "Anyway, the way he insisted on coming here with me, I don't think he's gonna leave until I do. So we'll both be fine. You two just go, but keep your phones close in case I need to call you."

Lana had moved first, leaning over the hospital bed to kiss Mama's forehead. Then she'd walked over to where Tami stood at the foot of the bed and pulled her into a hug. "I'll tell Gabriel to go and get you something to eat and drink from one of those machines."

"Thanks," Tami said, and then Lana left the room.

Yvonne moved next. She'd been holding Freda's hand, but now she placed it gently by her mother's side before doing as Lana had just done—leaning over to kiss her mother's forehead. "I'll be back in the morning, Mama," she whispered.

When she turned to Tami, it was to see her staring down at their mother.

"She looks so frail," Tami said. "I didn't realize she looked this way."

Yvonne moved over to her sister, taking Tami's hand in hers. "She's going to be okay," she said. "You know Mama's too tough not to pull through this too."

Tami nodded quickly, pulling her bottom lip between her teeth as she blinked nervously. Yvonne knew she was trying to keep back tears, and she wanted to tell her it was okay to cry. But Tami didn't need her telling her what to do. She didn't need her permission to feel whatever she wanted to feel or didn't want to feel in this moment.

Yvonne leaned in and kissed her sister's cheek. "Call me if you need anything."

Tami nodded again and squeezed Yvonne's hand before she left the hospital.

There'd been no calls throughout the night. Yvonne knew because she'd checked her phone in between the tossing and turning. She started to get up and go to the phone to send Tami a text asking how Freda was doing, but she didn't move, her mind still wandering.

They had another sister. That had been the most prominent thing on her mind last night. Daddy had fathered another child and had never told them. Grandma Betty hadn't told them. And neither had Mama, but Yvonne was certain now that Freda had known. That had been the moment when her mother's attitude had changed about their father, holidays—everything. His infidelity and the forever evidence of it had been living on that island all this time. The island Daddy and Grandma Betty had insisted Yvonne, Lana, and Tami visit every summer. Had they planned to tell them one day during one of those summers? Introduce them to Sallie so all the Butler sisters could be together on the island?

Last night, when they'd been sitting in the waiting room while Freda was in surgery, Tami had pulled out another letter she'd found in Grandma Betty's box.

> *This house is big enough for all of them. I wanted it built that way so that when they came back and found each other, they'd have a place to call home. Freda couldn't understand and I guess I don't blame her. Daniel made*

a mistake. Maybe I did too. We make decisions that are
best for that moment.

Tami had been right: Grandma Betty had always intended for them to come back to Daufuskie Island, to the summerhouse. Together. She'd known Sallie was there and that either with Grandma Betty's death or, as it had turned out, Ms. Odessa's death first, Sallie would learn who her parents really were. Those damn letters that they both seemed to write to whoever would eventually be the one to read them told the story. Yvonne sensed they all regretted it on some level. Not that, as Mr. Cab had said about him and Ms. Odessa, loving Sallie from first sight wasn't true, because she believed it was. She also believed that at the time those decisions were made, they'd each believed that this was what had to be done. Grandma Betty probably thought she was protecting her son and the family he'd built in the city. But Daniel had told Freda— and in today's world, that would've meant everybody knew about his side-chick baby. The dislike between both baby mamas would ensue, and the fight for child support and weekend visitations would commence in the open. Back then, she supposed it was easier on everybody to do what they'd done—sweep the secret under the rug and go on about their business.

Yvonne didn't think that had been easier on Freda or Sallie in the long run. Freda had suffered an immeasurable hurt, which she masked with negativity. Sallie had been deceived by people she'd loved and trusted and robbed of a sisterly bond that maybe she'd craved. Yvonne didn't know, since she'd had her sisters all her life. But lying here this morning, she had to wonder what it would've felt like to not have Tami and Lana in her world. To not know that they were part of her and that she could lean on them if she needed to.

With those thoughts, Yvonne stood and went to her phone. She picked it up and made a call and, knowing it was early, apologized as soon as the person on the other end answered: "Good morning, this is Yvonne. I'm sorry for the early call, but I thought we should talk."

⊠

Two hours later, Yvonne walked into her mother's hospital room. Tami was still there, dressed in the clothes she'd had on last night, and Lana was just taking a seat in a chair close to Freda's bed.

"It's about time you got here," Freda said. Her bed had been raised. "Tami said you were coming at eleven, but it's a little after now."

From the foot of the bed, Tami nodded. "Yes, ma'am, it's 11:03," she said, tossing Yvonne a knowing glance.

"Good morning, Mama," Yvonne said as she moved close enough to kiss her mother on the cheek. "How're you feeling? The nurses said your vitals were good, and the report the doctor gave Tami this morning was positive."

"If you mean them telling me I've got to go to a rehab hospital again is positive, you've bumped your head, Yvonne. Or got too much of that island sun," Freda said.

Yvonne ignored her mother's comments and folded her arms over her chest. "Well, that's exactly why I wanted all of us here this morning."

"This should be fun, then," Tami quipped, and eased her butt onto the bottom half of the bed.

"I'm not going back to the same place I was in before. They didn't check on me enough, and the food was horrible. Rosalee's told me about some other places friends of ours have been, so I already have a list of where I don't want to go," Freda began. "They have some home therapists that can come out. We'll look into that, and since you'll be home for the rest of the summer, Yvonne, it shouldn't be a problem scheduling them whenever they need to come out."

Yvonne sucked in a deep breath and released it, a silent prayer for strength easing through her mind. "I won't be here the rest of the summer, Mama," she said. "None of us will."

Freda's eyes went from Yvonne to Tami and then to the side where Lana sat. But Yvonne decided not to wait for whatever her response was going to be. She had more to say, and no doubt Freda would too. It was best if she simply heard all of Yvonne's plans right now.

"We're going back to Daufuskie in a couple of days, as soon as we can get you situated in a rehab facility. Then, Ms. Rosalee will continue to keep tabs on you until . . ." She paused and then cleared her throat. "Until Tami and Lana return to the city."

"Wait, what?" Tami asked, her brow furrowed.

After the first call Yvonne had made that morning, she'd called Lana next, so Lana knew what Yvonne was about to say. Tami would learn about the decisions Yvonne had made—and yes, for all of them—this time. Unlike how she'd reacted to someone taking the choice from her, she figured Tami would be on board with this new plan.

"Shh," Lana said to Tami. "There's more."

"We're going back to finish the renovations on the house," Yvonne said, and kept her gaze carefully focused on her mother. "And when that's done, I'll be moving to the island."

"What in the hell are you talking about?" Freda asked, trying to sit up even straighter in the bed. She winced in pain, and Lana stood, going to her mother's side to touch her shoulder and ease her back.

"You have to relax, Mama," Lana said. "Remember, the doctor said don't try to do too much today. They'll start getting you out of the bed and moving you around more tomorrow, but today he wants to make sure all the anesthesia is out of your system before you move around."

"I want your sister to tell me what the hell she's talking about," Freda replied after a heated look at Lana.

"I'm talking about doing something different with my life." Yvonne took another breath, feeling much steadier now. Convicted and, yes, excited about the way that storm of thoughts last night had come into focus this morning. "I've worked so hard for so long; I want to take some time to rest and enjoy the fruits of my labor. Daufuskie is the perfect place to do that, and the summerhouse—well, that's my home. It's *our* home," she said, looking over to Tami now. "And we're going to keep it that way."

"Oh my . . . oh my damn! Oh! Oh!" Tami couldn't get her words out before she'd jumped from the bed and was bouncing over to Yvonne to pull her into a hug. "Yes! Yes! This is exactly the right thing!"

"We're going to retain ownership of the house, and Yvonne's going to move down there to live in it so she can take care of it, and it'll be ready whenever we all go down for visits," Lana said. "And, Mama, after you're finished at the rehab facility, you can either come and stay with me and Isaac, or we can put in an application for the senior center where Isaac's grandmother stays."

Freda's eyes grew wider. "Who the hell said that? I don't know why the three of you think you can waltz in here and tell me what I'm going to do like I'm not a grown woman."

"We're not telling you what you're going to do, Mama," Yvonne said. "You have choices. Just like I do. Like we all do. I'm choosing to start another part of my life in a different place, doing a different thing. Lana and Isaac, well . . . they're starting the next phase of their family."

"The next generation of Butlers," Tami chimed. "And it has to be a girl so she'll be in line with the Butler women, like us."

"Like *all* of us," Yvonne added. "I talked to Sallie this morning. We're going to have brunch with her when we get back to the island."

"You talked to who?" Freda asked slowly.

Tami moved closer to the bed, taking their mother's hand this time. For a second, Freda looked like she would pull away, but then her gaze rested on Tami.

"Tell me what she's talking about, Tami," Freda said softly, her lower lip trembling.

"We know, Mama," Tami said. "We know about Daddy's other daughter."

Freda closed her eyes. Her fingers gripped Tami's hand.

"I told them never to tell you," Freda whispered. "Never to hurt my girls the way Daniel hurt me."

Yvonne's chest felt heavy, as suddenly all the sorrow that her mother had held inside her while she'd continued to raise three daughters by the man who'd caused her the most horrific pain came crashing down over her. She touched a hand to Freda's shoulder, and on the other side of the bed, Lana did the same.

"It's okay, Mama," Yvonne said. "We're all going to be okay."

And they were—Yvonne knew that without a doubt. Because now they had something that they'd each taken for granted before. They had each other.

✉

"I still can't believe you're here."

"Why? Because I didn't listen to you?" Deacon asked as he took a seat next to her on the couch.

She'd arrived home to her mother's house at just after nine that evening and had finished eating the chicken-salad lettuce wrap she'd grabbed from the deli after leaving the hospital. With a glass of water in hand, she was on her way upstairs to take a long hot bath and then settle in for the night. Lana was staying at the hospital with Mama tonight, so Yvonne had time to sit and think more about the decision she'd made. She'd planned to call Deacon and fill him in on the plan changes, but not until she had everything straight in her mind. Now he was here.

"I told you I'd text you," she said, sitting next to him.

His brows went up. "And did you?"

She pursed her lips. "It's been a very eventful day, and I'm just getting back from the hospital. I still had time to send the text."

"But you weren't going to, were you?" It was a question, but she suspected he thought he already knew the answer.

"In the morning," she told him. "I still needed to wrap my mind around a few things, and then I was going to call you in the morning to let you know when we'd be coming back."

He nodded. "Yeah, I figured you'd be busy today. That's why I called Tami to check on you."

"What? When?" Tami hadn't said a word about speaking to Deacon today.

The three of them had stayed in Mama's room until early afternoon, when Lana had told Tami to go home and get some rest. But Tami had left the room for a short while before then to make a Starbucks run to find them some good coffee. Mama had requested a matcha tea with lemon and one vanilla bean scone, which she'd eaten and drunk while Lana told them she'd scheduled a doctor's appointment for the next day because Isaac had insisted she do so before returning to the island.

"A little before noon," he said. "It was as long as I could wait to get an update. I'd already packed a bag and was just stepping off the ferry when she finally answered her phone."

Settling back against the pillows on the couch now, Yvonne felt an unusual lightness. She'd never had a man in Mama's house before. Had never liked one enough to bring him home to meet any of her family. It wasn't like she'd invited Deacon here, either, but he looked right sitting there, dressed in gray sweatpants and a matching hoodie, crisp white tennis shoes on his feet. This was definitely a different look for the handsome construction man she'd grown used to seeing in worn jeans and fitted T-shirts, but she liked it. She liked it a lot.

"So you were just going to ignore my wishes and come up here to do what?" she asked just as a flutter moved through her stomach.

"To do this," he replied, and leaned in close to touch his lips softly to hers.

This was the first time he'd kissed her somewhere other than her forehead, and she parted her lips to say something—what, she had no clue, but that was fine because he didn't let her speak anyway. He kissed her again, another brush of his lips over hers. A soft, teasing brush that sent those flutters in her stomach into a full-on frenzy. The next touch of his lips had his tongue slipping along the crease of her mouth, and before she could think another incoherent thought, her arms went up to wrap around his neck, pulling him even closer as she tilted her head and met his tongue with a hungry stroke.

His moan came quick, and then his hands were on her, and the kiss went deeper, lasted longer, and pulled to the surface every enticing sensation her private toy stash had never even come close to appeasing.

Epilogue

TAMI

One year later

"Do you see that, Sariah Elizabeth?" Tami asked the chubby-cheeked little girl with honey-brown eyes and curly black hair. "That is your legacy," she told her.

Extending an arm, she pointed at the little blue house. "That's where your great-great-great-grandfather, Riley Butler, was born and raised." Then she turned around, chuckling as the baby in her arms cooed. "Yessss, and this is the house your great-grandmother and namesake, Elizabeth Butler, built for us all to enjoy."

Sariah grabbed a handful of the micro-braids Tami was now sporting, and giggled as if she'd found a pot of gold instead. "Oh, girl, now you know we've talked about this before. You cannot be grabbing Auntie Tam's hair," Tami said in a cutesy baby voice. "You know how much this hair cost me?"

"I don't think she does," Gabriel said as he stepped out onto the deck.

It was a humid July afternoon, a perfect day for a Southern Belle Tea Party, as Mama Jo had announced when she'd arrived at the summerhouse earlier that morning. The woman had come in with cardboard boxes full of aluminum trays that she'd stored the food she'd cooked for the engagement party in. And now, as the festivities were in full swing, Tami had to agree with her.

White tents had been set up in the yard, with tables covered in pastel linen cloths. There were three tables of food—everything from Ms. Janie's fried corn cakes and Gullah rice to the caramel- and pecan-covered Cinnabons Lana loved—and trays of fried fish, which Deacon had requested. As the other half of the guest of honor, Yvonne wasn't to be forgotten, and since she'd declared today a "cheat day," Mama Jo had made her a special pan of Tummy-Yum Bread Pudding.

"Well, that's what aunties are for," she continued. "To teach her all the things she needs to know about looking good."

Gabriel eased an arm around her waist as he came to stand next to her. "Well, her auntie definitely knows about that."

Tami turned and grinned up at him. "You're really good at that," she said.

"At what?" he asked.

"Saying all the right things to me. I like it," she told him.

"Nah, you love it," he said, and she grinned even more.

"I also love you," she replied, and was rewarded by a soft kiss to her lips.

"I love you too," he said when he pulled back. "But I've been sent up here to—and her exact words were, 'Tell my child to stop monopolizing my grandbaby and bring her back down here.'"

Tami rolled her eyes. "Well, you can just go right back down there and tell Mama that she lives with this gorgeous little girl, so she's the one who needs to share."

Three months after her fall, Freda had been released from the rehab facility. By that time, the discussion of where she was going to live that would be conducive to her condition had been well underway.

Not surprising to any of them, Freda had chosen to sell her house and move into the in-law suite Lana and Isaac had built in their new house instead of moving into a senior home. Yvonne had even suggested that Freda move into the little blue house, where everything was on one level, but again, to no one's surprise, she had refused. It had taken her a couple of months to reconcile the fact that not only did they all know about Daniel's indiscretions and Grandma Betty's efforts to keep it all a secret, but that Tami, Lana, and Yvonne had decided to forgive everyone involved. It wasn't their burden to carry; the lies had been told, feelings had been irreparably hurt, but in the end they were all here now in the present, living the life they'd been blessed with, regardless of the circumstances of their birth.

"Not a chance," Gabriel said. "You are not putting me in the middle of you and Ms. Freda again. Remember at Christmas dinner, when you were supposed to be getting those glasses she requested out of the basement, and she sent me to 'go get my child'? Again, her words. But when I got down there, you had other ideas that took us even longer to return. Had Ms. Freda glaring at me with that I-know-exactly-what-y'all-were-doing look all night."

Tami laughed because she did remember that. It had been one of the best quickies she and Gabriel had indulged in to date. Of course, Lana'd had a lot to say about them having sex in her new house when she'd found out later as they were all cleaning the kitchen. Tami had resisted the urge to tell her sister that that had been the biggest part of the allure for her.

"Well, she's not at risk for that happening this time, since we've got company." She kissed Sariah's cheek. "Right, pretty girl?"

"Come on," he said. "I'm leading both the pretty girls back downstairs. But first, Yvonne also wants you to run upstairs to her bedroom and grab the gift she left on her bed. So I'll take her while you go do that."

Reluctantly, she gave him the little girl and paused for a second to note how good he looked with a baby in his arms. Then she went up on the tips of her toes to kiss his cheek as she said, "I'll be right back."

Tami went into the house and up the stairs until she came to the primary bedroom—the room that used to be Grandma Betty's but had become Yvonne's after her sister had decided to leave her job and move to the island. Tami, of course, had been elated that they were keeping the house, but she'd been overjoyed to hear Yvonne say she wanted to live in it instead of them renting it out.

She stood in the bedroom that was now painted a soothing gray, with navy-blue furniture in the sitting room that Tami liked almost as much as she had Grandma Betty's brightly colored fixtures. She went to the king-size bed, where Yvonne and Deacon, the newly engaged couple—as of about two months ago—slept, and found the gift box.

It was wrapped in pretty pale-pink paper and a darker pink ribbon, and was topped with a ridiculously huge magnolia. She grinned because she knew Lana had wrapped that box. It was way too artsy-looking for Yvonne to have done it, and Tami sucked at wrapping. Gift bags and gift cards were her friends forever.

Tami picked up the box and started to walk out of the room. She knew that inside the box was a framed picture of Daddy and Grandma Betty, taken at one of their grandmother's many award shows. When Daniel had died and Tami, Yvonne, and Lana had gone to his house to pack up all his belongings, they'd shipped some things to Grandma Betty but had kept some stuff for themselves. One of the things they each had was a picture of their father and grandmother together at different times. Living on the island had given Yvonne the chance to spend more time with Sallie than Tami or Lana had, so it was her suggestion that Sallie also have something of his. Yvonne had made the suggestion when they'd all, Sallie included, been at Lana's after she'd delivered Sariah five months ago. It had taken them a while to select the picture and have it framed, but now that it was done, they planned to give it to her today. Because today, they were all starting anew. It was the first time they were all on the island as a family. Mama, Sallie, Yvonne, Lana, and the memory of Daddy and Grandma Betty. Her family was sitting out in the backyard, where generations of Butlers had once walked. It was an amazing feeling, and one Tami was proud to be experiencing.

ABOUT THE AUTHOR

Photo © 2012 Lisa Fleet Photography

A. C. Arthur is the author of *Happy Is On Hiatus*. She has worked as a paralegal in every field of law since high school, but her first love is and always will be writing. The winner of multiple awards, A. C. has written more than eighty novels, including those under her *USA Today* bestselling pen name, Lacey Baker. After years of hosting reader-appreciation events, A. C. created the One Love Reunion, an event designed to bring together readers, authors, and other members of the literary industry to celebrate their love of books. A. C. resides in Maryland with her family, where she's currently working on her next book . . . or watching *Criminal Minds*. For more information visit www.acarthur.com.